Other books in the PROWLER BOOKS collection:

Fiction:
Diary of a Hustler
• ISBN 0-9524647-64
Slaves
• ISBN 0-9524647-99
Young Cruisers
• ISBN 0-9524647-72
Corporal in Charge
• ISBN 0-95246478-0
Hard
• ISBN 1-90264401-8
Virgin Sailors
• ISBN 1-90264403-4
Californian Creamin'
• ISBN 1-90264404-2

Photographic:
Planet Boys
• ISBN 0-9524647-13
Kama Sutra of Gay Sex
• ISBN 0-9524647-05

Travel:
New York Scene Guide
• ISBN 1-90264400-X

▶ active service

RICK JACKSON

PROWLER BOOKS

First printing November 1998
Cover photography © 1998 Glenn Studio

web-site: prowler.co.uk
• ISBN 1-902644-06-9

Printed in Finland by Werner Soderstrom Oy.

British Library Cataloguing in Publication Data.
A catalogue record for this book is available from the British Library.

▶ CONTENTS

SAFER SEX

Scenes depicted in this anthology contain unsafe sexual practices. These stories were written before the AIDS-era and represent sexual activities which, unfortunately, are no longer considered safe.

We urge you to always follow safer-sex guidelines. *Always* use extra-condoms and water-based lube when fucking. For more information on safer sex and HIV/AIDS in the UK call 0171 242 1010.

THE EXAM

I had been in Key West almost two years before I decided I was past due for a dental check-up. I'd never much liked messing with the dentist, so I had put my annual visit off much longer than was good for me. When a buddy mentioned he had just had some fillings put in, I asked about his dentist. I wasn't too sure how to read the grin that slid across the guy's face. He just said I should give him a try; but when I called for an appointment, I discovered I'd have to wait five months before they could squeeze me in. By that time, of course, I'd forgotten my buddy's knowing smile. Any dentist with a five-month waiting list had to be good.

As it turned out, the dentist was OK for a white-haired tottering coprolite three decades past simple senility. By the time I saw him, though, I discovered why I had to wait five months to get in and why the wait was worth it. His dental assistant was the most gorgeous single creature I have ever seen. The whole time he was leading me here and taking me there for X-rays and whatnot, I couldn't pry my eyes loose. He was absolutely perfect, possessed of a shimmering radiant beauty he seemed almost to ignore, as though he were aware of his magnificence but trying, for reasons of his own, to wander incognito among mortal men.

The dentist staggered in years too soon to give me the once-over, but I could only dream of meatier things than his gnarled hands shoved deep inside my mouth. I kept my eyes on Dave, at once trying to burn his image into memory and to decide what it was that made him so beautiful. He was about 24 and fairly well built, but was no weight lifter. I think what struck me first was the ruddy glow that made his skin seem almost florescent. It exuded youth and vitality from every pore. The long, boyish shock of brown hair that hung long over his brow highlighted his enormous brown eyes and nicely set off the gleaming smile one would expect from a pro.

Dave's epicene bone structure was a delicate as the bloom of his youth was sublime. Picture Charlie Sheen morphed with Rob Lowe, but lacking any Hollywood pretense or affection, and you have a rough idea of what an open turn-on Dave was. If Botticelli hadn't wasted so much time with Venuses, I could show you a picture. As it is, you'll just have to take my word that by the time the dentist was halfway through the exam, my dick was so stiff and cramped that Dave had to notice. I don't know whether the dentist was oblivious to my problem or used to his patients suffering impacted roots when Dave was around. In either case, he finished quickly because my mouth was in "fine shape."

I mooned around the outer office for a few moments, seeking any entrée to Dave's heart or any other organ he was willing to share. My batted baby blues and bulging basket must finally have done the trick. As he wished me good dental hygiene with a farewell wave, he mentioned that he often hung out after work at a bar around the corner on Duval Street. I was that bar's best customer for the next two hours until Dave swung in for a beer. I even let him drink most of one before I dragged his ass up to my apartment and out of his clothes.

Seeing him naked, I had to stop and stare again. Everybody in Florida has a tan, but Dave's naked body was a masterpiece of blushed alabaster with russet rosettes crowing each classically proportioned pectoral. His muscles were bold without being gaudy, rippling tightly down beneath soft, ruddy, hairless skin from his wide shoulders to a pygmy-sized waist. The ass that erupted off his pelvis was huge and hard and obviously hankering for what I had hard. He stood for a moment, watching me with an amused grin as I savored the spectacle and then the pulled my lips to his and made the fireworks begin.

The next hour is a jumble of deranged images and half-remembered ecstasies the sum total of which will remain with me, vigorous and alive, forever. Unfortunately, I was too busy to take notes and neglected to pull out my videocamera until later than night so the very frenzy of discovery blurred one sublime sensation into the next. I remember the tentative invitation of his parting lips as his hand, planted behind my head, pulled us together. Another hand slipped to my waist and forced our hips to mate, introducing our dicks to the driving pulse that pounded outward from both our hearts.

Soon our hands were everywhere. I couldn't get enough of the soft texture of his skin or the hard muscle that lay just below. My fingertips read the Braille begging me to satisfy his muscled need, slipping along his lats and up across his broad back and finally down to the finest ass any young man's wet-dream fantasy could crave. His soft-skinned glutes were coiled like steel bands that flexed and strained their yearning beneath my eager touch. As our dicks ground together, sharing their slick, oozing pre-cum, I let Dave's lips discover the taste of my neck and ears and shuddering shoulder. My fingers pried his buttcheeks wide, stretching at his ass-crack to prep him for my own in-depth exam. The harder I pulled his cheeks wide, the louder he said "Aaaahhhhhh" and the more his meat ground its way up against my belly.

I felt myself about to blow and knew we needed a break, so I pulled him into the bedroom. I'm not especially shy about doing The Deed in the living room, but I keep my party kit where I sleep. Besides, the wall along my bed is mirrored tile that reflects the sliding door and deck and Gulf beyond. The breeze wafting in from the tropical evening outside was nice, but I was more interested in how Dave's delicious bubble-butt would look reflected back at me. Somehow, with my hands full of his ass and my lips wrapped around his tongue, he was too close to seem real. Watching our naked young bodies thrashing about together in my mirrors gave me more than a better view. We looked for all the world like an award-winning fuckflick and somehow that reas-sured me that Dave was real and really mine.

His face was wrapped hard around my balls when I decided I should stop watching and get back with the program. I flipped down beside him and licked his crotch clean before I slurped his nuts into my mouth. They were huge and tender and when I bore down on them, Dave's whole body shivered in abject pleasure. I lifted one of his knees so I could peek out and watch us gobbling each other's nuts. The musky scent drifting up from his ass-crack as he humped his crotch against my face was so rich and masculine, it set my heads to spinning. Now and again, one of us would give the other's crank a jack, but we both wanted our period of discovery to last at least until forever.

Dave's suction picked up about the time his hand slipped back to my shank. I suddenly knew I needed something even more than I needed to slam my meat up his ass. Dave was so flawless, doing him first would have somehow seemed an act against nature. The way I felt made no sense whatsoever. He obviously wanted it as much as I needed to give it to him, but I knew down deep that Dave had to do me before I could really enjoy slamming the living fuck out him.

When I pulled away and stretched out onto my belly, he gave me a look that was easy to read. Then he reached down into my party box and came up with enough lube to grease Pakistan and squirted it along my crack as I arched my hole upwards. I kept my eyes glued to the mirror while his hand slipped between my cheeks to smear the lube everywhere he could reach. I expected a health professional to rubber up next, but he did nothing of the kind.

Instead, he slid his body down onto mine and slipped his slick, naked dick between my ass-checks. My butthole rose upwards on its own to slide along the underside of his swollen shank as he pressed that bone up between my clenching glutes and then pulled it back down again. His hips ground harder into my ass-crack with every hole-teasing stroke. My pucker leapt upwards to coast along his bone, so hungry for the ultimate sensation I could feel the ripples in his raphe as his rod rammed past. My butt yearned to be spread wide, yet Dave kept skidding along the very valley of my ass-crack, slip-sliding his good time from the naked press of bone against flesh.

My clearest memory of that long, tropical evening is the reflected image of Dave's gorgeous ass flexing and clenching at the air as he used my crack to jack him off. He kept his head down, perhaps too busy to enjoy the show; but my eyes stayed locked on his pounding, clenching, heaving ass. Those powerful hips reared up and down as though by magic, rolling his twin mounds of man-muscle upwards as my butt leaped desperately after to keep hold of his shaft. The slick probing of his thick dental tool between my cheeks teased ecstasy from my asshole, but my hungry pucker needed more than a tempting taste on the fly-by. I needed more than the feel of his lips along my neck and his wet, wriggling tongue down my ear. I needed his stiff dick slammed through my asshole and down through my tender guts until he ran out of inches and I could squeeze the hot, creamy marrow out of his bone.

The tease ignored my asshole. He ignored my cliché pleas of "Shove it in!" and "Do me!" and "Fuck me, bitch!" My hands locked back around his ass, as though by pulling it against me, I could force his dick down my hole and find relief. The mirrored image of my tanned hands clawing at his pale cheeks were just more of a turn-on that fueled my own rod's romp along the rough bedspread Dave was fucking me into. Between the harsh cotton below and the harsher hunk above, my hopes of keeping my load stowed were doomed to failure.

When Dave's hands slipped beneath me and I felt my hard, swollen tits digging into the palms of his hands, my balls started to cinch up. I begged for him to fuck me, but the bastard just kept humping away at my crack, grinding his thick bone across my tender butthole until I knew I would go crazy. His heaving bubble-butt and the feel of his hands on my tits and my asshole's impossible itch all blurred together and slipped me suddenly from sensibility.

I came back to life to find the gorgeous bastard still humping away at my ass-crack and me telling him what I thought of his priorities in the sack. He gave me a minute to stop spurting and spouting off, and then reached down for a rubber. He lifted his shank out of my crack and rolled me off my very messy belly and onto my back. Before I got with the program, he was rubbered up, had scooped most of my load from the bed and my belly to lube his dick, and had my legs in the air.

We were twisted around on the bed by then, so I had a perfect view of his back and ass as he snuggled his swollen knob against my fuckhole. His head was more or less hidden from view, but the whole world seemed filled with his broad, muscular back and that fabulous ass pulsing with puissant power. As he paused for a moment between my legs, his ass seemed almost a separate, breathing creature, rising and falling, clenching and opening wide in anticipation of the pleasure to come. While he had me pinned helpless against my bed, his crank had fucked away most of the lube he'd shot between my glutes, so I had no trouble feeling the slick, soothing froth of my own jism as it pressed against my hungry asshole.

I tore my eyes from the mirror for an ageless moment as my asshole nipped at the future. Dave's eyes were on mine, his head slightly cocked to one side like a puppy looking for love. His lips hung parted and wet with pleasure. The cool breeze wafting in from the deck had failed to staunch a slight dribble of sweat coursing down across his temple and into the shock of hair which lay draped across his forehead. I was struck for the hundredth time that day by the classic perfection of his beauty. What must it be like to be the cynosure of all the world simply because of the accidental arrangement of a few bones? As my eyes bore into his, though, I saw an even deeper, stronger beauty within and was about to reach my lips back up to his when Dave stabbed me in the back with a dick big enough to make a grown man howl.

I know, because I did. I howled and yelled and screamed and hung on tight with all my soul. For the first timeless instant or three, I was sure that swollen dick would split me open like an overripe mango. Even when I felt like the guest of honor at an auto-da-fé, my feet were locked around Davey's ass, pressing as much of his hard young body up my shithole as I could manage. Once his ram-rod had broken down the gates, my secret city yielded all to him. He rushed past the slick, clenching tissues of my ass so fast that his swollen knob left only a blur of frenzied confusion in its wake. When he finally boned home, I held him still for a moment so my prostate could scratch itself on the throbbing trunk of his tool.

When I was able to breathe again, I found myself moaning like a love-sick seal, but then his ass lurched backwards, dragging two thirds of his dick back out into the world. The mirror reflected the way his asshole flared open, his cheeks parted as though gasping for the air I needed. My heels pried at his butt and then slipped into that bucking man-crack to ride his asshole as he rode mine. As Dave found his rhythm and began a steady slam-and-drag, I tried to clench down to give him the welcome he deserved. My mind wandered again as his rubberized dick shed my sperm and started really rubbing my ass the right way. By the time his balls broke open to blast their creamy cargo up my ass, I had long since been fucked happy.

I thought for a time about jacking myself while he did me hard up the ass, but I'd shot years too soon the first time around. Once young Dave got his jollies, I knew I was going to flip him over and slam his gorgeous ass so hard he'd need to have his dental work adjusted. As we finally collapsed together into a tangled pile of satisfied, sweat-streak flesh and temporarily tapped-out bones, the tropic sunset had played out across the heavens, and the evening breeze cooled and caressed our naked bodies. I looked into Dave's eyes and pulled his body tighter against my own. Something clicked inside me something I'd kept buried so deep even I hadn't suspected its existence. As I felt his arms holding me tight and safe against the world, I knew I had finally found a man I could love long and hard and forever. Besides, dental hygiene is a very good thing. A man never knows when expert advice might come in handy. I decided there and then that I would just have to keep young Dave around.

GOOD SERVICE

"Can I get you anything else, Sir?"

I looked up from my omelet and coffee and thought right off of several things he could get me. Unfortunately, in these days of sexual harassment allegations, a Marine officer has to be careful what he says to Navy enlisted types. Still, we were alone in the wardroom; it was early; and I hadn't spanked the monkey in hours. I decided I was entitled to a little leeway and answered with my most winning smile, "No, not unless you want to choke down my load while you're at it."

Men on ships sailing at the edge of empire often joke about fucking ass or sucking dick; the trick is to know when the cocky talk really means business. I wasn't positive, but when I looked up into the gorgeous young crank's fraternal, semper-fi smile, I had a hunch I'd made contact. Well, let me amend that. To be politically correct, the seamen who used to be called cranks are now FSAs food service attendants. I wouldn't want to upset my anal-retentive Navy readers with improper nomenclature. In my experience, most of the Navy is anal retentive in both senses of the term. Half the trick about military life is remembering that what seems to be is more important than what really is.

As part of his character-building process, every young seaman spends 90 days as an FSA, generally slaving away in a steaming scullery or slopping food to his enlisted brethren on the messdecks. The best and generally most beautiful of the bunch score wardroom duty. They spend their three months of cranking bringing officers food, cleaning our staterooms, buffing our passageways, and generally being of service in as many little ways as we can imagine. I can imagine quite a few.

SA Darren Dillon, USN, was the kind of kid that makes a Marine lay awake nights. He was only about 5'8", but built solid as any recruiting poster. His body was pumped and buffed and tapered to perfection. His face was chicken-delight with huge blue eyes, a ruddy complexion that positively glowed with youth, a dimpled grin just this side of sin, and a thick shock of curly black hair that hung low across his strong brow. Even his uniform was always gunnery-sergeant crisp with hard edges and a crystal clarity that made him look tight enough to be a Marine. When I got back to my stateroom after my workout one day last August, Dillon was especially easy on the eyes.

The cocky shit was sprawled across my rack, buck naked, hard, and ready for a reaming. His grin and the chronic sparkle in his eyes shouted out his eagerness so I didn't waste time with small talk. I'd just spent two hours sweating my ass off in the weight room; but for what I had on deck, I didn't need ass and the way Dillon's dick counted cadence against his belly, the smell of a man in heat didn't do much to turn him off.

As any Marine leader would agree, my first order of business was to make Seaman Dillon choke down my big dick and his smarmy smile, in that order. Before you could say "Open wide!" I had moved to my rack, lost my T-shirt and shorts, and shoved my thick nine inches of untamed Marine meat through Dillon's cute little face. Those blue eyes bulged wide as my swollen knob prodded and twisted through his mouth and back into his tight throat. He gurgled and choked, but by then I had my hands on his ears and used them to screw his face down my dick as easy as mounting a bayonet.

His tight, hot throat surprised itself with how much commissioned cock it could take and how incredibly deep it could take it. I've had Marine master sergeants gag and hurl when I've reamed my way down their gullets, but young Dillon was a born cocksucker. Instead of fighting my knob, he instinctively caressed and enfolded and surrounded it in a warm, fuzzy mass of eager sailor service. His slick throat stroked every throbbing blue vein and rippled around my pulsing knob as his suction went into overdrive, pumping up enough precum to drown the average Saudi camel caravan.

As his full lips were stretched tight around the thick base of my dick and his throat was leaning how really to say "Ahhhhhhh," his hands were busy checking out how fine a Marine-built butt can be. If I do say so, United States Marines have the best butts on the planet and Dillon obviously intended to make the most of mine. His palms coasted across my glutes, massaging them almost worshipfully as his fingers pried open my hairy ass-crack. If the rest of me was dripping sweat from my afternoon workout, my crack must have been awash; but young can-do Dillon dug right in, coasting along the tight, secret high-way to my hole. His lips and throat and fingers all worked in tandem like some deliciously infernal boy-toy machine destined to do my every bidding.

I liked the way his fingers were coasting across my shithole, but the treatment his face was giving my dick occupied most of my atten-tion. Like any great cocksucker, he kept his beat building, always an inch ahead of the rolling rhythm of my hips as I force-fed him nine inch-es at a stroke. Dillon didn't bear down too tightly, but slurped across and down my shank like a spring cloud, foggy and humid and building towards a cloud-burst. Neither throat nor tongue nor fluttering lips were dominant; all coursed along in perfect unison until I felt his warmth nur-ture and spread to a glow and, suddenly, years too soon, the cloud rup-tured wide and my shower of pearly Corps-cream sprayed deep down his semen apprentice throat.

I humped his face hard, but he pulled my ass towards him even harder, determined not to let a single drop of my sweet protein escape his maw. After I blew the first violent blasts of my load down his hole, though, I came to my senses enough to remember his boyish grin and the gleam in his eye. Nutting down his throat felt fine, but it lack a cer-tain artistic closure the situation demanded. I think Dillon was confused when I arched backwards, breaking his lock on my log until my knob popped out of his face and started spewing spume where it really belonged. Within moments, his hair and face and chest were awash in thick white flocculent threads of Marine man-seed worthy of any West Hollywood fuckflick. Spooge hung from his nose and dripped from his lips and dimpled chin until he looked like an overflocked Christmas tree gone seriously wrong. His tongue darted out to scoop up what it could, but his combined beauty and serious suction had jolted loose even more jism than even I could have handled without help.

Fortunately for young Dillon, I was standing by and didn't mind helping a bit helping a shipmate out. Almost before I'd shot the last dregs of my dick into his face, I lurched forward, pressing his head down hard against my rack and smearing my hairy nutsack into the jar-head jism draped across his face. I splashed across his boyish fea-tures on pontoons still tender and aching, but the balm my balls found to grease their skids made short work of any priggish hesitation. Dillon made some odd sucking, gurgling sounds as I skidded this way and that across his face, but I knew instinct would out in the end.

Sure enough, long before I had managed to swab up the leavings of my load off his face, his tongue and lips were slurping into overdrive, licking my nuts and crotch cleaner with every stroke. Soon, in order to find more jism to play with, I had to drag my ass across Dillon's broad, hairless chest rather the way the family dog does across a carpet when he thinks no one is looking. In Dillon's case, though, he was looking plenty.

His hands had been locked against my hips while I rode his face; but once I had added jism to the musk and man-sweat nature had stowed up my ass-crack, he pulled me forward until I slipped my nuts off his forehead and would have kept on slipping if his tongue and chin hadn't reached up to snag serious ass.

Dillon's lips lashed along, bristling through the stiff hairs that guard my virtue and sucking them dry. His nose snuffled along behind, filling his lungs with the scent of man while his hands clawed at my glutes in a frantic frenzy first to chow down on my cock-cream and then to slam his head up my ass. He failed at his last objective, but only because nature conspired against him. Nothing human could have done more.

His tongue ripped along the hairy, sweaty trough of my crack like swarm of Jehovah's Witness killer bees on a rampage. Everywhere he touched, jism and musk and sweat smeared hard into his face, leaving only the supercharged electricity of raw, untamed man-sex lingering behind to tingle its way into my very soul.

When his tongue stopped skidding and his lips locked tight around my most private pucker, the fluttering, soul-shattering, mind-numbing rapture he sucked and tongued and prodded out of my Marine asshole shut my brain down hard for the duration. Call me a pervert or a weakling, but nothing comes close to the feel of a gorgeous man's tongue tickling its way up my tight, tender asshole. My heart might keep beating and maybe I even breathe now and again; but if you held a weapon to my head, I couldn't pull myself off a mouth locked onto my ass. Some distant corner of my consciousness stays on duty, standing its post to record every bump of the tongue as it grates across my pink folds so I can savor the experience in memory. That sensory sentry relishes the firm, darting pressure of the tip as it forces its wet way into the very center of my being. Then, when my defenses have been breached and lie open to the world and the thick blade of that invading tongue has pried my hole wide, some slutty something within me revels in every salacious slurp and twisting tongue-thrust, cataloging every twitch and jolt and clench of my ass while, for the rest of my world, time has licked to a stop.

I have no clue how long my ass writhed helplessly against Dillon's mouth while he sucked and licked selfish pleasure from my depths. It could have been thirty seconds or half a lifetime. I do know that when the bastard's jaw finally locked up tight and his face was no more use to me, we were pretty much a mess. For one thing, spit and drool had splashed out of his mouth and glazed his face and neck and chest all glossy like some naughty 3-year-old caught with the pudding. For another thing, I couldn't help noticing a slick substance dripping down my back. Once my brain slipped back into gear, I vaguely remembered his body jiggling about and hoarse gurgles erupting from the depths of my ass. Hard though it was to believe, the jism dripping down my commissioned Marine flesh seemed to suggest that while he should have been concentrating on licking me happy, the selfish little bastard was busy spanking his own no-load, enlisted monkey.

I was long since good to go again, but the jism dripping down towards my ass reminded me that even seamen apprentices have dicks, too. His was only about 6" tall and no thicker than average, but it was uncut and dripping with the last throes of his creamy devotion. I twisted around to gobble his squid dick and suck it dry while my ass wriggled against his nose and chin. Once his dick was threatening to blow again, I spit it out and moved onto his nuts. They were small and tender and nestled in a crotch that smelled of nothing so much as youth. I spent several very satisfying minutes slurping his fuzzy ballbag into my mouth and sucking at his stones while his hips thrashed and twisted and humped high against my face. Everything about his `nads reminded me of innocence and the puerile eagerness to please and, by extension, of his blue eyes and dimples and curly black hair.

At that moment, I needed to fuck him up the ass more than I needed to breathe. His load had melted on my back and was dripping down across my flanks, but it could wait. I wanted to hold him in my arms and whisper the wisdom of age into his ears, but that would have to wait, too. Once I bounced down between his knees and looked back at his muscular body and the eager purity of his eyes, I knew he needed It even more than I.

I gave it to him. Without even thought of tenderness or technique, I lifted his legs towards the overhead, rolling his enlisted shithole into targeting position. His eyes flashed blue and his full, dry lips parted in desperate anticipation as I put my dick hard against his shithole. I pressed and twisted for a moment, teasing him with the torment to come, and then backed off.

I kept Dillon's legs high but lifted his head enough to slam my knob back into his mouth. The taste of his own asshole on my meat made his mouth water gushers so that within moments, my dickhead had all the lube it was likely to get. I gave his face one last masterful jab and then dropped his head in favor of a finer hole. His hot spit began instantly to dry on my dick, but I didn't mind. My long, thick dick was so swollen and his trembling little asshole was so tight, he just plain had to hunker down and tough it out if he wanted my hard-charging Marine load blown up his butt.

The instant my huge knob rammed up into Dillon's ass was one of those times you wish you'd remembered the camcorder. Tight and hot as his butt had been wrapped around my butt-busting bone, the awestruck look of lust mingled with equal parts of panic and sublime satisfaction that galloped across his face was even more of a rush. Even before the base of my dick had reamed his raw ass wide enough to burrow in, even before my throbbing knob had slammed hard against his gizzard, even before his hands clawed helplessly at my back as I used his young enlisted butt as my own private drill field, his narrow hips lurched upwards against me, slamming his straining asshole up along my shank as I was ramming it downwards into his guts.

Our bodies crashed together like thundering elk at rut with the sweaty SMAAAACK of flesh meating bone. My unconscious grunt of animal conquest echoed off Dillon's gasp of ecstatic agony and hung suspended for an instant as both our bodies cherished the first sublime moment of total possession. Then gravity dragged Dillon's helpless body back down against my rack and I cycled out to piston my way back into his slick cylinder.

As Dillon's tight, boyish ass somehow managed to accommodate all I had, his body and mine found a common cadence to drive us onward. Once the initial shock of entry had passed, his eyes opened wide with new-found knowledge, glowing with pride that he had met the challenge and, somehow, survived. Dillon's hard body rippled with the impact of every fuck-thrust. His fingers became claws as he tore at my back and ass in a desperate attempt to lock his jolting body forever against mine. I tried to help, nibbling at his ear and reaching low to teach his hard tits what a man's teeth can do, but his young lust and my mature need kept us bucking together too hard for anything as civilized as love. Like any warriors, we took what we wanted in savage emulation of man's oldest principle.

I needed Dillon's fresh young body to bend itself resolutely to my will, to beg for my load up his butt, to learn man's deepest pleasure, the muted echoes of my naked warrior lust. He yearned to be tamed and possessed and conquered to have his pack's alpha male dominate him so absolutely that he would never again be the callow yearling lost amidst the many. Almost as though I were fucking self-confidence and maturity into his ass, every brutal soul-shattering stroke of my Marine dick taught Dillon more about the world and about himself. As I reamed him raw, I couldn't help thinking back over one or two of the men who had helped cull me from the herd and taught me a better, more independent way.

The thought that years hence, young Dillon would be reaming some other recruit raw and think back on me was just too much romance for this simple Marine to handle. My cadence fell to shit, The Void engulfed me, and I blew one of the best and biggest loads of my life smack down into Dillon's hot young fuck-hole. I slammed and twisted and held on the best I could while nature took its course, but just as my hips were stumbling to a stop, the damage I'd done against Dillon's prostate also took its toll. His dick erupted in epic streams of creamy pride that blasted high into the air before they splashed back onto both of us, my rack, and the bulkhead beyond.

I only let four or five go to waste before I had undicked his ass and slammed my face down over Dillon's jism-jet. My lips frolicked across his knob on layers of hot, tangy seaman semen until my tongue needed to pry his dick wide to scoop out the last, shy no-loads lurking deep. By that time, of course, I'd pivoted my hips around and shoved my own shank back into Dillon's face so he could discover the thrill of licking his own musk off a stiff Marine's big dick. We rolled back and forth from hole to hole for most of the rest of the afternoon until Dillon

Rick Jackson USM

was due back in the wardroom to serve dinner. He limped a little when
he brought me my food that night, but by the end of his cranking tour,
he was hard and ready for anything even some rough military service.

THE HAYRIDE

Driving through the Mid-West in the heat of summer, my shirt off and top down, I had started thinking off and on about Steinbeck anyway. When I saw Jimmy standing, lost in a hopeless, mindless daze beside his wreck of a truck piled heavy with hay, a windmill slowly spinning through the summer breeze in the field behind him, I did something I'd never done before. I pulled off the road and asked if he needed any help. Two things struck me about him right off: his goofy puppy-dog happiness at having me stop and the immediate impression that he wasn't NASA material. I'd known retarded people before and read his vague combination of otherworldly contentment and the slight strain around the eyes as a sign that if he wasn't functionally retarded, he had to be what teachers liked to call "slow."

Nothing he said right off changed my mind. He stammered and stuttered and did everything but scuff at the dirt with a sheepish toe. His engine was hot and needed water, and he still had several miles to go. Did I have any water? As a matter of fact, I did -- a couple gallons that had melted in my cooler the day before. By the time we'd managed to ease the radiator cap off and decided to let the engine cool some more before going any further, I'd decided a couple other things. For one, Jimmy wasn't as slow as I'd thought. He had the look actors always strive for when the do OF MICE AND MEN -- the vacant gaze and archaic smile, the loose-limbed slouch, and the gawky, big-boned affability of a shaggy sheepdog with a stick to fetch. When he talked of graduating from high school the spring before and of his plans for the future, though, I saw through my preconceptions. He wasn't slow; he was just a bumpkin.

The second thing that struck me about Jimmy was that more than his engine was getting hot. At first, I thought he was just curious about the city-slicker. As we stood shirtless together in front of his truck, I felt his eyes on my chest and belly long before I caught him looking. Even with sweat streaming from our bodies, his tits were hard enough to chip ice. I'd never had wetdreams of doing raw, big-boned rustics; but everything about Jimmy was so wrong, he suddenly pretty damned good. His sneakers and jeans were covered in dust and straw; great shaggy blond bangs hid most of his heavy brow. His nose and jaw were strong; crystal blue eyes suited his Slavic face. The ears, though, made the biggest impression. Even men as big as Jimmy usually have cute little ears at his age; his were huge and stood at perpetual, per-pendicular attention as though he were picking up Voyager transmis-sions from the depths of interstellar space. With those ears, he might well have been.

Goofy grin and sweaty farmboy charm notwithstanding, Jimmy knew what he wanted. His massive dick had already done everything but split his jeans when he asked if I wanted to relax while the engine cooled. I knew what he meant, but had no clue where he had in mind. I'll never underestimate farmboys again. One minute he was standing beside me, licking his lips and leering heavy-lidded at the bulge running three quarters of a foot across my left thigh; the next, he had scrambled atop his rig and was tossing bales towards the edge to form a straw bul-wark against prying highway eyes. He left it only one bale high, but as I climbed up to meat him, I realized the load of hay was already stacked so high we would be invisible but to the gods.

I've always liked being naked outdoors, feeling another man's hands slipping along my body and smelling clog the air. Life seldom gets better. Stripped naked up on that giant stack of hay, I learned a new appreciation for the outdoor life. At first I smelled only the sweet summer scent of hay, but its tickle on my back and ass as Jimmy knelt between my legs to lick the day's sweat off my balls inflated my crank as nothing had done in months. The sun sucked the sweat from my body until it poured in ticklish rivulets down into the straw. My calves slid along the slick bronzed muscles of his back as he lapped like a spaniel in heat at my nuts and the base of my dick and down, deeper into more dangerous country that even I've never seen first-hand.

Rube or not, Farmer Jim had been around. The slut knew where every nerve ending lurked and how to tease it to maximum effect with-out making me blow my load years too soon. My swollen dickhead throbbed and pulsed against the harsh rust- colored curls that carpet my belly. Instead of licking my bone to the flesh, he stopped with stalk and eased back south. As his tongue prodded ever deeper up my ass-crack, my hips instinctively curled up like cheap linoleum. Hands used to controlling livestock lifted my legs until my knees were in my face and Jimmy's rough tongue was sanding the musk from my tender, twitching asshole. His tongue on my shaft and balls was better than anything I'd ever felt; the constant snicker-smack of his insatiable tongue grinding and darting and slurping across my butthole was worlds beyond anything I'd imagined possible. I've always been a top, getting my satisfaction from using my thick nine inches on tight, dark assholes; but Jimmy's sappy, sunlit body up my ass was more pleasure than a busload of marines on liberty. Seconds after he tore into my ass, every sense except the one buried up my ass shut down to enjoy the show.

His bumpy blade rasped harder across my tenderest, most secret tissues with every swipe, but that was only the melody. The way his lips locked tight around my asshole, sucking at my tight butt like a love-sick lamprey, blended the theme into a harmony. The contrapuntal tip of his tongue drilled into the very pit of my pink pucker, twisting and turning to screw its way up my butthole until he was playing music up my ass that was bigger than Mahler and more consummate than Mozart. I listened and felt and lived his farmboy face up my ass until I knew I'd never really be alive again once he pulled it away. After minutes that seemed longer than a lifetime and shorter than a heartbeat, he tried to do just that; but my heels behind his ears like stirrups spurred the slacker's face back down on the job where it belonged. As though from a great distance, I heard my soul give up a long moan of bliss and joy and ultimate satisfaction that might have gone on forever if the selfish bastard hadn't pried himself up from my ass just to breathe.

My legs collapsed onto the straw again. He knelt between my legs, panting and licking the scent of my ass from his lips, shimmering in sparkles of sweat in the hot summer sun. His chest was farm-hand broad and hairless besides. Those twin stalks of man-tit that had first shown me his need still stood tall, but now I moved my gaze down across his cobbled belly to the bull-sized dick between his legs. One look at it reminded me of my own throbbing joint, now leaking love- lube onto my belly and chest like an oil tanker in an oyster bed. My eyes met his and I read in them what he had in mind; I just didn't know whether I would give it to him -- or whether I could. Sure, his crafty country tongue taught my asshole some new tricks, but that didn't make me a bottom. Besides, even assuming my spirit wanted him to breed my butt; my flesh was weak and tender and very, very tight. His monster joint was at least an inch thicker than mine and maybe an inch longer. I'd seen enough of the damage my dick could do to a tight end to know how receiving his field advance would tear the living shit out of my Astroturf. On the other hand, those blue eyes were hungry; that young body was hard and fine; and that big, thick untrimmed dick oozed its stream of pre-cum through the floppiest, friendliest foreskin I'd ever seen. Maybe he'd get me in the end, but first I had to wrap a tongue around his tool and see what I could do to tenderize his meat.

As he lay back against a bale and let me slide my face onto first one tit and then the other, I felt his body shudder like colt in a cool rain. Greedy hands slipped across his hard flesh and learned the bucolic certainty of firm muscle and supple skin. Once his tits were too tender to chew, I lapped my salty way down across his bare cobbled belly to find his wellhead and quench my thirst. If his hay-flavored sweat had been savory, the love-lube trickling out of Jimmy's thick, throbbing country spout was artesian pure and maple sweet. It dribbled out of his fleshy crown and down in a crystalline vein that twisted around his massive dick until his low-slung ballbag collected the overflow. I started low, working my way up from his cum-clogged nuts, stripping the stud-syrup away with in one relentless swath after another. By the time I reached the underside of his dickhead, the whore had pre-cum smeared across his belly like black ice on a mountain road.

My lips nibbled at his cocksock, sucking one tender wrinkle after another up into my mouth while Jimmy put his hands on the back of my head and tried to force feed me. His hips wriggled in pleasure beneath me, but cocksucking is an art not to be rushed. As I worked his fleshy thrum up into my mouth, I made a conscious effort not to think about the perfect dick I had my lips wrapped around or about the studly young farmboy it hung off. I concentrated on the heat of the summer sun and the tickle of my sweat working through the thatch on my chest. I breathed deep of the scents of hay and the musky man-crotch. I listened to the muffled noise of traffic whizzing past, to Jimmy's moans of pleasure as each new fold slipped up into my mouth, and to the third-rate fuckflick shit he was unconsciously talking: "Oh, Jesussss. Suck that `skin. I've got more where that came from. Y'all go ahead and clean my cock."

By the time my tongue tip had worked its way through his fleshy overhang and was slipping along the secret, super- sensitive bounds of his cum-slit, Jimmy's hips were arching upward like a run-away riveter trying to pound his selfish prick up into my face. My fist locked around his cock's collar and jerked down with a vengeance, peeling his protection away and leaving his purple knob open for all the abuse I wanted to administer. His crotch had smelled fine. I'd like the taste of his dick-lube; but nothing prepared me for the indescribable taste of his naked dick. Aged sweat blended with man-musk and was tempered perhaps by some salty remnant of a carelessly shaken roadside piss. The tang of his tool was intense, but welcome as a half-forgotten childhood memory. I've sucked other uncut dicks and most tasted fine, but Jimmy's rustic rod defined the cocksucking experience. He was strong and exotic, yet familiar as a classic banana split. Now that I'd gotten through the toppings, I slipped my wet lips hard across his peeled pride to lick up the cream.

I don't know how I got all his dickhead into my mouth, but lust will find a way. My lips locked tight around his rim while my bumpy tongue set to work showing one ass-lick what damage a misplaced tastebud can do. Jimmy's hands pushed down hard on my head, stuffing his dick down my throat as he started screaming at hog-calling volume about how good he felt. His heels trapped my back; his selfish hips flew even faster upward, fucking everything he had down my gullet. I couldn't breathe; I couldn't see; I couldn't even suck. For one terrible moment that stretched on as my throat stretch out, Farmboy Jim treated me not as a person but as a thing to fuck, a convenient hole to shoot his load into. The more he ground my nose into his soft blond pubes, the more his swollen dickhead tore at the very limits of my throat, the more his hands twisted my hair and his hips slammed my face and he howled like a chainsaw murderer at a revival meeting -- the more I learned to love his abuse. Maybe there was something to this bottom shit, after all.

I'd always enjoyed being in control, dominating my partners and teaching them how to give me what I needed. With Jimmy in charge, though, I didn't have to think. I didn't have to act. All I had to do was be -- there and tight and ready to take what he needed to give. I'd no sooner decided that being treated like a blow-up sex doll was a pretty good thing when Jimmy proved how little control adolescent dicks can have. His hands and legs clenched up tight, pulling me far enough down his dick it should have gotten acid burns. Then his rhythm went to shit, he started to gurgle and howl at the same time, and I knew I was gaining protein. I couldn't taste it; his dick was too deep for that, but I felt his cum- tube pulse as one blast of non-dairy cream after another jet down my throat. Once I knew his heads were occupied, I grabbed a handful of balls with one hand and shoved the thumb of my other up against his butthole. It didn't want to give at first, but I felt his body shudder with mingled fear and excitement against the background of his breeding frenzy. Suddenly, my hand tightened around his nuts until they threatened to pop, his dick gave a leap that popped it clear of my throat and jetted sweet jolts of jism against the back of my mouth, and his ass relaxed enough to take my thumb up to the hand.

I twisted and turned up his ass the way he had down my throat, but Jimmy didn't mind. Just then I could have cut his liver out and sold it for research and he wouldn't have minded. With his creamy cum fill-ing my mouth, streaming across my tastebuds and out onto my chin with every frantic thrust of his hips, I had enough to worry about myself. As the last of his load gushed out, I locked my lips around his lizard's snout and sucked his balls flat. I kept on sucking until he had passed through howling, begging me to stop, and trying to pry his butt off my thumb and my face off his outraged root. The goad I had up his ass started him thrusting away again, intent now bringing in the second crop of the season. I'd had my chance to escape; but once his dick dug in for the duration, I had little choice but to reap whatever he sowed.

I suddenly realized what it was about him that was such a conta-gious turn-on. His monster dick was as gorgeous as it was huge, but I've seen plenty of big dicks. Shit, I use one to pee a dozen times a day. His body was as good: strong, well-built, and tanned. His classic blue-eyed farmboy innocence would have melted any pervert's heart; I had no choice at all. What really turned me on, though, was the utter-ly uncomplicated way he approached fucking. Jimmy knew absolutely nothing about pick-up lines or glory holes or cruising. He didn't need to bother with them. Sex was the most natural thing in the world -- and the most fun. After seeing livestock fuck his whole life, he had no big-city hang-ups or hesitations. If he wanted to plug a hole, he pulled out his dick and did it. He went at a man with a grin on his face and a sparkle in his eye, ready for the best time any man can have. A lot of the men I'd taken home ended up being neurotic or timid before and ashamed or bashful after The Deed. No one I'd ever met had grabbed hold of sex with the gay abandon young Jim did. With him, sex was spontaneous and instinctive -- which meant he didn't especially worry about whether you were having fun or not. Ayn Rand would have approved of his unspoken philosophy: only when absolute egoism drives a dick can sex be good. If both men are after the best possible time, the result is guaranteed to be seismic-quality bone-crunching sex. As he slammed my way back down my throat and I reached up to hold onto his powerful ass, I knew the first load he'd pumped down my gullet had only succeeded in getting the selfish dick worked up into one serious lather.

Once he was plowing away again with his steady, relentless rhythm, though, I couldn't help thinking about how Jimmy's stiff dick would feel cutting up a finer furrow. If having my throat reamed raw was such a rush; what would it feel to take his monster dick and the load it could deliver up my tender ass -- to feel his sweaty balls slam against my butt until they broke open, gushing spurt after spurt of country cream up into my guts. What would his jism feel like sloshing around up my butt as I carried it away with me like some breeder sow? The scent of his sweaty crotch in my face and the lingering taste of jism melded with the summer heat and the feel of hay and his sense of animal power to push me over the edge. I left sanity far behind, but saw quite suddenly that the Duke was right. Sometime's a man's gotta do.
. . .

I didn't care how much that fucking dick hurt up my ass. I didn't care about anything but getting Jimmy's farmboy bone up my butt and watching his goofy floppy-eared face as he gleefully pumped his load up into my guts in one butt-busting gusher after another. At first, as I struggled to break free, he kept me screwed down tight on his dick; but when I rolled backwards, pulling his dick with me and lifting my legs towards the clouds, he got both the idea and the dictionary illustration of a shit-eating grin.

Minutes before, when I gave his asshole a thorough thumbing, I had been planning to follow it up with a meatier member of my own. Jimmy had so busy using my face, he hadn't shoved anything up my ass since he'd pulled his tongue out. He wasn't exactly in the mood to worship at my shrine now, either.

What did happen was swift and remorseless: Jimmy popped his dick out of my face and let it slam with a wet SPLUNK up against his hard, sweat-streaked belly. His hands grabbed my ankles and parted them like a Thanksgiving turkey at a boys' home. Immediately my toes were in the air, his hips arched backwards and then curled cruelly upwards, slamming his impossibly swollen cannonball into my tender target like the original wrath of Doom.

The impact skidded me backwards half a bale and rubbed my back raw, but I had more important things to worry about. I'd been fucked once in the past couple years -- and that by a six-inch number who'd almost put me into traction. My butthole stretched and strained and bounced back, but Jimmy's blade was as whetted as his appetite for ass. On the next thrust, he picked up the speed towards Mach 3 and then ground rough and ready against my hole. His hands pulling hard on my shoulders and the breeding power of his hips caught my ass in a vice that guaranteed its exit-only days were over. Looking up at those intent blue eyes, crinkled with strain and sparkling with lust, I almost wanted to pat the kid on the head and tell him to run along and play. Then his rabid dick bit me in the ass and the impulse passed along with any real claim to consciousness.

The next two minutes were the most terrible I can imagine. Aeschylus claimed that "Man must suffer to be wise." If that's even partly true, I deserve a fucking Nobel. I expected my ass to burn; the thing didn't burn. It exploded in one white-hot cataclysm after another that started off at complete demolition and went rapidly downhill. Every cell self-destructed at once as his dickhead rammed its way through the tatters of my butthole. As the crest of his head plunged past, the pain grew almost exquisite. The shank of Jimmy's farmboy joint was nearly as wide as his head and by the time he'd slipped all of it to me, rippling his throbbing vein and twisting the length of that dry pole across the shrieking shreads of my shithole, I was helpless and howling with agony. Time seemed to slow as the dick dug its way deeper and harder into my guts until every throb of Jimmy's heart ricocheted through my ass. As though the outrage to my hole weren't enough, those ten inches of thick farmhood manhandled six or eight vital organs out of the way and crammed me fuller of dick than any mortal has a right to be. Every muscle I had was knotted up tight; my legs convulsed, pulling Jimmy's ass toward me as though I wanted more than what he had to give. I remember trying to breathe through the fire and wondering if there was any point.

I somehow forced my eyes open again as the broad base of his impossible dick finished off my fuckhole and his blond bush set to grinding away at the ruins. What I saw made me remember my nasty need to have him deep up where he belonged. His eyes were rolled back in his head, his tongue was hanging boyishly out of one corner of his mouth, and a shock of sunbleached hair flopped low over one strong brow as his body rippled with excitement. Jimmy was so fucking cute, his arms so strong, and the scent of sex and summer so filled the air that my body somehow forgot the agony. Rather, it used the agony, blending it with the unyielding feel of that bull- sized dick up my ass, the power of the arms holding me down to be fucked, and the glorious goofy good looks of the stud who was using me as his hole. Agony became ecstasy even before Jimmy decided I was ready for more abuse and started to pull his poker out of my flames.

My guts had been screaming for relief from the pressure, now they collapsed around his retreating rod and begged for more. He stopped about half way and gave me the second five inches again -- harder. My body erupted anew from the glow up my ass, now stoked hotter than ever by the way his hips slammed into my butt. The next stroke took away about eight inches and gave them back with interest. In no time, the selfish bastard had remembered the rhythm he'd used on my face and was fucking me faster and more furiously than ever. One distant corner of my brain felt my hands claw at his back and my heels snag his butt. I know I clamped my teeth into his shoulder and vaguely remember moaning like a punctured tire. Most of all, though, I remember the power of his arms holding me tight and of his dick doing me hard.

For the first time since childhood, I was completely under the control of another -- and I liked it. The harder he fucked me, the more my guts flamed out of control and the more I needed. He was brutal. Savage. More than beastial, for the beasts have never known civilization. Jimmy knew something of the idea; he just didn't give a shit. Time slowed to a stop as that beast of the fields chewed up my ass. I could happily have lain there in the summer sunshine and begged him to plow me into the hay forever. Unfortunately, Jimmy didn't need forever.

After minutes or hours of soul-numbing bliss, my fuck-fugue was shattered by the noise of a farmboy going off in my ear. My teeth were still sunk cat-like into his shoulder, which put my ear next to his mouth, but I did get my hearing back -- eventually.

One wave of cooling balm after another shot up my butt as Jimmy's body started heaving and twitching and flailing about as though he were the one with a live wire up his ass. I held on tight, eager for his hosing down and happy to eat his load up a second hole that day. Mostly, though, I watched his face as his body arced and shivered and thrashed and pounded in satisfaction so sublime it bordered on the obscene. His greedy eyes and parted lips, his floppy ears and the sweat pouring off his tanned face, the taste of his sweat and smell of hay, his strong shoulders and the thick uncut dick up my cream-soaked hole -- these and a thousand sensations besides etched themselves in memory where they will linger, undiminished, until my final hour.

I kept him inside me as long as I could, but when he finally flashed me that goofy grin and said "Thanks" on the way out of my ass, I got another surprise. At some point during the afternoon, I had shot the load of my young life up between us, sinking my chest and belly in a swamp of creamy froth and red curls. Fine as the experience must have felt, those thick strands of white were already melting in the heat and running down my flanks. Throbbing against my belly, my dick had never been so brutally swollen or so ready for love. When Jimmy hopped to his feet with a grin and started to stuff his dick into his jeans, something told me I wasn't ready for the afternoon to end.

I thought about his egoistic take-what-you-want philosophy and I knew one savory young farmboy who wasn't going to mosey on back to the barn just yet. I tackled him and spent the next ten minutes wrestling naked atop the haytruck. When I finally pinned his ass down and, sliding my cum-incrusted cock up and along his butt-crack, suggested that I was going to show him what it felt like having some stranger rape the living shit out of you, he just gave me that grin again and asked whether I thought I was man enough.

By the time we were both rubbed too raw to rise, the late summer sunset had come and gone, and the engine in his truck had cooled off nicely. Jimmy was late getting the hay home; but the delay served his family right for letting a horn-dog like him out without a keeper in the first place. Looking back on the afternoon, I can't help wondering which was more fun -- having that monster farmboy meat up my ass or watching his eyes sparkle as I harrowed his hole. I'd say it was about a tie. In any event, I solved another mystery that day. I'd always wondered why anyone in his right mind would want to live in the Mid-West, miles from the nearest towns -- what Steinbeck found so fascinating and noble about the people there. Now I know.

INTO THE BREACH

My brother had warned me that his landlord had hired painters, but halfway through my first annual leave since Desert Storm, I had more important things on my mind than routine maintenance. The morning before, I'd dragged my raw dick home to bed about dawn and somehow still managed to roll out of my rack about 1430 for more adventure. I was digging through my duffle bag in search of a clean pair of Levis, naked as an impure thought and groggy as a politician on the witness stand, when I noticed the kid peering in from the deck outside my guest room.

I couldn't tell whether he was impressed with the Marine Corps seal emblazoned across my hip or the way my raw Marine unit was belatedly saluting reveille. Maybe he was even enchanted by the way the five years in the Corps had built my commissioned butt into a thing of utilitarian beauty. One quick glance told me that whether from the results of my PT or his patriotic fervor, I just generally impressed the hell out of him.

Standing about not eight feet away, he wasn't so bad, either. His torso was naked to the summer sun, his mouth agape with serious craving for my cock, and his eyes wide with admiration for my hard war-rior body. I twisted around slightly to give him a better, three-quarter view while I finished taking stock of the charms he had to offer. A ban-tam-sized 5'6" 19-year-old with muscles out the ass, wearing the same loopy gape of innocence as every boot camp recruit I'd ever seen, he had obvious and potent potential.

Officers don't generally get to break recruits in that's why the Corps has sergeants and barracks showers. I've heard enough stories from gunnies I'd done up the ass, though, to know what I was missing. Looking at Tony's lean young body, his cat-green eyes and coal-black hair, I decided to ignore how raw the Aschenbach brothers had rubbed my rod the night before and go once more for the gusto.

He was lost in brain-lock when I slid the door open and suggested he come in out of the sun. Hungry green eyes raked down my body and focused, as though it were a holy relic, on the slab of tenderized meat that swung low between my thighs. Then they moved for a few fervid seconds of admiration to the eagle, globe, and anchor tattooed into the flesh across my hip. His gorgeous eyes all but slurped their way back towards their prime target, and I knew I wouldn't at all mind sacrificing some of my precious leave time to promote better Marine-civilian relations.

When he finally broke free of his spell, he looked dumbly about, dropped his brush to the deck, and teetered towards the open door as though obeying some private, otherworldly command. The moment he was through, I slammed the door shut against the oppressive heat outside and kindled a fiercer heat within.

His firm, young body shuddered as I reached low to cup his ass and force his sweaty body against me. His day's work had brewed up the gamey, musky smell of man that enveloped him like a nimbus. I reached my lips low to his neck and licked up a stream of liquid sweat before the AC had a chance to steal it from me.

The bantam's body shivered again in delicious reflex as my hands coasted upwards from his denim-clad ass and across the rippled muscle of his back and flanks. By the time my fingers found his swollen tits and were stroking them with a Marine officer's usual insistence on obedience and attention to detail, his full, foxy lips were mute no longer. One animal squeak after another surrendered his humanity until he lost all thought of language in favor of grunts and moans and rabid whines of feral pleasure suddenly loosed upon the world.

His hands were with the program from the beginning, splaying wide across my shoulder blades as though clinging to his last lock on sanity. I felt his firm, bare belly grinding hard against my thick nine inches of commissioned pride and knew he needed me to possess him absolutely. I also knew I was about to prove why they say Marines are "in the service."

As my hands rode hard across his rippled flesh, the quivering in his body echoed the quavering in his masculine moans of rapture. For a moment of pit-sucking frenzy, his face disappeared beneath a bicep and then emerged to suck at my left tit like a stray calf fresh from some foreign famine.

Tony's talented hands soon reconnoitered my back, coursing down my spine to cup my hard, naked glutes with a continuing reverence that would have been comical if it hadn't made my sore dick swell so impossibly to meat his advances. I wanted to hold his musky male body against mine forever almost as much as I wanted to fuck him deep enough up the ass to rupture his larynx.

As my lips teased his, I upbuttoned his jeans and let his lizard leap hard up against his belly. The kid wriggled his ass in a vain effort to shed his Levis, but the cowboy boots were too much for him. I tossed his ass backwards onto my bed and plucked him naked enough to make a master sergeant drool.

His sun-bronzed torso was pumped to manly perfection, yet gloriously hairless and innocent. Except for the black curlies that crowned his thick seven inches of teenage tool, his only fur led from his belly button down into that sweaty crotch. Tony's balls were surprisingly large for a lad his age, and so inviting I couldn't help myself. My face dipped down between his thighs to lick those sweaty nuts clean enough for a command inspection.

The musky smell of his stale sweat sent my heart pounding into overdrive until I was lightheaded enough to forget patience. I leaned low, cupping his knees with my elbows and lifting his body off the bed to chew at his tits and slash my tongue into his ear. His muscle-packed body was surprisingly heavy for boy of his size; but the way my adrenalin was pumping, I could have given the whole 13th MEU a serious clean and jerk. His strong arms wrapped around my neck as his feet found their rightful place in the small of my back leaving his tight civilian shithole just an inch or two from my lust-swollen lizard.

I held off as long as I could, but avoiding bone-crunching, butt-busting sex with delectable young men has never especially been one of my strengths. My dick had long since been belly-up and good-to-go, so a simple flex of my arms and roll of my hips sent that tight teenage pucker pounding down my swollen shank like the veritable wrath of Doom.

His dry shithole raked down my raw meat until every nerve ending I had felt like preparing federal sexual harassment suits. Even if I'd taken time out to lube the log, his sphincters clawing at my meat would have taken a fearful toll. Doing him dry and unfingered showed gungy, hard-charging Marine commitment to the cause but nearly ripped my dick off until the juices of his ass came to the rescue.

If anything, of course, my impetuous lack of lube gave young Tony even more of a pain in the ass. I've always liked watching a man's eyes as my egg-sized knob slams up into his guts and starts teaching him about the sweet limitations of physics. My sweaty young painter was even more than the usual rush: Green eyes have always been a special turn-on for me. His face evolved in seconds from a mask of puerile beauty and perfect innocence, through the blind reflex grimace of unspeakable agony that proved what a fucking stud I was, to the very image of a profane buddha with nirvana glowing bright from every pore.

Once he had discovered the transcendental, soul-centered peace that only great gurus and guys being reamed raw can know, his shit-chute rippled up and down my swollen shank, squeezing here and dragging there, desperate to lure me farther into his depths and determined enjoy me along the way.

The moment his eyes slammed shut and his jaw clenched to, every other muscle on his body knotted tight. His body shrink-wrapped itself around mine as his legs and arms convulsed to lock us together with our lust and take my breath away. Even before the eyes opened to brag of his new-found pleasure, his mouth imploded inward in a great, gut-wrenching gasp of indescribable pain and ineffable ecstasy. By the time my shank was buried bone-deep up his ass and the ruins of his shithole were grinding into my stiff curlies, Tony had broken through the bonds of pain and was growling and panting like a lioness in labor.

I wanted to snake my tongue along his until our kisses could short-circuit time itself, but Tony's perfect pucker of a mouth was too busy sucking air to bother with mere romance. Instead, I went back to his ear, slurping at his lobe and darting deep enough into ear to give him a spinal tap. My aural sex play made my civilian boy-slut screech all the more and levitate up my dick like a cheap magic trick.

He kept climbing until my swollen knob caught on the very insides of his sphincters and jerked his ass back down where it belonged at the broad, brutal base of my thick jarhead bone. I gave his tortured asshole a good grinding with my pubes and then held him tight, rolling my hips back to draw my sword from its sweet sheath so I could slam it in again harder and deeper and faster.

Before I could really plan the mission, I had his body backed up against sliding glass door and was slamming the living shit out of him for all the world to see. Fortunately for my police record, the world didn't seem to be watching just then.

Every cell in my body glowed brighter with pleasure as inch after thick, relentless inch rammed home where it belonged. The cruel rolling motion of my hips drove my dick like a nuclear-powered pile-driver with a broken throttle. I must have let my eyes slip shut in ecstasy, because only fleeting images remain to me of what happened next. At one point I was conscious again of his incredible musk and realized my head had somehow become wedged in his left arm pit. I remember the feel of his teeth tearing into my shoulder as our bodies bucked relentlessly together. The frenzy of our workout soon overpowered the AC and sweat poured from both our rutting bodies, slipping between us and greasing the skids of our flesh and muscle and brutal, butt-reaming bone.

Some priggish perception deep within me fought through the fog of my fuck-frenzy to warn we were about to slam the sliding door off its track. Looking back, I don't think I'd have much minded. Something about the image of fucking his hard teenage body out into the sunshine, as we rolled around on my balcony and let the neighbors hear his howls of animal pleasure while I did him deep and hard enough to make the gods themselves weep with envy, appeals to me. My brother always worries about what his neighbors think, though. Besides, the way Tony was gyrating up and down my jarhead joint was getting seriously out of hand.

I twirled around and fucked him to the floor. Once I had his back pinned, I taught him more about wrestling than he had ever wet-dreamed possible. My hands locked into great fistfuls of his long, black hair. My forearms kept his broad shoulders down while my body fucked itself into overdrive. My ass rose and fell, clenching my load closer with every fierce fuckthrust, but my eyes were opened at last and locked hard onto the green gateways to Tony's young soul.

As his man-hungry guts tore at my slashing shank and his mouth howled obscenities worthy of a tax collector, I saw myself reflected in his eyes, blurred by circumstance and ennobled by Tony's reflected hero worship. As sure as in any Vulcan mind- meld, I felt Tony and I become one, at least for the brief, timeless moment of our joining. As my thick Marine tool taught him much about life, the view from his eyes reminded me how I, too, had once been before travelling the world and commanding men in battle and feeling the recoil of my rifle as Death leaped from my hand.

I had been bright-eyed and open. In a very real sense, I was Tony in an earlier, less complicated time. Maturation implies losing the simplicity of youth as much as gaining the wisdom of experience. With my raw dick nailing Tony's fine, firm ass to the deck as he screamed and twisted and swore like any trooper, I realized that I had finally come home again.

With our eyes locked tight and his body riding fast along my meaty monorail to ecstasy, our souls joined for an instant of intimate revelation. The moment was broken years too soon as my dick dug deep against Tony's prostate one too many times. His eyes crinkled shut again as his hands clawed at my back and seven solid inches of untamed youth exploded between our heaving bodies, spraying one frothy glob of pearl-white pleasure after another up across the tanned canvas of his flesh.

The harder and farther he shot, the more his sperm-nozzle bucked out of control until I was also dripping with his load. By then, Tony was totally out of hand and had made me lose my bearing as well. Watching Tony's face distort in the torment of man's greatest gift was a world-class rush. Listening to his soul shrieking in sublime submission was fine beyond words. Feeling the tight heat of his guts purring along my dick as I pounded him even harder was the high point of my leave.

When his steamy teenage jism ricocheted off my chest and shoulder and face, though, I lost all contact with reality and felt my body turn itself inside out like some science fiction experiment gone horribly wrong except that every fiber of my being knew that pumping every ounce of jarhead jism I had up into Tony's hot young ass was incredibly right.

As his thick, spunk splashed off my body back down onto his, the savory stench of man-sex joined our animal cries to saturate the air with rapture. The sweaty smack of my hips pounding his ass as my bone drilled deep quickly staggered into a surreal, syncopated cadence no platoon could march to except in dreams.

One impossibly thick pulse of jism after another blasted up out of my overburdened balls until my rod felt about to rupture and Tony's tight ass was awash in enough Marine protein to keep a Recon company delirious for a month. I'd like to say I took careful notes of every careening cum-stain in the making, but the truth is that I could only hold on tight, having long since surrendered to man's most ancient, most primitive, and, yet, most exalted master.

When I humped my way back to life, Tony and I lay in each other's arms on the deck as our jism melted and we caught our breath. I licked his broad chest and hard belly clean before I started on his dick and made him lick his musk from my government- owned meat before I carried him to bed for an encore. My brother finally got home from work around 1800 and was surprised to find the painter still around.

When the thoughtless bastard walked in on us without knocking, he took one look at Tony and shook his head. I heard him mumble to himself as he turned and left that he hoped the landlord had arranged to pay by the hour rather than by the job. As I pulled Tony close to stop his giggles and let my hands read the braille poetry of his broad back and bubble-butt, I realized at least one house-painting job was going to take a long fucking time.

THE FIRST NIGHT

I usually try to score shore patrol duty the first night in a liberty port. When you pull into a fleshpot like Phuket, Thailand, on an LHA with 3000 other marines and squids; you know the first night is going to be a brawling clusterfuck. Most marines on liberty love to do two things: drink and fight. Nothing gets gungy marine shore patrol pumped up like slamming a drunken buddy back in line with a sharp thump of the baton up the side of his head -- well, almost nothing, but I'll get to that directly. Marines who pull shore patrol duty dress up in slick military uniforms and wander, paired like nuns, through all the bars and massage parlors looking for mischief. Since one of our special jobs was to check inside the three gay clubs to make sure nobody off the ship inadvertently wandered into joy, by the shank of the night I knew just where I belonged.

When my shift ended at 2345, I told Gonzales I was going to change clothes and hang for a while. He could go back to the Beach Guard to check out for both of us. What I really did was head back down to My Way -- a club we'd checked out early on. My idea was to rent one of the scrawny Thai boy-whores I'd seen dressed in jocks and dancing with all the verve and style of a broken marionette, take him upstairs, and bust four month's worth of palm-driven nut up his ass. I gave a glance around to make sure no one was watching, ducked into the dark hole in the wall, and changed my nasty little mind in one quick hurry. Scrawny was the last word you'd use to describe Corelli -- and he was sitting in that off-limits club surrounded by half a dozen gaunt boys trying their best to be charming -- and to admire the sequoia-sized woodie making a tent of his shorts. When he caught movement by the door, his glance met mine and transformed itself, in one gut-crunching moment of terror, into the look Bambi would give an 18-wheeler's headlights just before the impact. The uniform and SP armband told him he was as fucked as he'd ever been -- until then.

Rick Jackson USM

Don Corelli was a PFC from an AAV platoon and I'm a grunt, but we shared a berthing area and head so I knew all about him. Sailing the Gulf in summer, berthing temperatures hover in the 120s and 130s so we more or less live naked off duty. Of my hundred roommates, he owned one of the two or three bodies that had most often over the past months found its insistent and insidious way into my dreams, both waking and sleeping. He was 5'11" of firm Wisconsin farmboy tightened by the Corps into a hardened killing machine. Correli's musculature wasn't the best aboard, but his fresh chicken- delight appeal was worlds better than any of the weightlifter caricatures the ship's gym turned out. His broad shoulders and narrow waist, his flat gut and fine natural pecs were covered by soft, tanned boy-skin pumped my `nads just fine. I'd long since learnt every mole and freckle of his body from his hard, tight, marine-built butt; up across his cobbled torso, hairless save for his pits and pubes; to his foxy, fuckable farmboy face.

That face was round, with little ears just big enough for my fantasy to use as handles as my hands guided his head along my shank. Spaniel-brown eyes lived beneath a single strong brow and above a cute little pug nose. Best of all, though, was that tight mouth with its thin upper lip and lower pout that had begged for everything I had each time I'd closed my eyes and pictured Corelli as my little marine love-monkey. If I'd found nearly anyone else off the ship in the bar, I'd have had to give them a warning and run them out before I took their place; but after all the sweat-soaked desert nights of naked, unfulfilled lust Corelli had put me through, he wasn't about to get off with any warning.

Almost before his jarhead brain could slip into action, I'd grabbed the scruff of his t-shirt, pulled his ass through the bar and into the head, and cuffed his hands around a florescent light fixture hanging low from the ceiling. When his lying mouth finally came on line, I wasn't interested. I moved behind his ass and pretended to pat him down, using the quick feel to prove his young marine body was as hard and savory as I'd tasted in my dreams. My joint was already jumping out of my trou so I didn't waste any more time. Even straight marines (mythological creatures I've read about but never positively identified in the real world) are used to being fucked up the butt by the Corps. As the rabid stink of his terror evaporated, it left only the sweet, musky scent of a young man's cravings. Correli obviously needed what I had to give so there wasn't much point in tender words of courting.

I jerked down his thin cotton tie-dyed shorts and kicked his right foot out of them. A single stroke of my hand had the back of his t-shirt over his head and into his mouth as a gag, just in case he turned out to be a noisy fuck. Any other time, I'd have taken the time to travel the glorious landscape of his flesh before I boned his butt. That first night, though, was definitely not any other time. I'd caught his ass in an off-limits area; we both knew I should haul his faggot butt back to the ship for office hours and, at the very least, a massive loss of rank and pay. That night, though, I was feeling the generous semper fi spirit to the Corps. We'd handle his crime the marine way: man to man. I'd dish out his punishment, and he'd take it until I had nothing else to give.

I popped my web belt and unzipped, letting my massive marine mastiff slip his leash and leap up for a moment's freedom before it took a bite out of Correli's butt. My bulldog head, already slavering with thick, clear pre-cum, had no sooner chomped its way between his tight cheeks than his devil-dog butthole was nipping away at my milkbone like the bitch he was. As my hands gripped his narrow hips, the slight tickle down my tool told me Nature was giving Correli the only lube he was going to get. I slammed my swollen marine manmeat hard up his tight ass and felt both our bodies shudder with the promise of pleasure and the terrible threat of palatable pain.

The slut's strong arms tightened around the light fixture, lifting his body slightly off the floor and down again onto my pole, seating his butt-hole around my base, grinding his tender tissues against my wiry rust-colored bush, and begging for hard PT with every horn-hungry inch of his hole. I slid my hands up his lean flanks, glorying in the shivers that rippled through the hard bedrock of his firm flesh. By the time I'd found his passion-pumped tits and begun to give them the tweaking torment they deserved, my hips were more than good to go. They curled instinctively upward, slamming my meat up into his guts with a gusto they hadn't felt since bootcamp.

Correli couldn't decide whether to grunt when I reamed his butt hard or moan as I lay deep inside him, stirring his sea- pussy to life. His hot, bare back ground backwards against the thick red pelt that covers my chest and belly, scratching the terrible, unspoken itch he had kept buried secret and deep up inside him all those long months underway when I could have used a tight hole to nut.

As I made up for lost time, the last thing I was just then was a kind, caring lover. I needed to blow a load up his ass more than I'd ever needed anything in my young life. My pelvis took control of our destiny and laid enough pipe in the next five minutes to drain the North Slope several times over. My little marine fuck-buddy wasn't really content just to hang around and be used like a side of beef on a hook, but his options were limited. About all he could do to help was lift his torso along my crank in a series of small, feckless countrapuntal chin-ups that kept him feeling useful without getting in the way of my rhythm.

Once our bone dance was seriously underway, I dropped his tits and slid my shore patrol baton in front to master his thighs. Holding onto either end, I kept him pinned against my hips as they slammed up his tight jarhead butt the nine best inches of marine meat he'd ever fucking dreamed of. With each thrust of my tool up his hole, I instinctively pulled my other baton harder against his lean thighs, smashing his cum-clogged balls up towards his belly as though they were dough and the cruel, space-age plastic were a rolling pin guaranteed to get a rise out of him.

The racket of his sweaty flesh and muscle slamming along my bone soon drowned out the shitty music leaking in from the bar. The shirt in his mouth did little to keep him quiet, so I wasn't especially surprised to see the door open and heads pop in to investigate. What those skank bar-boys were doing was the last thing on my mind as I lifted Correli's body from the deck, pulled his butt back into a better angle, and got righteously busy.

If he'd been groaning and grunting before, once I'd swept him off his feet, the slut sounded like a cougar with his nuts caught in a blender. My dick had forgotten how fine ass could feel, but Correli's slick shitchute reminded me. His butthole was tight locked around my swollen shank -- but after four months of the float it had to be. The real revelation of his need lay inside his ass: the satin slickness of his guts rippled along my crank in endless waves of soul-searing caresses, pulling me harder and faster and deeper into his hole with every fierce ream of my rod down his farmboy fox hole. Swinging slightly from the fixture, the trackie whore summoned up some magical reserve of consciousness to vary my angle of entry with every stroke, exposing new and tender territory to each terrible assault of my gungy grunt tool.

I used his ass for fucking ever -- slamming my swollen dick up his guts, feeling his sweat drip against my flesh and splatter between us, listening to the echos of our rut ricochet off the tile walls of the head and count cadence for our pleasure. Our tattoo grew ever more frenetic and his butt hotter and tighter, until my balls turned on me and, years too soon, shot busted the original nut of creation up into Correli's PFC shitchute.

I dropped my baton and clawed helplessly at his hard, heaving body as we flailed about like cherry boots, my ass clenched tight, pressing every drop of the jarhead jism I'd been saving up where it belonged. As I came somewhat back to life and found he'd spit out his gag, I felt my pubes tearing the living fuck out of his shithole and heard his screams and profane anthems of ecstasy as we loved life together. By the time he'd begun to settle down, I'd ground everything I had up his ass and wanted a break before I dug down deeper to stir my load. My joint was still hard as a gunny's head, but while I had Correli hanging around helpless and horny, I was going to make the most of the situation.

When I dropped my news bitch's feet to the floor and unplugged his hole, I noticed our crowd of bar-boys had swollen -- but they seemed content to watch so I didn't care. I'm sure before we were finished, we taught them a world of new maneuvers. Correli was still panting and talking dirty so I stood in front of him like a DI with an especially retarded recruit. He was on about how good he felt and how much he'd needed my thick dick up his hole, but his mouth was getting on my nerves. I reached between his thighs, grabbed a fistful of nuts, and shut him up quick.

Then I sucked his body as he hung before me, twitching and helpless more with need than from the cuffs. I started with his pouty lower lip, wrapping a firm hand around the back of his neck and grinding his face to give my mouth what it craved. The hot breath jetting from his pug nose and the sweat dripping from his boot face did the impossible: they turned me on even more. I lapped my way across his neck to suck for a time at his left ear lobe. Once my hands were on station behind his muscular back to keep him from completely losing his bearing, I tongue-fucked his ear until he was ruined for other men for all time. When I'd finally tired of holding him steady to keep him from spazing, I left his ear and worked my face slowly down to his tits. They were hard and tender and just the thing for a meaty midnight snack.

As my hands slid along his flanks, across his rippled marine gut, and up the cobbled lane of his spine, I chewed his tit-stalks like a cur with a fresh bone. The slick texture of his sweaty body and the glorious stench of man kept me from concentrating, but the ageless autopilot of our kind had never failed me. When one tit had been chewed numb, I moved on to the next, and thence down to his belly button and below. As the whore thrashed about, trying to hook one naked leg about my body without losing complete control, I licked and slurped and gnawed my way by slow, insatiable stages down to his ballbag.

Once on station, I chowed down on the same fuzzy protein pips I'd just cracked open with my baton. The mongrel devil-dog lifted one leg so I could lick everything he had, but I passed on the impulse to slip my tongue up his ass -- not because I didn't want to, but because I knew I'd rim his ass raw before the night was over. Right then, though, I had other things on my mind: sucking his thick, leaky dick.

A thick stream of syrupy love-sap had been oozing out of his log since I'd stripped his ass and used it to clean my weapon. His wrinkled ballbag was so sweet with his love- lube, there was no fucking way I could keep from lapping my way upward and locking my lips around the head of that dinosaur-class lizard. My hands instinctively locked themselves hard around his firm, marine ass as I my lips coasted across the hot, swollen surface of his purple head. My palms burnished his butt, my fingers pried deep down his ass-crack towards my load, and my face wrapped itself around his pulsing pecker like a glutton with an extra chow pass.

I was too busy having a good time to take notes, but if you've ever had your throat stretched wide by a leaky jarhead dick as you've molested the meaty ass already sodden with your jism, you know how satisfying life can be. If you haven't, let's just say I recommend the experience. Some distant corner of my brain heard him cooing shit again and vaguely registered my own jungle grunts of pleasure, but it wasn't until I felt Corelli's ass clenching tight against my fingers and his ballbag pressing against my chin that I came back to my senses. The slut thought I was going to swallow his load -- rather, we both knew I was, but not there. Not then. We had four days left in Thailand and for the duration, I'd already decided Corelli would be confined to quarters -- mine. Long, slow, easy love would alternate with rough marine grudge-fucks once we were together in my room at the Patong Beach. I'd use his body every way but upside-down in the closet; but as he fucked my face with his desperate dick, I had to make sure we both remembered who was on top.

In a classic example of military heroism and self-sacrifice, I pried myself off Corelli's meaty marine weapon and left him hanging. His jaw dropped in disappointment; but when I moved to the rear for some classic entrenchment, that trackie fox hole welcomed my troopie tool home from the front with everything but yellow ribbons and a ticker-tape parade. His arms lifted his body back into the air and down on my shank again, his feet reached back to pull me harder into his body, and one seismic jolt of animal satisfaction after another rippled through the hard, naked bedrock of Corelli's desert warrior body.

If my dick was stiff and swollen the first time I'd shoved myself up his ass, now I was one gone grunt. My frothy jism greased the grooves of lust as his gluttonous guts gripped my meat and my body humped his hole like a Homo erectus with a bad attitude. I may have heard the cuffs grate against the light fixture as I fucked his hole; once when I was chewing on his ear lobe, I opened my eyes to see every scrawny rental unit in the bar standing in the doorway spanking Frank. The smell of mansex saturating the air, the sounds of our beastial rut, and especially the perfect feel of my peg in his hole working like the perfect military machine conspired together to shut down the last remnant of mammalian consciousness. I slipped into the delicious agony of a nirvana so complete that perfect pleasure destroyed desire and I reamed that mean marine machine forever.

When forever jerked to a stop and I recovered my bearing, I'd lost enough protein to feed Poland for the winter, but I was far from wanting to stop. I kept humping that hungry hole, not because I had anything left to give, not because I thought either of us could take another stroke, but just because it felt so fucking fine. By the time the boy in me had died and I remembered senseless civilized shit like treating my bitch right, I was dragging tail anyway.

I slipped out and staggered around to give Corelli a sloppy kiss by way of reward before I pulled his ass off the light fixture -- only to find he'd been a bad recruit. Whether because of my talented tongue or the tight need of my throat or the hard boning I'd given his butt, the boot bastard had lost his own bearing and sprayed spume all over his sweat-streaked torso and the floor beyond. I was tempted to order him to lick his load off the deck, but by the time I had his wrists temporarily uncuffed, I'd thought of someplace better for him to put his tongue. It took nearly ten minutes for us to get to the hotel and register. Somehow my ass kept from raping his face before the door shut behind us, but you can bet your Sharpshooter medal I made up for lost time was I had him alone, just where I wanted him -- in my bed for the duration.

In a lot of ways, each of the nights that followed, and the long days back to Pendleton, and the months that have followed since have all bred even better love. Now I can make him quiver with a look and there's not a hair on his hide or a pore on his pecker that I don't know and love repeatedly. Somehow, though, that first, frenzied, desperate night will always burn brightest in memory. It was then I found how fucking fine two young animals in heat can feel.

THE BLACK AND TANS

Let's face it, when you're young and built and hung, getting laid is no adventure: it's inevitability. The adventure comes in discovering things about the meat you're molesting or letting it teach you something new about yourself. Everybody you cum across is different one way or another. Drilling away to find the core of that difference is the main thing that makes slam-bang buttfucking sex more interesting than a quick handjob on the sly.

One sample sea story should show what I mean. About halfway through the Desert Storm I was on a ship that pulled into Dubai for a three-day liberty. The first day out, I sniffed around town plenty in search of adventure. The whorehouses were easy enough to find, but nobody could give me a line on where a young sailor could tickle some tight Arabian tail. If you know anything about the Middle East, you know how unbelievable up that sounds. For gay young bachelors in the mood, the Middle East is Party Central.

The second day I scored big. I walked off the ship at Port Rasheed, crawled into a taxi on the pier, and told the pair in the front seat to take me back over to Deira. Since that's where the cathouses were, I thought it was as good a place as any to keep looking for something tighter than whorettes. Playing a hunch, I asked the young Arab in the front seat (who seemed to be translating my English for the Sudanese in charge of the driving) where I could find some boy-butt to fuck. His eyes opened wide and he let off a stream of Arabic that must have meant something because the driver's gaze richocheted off the rear-view mirror until I felt as though my ass had been scanned by a Romulan bird of prey.

The driver jabbered back at the Arab, and I got asked over for the day. They shared what the Arabs called a "villa" and we would call a "condo." I guess the place was OK. I was only there for two days so I didn't see much except the bedroom. That was more than worth a trip around the world. One whole wall and the ceiling were done over in mirrored titles. A videocamera on a tripod stood in front of the window and two TVs straddled the foot of the bed. The Arab introduced himself as Abdul-Rahman Zayad Al-Kanoo and his tall, very black Sudanese friend as Feisel Sultan Al- Nahareesh. I had already starting thinking of them as Tom and Conan, so that's what I'll call them for simplicity's sake.

Tom rather looked the way Tom Cruise would look were he Arab. His skin was a dark tan color, rather like coffee with just the right amount of non-dairy creamer. A shock of hair over one brow, a perfect nose and jaw and, especially, teeth continued the similarity. Once he pulled off his thobe, I saw his body was also aces. I've never had the pleasure of doing a probing investigation of the original, but, except for the Islamic abbreviation of his manhood, this Tom more or less fit my idea of a perfect good time.

Conan, on the other hand, looked nothing like Schwarzenegger except for his size. He must have been 6'4" and was filled out with more muscles than an Olympic triathlete gold- medalist. Once his white thobe hit the floor, I was amazed at his blackness. I'd done plenty of American blacks, but this guy was so dark he seemed to be a hole in space. Up close, his face was, after its East African fashion, as strong and well-defined as Tom's -- maybe a young Sidney Potier built like the Washington Monument.

Since I was the guest, they started off tongue-tickling me, tearing into my body like a swarm of locusts after the big sleep. Tom's specialty seemed to be ballbags, while Conan was more into tits and armpits -- but they both got around. The Navy's free rubbers and free mail are about the only bargains left in military service, so I'd thrown a couple dozen of the former into my backpack before I left the ship. The guys thought they were great fun -- or, at least, Conan did until he tried to squeeze into one. He finally made it, but that was a show in itself.

I lay across their bed, watching their reflections off the ceiling as they licked me raw. Even if they hadn't given me a videotape of the action, I'd never have been able to forget the picture we made: my untannable redhead's skin and rust- colored bush; Conan's great black presence as his head chewed on a tit, my white hand standing out stark against his black curls; and Tom's black hair and coffee-colored body stretching away between my white legs as he licked my balls like a spaniel and made me wag my tail and bark with pleasure. Both their backs and asses extended out away from me, catching the glint of sunlight streaming through the windows and teasing me with dreams of the Afro-Arabian assholes buried deep between deliciously dark sets of manmuscles.

I could have stayed there forever letting them chew their way into my affections, but their dicks needed relief. I'd long since learned that Arabs like to be tops, to show that they're in control. I like to sink a shaft; but if I end up on the bottom, that usually works out OK, too. In Conan's case, though, I wasn't so sure. I'm something of a stud aboard the ship, but this guy could pick my ass up and ruin me for other men. I asked Tom what they usually did and he smiled as told me that Conan was hoping to do me but understood I wasn't man enough to handle him. Later on I learned that Tom had never let Conan near his ass, but just then I felt the need to sacrifice my butt on the altar of American manhood.

Before I got that involved, though, we lay in a tangled heap upon the bed, caressing one another in a way foreign to most American men. I've heard that women are good holders and strokers, but most men in my experience want to suck or chew or fuck. These two were perfectly content to spend the afternoon holding me in their arms, brown and black and white all tangled together in a muscular montage of shared scents and textures completely unlike anything in my experience. The heat from their bodies, the musky scents from their pits, their exotic accents, the mid-afternoon call of the muezzin drifting in through the open window with the scent of unfamiliar spices, and a myriad other details of that sublime afternoon have blended together like those multihued arms and legs to form the most treasured memory of my sexual life.

If, like Conan, you've been waiting for the down and dirty, it did happen, though not quite as I'd expected. Tom started things off, straddling my face, dragging his dusky ballbag across my face until decency demanded I suck his nuts like a squirrel with rock candy. In another lifetime, I'd have sunk my face up his butt to lick his shivering pink pucker. I did check it out, but until somebody can fix me up with a vaccine that works, I've put a reluctant but firm halt to my inclination to be an ass-lick. As it was, the action I gave his balls made him squirm as though they were caught in a bear trap instead of my loving, tender, ball-crunching embrace.

All the while I was watching myself chewing on Tom's ballbag, Conan was between my legs, licking my own nuts, lapping his way long my crotch, exploring the novelty of my stiff, rusty pubes, and getting ready to do me hard. He started out slowly, dipping his fingers into a tin of something super- slick that looked like camel snot, but probably wasn't. Only one massive hand was necessary to lift my legs so he reached between my cheeks with the other, shoving one giant finger carefully up my ass. The finger was twice the width of mine, but Conan wriggled and prodded so gently that the camel snot let him fingerfuck my hole with less of a strain than a few clumsy needledicks of unpleasant memory. Since I had a mouthful of his buddy's balls, I brought my teeth together as a gentle reminder to Tom that if his Sudanese sex-kitten made any wrong moves, he could end up a eunuch. Unfortunately, my ball-busting had been so successful, and Tom was already squirming around so loudly on my face, I doubt Conan noticed much difference.

He kept at it, easing my ass wider by the minute. With my legs in the air and him at my hole, I think I learned how women in delivery must feel. By the time he had two of his huge fingers up my butt and was stretching them wide, I was plenty uncomfortable. I didn't hurt, exactly, but I wasn't about to break into Broadway show tunes, either. Only the image of those two studs going at me head and tail kept my mind off my troubles.

Then my troubles mounted -- along with Conan. He spread my legs like a parakeet's wishbone, wriggled up to my hole, leaned forward to give Tom a sloppy kiss on the mouth, and jerked my legs south and my body onto his joint. Fortunately for Tommy, I'd stopped gnawing on his `nads as soon as I saw what was up. Once Conan's monster meat was up my ass, I wasn't uncomfortable any more. I was fucking devestated. Just looking at his dick -- and, believe me, I'd done that a lot while he was prepping my sea-pussy -- I could tell that the rubber was holding him in the way a girdle used to do a fat lady back in the good old days when they wore such things when they went out in public. Even packaged as it was, his Sudanese meat was more than I could handle. One wave after another of gut-wrenching, mind-numbing pain shot up my spine and enveloped me in seizure after horrific seizure of agony being description. I was about to tell him to get the fuck out of my ass, when I looked over at the wall and then up at the ceiling. My white legs wrapped around that huge black butt were so foxy I didn't at first notice the brown hand massaging Conan's asscrack. I got so tied up in the look and smell of our little live sex show, I was able to put off thinking about how fucking much I hurt.

Conan kept my body more or less steady for a few minutes, spitted like a goat at a family reunion. He probably hoped my butt would loosen up enough for a good time to be had by all. By the time he was ready to slide me up and down his pole, Tom was slipping him his own fine Arabian pipeline. Maybe that's what he was waiting for, because once Conan got a dick up his ass, he started to breed me hard. My butt had just settled down to a dull burn when I felt Conan's hands slide me along his pole. When I do a dude, I keep him more or less steady and slam my joint up into him. Either because Conan was too much bulk to move without setting off the local seizmographs or because Tom was hard in the saddle, he didn't much move his hips. He just held me suspended in his forearms a foot off the bed and pounded my ass against his pelvis, impaling my guts on his glorious, grotesque ebony dick. Even straining as I was, I could tell how thick his shaft was. In other men, I'd relaxed once their thick dickheads were inside me and I only had their shafts to shift. Conan's head was enormous, but his shaft was thick and firm and rich with veins that throbbed beneath the thin rubber skin and carried on the tradition all the way down to his even thicker base. As I jolted along his Sequoia-sized log, only the sight of his broad chest above me and my legs wrapped between the sweat-shining small of his back and Tom's rich coffee belly kept me on even keel. I looked round to a TV monitor to watch Tom's tan ass clench tight as he drove his dick hard up into Conan's beautiful black butt. I tried to yell to him to fuck the glorious bastard harder to get some of my own back, but I was sliding along the bar up my butt so hard the breath just wouldn't come.

I did, though. Whether from the general torment or the sublime visual images or the punishment my prostate was taking, I felt my balls flush free -- but not in kind of the mind-blowing, gut-wrenching, rockets-exploding jism jam I'm used to. Instead of blacking out when my insides started to flip over, my consciousness was fine-tuned. I was aware of every sight and whisper and scrape of African bone against each exposed Irish-American nerve up my ass. I saw my balls clench and my dick launch jism up onto my belly and chest and the bed beyond. I felt every glorious wave of cock-snot zip up through my dick, stretching it wide to flood past, and then zoom out my jism-jet like AFFF out of a fire hose. I felt it splash against me and splater and slowly liquify to run down in ticklish rivulets that would have bothered me any-time I wasn't being slammed up along the biggest, thickest, angriest looking piece of manmeat I'd ever seen.

After I blew my load, Conan dropped me onto the bed so he could use one hand to do a body fingerpainting with my load. The cream white would have looked better on his velvet-black canvas, but, hunching over my ass, drilling away faster and deeper and harder than ever before, he seemed contented enough. A look at the mirror showed Tom, standing now to keep his dick up Conan's ass. They both slammed away while I lay there watching, more a spectator than an actor in the best show of my life.

Both the boys had been making so much noise all along, that it wasn't until I felt Conan grinding his short culies up my ass that I real-ized he'd come up with a load of fingerpaint, too. He ground some more until Tommy let loose a jackal-like howl and blasted his Arabian load up his buddy's black butt. A giant hand reached back to grab Tommy's head and pull it against his shoulder for a last hug of love or friendship or, maybe, just shared accomplishment before we collapsed together onto the bed to sort things out.

I liked the fingerpainting idea so I stripped Tommy's cum-clogged cocksock off his bone and dumped his load onto Connan's belly. Connan's cum was considerable -- but misadventure had back-washed it out of his American-sized rubber from lack of room. His gooey balls had dripped down onto my ass and thighs, making me plenty messy but wasting the crop I'd sacrificed so hard to bring in. We mucked and mired about until the boys thought it was time for a long, sloppy, very confused shower.

They lent me a thobe so we could go out to dinner, though I don't think I fooled anyone into thinking I was Arab. The excellent meal was mainly mutton and sauce, eaten with scraps of pita bred. After they took me home and reclaimed their thobe, they showed me how to use an Arab crapper to advantage, taught me a few new positions and tried out some of mine, and let me see some of their other home movies -- not that I needed video skin to get me in the mood with those two naked beside me. The next two days are a blur, but whenever I think of them, the distinct particularity of our skin shades and body types and cultures stands out in memory, even as our bodies merged to share who we were. I suppose Tommy and Conan were guys I'd have done if I'd seen them in Kansas. The exotic thrill of mixing cultures and the glorious image of black and tan and white all wrapped up together, though, is what made those two days in Dubai the high point of this desert defender's young life.

THE BLACK CAMEL

I re-read the letter for about the thousandth time. Just looking at Dave's handwriting game me a rush -- knowing that the hand which held the pen also beat him off. Every time I got to the part about him coming to town, I got hard. The letter was couched in the careless, profane, abusive language we sailors use with one another, but the tone was unmistakably affectionate. We hadn't seen each other since I left the NEW JERSEY months before to transfer to shore duty at FTG Pearl Harbor, but we'd spent almost two years together in the NEW JERSEY's Combat Information Center. Since we were both STG2s [second class petty officer sonar techs], we worked side by side, slept in the same berthing, and grew ever-closer together as the CIC duty roster slowly changed over the months. By the time I'd asked for my transfer, I'd become Davy's best friend; he had become the center of my universe and the cause of my greatest torment.

I was in my rack reading a Charlie Chan novel when Dave reported aboard. Combat Systems berthing aboard the NEW JERSEY was always hotter than a marine's butthole, so we usually kept our rack curtains open when we weren't sleeping. Every little breeze the ancient fans could crank out helped some. Because we'd just come back from a week's sea trials, I hadn't been on the town for awhile, and my ball-bag was swollen tight. When I looked across at that ass, I lost all interest in solving helping Mr. Chan solve his pesky tropical murder. Dave's middle rack was right across from mine so when I looked up from THE BLACK CAMEL and found him stowing shit into his rack-pan, all I could really see was that beautiful bubble-butt. He was wearing his cracker jacks and, bent over as he was, that ass was an outrage against modern morality. Two tight clumps of muscle, each a man-sized handful, stuck out at the world. When he straightened up and said his name was Dave Dalton, I saw that the eyes would be a problem, too. They were as green as a cat's and surrounded by long, doe-like lashes the chestnut color of his thick, wavy hair. His face was OK -- a strong jaw, high cheekbones, perfect nose, blinding Hollywood teeth, and all the rest that goes with the All-American face -- but it was set on that awesome body besides. The gorgeous bastard was the avatar of my dream-hunk. I was fucked.

After four years in the Nav, I'd gotten really good at pretending studs didn't inflate my crank. For the first several months Dave was aboard, I had no problems. I kept my lurid little mind busy with jerk-off fantasies involving that tight ass and those green eyes. The more I got to know Dave, though, the more I liked him. I think our real problems must have started when I noticed him after his shower. I made it a rule to save my pecker checking for the baths because I figure there's no percentage in tormenting myself with USN meat. When I woke up from a nooner to find his freshly showered dick practically in my face as he was towelling his hair, I nearly reached for the gusto. It was only in front of me for seconds, but all I've had to do ever since is close my eyes to see it -- beautiful, uncut, thick, about eight inches long, and complete with a generous flourish of skin at the tip. That perfect peter stretched out over his egg- sized balls like a snake over a log. From that day on, life grew progressively harder.

The next few weeks were tolerable because we were about to go on WESTPAC, and the CO was working the living shit out of everybody. Aboard, I didn't have time to think of dick. On my few days off, I'd go to the Castro and find some fine young face to fuck until the image of that snake faded back a bit into the jungle undergrowth. Once we got underway, though, my cool turned to shit.

For one thing, Dave and I were in the same duty section -- working side by side at the sonar console. We were off at the same time so when he wanted to hang out, play UNO or Trivial Pursuit, or just shoot the shit, I was generally around. The nights were obviously the worst. Like most guys aboard, he slept naked in the heat. He often kept his curtains pulled shut for privacy's sake and so he could ready himself to sleep without bothering others; but when berthing was unusually hot, I'd look over in the middle of the night to see the red battlelight reflected off his hard, lean body. Dave is usually a belly sleeper. He liked to curve his right leg beneath him and face the bulkhead -- which meant that those two handfuls of ass were pointed directly at me -- begging for it. Four feet away, I'd try to sleep and fail. The muscular back running from his wide shoulders down to his narrow waist would have been bad enough, but that ass was just too much. I'd shut my curtains and swelter until I'd spanked a couple of monkey loads into a handy sock. Those were the good nights.

After an unusually rough day, he'd be restless. He'd pitch and turn and usually end up on his side, arms wrapped around his pillow with his dick sprawling out across the mattress from under his chestnut curls and his nutsack draped down across his solid thigh. Then I didn't have to deal with the ass, but his massive, hairless chest crowned by gorgeous tits was even worse. His stomach was so flat that even when he was asleep, it seemed rock-solid.

One night around midnight, three weeks or so out of Alemeda, my crank was rubbed raw so I was trying to sleep without shooting off again while I watched him toss and turn. Sure enough, he clutched his pillow and began to smile as his dick started swelling. The head was first, creeping out like a reclusive cyclops as the skin ruffle slowly stretched back over the head I'd never seen. In no time, he was up off the mattress and had grown to about ten inches. By the time the skin had completely exposed his plum-sized head, that cock was stiff as iron, and standing tall way past his navel. With every beat of his heart, the dick would throb, and pound itself against the center of his belly. The larger he grew, the more he throbbed and the wider the bastard grinned. I was nearly cumming from watching the show when I saw him jerk awake.

His eyes darted around the compartment to see whether anyone else was awake and, once reassured, pulled his curtains shut. I heard him spit into his hand a couple times and then all was quiet save for the glorious sound of flesh against bone. After about five minutes he started to hiss something like a steam locomotive running dry. I heard his limbs jerk, his breathing stop, and, after a few minutes, the rustle of cloth. Soon afterwards, Dave opened his curtains, rolled over onto his belly, and drifted off into the sleep of the just with his pucker peeking out at me from the smile of those tight cheeks, leaving me to put another blister on my dick trying to squeeze out enough spunk to get to sleep.

The next week, we pulled into Pearl for four days and Dave and I did the tourist bit. That was my first time in Hawaii and I loved it. During the day, we drank, hiked up Diamond Head, swam, lay in the tropic sun, drank, and cruised Waikiki. Nights, we spent drinking. Our last night in town, Dave said I was on my own. I suspected he was headed for Hotel Street and some cheap, meaningless sex -- just what I needed myself. I'd looked up the number of the local gay information service our first day in port, so I knew about the Kuhio District and its bath, bar, and other family businesses down in Waikiki -- just a 60õ bus ride from Pearl. That afternoon, evening, and until six the next morning, I fucked everything that would move -- asses, faces, hands. I went through more Trojans than the Mycenean armies, but when I got back to the ship, I knew I could handle the pressure -- for awhile.

The following months strengthened our bonds. When we stopped in Chinhae, a pack of us hired a taxi for the trip to Pusan. Dave and I ended up in the Florida Club. The "hostesses" were insistent and I'd had enough to drink that when Dave suggested we take them upstairs for the evening, the idea seemed to have merit. We ended up in bedrooms separated only by a curtain so I was able to enjoy the sounds he made as he humped. I'd gotten excited enough to hop into the saddle myself and was riding away, dreaming that the slack hole beneath me was really Dave's tight virgin ass, when who should burst in with his monster cock waving about but dangerous Dave himself. He was yelling some shit about a rat roughly the size of a pony, which was supposed to have run through our rooms. I hadn't seen anything, but then I'd had my eyes closed in fantasy. I could easily have missed a circus troop of three unicorns and a mastodon. All four of us spent the next ten minutes looking for the phantom rat.

Dave finally tired of the safari and dragged his still-rigid dick back to bed. Fortunately, he neglected to close the curtains -- so for the rest of the night I was able to watch his ass in action as it rammed that monster man-meat home. He pronged the wench four times before we left; I was more or less constantly in the saddle. She certainly wasn't much -- loose and gushing the whole time and interesting as a theology seminar, but Dave's example was inspiration itself. I hoped against hope that I could pump enough socially acceptable spunk to dry up my pump. Besides, there's something about two guys going wenching together which strengthens the ties of male bonding.

We went on to Yokusuka, Hong Kong, and the PI, but I was able to avoid wenching until we hit Subic. The Philippines was a kind of Disneyland for sailors, so I knew there was no way to avoid doing it there. The night we got in, I streaked out the gate and down to a famous gay bar on Rizal Boulevard. I found a meaningless, transient relationship which was consumated in a flea-trap hotel down by the Olongapo Casino. The guy was nearly as bad as the Korean bitch, but at least I got off enough to be sure I could trust myself the next night. I'd already promised to go up to Bo Barrito with Dave. A three-peso, thirty minute jeepney ride from the base, "the barrio" comprised a quarter-mile stretch of highway with cheap, well-stocked whorehouses on either side of the dusty road. For about seven bucks, a sailor could get wasted, hire a girl and room for the night, and still have money left over to get drunk the next morning. What the Ka'aba is to Muslims, Bo Barrito was to squids. Dave and I started off with other guys from the ship but ended up in a joint called The Buzzard Inn. The rooms were better than usual, but Dave apparently had trouble with his wench. We parted about midnight and by 0030, he was at my door, fuming about the static he was getting from "his bitch." I thought fast and invited him in, suggesting that the two of us spend the night pronging mine.

I'd started off already, dreaming away of Dave's tight, hot little hole as I got the girl (who had the sweet, if inaccurate name of Baby Ruth) warmed up. As Dave shucked his clothes, I suggested he take up where I had left off. When the girl saw Dave's tool, she shied away, but I gently reminded her that I had paid her "bar fine" and had the documents to prove it. She let Dave have his way -- with me watching every fucking move. With my running commentary, constant suggestions, and encouragement, Dave set to. I saw at the end of the bed, watching his dick sliding in and out of her and dreaming that it was me.

Once he was underway, I moved even closer and played with them as they fucked. By this time, I was impressed and moved around so that the wench could suck me off as Dave was ramming his swollen rod into her. It wasn't the kind of blowjob I would have liked, but certainly was better than nothing. He lasted about ten minutes the first time, then I hopped aboard while he did the color commentary. I insisted that he move up to let her blow him, just inches away from my face. The vision filled me with a passion unlike anything I'd ever known, but was frustrating as hell because I knew that was as close as I would ever get to his dick. For our second go-round, we used the ever-popular sandwich ploy: Dave on the bottom impaling Baby Ruth, me atop her fucking her ass as though all I needed to do was ram hard enough and I'd be through to him. Looking past her at his face as his lips parted and eyes clinched shut while he shot off inside her, I delivered the best load of my life. We bucked and thrashed like animals. It was great! One or the other of us was at her for the rest of the night. By the time we caught a jeepney for the base the next day, we were almost as intimate as I'd have wished.

As I re-read the letter yet again, that night in Bo Barrito, the high point of the WESTPAC, lived in my mind over and over, like some loop-projector gone wrong. We'd had other fun times, but for weeks afterwards, that night haunted my sleeping and waking hours until I knew I had to get away from the NEW JERSEY before either My Secret spewed out or my sanity unraveled. I'd liked Hawaii and, since I was about due for a shore billet, I decided to ask for a transfer to Pearl. We had one last blow-out at the Terror Club in Sembawang, Singapore before I left -- and promised to keep in touch. Since then, I'd gotten a few cards, and now The Letter.

When I picked Dave up at the airport the next Saturday, I had fears on several counts. First, of course, I didn't want to let My Secret slip out after keeping it hidden for so long. Not only would I lose his respect, but if anyone else found out who I was, my career could end in mid-stroke. Then, too, one always feels awkward when meeting old friends after you've grown apart. By the time we'd downed our first brews, though, I knew that nothing had changed. We were still so close that I could often tell what he was thinking from a glance. We spent the rest of the night drinking and, by the time we finished off the last of the case at my apartment, we were the dictionary illustration of "shit-faced."

I'd taken digs in Salt Lake, but hadn't gotten around to finding a roommate yet, so there was plenty of room -- but only one bed. Dave insisted that I use it. After all the beer I'd drunk, I more or less passed out as soon as my head hit horizontal. Dave was still up, finishing his shower and turning off the lights. I hadn't been out long, though, when I felt Dave shaking my shoulder. I looked up and saw him starkers, with his hair still deranged from the shower. He mumbled something about the air conditioner being too cold on the floor and did I mind if he climbed in with me.

If I'd been sober, I'd have come up with some reason why it wasn't a good idea. Fortunately, I was drunk enough that I thought I'd be able to sleep through the night without raping anybody. I rolled over and he slipped into the bed in his belly-down position. I winked out.

I think I woke up once to feel his arm lying across my chest, but otherwise slept like a drunken sailor. The next morning, I drifted up to the twilight state between sleep and life with a piss hard-on. My subconscious was debating whether I could put off waking up to pee until later when I felt a fly on my forehead. I brushed it away and discovered that the guy with me was brushing my hair out of my face. I automatically snuggled closer, put my arm around his waist, and asked how he'd slept. The nickle only dropped when I heard Davy's voice. I opened my eyes and remembered who the guy was. I must have turned about nine different shades of purple trying to straighten things out. He just looked at me with a crooked little smile as I was blathering about thinking he was some lady I'd brought home to pleasure. When I ran out of spiel, he reached over and put my hand onto his mammoth, blood-gorged crank.

As those green eyes bore into my soul, David said he'd been trying since his second week aboard to penetrate the veil which separated our souls. Often he was sure he could feel my lust burning, but he'd never had the guts to put his ass on the line. He asked if I'd noticed that he slept naked, with his curtains open. He asked if I didn't think it strange that he'd chase around a Pusan whorehouse while I was trying to screw. Didn't I think his coming to my room at the Buzzard Inn mean SOMETHING? Why hadn't I had a fucking clue? Surely I must have known when he climbed into bed the night before what he had in mind? As he reviewed our past, propped up on one elbow, looking into my depths, he explained how he'd gone slowly ape-shit while we were aboard. Now, however, he'd decided he had nothing to lose.

As quickly as I realized how lucky I was, I began to mourn the time we'd wasted. I asked the bastard when he had to report to his new command and when he said he only had until Thursday, I was desolate. Then he smiled and suggested that I get a roommate. His new command was NAVCAMEASTPAC in Wahaiwa -- about twenty minutes away from my joint -- from both of them. When I was trying to adjust to this new set of affairs, he began a gentle rocking of his hips, pushing his huge hump-horn into my hand. As I figured out he was using my paw to beat off, I also discovered that the candy store was open and unguarded -- and I should let rational thought wait until much, much later. I ducked down under the sheet which had trapped the warmth of our bodies in against the morning coolness and gave him a licking. I used my tongue on his nuts, his stem, his head, his butt and tits -- and everything else I could reach. Starting slowly, I grew wilder by easy stages until I was gagging myself on his impossible peter and he was working me over better than any fistfucking fantasy.

He lifted his mouth from my meat and pulled me above him. His legs grasped my ass as he practically forced me into his ass. My hands on his shoulders, looking down into those eyes of joy and need, I felt myself lose control before I was completely inside him. My hips went wild; I slammed against his beautiful butt, driven forward by nearly three years of unproven passion finally released. When I had filled his ass with my load, he grinned and taunted me that was a one-stroke artist. He seemed to recall it had taken me 45 minutes with a certain wench in The Buzzard. I ground my hips into his ass some more and tweaked his tits while I reminded him that while he was a world-class bitch, he was no fucking wench.

I think Davy must have liked that, because he nodded, laying his hands on my ass with a smile. I managed to wriggle from his embrace and insisted it was his turn to show his stuff. I reached under the mattress and dug out my KY. Perhaps someday he would stretch me out enough to just hop on, but until then, we were going to take things slowly: I was going to do the work. I slathered his pole with enough KY to lube a small Harrier before I climbed up. As I began to play with my stiff meat, I lowered myself onto his as gently as a love- struck guy could. At first I had no luck, but quite suddenly he gave a little shove with his hips and rammed himself through the gates. I yelled like a stuck motherfucker on speed and reached round to squeeze his nuts, reminding him that I was in charge of this fucking evolution. He lightened his grip on my dick and told me not to get cute; but he kept still and let me take what he had at my own pace. I didn't want anything to rip that would take too long to heal. If he was going to be around, I wanted tomorrow to be as good as today. Straining to the max, my guts on fire, I finally worked him inside my and began the slow rocking motion that forced my prostate against him.

I let him begin a slow rotation as I applied myself to playing with his tits and, leaning far enough forward, kissing him as I'd never kissed anyone before. This time he was the dickhead that shot off years too soon. I'd just put my tongue into his mouth as his hips seized control of his stock. It flew in and out like a piston, drawing my guts on the down-stroke, making me want to explode on the up. The pressure on my prostate was so great that, for the first time in my life, I came from anal agonecstasy alone. As he forced his juices into me, mine surged from my meat and flew against his chest, into his face and hair, and onto the wall behind. As his dick grew still, I squeezed his ballbag again -- this time to force out every drop. I forced what was left of my ass as tight as I could when I pulled myself upwards, squeezing him dry. I lay atop him, wriggling about on his hard body, separated only by a thin layer of my own spunk. We kissed and cuddled until, stilled wrapped together, we feel into a deep, profound sleep for a few more hours.

I was first to wake when the sun hit our bed and woke him with my dick. Since that day, I have thought of no other person. Except for duty days -- which we have arranged to have in common -- we have made love at least once every day. After work, we have a couple beers, jog or work out, take a long shower, and spend the rest of the evening in bed, making slow love as we chat, watch TV, or just watch each other and admire nature. We have become more than lovers, more than friends. We have become one spirit in two vessels, whole only when linked together and, once linked, needful of nothing else.

We both have two years before our next rotation, and it looks as though we'll both leave the Navy then unless there is some way they could guarantee us the same duty station. Although I can't believe it could be true, Davy seems in love and in lust with me as much as I am with him. One night last week, as we lay in each other's arms to let our bodies recover and our spunk dry, we finally finished THE BLACK CAMEL together. I'd lost interest that day in my rack when Davy's ass burst into my universe, but he ran across the book in the closet and thought we should make it ours. Tomorrow we're going to have little black camels tattooed on our butts. We've talked it over and think every sailor should have a tattoo where it counts most. Charlie Chan might even agree.

CLAN MATES

Even when we deploy together on amphibious ships, sailors and marines usually don't hang out together. Our schedules are different, we sleep in different berthings, and we just plain don't have much in common -- as a rule.

We squids are plenty busy underway; the grunts mainly try to keep out of the way. Sailors are often working twelve on- twelve off for months; jarheads have dick to do but work out and wait for battle. Ashore, the troopies have it rough, but an average grunt day involves rolling out of the rack at 0600, chow at 0700, PT at 0730, lunch at 1100, and maybe a few laps around the flightdeck or some time with the Universals in the weightroom during the afternoon before chow and bed. Marines come aboard looking choice, but their underway workout schedules would turn a mob accountant into a stud.

As Desert Shield blew up toward Desert Storm, we floated around the Gulf so long that the lines between Navy blue and cammie green started to blur. I'd seen Lance around the ship, but I got to know him in one of the classes the Navy brought aboard. The idea was to earn college credits and keep from being bored as our world drifted towards war. Some squids signed up, but the marines eager for some-thing to do that didn't involve heavy lifting, registered in packs. Contrary to what you've probably heard, marines are sharp guys. At first, though, Lance and I had little in common except the coincidence of having the same last name. I'd run into other members of the Jackson clan before, but none of them had been built like Lance. Before we realized it had happened, we were fighting for the top of the class and the prof was making cracks about "the over-achieving Jackson broth-ers."

I wished. Underway, I tried to my fist-fuck fantasies, but Lance made it rough -- especially since we were all stroking around the ship in just t-shirts and shorts because of the heat. Every time Lance and his troopie buddies were around, my shorts just naturally climbed towards the overhead. Lance was a 19-year-old PFC during the War -- and about 6'1" of the foxiest preppy young marine meat you could hope to wrap a lip around. His face was something of a blend between Chris Reeve and Schwarzenneger, with close-cropped temples and a crest of dark blond hair on top. Doe-brown eyes with lashes into next week, a perfect Ivy-league nose, high cheekbones, a strong jaw, and enough sparkling white teeth to make a Hollywood agent cream his trou were just the beginning of his Jackson charms. Daily PT had broadened his shoulders and chest, narrowed his hips, and pumped up his perfect, tight marine ass to the point I'd have gladly licked his mama's pussy just because he'd once passed through naked.

After that first history course, we found ourselves in a couple of math classes and finally one in marketing. The folks at home called us war heroes -- but during Desert Storm, Lance and I had dick to do. Even our role in Desert Shield was pretty minor: practice maneuvers in Operation Imminent Thunder, a couple of SCUD false alarms, and a great Christmas liberty in Bahrain just before the war started.

We were half-way through the marketing class when we pulled into Bahrain for Christmas liberty. Lance had been friendly for weeks, always eager to kick back and chat when we ran into each other around the ship. I had tried to keep my distance so I wouldn't warp out and shove my good news up his ass without an invitation; but when he asked the day we pulled in if I'd show him around town, I couldn't say no. At least ashore, I didn't have to put up with the sight of his hard marine butt grinding away inside his skimpy UDTs -- the tan shorts marines wear, more designed to show off their butts and baskets than cover anything.

We might as well have been brothers, we got along so well -- as long as I could banish the image of his face being skewered on the end of my joint or him bent double, ass to the sky while I used his hole like a cur bitch in heat. This was my second float so I showed the bootcamp around the Bab souk, we ate Pizza Hut at the Yateem Centre, and then spent hours at the gold souk. By the time evening prayers screeched across the sunset, we had shopped. Lance was bitching about sore feet, and sounded more like a pooped preppie than desert defender. Like any good squid on liberty, I suggested we stop by the Holiday Inn for a couple beers before we caught the bus back to Mina Sulman Pier.

Lance was studly, clever, and charming; but the guy had no more idea how to limit himself to a couple beers than the village dog does how to conduct Bartok. Even at $4 a brew, we were both shit-faced inside an hour, but Lance wasn't about to let up. When I told him the last bus back to the pier was about to leave, he just snarled, "Fuck the pier." His VISA card appeared as he staggered out to the desk for a room. It cost him almost $200, but he was able to drink for another hour before he got sloppy. I managed to propel him upstairs, out of his clothes, and into the shower before he got really messy. Once I was sure he was on the mend, I left him under the water for nearly twenty minutes, not so much because I didn't like watching him heave, but because the sight of water splashing off that classic male body was more than I knew I could bear. The gorgeous bastard was retching like a bootcamp on moonshine; but anyone seeing his hard, hairless pecs heaving under the cold spray or his massive marine bubble-butt begging unconsciously for what I had as he unselfconsciously leaned against the tile would have seen too much to keep from jumping his humps.

When he'd sobered up enough to dry himself off, I rinsed down the shower, and used it myself. By the time I came out, he was safely in his rack and, I assumed, passed out. I was about ready to crawl between the cool white sheets of the bed across from his for my first night ashore in months when I heard soft, wet, ugly choking sounds coming from his bed. The shower should have sobered him up, but the first thing you learn in the Navy is not to take chances with buddies aspirating puke. That Christmas the War was still two weeks away. Nobody was sure we would make it home alive, but the idea of a perfect young animal like Lance being shipped home in a bag because he'd choked to death on puke scared me so shitless I forgot about keeping my distance. I'd grabbed his shoulders and was trying to roll him over before I realize the difference between chokes and sobs. For about thirty seconds, I was shocked rigid. I'd never thought of Lance as the maudlin drunk type. Then, my eyes double-crossed me, drifting from the tears streaming across his cheeks to really notice the rest of his body; I went seriously rigid.

I babbled something about being sorry and pointed my peter back towards the other bed, relieved he was too torn up by whatever to notice my nine plus inches of swollen solecism pounding away, belly-up and ready to wrangle. Before I could move, his hand latched around my wrist and pulled my ass down onto the bed. All sobs and snuffles, tears cascading down his classic cheeks, he somehow managed to sputter, "No. Please. Just-- Sorry. Can you just . . . hold me a minute." I wanted to hold him all right. He obviously had some macho marine male-bonding crap in mind. Since I've never understood EST or encounter groups or even pretended to understand foxhole psychology, I had no clue what he was after or how to react. I let him pull me down to the mattress, but lay stiff and uncomfortable beside him, feeling a little like a prom king at a coroner's carve-up. Not knowing what to say, I kept quiet and just hopped he wouldn't see my joint beating cadence against my belly. He sobbed on, choking out drivel about not being a good marine because he was weak. Clamped onto my arm, he certainly felt strong enough. When I tried to back away, he twisted about, tossing a leg over to trap mine -- and giving me the shock of my squidly young life. His dick was not only a match for my nine thick inches of Naval pride, the bastard was cocked and ready to fire. At first I thought he had his hand down there, but his hands were both busy holding me hard beside him. Besides, even through his sheet, the heat and swollen, throbbing need of his first class privates grinding into my flank was inescapable.

Despite sharing the same last name, I still didn't think he was family. Everything about Lance shouted out cocky young marine stud on the way up. He couldn't be gay. The gods weren't that kind; they were just fucking me hard. Then, after I tried to comfort him for what felt like forever, he managed to whimper out the good news: Would I do him a favour and keep it between us. He couldn't let his buddies on the ship EVER know, but -- Would I -- do him?

He'd have warped out completely if I hadn't; but once I knew how much a Jackson he really was, he didn't need to beg twice. Faced with such need, I knew what I had to do to help out a shipmate. I reached down to grab his swollen service member and used it to shift him from neutral into first. The rough linen sheet was already wet with pre-cum oozing out in a relentless stream of encouragement. He didn't believe at first I'd was really going to give him what he needed; but when I shoved his body back onto the bed and jerked the sheet off him, his marine instincts recognized I was in charge. The problem was, I wanted him all at once and couldn't decide where to start.

My hands took a slow, careful measure of his flesh. They glided deliberately across his pecs and flanks, and down across his hard, flat belly until he was trembling like a colt and groaning, slack-jawed, like a Tijuana whore. His tits were swollen tall and eager, teasing my lips into tormenting them. Fierce and spit-slicked, they took up the challenged, sliding roughly up and down his nubbins until i was whistling up a desert storm of my own. His broad chest bucked upwards, hard against my face as though eager for the dangerous feel of my teeth and the delicious torment they could deliver. My right hand slid down to his messy, love- lubed crank and held him fast.

With anyone else, I'd have long since chowed down his dick until I choked on his load. Lance was a surprise, but I'd been around marines enough to know what they need: a hard fuck up the butt. I knew before I left his bed, I'd swallow his joint so far down my gullet he'd get acid burns; but first, I had to do him hard. He yearned to be taken, to be shown someone else was in charge. I'm normally a gentle, easy-going cocksucker. I've never much liked being done up the ass myself, and enough men have run screaming into the night at the sight of my Jacksonian joint that I'm usually content with much less than the brutal buttfuck I knew Lance craved. He'd begged for my help; I was going to give it to him -- and keep on giving it to him until he had my frothy naval jism spurting out his cute little ears.

I hadn't left the ship with cruising in mind, so I hadn't brought any lube along. We didn't need it. Lance had enough clear, organic lube for the Seventh Fleet. I slid my fist up his crank and down mine, leaving a crystal-pure coating of the slickest dick-do I'd ever worn. Lance lifted his feet off the mattress to show he was ready -- but not nearly far enough for what I had in mind. I grabbed his ankles and spread him like a stubborn wishbone until he popped his ass into range. I would have loved to slide my tongue up his crack first, stripping clean the scent of man his sloppy shower had doubtless left behind; but I had to play the butch marine-rapist -- at least until he'd been broken to the saddle. Once he'd learned to bear my load, I could haul his ass back to the showers for a clean up so I could rim what I'd reamed.

He was more frantic than eager. His ass arched high; his legs locked tight around my chest and slowly worked their way down towards the small of my back. I planted my hands beside his armpits, dug my toes into the bed, shoved my dick hard against his tight marine pucker, and hovered above his face, memorizing every perfect preppy line. I'm not normally much of a thinker while I'm on the job; but even then, excited as I was, I knew that years hence I'd look back on Lance as one of the high points of my life. I wanted to remember every hair and pore, every twinkle and twinge so that whatever else life had in store for me, I'd have that night, always.

My slicked, throbbing dick pressed harder against his twitching, pink marine pucker, half psyching him out, half hoping to stretch the moment past forever. The slut parted his lips to echo the hunger that lived deep in his Bambi- brown eyes, but my swollen nine inches fucked him mute. His lips and lashes both clenched shut to meet the waves of pain I knew would be ripping his guts apart. I also knew when the muscles of his temple unknotted and his mouth gaped open to suck at the air, he felt good like a marine should.

One of the first jarheads I'd done while I was still in bootcamp explained how they felt. Some marines never go near dick, mainly because they're afraid they can't handle the strain. Only the hard-Corps jarheads need to prove themselves enough to risk everything from their asses to self-respect. Nobody wants to think he can't handle pain, but each of us has his limits. The first couple times a marine spreads wide, he just needs thick dick up his butt to prove to himself he is man enough to handle the pain he's heard so much about. Then, slowly, the more dick he does, the more he realizes how good that having his shithole stretched feels. Slutting becomes so habit-forming he isn't content unless he has swollen milkbone slammed up his slick shit-chute and pubes ground hard into the ruins of his fuckhole. My marine mentor confessed that most grunts stroke around all macho and trim on the outside, but empty as a politburo's promise on the inside. Only with their legs in the air and their shit-chutes stretched tight around thick dick slamming their guts to tapioca can they be happy. Even then, as soon as their butts are flushed full of jism and the meat of the minute is reclaimed, they start craving their next fuck-fix.

When Lance opened his eyes and looked up into mine, lost in the worshipful pleasure of the moment, I knew he hadn't put out in ages. My rod had rammed had up into his tight foxhole in one swift, greedy, relentless stroke. Lance's muscles had seized up, but his slick hot marine guts latched around my lizard as though it were a holy relic. I'd lain still inside him for the moment it took his body to adjust to pleasure, but the dry heat of his guts swelled my meat deep within him and called me to action. His hands slipped back to polish my glutes like crystal balls that held his destiny. His hands and heels pulled me deeper into his ass until I was scratching at the twisted end of his fuck-tunnel buried nine inches up his need.

He moaned soft and low, shamelessly wallowing in the rare pleasure of being stretched tight around another man, yielding up his body in exchange for a few moments' peace. His spaniel-like gaze of devotion was so absolute I had to look away, half embarrassed, down to his parted lips and the strong jaw slackened by sensuality. My lips slipped to his shoulders and neck -- and would have returned to his tits if he hadn't pinned me so tight in his cock-hungry clutches. As it was, I was able to lap at his neck, slurping up the remnants of the day's sweat-bred musk his sloppy shower had missed. Caught head and tail, his body shivered helplessly in pleasure as my lips moved to his left ear lobe and my tongue trilled beyond into the deepest secrets of his ear,

His moans had grown to grunts, but shivering and quivering though he was, the last thing the slut wanted was for me to stop. The arch of his ass proved that. His hole pressed tighter against my crotch, fucking himself even deeper up my dork, begging for more. Never one to give a bootcamp his way, I took back about seven inches of what I'd given him -- and then slammed it back down through his ass with interest. If anything, his guts were greedier than ever, riffling along my rod like Nebraska wheat teasing the wind. I felt his massive mounds of marine manmuscle clamp shut along my shaft to hold me hostage. I pulled completely out again to teach his ass a lesson, popping his shithole like a balloon when my super-swollen dickhead flew through. Then I drilled deeper, angling hard against his prostate on the way past. Once more his body seized and shivered, but I had forgotten mercy. If he was going to sob and beg, it was time one marine asshole learned a few things about life.

My hips knew what to do. I turned them loose to slam my rapacious ramrod down where it belonged while I took stock of the hard male body that quivered below me. I felt my spine flex in and out, flying along in the breeder's arc evolution had taught our kind before we made it down from the trees. His hands had left my ass by now and were clamped tight around my shoulder, as though he were afraid I might remember something more important I had to do than keep fucking him hard up his tight marine ass. Well, at least it had been tight marine ass.

My eyes returned to his for a long moment before I ignored his need to breathe and slipped my Jackson lips against his, sucking gently at first and then using his mouth the way my dick was using his ass. The savage smack of my hips slamming against his upturned butt and driving dick deep enough to jar feral grunts from his parted preppy lips wove a hypnotic spell stronger than any opiate. If my marine was addicted to dick, I had already been seduced by the tight, masculine nature of his ass, I smelt his sweat and mine as they mingled in pools between his pecs and along his cobbled belly. The glorious stench of mansex thickened the air until our lean, hard bodies were thrusting and heaving together, lost awash in a sweet, stingless honeyed sea which threatened to pull us, unrepentant, into its lush, limpid, languorous depths.

One sensation blurred hopelessly into the next. A lifetime too soon, I felt my balls clench in a seizure of their own. I tried for an instant to hold back and knew there was no point. Lost, I picked up my speed, determined to teach his foxy bootcamp butt what real men feel like. He felt my Jackson jism jetting upwards, too; his hands clutched at my head, smearing my lips against his while my dick drilled deeper into the marine ass climbing to meat it.   The taste and smell and sound of sex wrapped around us like a deafening cocoon; sensations were at once unbearable and inexpressible, deep enough to shatter the soul, yet ephemeral as perfect youth.

When my thick frothy load of seaman's semen blasted up into Lance's marine guts, I felt closer to him than any brother. His hands and feet clawed at my body, holding me tight against the world; but he was helpless against my own limitations. Fine as I felt humping his hole, feeling wave after prick-pulsing wave of spooge slam up through my dick to splatter off the deepest, most secret corners of his being, my pods eventually ran dry. Even then I didn't stop at once but slid on, snicker-snack through his hole to savor the slick texture of my load coating his ass and the spurts of spooge that sprayed back out to Spackle my thighs and balls with spent splatter. Eventually, though, I collapsed onto his chest and lay in his arms, only the bottom few inches of my crank still up his hole as though, like a bookmark, the end of my dick could remind me where I'd left off.

When I had recovered enough to think like a human again, I remembered his powerful Jackson joint. I ground my gut into his as I sucked at his lips, but wasn't able to tell whether the goo that bonded our bellies together was sweat or something more sinister. I've had more marines than I can count shoot off on their own, whether from the pressure on their prostates or the massive thrill of being juiced themselves. I needed to suck Lance's marine meat; but before I could open myself up to him, I needed to prove one last time who was in charge. He sighed a bit, accepting the inevitable, as I eased the rest of my rod out of his foxhole. I think he was surprised, though, when I turned about to straddle his chest, shoving my ass into his face with a harsh "Lick my hole, marine."

Marines do love to follow orders. His hands pried my glutes apart to give his nose and tongue free access to my virtue. He may not have gotten any lately, but Lance was no apprentice asslick. His tongue flew straight and true as a Tomahawk toward my pucker and the impact was just as dramatic. His warhead drilled deep through my hardened muscle while his bumpy blade flared outward, stretching my tight hole for maximum effect. Once he'd made himself at home, his preppy lips locked tight around my fuckhole and began sucking lightly, urging my pucker-lips up along his tongue. My hold on sanity slipped.

I ground my butt hard into his face and heard him snuffling up my ass, contented as a hog, dexterous as an anteater, and horny as any young Jackson should be. The whore had shot off while I was up his ass; great clumps of white threads were marooned now on his chest and belly, drying as his sweat evaporated into the chilly, processed air of the room. The way his tongue was tearing into my tush told me I could get a piece of him at last. I sat harder onto his face, feeling my nuts droop down across his chin, as I reached down to pull up on his knees and bring his balls into range. I started on his `nads to make sure they were cranking out another load. My tongue slid deep between his thighs and balls, licking clean his musky scent and, finally, slurping one nut at a time into my mouth for some serious ball-handling.

Lance seemed hardly to notice when I moved down to his crank, licking along his shaft, stripping it clean of its pearly load of old pre-cum and fresh jism salted with mansweat. The tongue-lashing he was giving my shithole was almost enough to make me forget this ten inches of marine weapon -- almost. I had to pry the fucker out of the goo that coated his belly; but once I was able to look him in the face, I was more than ready to suck serious dick.

My lips slid swiftly across the hot, purple head of his dick. My mouth was watering a Niagara so slathering spit across his head to slick my way was no problem at all. Once I had his snout between my lips, his hips reacted, arching upward to slide more of what he had into my face. His tongue still twirled away up my asshole, but Lance was marine enough to handle two things at once.

My lips locked behind the pulsing trigger-ridge of his plum- sized head; my tongue tore into overdrive, slicing across his super-tender tool until moans and grunts joined the contented snuffles rising, muffled, from my ass. I slipped my suction up past MAX and eased my face even farther down his dork until, almost before I knew it, I'd used the curve in his stiff dick to match the curve in my throat and lock his Jackson dick down my gullet. I twisted this way along his shaft and pumped that. My chin ground into his golden pubes as though I could massage another load of marine cream up from his balls.

Between my butt and throat, Lance was getting more fun than any young marine deserves to have on liberty. We'd been deployed long enough, even after spunking with me up his ass, the slut didn't take long to prime his pump for another gusher. My fingers slid down to the mire up his asscrack to massage his butthole while I worked. Almost immediately, I saw his nuts rise into view and knew what was coming. Just in time, I jerked my jaw off his joint far enough for his massive meaty head to pop out again into my mouth. My tongue was on it like wasps on a company picnic the whole time my suction was slurping up his sweet, cream marine load.

Lance let loose an ancient scream of ecstasy bred to triumph as his body seized up even more solid. I slammed three fingers far up his shithole to tickle his gizzard and his fancy at once. That's where I stayed, splayed out inside him, pulling down with my paw and stretching his spooge- packed butt as I sucked upwards with my mouth, pulling the long, pearly ropes of more Jacksonian jism up from his nuts. For a moment, the lazy bootcamp slut was too busy having a good time to keep tonguing me up the hole. I slammed my ass back against his mouth and gave him something more to think about.

What with relishing the feel of his tongue up my ass and the taste of his load rolling across my tongue and the hot, creamy texture of his mouthorgan, I was one busy surface warrior. Fortunately, Lance was an even busier desert defender. I'll never know how long I spent sucking wad after glorious jarhead wad out of his swollen dick. I know long after he ran dry, I kept up the pressure. I had to. That magical tongue up my ass dropped me into brainlock so complete that my entire being seemed bound up with the raw, tingling nerves of my asshole. Now and again I would feel his nose on my cheeks or more of my jism leak out into my hand, but I rocked and wriggle and squirmed about on the end of his butt-licker until half past forever. When his jaw finally locked up and I snapped back into the world enough to ease my face off his crank and unhand his hole, I collapsed atop him. Now it was his turn to hold me awhile before I taught him what a Jackson buttfuck would feel like once the pressure was off my balls and I could take my time. He held me tight against him, the sweat and jism drying on our bodies, until I pulled his ass back into the shower to prep it for Round II. During the rest of that night and the days that followed, we continued the match, ringing chimes to end round after round of brutal, heroic, glorious fucking without ever coming tot he final bell. The next day we found a cheaper room so we could stay off the ship until it pulled out to await developments. Most of the marines aboard were pissed they never got to storm ashore to liberate Kuwait. I see their point. They've probably missed being involved in the war of their generation by just a few miles. Lance and I weren't bored during the long spring months that followed as we floated about the Gulf waiting for history to happen. We were busy finding new gear lockers and fan rooms and other out-of-the-way places to tend to business. It wasn't the business of making war; but by the time we sailed back east to the States, we were the best-trained pair of buddy-fuckers in US military history.

A COWPOKE DOWN UNDER

I lay there wishing the creature would hurry the fuck up. My ankles did-n't hurt, but the fishing line had started biting into my wrists as I twisted about to get comfortable. More to the point, I felt more goofy than sexy all staked out on the bed. My position did bring to mind an image I had-n't thought of in years even though it had teased ceaselessly at my nasty adolescent little mind the whole time I was growing to studhood. The clip ran relentlessly through my teenage fantasies as I shanked my crank. I'd seen it in some bad western movie where the Indians had staked a lone cowpoke out to die of exposure in the cruel Arizona sun. I remember nothing about the movie except the Technicolor image of the guy -- his blond shock of hair cast carelessly down over a heroic brow, a boyish dimple or two, and a lantern jaw. I'd always started my workout sessions with his face and then slid down across his powerful tanned pecs as they broiled under a sexy dapple of glistening sweat in that harsh heathen heat. His belly was flat and hard, but for reasons past understanding, the idiot Indians had neglected to pry my hero from his trou. If I'd been the Indian chief, I always told myself, things would have been done right. The camera would travel across his gorgeous torso, down along his hard flanks, and end showing his toes wriggling, bootless, in the harsh glare of relentless doom.

As I lay there staked out in the bedroom of the small apartment in suburban Perth, I returned for the first time in years to that central fantasy of my youth -- and remembered what the B-movie had left out: how I would happen across the poor cowpoke. I'd save his ass from the ants or scorpions or whatever, and he would show me how grateful a good western buddy could be.

After I lost my cherry to a girl in high school, I decided I'd just been going through a phase and stopped dreaming of reaming out sun-fried cowstud. Pussy was more immediate than the lost glories of the Old West and, besides, by then I knew what was socially acceptable and what wasn't. In the years since, I'd often compared my body with those around me. You don't spend four years on a `gaitor in the US Navy without seeing hard, naked manhood in its prime; but I was always able to banish the occasional quirky idea about my shipmates as a relic of that unfulfilled phase of my youth.

Lying there, staked out and helpless that day in Perth, I knew one thing for sure: the slattern I'd picked up was taking for fucking ever to come out of the crapper. Maybe because it had taken me so long to get to women, I'd never been as interested in sex as most of the guys on my ship. Still, after five months floating around the Indian Ocean with nothing but the usual strained faggot jokes and my hand to keep me company, I needed relief bad enough to try Claire.

A pack of us had gone to a bar our first day in Freemantle. The quail were all over us, fighting to buy us drinks and get us home to bed. I'd held out for something a little fresher, a little more stimulating, but finally, when just she and I were left, I decided it didn't really matter what I blew my load into. I let Claire drag me home. My plan was to pop a nut and run, but she wanted to play cowboy and pioneer wife. At first, I couldn't be bothered with her bondage crap; but it was soon clear I'd tap a gusher a lot faster if I played along. Sweetie had no sooner gotten me staked out, than she had to pee. They always do, for some reason, and never think of it until they start.

I lay there, my mind drifting back again to the sweaty cowpoke meat hidden inside those dusty pants, and came back to reality to find my dick harder than a rustler's heart. After what must have been five minutes, I yelled at the bitch to get her ass into gear. At the time, of course, I had no way of knowing the crapper had two doors or that she was long gone.

I nearly shat when the dude ambled out of the john. First a quick thrill surged through me: he was fucking gorgeous. Then my wrists and boner reminded me of my position and made me hope the guy wasn't the husband wronged -- though I couldn't imagine what else he could be. Something about the leer on his face didn't seem to fit, but I was past noticing subtleties. I started to babble an explanation of sorts when I noticed his dick. Then I really got confused.

He'd shambled about half way between the door and me and just stood there watching, feet apart, hands by his sides, dick belly-up and beautiful. I felt my own meat pounding against my gut like a Morse key in an lightening storm. Like a fool, I stopped babbling only to ask him where Claire had gone. His grin grew as he pried his dick down away from his flat, hairless belly and let it slap back up with a meaty thwack. I needn't worry about her. She was gone. We were alone.

I asked him what the fuck he was up to -- and silently felt sure of the answer, deeper within me than I'd known I could feel anything. Something about his stance and manner and, especially, the hungry look on his face as he took inventory of what I had told me the whole story. I never did learn the details -- who Claire was, what their relationship was, and or where she fit in. Just then, I was too busy learning the shape of his studly body Down Under to bother about trivialities and later -- well, never mind later for now.

I showed him my pissed-off defender of freedom persona, explaining what I was going to do to the bastard if he didn't get me up off the bed on the double, The more I ranted and threatened, the wider his grin got, the more his eyes sparkled, and the quicker his dick did a tom-tom imitation against his tanned belly. When he finally spoke up again in his foxy Aussie accent, he ignored my tirade as irrelevant to our present circumstances and sounded almost as though he were making idle conversation on a bus: "What's your name, Yank?"

I tried not to think about his swollen dick -- or about my own. I'd never been harder. Despite my cocky talk, I was afraid of what was going to happen; yet every part of my body except my brain yearned for whatever he had in store. Here, at last, I was out of control. Whatever delicious perversion he had in mind was his karma's problem. I was off the hook. At last, those adolescent fantasies seemed close to reality. My dick was so swollen it seemed ready to split down the middle like a frank left forgotten to simmer to bits in a picnic pot.

I growled my name and repeated what I was going to do to him when I got loose, but the gorgeous bastard only grinned harder and told me his name was Alec. He didn't look much like an Alec; he looked more like a fucking Apollo. Looming over me, he was about 6'1", 200 pounds of pure surfer-stud muscle. His hair obviously started out a dark blond, but was bleached golden above the neck. Like my dream cowpoke, he had a shock of hair hanging low across his forehead, setting off thick blond brows that seemed almost to merge above his classic nose. He, too, had dimples and a strong jaw filled with sparkling teeth; but he had more hard muscle than my cowpoke had ever seen.

A thick neck lead down from his cute little ears to spread into shoulders wide enough to throw an ox. The bastard obviously lifted weights as much as he surfed; his massive chest and bulging arms set off a belly that would have almost disappeared from sight except for the meaty signal pulsing in front. Before long, I was to see his world-class butt, hard and firm, hanging off his hips like some futuristic anti-gravity fuck-machine. I'd see his strong legs and feel the hard muscle of his back. Just then, though, my universe was filled with the biggest, hardest, meanest-looking dick I'd ever seen.

I don't know whether Aussies are usually uncut, but Alec made me hope so. At first I could see much of his dick except the bottom, but that was enough. Impossibly hard as he was, a great ruffle of soft, wrinkled skin peeked out from between his dick and belly, making my mouth water as though I were one of the faggot cocksuckers squids always joke about underway. His huge balls hung low and heavy between his legs, swaying slightly as he stood silently before me -- waiting, looking, savoring the moment. When he spoke again, almost drooling with every syllable, my last doubts about what lay in store for me vanished: "She said you were the best bit of meat about, she did."

The more I growled about his slut of a bitch and about how he was a faggot, cocksucking, ass-wipe, the harder we both got. He didn't say dick as he eased his way the last few feet to the bed and looked down at me twisting about. I writhed and thrashed, struggling with the physical bonds that held me, yet snapping free the last vestiges of my priggish inhibitions as I inwardly yielded absolutely to the demands of the moment.

His right hand reached out slowly, as though relishing a slight delay to intensify his ultimate pleasure. Deep brown eyes that seemed at odds with his bright, golden hair glowed with a primal hunger. When his fingertips ultimately made contact with my thigh, he might as well have been hooked straight to a nuclear reactor. A spark of lust and excitement and deliciously forbidden pleasure jolted up through my leg to disorient me. Flat on my back, I felt myself swept away by a maelstrom of fears and joys past my understanding. One part of my brain heard a low, beastial groan of exquisite pleasure escape my lips and I knew for certain that I was lost.

His hand on my thigh slid slowly upwards, sending shivers and gooseflesh before it. He stopped inches from my balls and started back down again, murmuring something to himself about softness. His left hand reached out next to glide across the very top of the rust-coloured thatch that grows thick on my chest. I've always found it wiry and harsh, but Alec's palm was obviously fascinated by the texture. His own hairless, brazen chest was dappled with sweat and stippled by gooseflesh of his own. Those spaniel-brown eyes slipped shut as his hands continued to take the measure of my body as though every hair and bulge were a religious relic to be venerated.

The smile was gone from his face now; he was beyond boyish smiles. Short, shallow grunts jolted a jerky melody from the very depths of his soul. As his palms eased across my flesh, as his fingers pried away my past prejudices and inhibitions, as my flesh surrendered to him, I stopped resisting the inevitable and lay still beneath his touch. I gave myself up to an enjoyment that far surpassed any spit-palmed adolescent fantasy. His touch glided across my flesh, slowly, reverently, deliciously. His grunts of appreciation grew louder, teaching me to meet his touch with my body, pressing my muscle against his hands, giving him my body as I had yielded up my soul to the wicked, wonderful world he represented.

My own groans of pleasure soon rivaled Alec's and seemed to seduce him from his trance. Those brown eyes opened again and he said something about my knowing what I wanted after all. Like an idiot, I strained at the bonds that held me down; but now I was struggling to reach his massive dick. Escape was the last thing on my mind. I had become a slut.

Right then, I was willing to give Alec anything he wanted, but he wasn't about to accept any gifts. Unless he could take it, he didn't want it. I twisted and torqued my way toward his hands and he pulled backward to take stock of the possibilities. I wasn't sure what to expect. I'd heard about faggots being done up the butt, but he'd have to untie my ass from the bed first. If I was thinking at all, I probably expected his monster dick shoved down my throat. When he really got going, I discovered how sick a bastard young Alec really was.

He started off on my right tit -- with his tongue. Alec slid his face over my chest. His breath came in short, hot spurts that chilled the sweat oozing out of my pores. My chest hair rippled like Iowa corn as his panting grew more frantic. When his wet tongue tip slashed down through the forest of rust-coloured hair to snipe down at my nubbin of passion- pumped flesh. I'd never thought of my tits as sexy, but Alec's bumpy tongue slid across raw nerves I'd never known I had until I was sure I would come from pure shock.

Somehow I stood up to the tit-torture, even after his tongue slid back between his lips and they went into action. His nose snuffled through my chest pelt while his lips, as slick with his spit and as they were experienced in what young American seamen need, locked around my nipples like a vampire dervish in a blood bank, twisted and tugging, determined to suck up every possible particle of pleasure. His furrowed lips tightened hard with every up-stroke along my blood-gorged stocks and then released their grip to glide down on a hot layer of spit as his bumpy tongue darted deep down my shaft to torment me.

At first, only his nose and lips and tongue touched me, but I was able to smear my chest against his face, begging for more like the slut he had made me. My overpowering urge to grab his blond locks and shove him hard against my chest kept me jerking at the nylon line despite common sense. The bastard had me where he wanted me and was in no hurry at all.

His tongue and lips alternated between teasing my tits and rougher play. Now and again, he'd let a dangerous edge of tooth glide down my stock; but just the raspy, cat-like torment of his tongue was enough to set my every nerve alight. Alec kept using my right tit and then my left until they both numb with delight. Then the sick slut slipped his face into my armpit and began lapping up the sweaty musk that lived there. Now his tongue slid across my flesh in great canine swaths of wet love that taught me yet another lesson about how a man's body can be used. Too soon for either of us, he'd lapped me clean and moved up across my shoulder to my neck and, ultimately, across to my left ear lobe.

His face pinned my head to the pillow while he went to work. Lips and tongue alternated again, sucking, pulling, scraping, urging my flesh into him as though he were a hyper-attractive man-magnet. The feral snorts of breath that escaped his nose roared into my ear just ahead of his tongue, drilling deeper into my head than any human should have been able to reach. Like a starving ant-eater, he flicked his tongue deep and curled it upwards as he sucked at my lobe with one lip and I cried out every filthy thing I knew. I was past knowing what I wanted. His tongue-fucking was so perfect, so brutal, that I knew I would go mad if he didn't stop; yet, once I'd felt what he could do, I knew I'd never be able to get enough. Almost as though I were watching from outside, I felt my body shiver and thrash, my hips convulsing upwards as they fucked the air and wished it were him. The louder I screamed, the faster his tongue snaked in and out of my ear and the more self-satisfied his porcine grunts of pleasure grew.

Whether to take my mind off my ear or maybe just to be a dick, he slid his fingers down to my left tit and started twisting -- hard. The delicious brutality of the moment transformed what should have been agony into something even worse. I'd been close to a breakdown before; now I slipped over the edge. Sensation blurred into surreal sensation; I was helpless to do anything but clench my eyes shut and wait for the universe to steady itself. I heard myself screaming again but as though at a great distance. One convulsion followed another, each fiercer, more sadistic and pure than the last. Then my brain just fucking shut down.

I remember drifting back to consciousness and thinking how wet I felt. My ear and neck were cold and clammy now; Alec had moved south. I lifted my head and saw him lapping a gigantic and very messy load of my best work from my chest and belly. I'd apparently lost it entirely and blown a huge cargo of Yank seaman semen up into the dense thicket of fur that covers my torso. Alec wasn't letting it go to waste. His lips had surrounded the nacreous globs of goo and was busy sucking them out of my hair. Then he went back, using his tongue to round up any strays that had escaped from the herd.

Turned on as I was, I couldn't do much at that point but breathe. I'll never know how long Alec had been up my ear, but it took me five or six minutes before I could gulp down enough air to live. By then, my captor had finished harvesting my sperm-farm and was ready to get serious -- but he wanted an audience. When he saw I would live, he went after the last thick threads of jism left -- dangling from my cum-slit and down across my dickhead onto my belly. He started low near my navel and slurped upward. His terrible tongue-tip tore into my jism-hole, drilling out the last of my load before his lips slid slowly upward to encircle my throbbing meat.

If his lips had seemed possessed as they sucked my tits; once he proved what a cocksucker he was, I was ready to nominate him for a Nobel fucking Prize. He used the same basic method: letting his lips sneak up on my nerve endings on a layer of hot spit and then ripping into my weakened defences with his bumpy tongue. Now, though, his suction went into overdrive as well -- all while he was working his face steadily downward along my nine thick inches. My dick was so stiff and lying so tightly against my belly that he had trouble bending me high enough to handle -- but by now he'd moved between my wide-spread legs and was taking his time. I'd just shot the finest load of my young life, but every throb of my naval weapon brought me closer to doing it all over again. Through the fuzzy cloud of pleasure that obscured reality from fantasy, I remember his snuffling slurps and the shit I was talking. I'm sure I sounded like the worst-written fuckflick of creation, but the torment his face was giving my dick was too serious a rush for me to consider coming up with anything creative.

He worked my swollen dickhead deep down into his throat and locked me in place, scraping the tender pink tissues of his craw across my head, pulsing his suction like an organic milking machine stuck on overdrive. I saw his head bob up and down along my shank and felt his lips at work but my head stayed locked tight and deep inside this throat until I knew I was about to shoot off again. For the first time ever, I felt my load being sucked up from my nuts and knew I was going to hump Alec's perverted, cocksucking, faggot facehole until it bled.

I was wrong. He did fine until my balls tightened against his chin. Then, just as I was ready to have one seriously fine time, he eased his face off my dick and knelt between my legs, grinning down at me, hoping I'd beg for his service. I did, too -- but the bastard wasn't about to swallow my load again -- yet.

He watched me squirm for a few minutes and then sank back down to my crotch. Now that my weapon was loaded and ready to fire, he concentrated on my spooge-magazine, sucking first one nut and then the other into his mouth for some rough ball-handling action. They were already slightly sore, first from long, underway weeks of relative inaction, then from the strain of spewing my personal-best load of spunk. His lips locked around my nut-sack and his suction started up, pulling blood down into my nuts and making them swell and throb and ache with the unbearable weight of their next load. I started moaning again and kept it up as he switched back and forth between balls for the next twenty minutes or so.

Now and again, he'd stop and lap the outside of spooge- factory as though he were some cur dog going at his own `nads on a dusty country road. He took time out to slurp along my thighs but the absolute limit in kink came when he used his nose to lift my nuts aside so he could snake his tongue back underneath me. The farther back he got towards my butthole, the better we both felt. I'd have given a nut to give the ass-lick what he wanted, but my legs were tied too tightly for me to arch my hips up enough off the mattress to manage.

When he'd sucked my second load of the day back down where it had started, Alec moved back up to my dick and swallowed me again. He was an old friend and my dick knew what to do. I slid straight down past his tongue and let his throat lock around the head of my joint like a family dog slipping into a collar. This time around, though, he had less chance of escaping my spray. My hips were loose enough to fuck his face, slashing upwards, driving my dick home where we both knew it belonged. His head met my meat on the up-stroke and tried to hang on on the down, but now instinct took control of my dick -- and his face.

I reamed and twisted and slammed dick deep down his throat until I felt my load being sucked up again. This time it happened faster and with a violence and frenzied ecstasy bred of Alec's need as much as my own. Once again, though, he jerked his head up off my joint; but now he was too late. My plume of spooge shot out, spraying my belly and chest with more thick threads of pearly mancream than I'd ever seen. Alec knew when he was beaten.

He wasn't going to slurp his load of seed up, but his lips puckered tight and pressed my dickhead down into my belly fur as I shot spasm after glorious spasm up onto myself. As soon as I was pinned and knew it, his tongue flicked out through his lips, fluttering along the super-sensitive V beneath my dickhead, at once forcing me even harder against my belly and raking a whole other set of nerve-endings that were already exploding. His lips and tongue worked harder, feathering frenzy against the bottom of my dick as one jolt of jism after another spewed out the top. Pressed hard against my belly, my dick pumped the last half dozen blasts of spooge into a pearly pond that formed right at the end of my dick.

If anything, the second load took me longer to lose and was more fun. At least, I suppose it was; since I remember dick about most of the first gusher, I can't be sure. When, at long last, I humped out my last few threads of jism, I was ready to lie back content while Alec licked me clean again. He had other plans.

The moment he saw I was dry, he hopped to his feet, straddled my waist and started to shit on my crotch -- at least that's what I thought he was doing. Instead, he slipped his asscrack along the underside of my dick, just grazing the surface and keeping it from going limp. Within seconds, he was gliding along my meat, dipping low enough to drag his ass through the pool of jism that lay just north of my dick. Then on the back stroke, he dragged his butthole harder along my dork -- scratching his ass like a dog scooting across a new white shag carpet. Each trip got his butt slicker than the last and made my bone the more ready to see what he had in store.

Now, of course, I'd know what to expect; but when he reached down with his hand to pry my joint away from my belly and eased his asshole around it, I figured my life was just about perfect. In the fear and discovery and mind-numbing ecstasy that had come before, I'd forgotten about my cowpoke fantasy; but the moment Alec slipped his tight shithole past my trigger-ridge and I felt the thrill of reality after so many years of fist-fucking fantasy, that Technicolor cowpoke popped into my head one last time. Looking up at Alec wobbling back and forth as he worked himself down my shank, I knew I'd never have to conjure cowpoke again. From now on this bizarre afternoon would be the yardstick against which all my future fantasies and realities would be measured. As his shithole stretched its way along, I also knew I'd never bother with the Claires of the world again, either. Some assholes might not like the idea of guys doing guys, but now that I'd felt what a hard young body like Alec's had to offer, there was no fucking way in hell I'd put up with the nasty slackness of slatterns. In fact, watching one expression after another slide across Alec's face as my pole disappeared up his hole, I was even ready to see what his impossible dick felt like stretching my guts apart.

It was at least ten inches long -- and probably more. His head was swollen enough now that I could see his cum-slit oozing a steady flow of pre-cum. Soon the crater formed by his foreskin overflowed dicklube and a thin trickle rippled down his joint to drip onto his balls and then onto my belly. Almost at the same time, Alec's asshole seated itself around the broad base of my dick, grinding this way and that across my Brillo-like pubes, and his soulful brown eyes rolled back in his head. I made up my mind to find out what it felt like to have a man up your ass.

I lay silent for a moment or two but some ancient instinct set my hips back to work. My ass arched upward, driving my dick even deeper into Alec's butt. His eyes eased open for a moment so he could look at my Navy-issue body one last time before he slipped from into a world of his own. His lips parted slightly and the moment was passed. He was on auto- pilot now, stroking up and down my joint, scratching the itch that lay buried deep within him like a bear against an even thicker log. My dick drilled upwards as his ass matched my rhythm, twisting slightly to screw himself along the throbbing blue vein that guided me up into his guts. Every movement stretched my shaft tighter, pulling the twin lobes of my head tighter and bringing me closer to launching an impossible third load up into the secret depths of his guts where it belonged.

Suddenly I felt something hard bounce off my dick as I slipped into him; Alec shivered in a spasm of shattering sensuality so severe that for a moment I was jealous. I didn't know about prostates at the time, but I knew what made him feel good and was determined to deliver. My ramrod changed its angle of entry just enough to slam hard into his explosive buttnut on nearly every stroke -- sending one ripple after another of gooseflesh across his body and ripping one animal moan after another from the very depths of his being. Alec was still grinding his ass along my crotch, but now that I knew what to aim at, I went to work pounding his prostate for all it was worth.

My dick loved the firm, slick texture up his ass, but Alec went ape-shit. His head flew back and he opened his mouth for a soundless scream fierce enough to deafen mankind. His gasping breaths stopped dead and, while I slammed harder and faster with every butt-lashing, gut-wrenching stroke, my captor proved he had more than pre-cum down his dick. I'd never seen another man shoot off before. Alec was an impressive place to begin. At first he seemed to be having a seizure, but as his lungs clawed at the suborn air for breath, his massive manmeat exploded, shooting globs of iridescent white shrapnel up onto his body and out onto mine. Some of the larger globs splattered against his hard, hairless flesh and began the slow, easy drip down. Many arced through the air to land on me or on the bed beside me. Once his gusher had come in, Alec reached down to get a grip on himself and pumped his well dry, sending his Australian cream up like an explosion in a fireworks factory. My rod was ready to keep reaming his butt, but once his body seized up, that tight Australian bunghole clamped down tight enough to break my joint off at the nub. The sight of his jism arcing through the sky, the strangle-hold he had on my meat, the noise he was making, the fierce friction of tender flesh against hard bone, and, especially, the perverse thrill of having my dick up a man's tight ass while he shoot off, all conspired to send me over the edge again as well.

I couldn't see my watch, but this had to be my third cum-crop inside as many hours. Alec had taken his time; neither of us seemed in any hurry other than the one built into a man's nature. Now, at least, I was putting what I had where it would do some good -- up his ass to lube it out. My first jolt did just that. I couldn't feel my spooge splash off the inside of his guts, but his butthole magically started slip- sliding along my shank so I picked up my speed and really let the Australian asshole have it.

Alec must have crested first, because when I opened my eyes, he was all doe-eyed and grinning. He was also seriously dripping jism, but at least none of it was mine this time. I knew where mine was. He fucked with my dick for a few more strokes and then leaned forward, smearing his chest and belly against mine. The remains of my second load and his fresh first melded together in milky satisfaction as he eased off my joint so we could get in some quality bellyfucking time. Over the next eight or ten hours, we kept each other from getting bored. By the time I finally fell asleep with Alec lying atop me, I'd learned a life-time's worth about lust and love -- and where a man fits in.

Probably the major disappointment in my life was that I never felt Alec's gorgeous uncut dick up my ass. At one point he did tease me with it, sitting on my belly so I could suck on his `skin and the very tip end of his crank. Why he wouldn't let me treat him the way he deserved, I'll never know. I'm sure he had good reasons -- in any case I was bound to do as he wished. I only know that when I awoke the next morning, he was gone with nothing but dried jism on my belly and a lifetime's worth of memories to prove he'd ever been there. I found a knife by my hand and cut myself free. Every muscle I had was cramped and stiff, but at least now I knew how to uncramp the muscle that matters most.

I took a long, hot shower and decided to wait until Alec came back. He never did. I should have wondered why Claire brought me through a door that led directly from the to the back bedroom. I discovered why easily enough: the rest of the apartment was vacant. Whether it was a model apartment or one Alec just kept rented so he could screw Yank sailors or what I never figured out. I obviously wasn't meant to. Alec had shown me what I wanted out of life and how to get it; if he wanted to be a tad kinky with bondage or shy about the rest of his life, I guess that was all right with me. I left the apartment on his terms -- knowing nothing about him other than that he and the single, glorious night we spent together, slavish master and devoted bondsman, would remain with me bright and alive until my final hour.

A DAY AT THE ZOO

Even in San Diego, you don't see many military uniforms out in public. When you wear the things 36 hours a day, the last thing you want to do is take them home with you. That's why I was surprised to see the marine at the zoo in his cammies. I supposed he had just gotten off duty and had stopped by the zoo to pick someone up on the way home. In a way, I was right. He was looking to pick somebody up all right, but he hadn't gotten off yet. I was to help him take care of that.

The San Diego Zoo in Balboa Park is one of the best in the world. I'm on a carrier out of Alameda, but whenever we pull into San Diego; I always stop in to visit the animals. Spending four years on a Navy ship gives you a certain sympathy for zoo creatures. I was especially sympathetic when I saw Mike lounging against a tree over by the gnus. His hands were in his pockets, his cute little cammie cap was pulled down over his eyes so he looked something of a cross between John Wayne and James Dean: a soulful, modern-day, misunderstood killing machine.

Squids have a long history of loving marines -- hard and often. Mike would have attracted my notice regardless of what he was wearing, but something extra-special about the way his gaze slid seductively out from beneath his cap tripped my built-in asshole alarm. Walking down the slope in his direction, I felt his eyes scanning everything I had but my blood type. I was dressed in a t-shirt and shorts, but grunts and squids can't hide from each other. Before I got too excited, though, I wanted to see what he looked like up close.

He was choice. The baggy cammies hid a lot, but the way his ass flared out against the tree from beneath his blouse was the best recommendation a young marine could have. Butts are the first thing to go when the body starts to flab up. Mike's jutted out hard and firm and inviting. Something subtle about it promised experience and a meaty hunger rolled up into two, compact mounds of mean marine muscle. My dick awoke from a week's hibernation and began twitching at my shorts, ready to romp.

When I got close, I saw his face was an added bonus. His head was almost square, but his blond hair and pug nose and strong jaw seemed at once Teutonically tough yet begging to be tamed. His mouth was on the small side with a Ricky Nelson lower lip, but I knew I had just the thing to stretch him into shape. I couldn't figure why meat like Mike had to lounge about in the park to find love -- or why the Seventh Fleet wasn't lined up waiting to choke on his load. But I knew enough about military service to volunteer.

By the time I reached him, my shorts were stretched painfully tight across my crotch and his punkish pout had turned to a leer. When I asked if he had a place, he turned and started to walk down the slope, away from the gnus. At first, I wasn't thrilled. I don't mind the occasional midnight roll on the beach or even a romp on the sands at Black's where you entertain only your own; but it was 1400 on a Saturday afternoon. The park was clogged with kids and other civilians who didn't need to get caught in the crossfire once we started shooting. Heading for a john or a bush for a quick fuck wasn't my style. Besides, the truth is I'm a noisy fucker.

Public or not, I followed that cammie-clad ass halfway to forever, down a little trail that wound into a canyon separating the Zoo from Balboa Park proper. The vegetation turned wild and then completely took over, shutting out the sun and making progress difficult. When he came to an open clearing on the hillside, my marine finally stopped beside a huge tree that forked at the ground, one trunk growing straight upwards until it lost itself in the canopy overhead, the other twisting out at ground level for five feet or so until it started its march upward toward the sky. Mike had obviously been there before. The effect, snuggled away in what might have been endless forest, built a little alcove against the hillside, complete with a view across the narrow canyon and a love seat formed by the massive trunk. Even standing beside me, Mike was nearly lost in the jungle background; from a distance he'd be invisible until he shucked his cammies. Fortunately, the chirp of birds and occasional rustle of squirrels promised that only the gods were there to watch what happened as I pulled my thick nine inches of service member out of my shorts.

Marine Mike had stood silent, feet spread, waiting. Once he saw what I had, he collapsed to his knees at my feet, one hand pulling off my shorts as his face slid hard enough into my crotch to knock his cap off his head and shove my naked butt back against the hard bark of the love seat. The bark was as rough as Mike's tongue and, trapped between the two, I discovered how unyielding nature could be. He started low, licking up my thighs like a kid with a melting chocolate cone. His blond, Corps-cut hair bristled against one leg as his face worked on the other, sliding his tongue deep up between my ballbag and thigh, slurping up into the tight, musky fold of my crotch.

I lifted one leg slightly to give him room to work, but he took advantage of my kindness, snaking his tongue back below my balls to worry away at the crack in my ass. He flicked and fluttered against the back of my nutsack, so I tried to help out by lifting my leg higher and still higher until my heel was resting across the trunk like a ballerina with an exercise bar. By then he was below me, slurping at my balls as they hung low and heavy, clogged with two weeks' worth of American naval prime. His nose dug away at my butt until I turned my back on him in self-defense and leaned my chest across the tree, ready for anything. If he was a typical marine, my virtue was safe; if he wanted to fuck me up the butt, I was ready then and there.

As I expected, he had laid out another plan of attack. I felt his fingers, ripping at my buttcheeks, prying open the way for his tongue. His high cheekbones pressed hard against my low ones as his nose snuffled its way along my ass-crack and his sandpaper tongue followed along behind like a frenzied platoon of pira§a. When he hit bottom, all I could do was wrap my arms under the trunk and hold on as the jungle started to spin. One wave after another of mind-numbing, gut heaving bliss swept up my spine and through my consciousness. I felt his lips lock low around my butthole and start sucking -- first lightly so his lips collapsed onto my pucker, then harder as his tongue began dancing about the wrinkled edges of my hole.

His face was all the way up my ass now; his hands clasped tight to the front of my thighs. As he grunted and snuffled away, some remote partly-functional corner of my brain recorded occasional images of a brief, cool breeze wafting up the canyon to chill my sweaty flesh or woodland sounds or the leafy dapple of sunlight against the ground. Mostly, though, I remember his marine need to feed: The feel of his cammie- clad arms on my legs. The strong feel of his huge hands on my thighs. The rhythmic back-and-forth motion of his face as he kept fighting to hold his victory against my butt as it countered with one muscular shudder of animal delight after another. Most of all, until my final hour I will remember the feel of his wet, bumpy tongue drilling its way up my asshole. Not content with a sly swipe down my crack, he prodded and poked, screwing the tip of his mouth-muscle deep past the first folds of my butt to get at the heat that lived within me.

I fought to hold onto full consciousness, but there has always been something about the feel of a tongue up my ass that sends me straight into brainlock. I didn't pass GO. I gave the $200 a miss. While Mike licked my asshole raw, I just hung onto that tree trunk, my eyes shut and mouth open in one long, low, eternal moan of pleasure. Like some bad sci-fi space alien, man's most ancient instinct took control of my body, wriggling my ass up into that hot young marine face, fucking myself up his tongue until his whole head seemed to be up my butt. Of course by then I didn't feel his tongue or the lips sucking away at my hole. I didn't feel his massive hands or even the rough texture of the bark scraping across my flesh as I writhed and twisted in mindless delight. In a very real sense, sensation was too civilized a concept for me. All I knew was the perfect glow of contentment. Centered on the tongue sliding snicker-snack in and out of my asshole, that glow spread by easy stages to every fibre of my being until time itself slowed to a stop and I might have been some prehistoric creature, frozen, stingless, in a sweet sea of amber. His honeyed glaze grew thicker and more seductive until I slipped beneath the sticky golden surface in delicious, sublime surrender.

If Mike's jaw hadn't locked up on him, I'd be there still, wrapped about that rough tree trunk, entranced as by a wizard. As it was, it took me awhile to recover after he pulled his tongue out of my ass. Gasping for breath, I twisted about to lie against the trunk. I guess marines don't need to breathe; mine certainly didn't waste much time. My weapon was no sooner within range than the grunt slut swooped down to cock my hammer.

I looked down as I felt his wet lips slide across my dickhead. They quickly skidded through a river of pre-cum his tongue had coaxed up from my depths and kept on skidding -- all the way across my head, over the hump of my corona, and down the seven odd inches of my shaft. His lips crashed to a stop around my thick base, but his cute little pug nose didn't even want to stop there. It twisted and pounded into my stiff, rust-colored pubes as though he could tear free another inch or two of dick to suck.

He didn't need it. My egg-sized dickhead was buried Adam's apple deep down his gullet. I felt his hands spread across my ass, smearing his face into my crotch and scratching his deepest, most primitive and secret itch with my cum-slit. I slipped my hands down to the back of his blond head, delighting in the Velcro texture of his cut and the sensual streams of sweat that poured from him in the stifling summer stillness. He was snuffling and grunting again -- or maybe it was me. I distinctly remember a racket and hoped we were far enough from the crowds so they wouldn't hear our animal noises and wander down to investigate.

Unfortunately for my memoirs, my brain was too busy enjoying life to take notes here, either. I can't give you a blow-by- blow account. I know I latched onto his cute little ears and used unconsciously used them to slide his foxy face up and down along my pole, slamming him harder into my crotch with every stroke. I know I felt his pouty lower lip scratching at the top of my balls. I know his cock-sucking throat clenched and stroked at my swollen member like a 110-volt milking machine operating on 440. Mainly, though, all I felt was good. Inside the tight warmth of his throat, my aching bone seemed to dissolve away as sensations came too quickly for mortal nerves to carry the good news past his lips. Instead of my dick and his throat, I felt only warmth and pleasure and a fierce vortex of suction that lured my guts down into his bobbing, grinding marine maw that slid up and down my thick nine inches of throbbing pleasure.

Then I made the ultimate mistake. I let my hips start slamming forward to meat his face. My ass instinctively began clenching at the front of every stroke, driving my load up to its doom. I listened to the slurpy grunts and growls and felt the texture of the forest around me and eased an eye open enough to see his Apollonian head and cam-mie-clad marine body dangling off the end of my dick. A marble statue couldn't have held back its load so what chance did a lust- struck, nature-loving squid on liberty in San Diego have?

I felt a howl rip upward from the very depths of my being to keep a week's worth of creamy naval spooge company on the way off the launching pad. Mike was a marine; he knew how to swallow spunk in style. My dick had been buried far enough down Mike's throat it could claim out-of-state residence; but when he felt my balls clench and heard me going off, the bitch eased his face off my bone enough to pop my head out into his mouth. His tongue tore into the underside of my dick while he did a perfect rag-doll impression with his head, grinding the top and sides of my shank against the back of his mouth. Not only did I get the living cock-snot pulled out of me, but the sadistic slut managed to tear loose every nerve in my joint while he was doing it.

I screamed and spooged and clawed and just fucking held on until I was sure he'd finished taking my load. It took some time for him to suck the lumpy white worm up from my balls, but I did eventually splash down and collapse again against the trunk of the tree. Mike slid back down to latch his lips around the base of my joint and then slid upward, careful not to miss a drop. By the time he'd picked up his hat and stood beside me to say an awkward farewell, licking his chops like the cream-sated pussy he was, I knew I wasn't nearly ready for the afternoon to end.

He probably couldn't wait for me to leave so he could take out his crank and beat off, the taste of my jism still rolling fresh across his tongue. Like most marines, he didn't expect any help from me. He expected me to splash and run. Unlike most squids, though, I love to give as much as I lust to take.

My hand had no trouble finding his dick, and the stunned look on his face was worth the Denver mint. He stood silent, as on parade, while I pressed his dick against his body. His huge hand clasped itself across mine by way of consent and fellowship and thanks. Now it was my turn to sink to my knees, but his gear was harder to get through than my shorts. Unbuttoning the blouse, unbuckling the belt, and freeing that glorious uncut piece of marine meat from his pants took some time; but I was enjoying my afternoon at the zoo just fine. I slid a hand up underneath his t-shirt and across his flat, hairless belly. As his trou dropped with a brass clank to his ankles, I moved my other paw around to cup the classic ass I knew would feel marine hard and ready for action.

But first I had to tend to business. His cammies had kept the day's sweat alive and well inside his crotch, brewing up a man-musk my tongue couldn't resist. Now it was my turn to lap the sweat from his balls. When he was marine clean, I pried his dick away from his belly and took my time memorizing what I saw. The thing was a fucking masterpiece. Mike was only about 5'9" so his dick was an inch or so shorter than mine -- but just as thick. His real bonus was what I didn't have: the softest, foxiest, meatiest foreskin any young squid could hope to suck.

Sweet, clear dick-lube must have trickled from his dick the whole time he was doing me because his `skin and shaft were both soaked with the stuff. I tidied him up with my tongue and then tore into his cocksock, swirling around inside to scarph down every particle of his pure, unadulterated, prime vintage man-musk. If his crotch had been fine, the scent of man I discovered locked inside his dick were worth a Nobel Prize. I lost track of the groans he was making as I slurped and sucked my way along his joint. My tongue slowly stripped back his `skin until his soft, purple meat was at my mercy. Then I went in for the kill, stroking down all the pole he had. My hands on his ass pulled him farther and harder into my face until his butt started clenching in rhythm to my suction and I knew I was about to taste one fine load of marine cream.

I was wrong for once. The bastard suddenly leapt back, taking his dick with him. I looked up, hoping he was going to be stupid enough to waste his load by pumping it out himself. He looked confused and half embarrassed, but then, for the first time, he spoke and was a classic grunt: "We can do . . . You can chow down if you want, but first. . . . Could you . . . . Why don't you. . . . While you're still hard, would you -- fuck me, please."

The poor sap's tone was about halfway between a beg and abject tears. What can I say? The guy had just given me the blowjob of the year. Could I turn him down and make a grown marine cry?

I haven't disappointed one yet. I've been around enough grunts I should have know what he wanted. He wanted it hard up the butt and, fortunately for us both, I didn't mind helping out a service member -- his or mine. By the time I'd gotten to my feet, I had slipped into the butch D.I. persona he needed to yield his ass to. A rough hand on his shoulder shoved him over the tree trunk. His gorgeous marine-built bubble-butt crested toward the sky and took my breath away. I slid a hand between his cheeks to feel the heat of his need and enjoy his hard mounds of muscle before I rammed my way through.

My fingers slid along a slick layer of sweat until they found his fuckhole. A single touch sent him into a rolling spasm of shudders and moans and dirty talk. I longed to take my time, to treasure his ass the way it deserved; but I knew that wasn't what he wanted. I pinched his pucker between my thumb and index finger and pulled upward, making him squirm like the slut he was. As my fingers tore into his hole, I decided to fuck with him before I fucked with him: "No, on second thought, I'm not about to get jarhead shit on my dick. Let's call it a day -- but thanks for the blowjob, cocksucker."

The look on his face was almost as classic as his ass. I had to laugh and leaned over to tongue-fuck his ear while I played with his shithole. Between the action his ass was getting and the toll my mouth was taking on his sanity, he was already having a good time. I was slurping the sweat off the nape of his thick, close-shorn neck when I got yet another idea I knew would ring his jarheaded chime. I saw that his dog-tag chain had worked its way up above his blouse. I'd thought briefly about making him strip out of his uniform, but the idea of doing a marine in the uniform of his country appealed to me even more than doing him out of it. He obviously got off on my fucking the Corps and him at the same time. His dog tags were a different matter. Grunts feel about their tags, the way squids feel about their nuts. When I latched onto the chain and pulled his tags out from under his blouse and on over his head, I expected him to shit.

He looked plenty worried, but we both knew I was in control. I glanced at the tags long enough to remember his name and then made his fucking year. I wrapped the beaded chain around my dick and balls like a pervert's handicraft project, looping it here and tucking it there. When I was finished, Mike's USMC cockring had swollen my already mean meat to world-record size and was putting enough pressure on my nuts to slip the San Andreas. Best of all, his tags dangled below my balls, banging against my thighs while GI wind chimes, clanking at the slightest hint of motion.

"You have any last words, marine?" was all I said as I kicked his legs apart and slid my dick into position. He gave a half-grunt/half-whimper that begged for a hard ride. That's what he got. I slammed my swollen purple monster against his tight marine ass and was nearly through on the first try. He was so hard that even bent over with his ass to the sky, I had trouble working my way past his championship gluts. I eased back a moment and dropped a huge dollop of spit into his crack. My dick slid through the mix of my spit and his sweat until I was sure I was lubed enough to get inside. I'd hurt him like living hell -- but if he was man enough to stand it, I was, too.

I grabbed the shoulders of his blouse and used them as reins on my second attempt. My hips arched backward and then slashed forward again, drilling my savage stake into the heart of that marine's hard young body. I felt his butt straining for a fraction of a second; my monster meat was too much for him to take -- but he took it anyway. Before my pelvis slammed into his ass, the first several inches of my joint were up his shit-chute and drilling deeper. The chain around my crank felt fucking weird, but the jingle of Mike's tags between my legs and slamming into his balls as I did him up the ass were a classic rush -- as if I needed an extra one just then.

I gave my meat a few seconds to set up housekeeping and then went to work. With other squids, I'm the world's gentlest guy. Since marines don't want gentle, I give them hard. I was more turned on than I had been in years. What I could see of Mike's body were reasons enough: that beautiful butt, the classic uncut dick, the farm-boy face with his cute little ears and pug nose, and a hundred other tiny things too small to mention but impossible to miss. The idea of doing him hard in his cammies was that much better. Add the kink of having his precious fucking tags wrapped around my `nads and clanking cadence, the forest primeval setting, the scent of sweat and musk and sex in the air -- well, I was one happy camper. Normally I do marines a little rough; I got carried away.

As my dick ripped faster and harder through Mike's straining butthole, he couldn't help grunting every time I hit bottom, and jolted the fuck out of his liver. I pulled up on his shoulders, dragging his ass harder into the line of fire so I could ream him even cleaner. One hand dragged the collar of his blouse back against my face so I could nip at his neck as I used him up the ass. His tight butt arched out and up, giving my dick a perfect angle, and I made the most of it. When I got the range on his prostate, I really went to work, recalculating my fire solution on every brutal stroke, pounding it to jelly and making Mike love life. Sometimes I'd slam my dick so far up his ass that the chain wrapped around my base would stop me. Now and again I'd pull my dick out on the up-stroke, just for the brutal pleasure of stretching Mike's shattered fuckhole twice more -- once popping upward from the inside and against as I slammed my meat home where I belonged.

The CLANK-CLANK of his tags as I drilled him faster gave me my best idea yet. The slut was barely conscious now, a bundle of hard muscle held together only by the need for the meat I had to give. Every nerve he had was stretched to the breaking point; like any classic bottom, he was rapidly slipping toward the mindless contentment I'd felt with his tongue up my ass. The last thing in the world he needed was something to keep his mind occupied. That's why I gave it to him.

If you've seen marines jogging along early in the morning, you know how hard they get over counting cadence. I ordered the buttfuck to count cadence for me and he knew he had to obey. The problem was, of course, he couldn't think. Instead of letting himself slip gently into a fuck-fugue that would mercifully ease the intolerable burden of his pleasure, he kept trying to concentrate on his cadence and, as a consequence, felt every perfect fuckstroke slashing up his tight marine ass.

He didn't believe I really expected him to perform, but I fucked some sense into him. Soon he was trying, grunting through clenched teeth what I took to be attempts at poetry. The CLANK-CLANK of his tags, the SMACK THWAP of sweaty skin against hard muscle, and the cruel SWOOSH of my butt-buster splitting open his ass drowned out most of his rhyme, but he did try. Something like

    1-2-3-4

    Who's the tightest fucking whore

    5-6-7-8

    Ream that hole, don't hesitate

doesn't even scan right, but Mike had other things on his mind. Now and again he'd forget and slip into long, drawn- out drivel like "Yeeeeeeeeesssssssssssss" or "Jeeeesssusss!" but an extra-vicious jab up the bung got him back with the program.

The flip side to all this shit I was giving him was that I wasn't able to let myself go, either. Probably for the first time in my life, I was fucking a prime hunk and keeping my wits about me. Looking back, I can remember the incredible feel of Mike's shithole stroking along my blood- gorged joint. I remember the chain biting into my balls and the slick feel of his guts as I slid through them. I remember a hard wall of muscle somewhere up his ass that kept snagging my dick on the way by and, most of all, the way his butt twitched and torqued on my tool while I did him. Most of all, though, I remember the solid THUD of our bodies slamming together as Mike grunted his cadence and his tags kept counterpoint.

I'm surprised I lasted as long as I did. When I finally knew I couldn't hold off another moment, I picked up my ramming speed and fucked Mike's body back over the tree trunk, nailing him down like a pile driver run amok. I had one hand back up under his t-shirt molesting a hairless tit and the massive pec it crowned. My other kept his neck in a head-lock; then when I lost control. About two dozen thrusts later, as his guts were filled to overflowing and my nuts felt about to fall off, I discovered I'd clamped my teeth into the back of his neck like a tomcat. I untoothed him, slowly undicked his ass, and wiped my gloriously messy meat back and forth across his ass while he was collapsed over the tree like a pricked balloon.

Yes, I did finish sucking his dick. Yes, it was even better than I'd expected. No, as good a cocksucker as I am, I don't think Mike really enjoyed blowing his load down my throat as much as he did getting mine up the ass. Go figure grunts.

We tried for about twenty minutes to get his chair off my dick, but we finally had to break the thing to do it -- the chain, that is, not my dick. I had plans for my dick. Mike had to make formation later that day at 32nd Street, but we made arrangements to get together the next afternoon. When I showed ten minutes early up back at the tree and discovered that the slut had brought a friend along and had already stripped him buck naked and tied the fucker to the trunk with his web belt, I knew that Sunday wasn't going to be my day of rest. They don't call young grunts "lance corporals" for nothing, you know.

DESERT MANEUVERS

I'll always be sorry I missed the war. Watching the Desert Storm blow itself out on CNN as I sat on my ass at Pendleton wasn't much fun. Just as I was hating life because I'd missed the war of my generation, I heard we were deploying for the summer to the UAE, Bahrain, and Kuwait. We'd missed most of the show, but maybe Saddam would pull another boner out of the bag and we'd see some action after all. Here was my chance to finally make up for lost time; I was excited as a boot-camp who'd just figured out to do with his weapon. I was also fooling myself.

They may have been war heroes and all, but the Desert Storm troopers had six months off and then worked for four days -- during the season when Arabia wasn't much warmer than Akron. I'm sorry I missed those four days, but I very deeply regret the months after the storm when our company was called in to stand guard duty -- in the hottest weather on the planet.

When our unit got to the Gulf in mid-July we started humping our shit across one stretch of stand after another -- in temperatures hot enough to make the fucking sand sweat. Maneuvers in the UAE's 135⁻ were unbearable, but at least the Emirates are dry. In Bahrain and Kuwait, 120⁻ seemed twice as hot because of the humidity and choking white haze. The Kuwaiti oil wells belched our smoke into the furnace-like air already choked to capacity with water and sand dust. Instead of blowing away as it would it any decent Christian country, the smoke simmered to a white, oily soup, too heavy to rise far above the sand, too dense to creep away on little camel's feet. Bad news with nowhere to spread, the noxious shroud wound its wet, choking way across our eyes and mouths, holding in the sun's heat and blocking the slightest breeze until the very air glowed with a persistent, palpable, pernicious presence.

Our desert cammies were khaki-colored to hide us in the sand, but were thick as a Midlands' twill. Even at midnight, they hung heavy with sweat; in the afternoon the sweat dripped from our blouses until we left dotted trails behind us in the sand like incontinent snails. Even swallowing our required five gallons a day, we lost so much water that pissing was a major operation. In the beginning, getting us acclimated, they'd give us a few hours off around 1400, but there wasn't much point. From our cots and canteens to our weapons, everything we knew, everything in our world, was hot to the touch.

Just sitting motionless at 0300, life was unendurable. Humping our gear along on endless daytime maneuvers across Satan's desert playground, the men who had come to the Gulf as America's studliest warriors wilted away to withered Dantesque caricatures.

Sex was the last thing on my mind. That August afternoon, Miller and I pulled watch at a check-point miles away from the nearest other lifeform. The little guard shack promised some minor pretence of shade, but it lied. The half walls and tin roof were as innocent of comfort or hope as the rest of our lives.

I lay panting quietly in what shade there was, making a sweat-puddle in the sand, trying to keep from passing out. Miller, doubtless dreaming of breezes from a time before the Gulf, had draped himself across a window frame a yard away. I found myself watching the steady drip-drip-drip of sweat off the back of his blouse. My eyes followed the darkest river of sweat down his cammies and into his boots. One idle, unguided thought led to another until I realized I hadn't so much as jerked off in at least six weeks.

Looking back, I don't think I saw where events were heading, I'd just finally had enough fucking semper fi uniform code crap for awhile. Our reliefs weren't scheduled for hours; the air was so hot not even the vultures were aloft to see what we looked like. I said a naughty word, went into the shack to get another bottle of 125⁻ drinking water, and stripped off my blouse and t-shirt. I'd have lost the pants, too, but I'd long since given up on shorts and I knew I'd feel like an idiot hanging out in the desert in only my boots. As I wrung out the t-shirt and blouse, if I wasn't a whole lot cooler, at least I was lighter and more comfortable.

Troy Miller was my sergeant, but no one had ever accused the guy of being a Nobel laureate. His job demanded he keep me good to go, but he was so dead on his feet himself he could barely pant. I saw a 'entative, censorious shadow flit across his face, but when he started unbuttoning his blouse, I knew I wasn't the only marine around who wasn't feeling much like John Wayne.

I didn't seriously think of doing him until I saw his naked torso. None of us had been working out much in the Gulf, but Troy was choice enough goods he could coast awhile. Marines break down into three general types: R2-D2, C-3PO, and Wookie -- short and compact, tall and well-built, and gigantic but not overly bright. Troy was R2 all the way: only 5'8" but well- designed, usually full of energy with a quick lip and quicker grin. His blue-green eyes and chestnut crest of hair were prime recruiting-poster material.

As I stood beside him and watched the streams of sweat roll from his neck, down across massive shoulders and disappear into the thick, chestnut band of thatch that lives across his strong pecs, my crank started to climb north for the first time in weeks.

Troy had come to the First of the Ninth several months before, but I'd never bothered to find out if he was family. Back before the Gulf, when I still though about sex, no marine had ever turned down what I had on offer. Usually, though, we tend to be conscious of rank. I could be fairly sure of another lance corporal and dead sure of doing a PFC, but lances don't usually go around dicking their sergeants. Besides, you never know. Troy seemed a regular guy, but he could have turned out to be one of those up-tight so-called straight assholes you read about in the Reader's Digest and Jesse Helms' newsletters.

My eyes slipped down to the crotch of Troy's sweat-soaked cammies and learned that regular was the last thing he was. The horny bastard must have liked the sight and smell of my firm, sweat-slicked marine flesh, because his pole was poking his pants as proud and tall as a Commandant's parade inspection. Suddenly, all the molten loads I'd forgotten about for so long bubbled up from my balls and I knew I was going to erupt. I could do the inside Troy's beautiful butt or the uniform of my country, but the nasty was about to get done one way or the other. As I moved around behind him and admired his powerful pecs give way to perfect lats and then the back and hard, sloping shoulders of a Greek god, I hadn't much doubt what meat was fit for my creamy sauce.

I took my time. Miller just looked at me with his bright, azure, tomcat eyes as I eased my face down to his biceps. A glorious stench

...g about his body, inviting as an oasis. I didn't say a
... I was being a Valentino shaikh, silent and sultry; maybe
...were necessary. Our eyes had already asked the question;
...ks knew the answer.

My nose slid along the soft, slick surface of his bicep until I
reached his shoulder and my tongue went UA. His hard marine body
shivered as my bumpy tongue slid across the perfect country of his
shoulders. Muscles rippled and quavered beneath soft skin as I licked
him cleaned, starting low and moving by easy stages up his thick,
wrestler's neck. By the time I was tongue-fucking his ear into surrender, his hands were all over me -- pulling my body hard against his, sliding along my knobby spine down into my cammies, following along my
flanks, fiercely grinding the back of my head forward until my face
honed itself against his, lifting my hot, incredibly sweaty ass as he
locked our bodies together.

Gooseflesh ricocheted across the soft skin stretched tight across
his man-muscled frame. Lust carelessly smeared one sensation into
the next until our clutching, heaving bone-dance threatened an immediate good time. My weapon was cocked and ready to fire when some
passing god whispered "At ease." We had the whole afternoon.

I broke Troy's love-hungry grip on my grunt ass, pushed his panting beastial body away from mine and showed disrespect to a superior
officer: "Faggot bitch." His arm snaked out and savagely pulled my
face hard against the powerful pecs which rose to meat me, pressing
his hard, thick man-tits between my lips.

His naked, sweaty chest ground about in such pleasure even I
thought it looked obscene until his tit-stalk found the sharp, delicious
danger of my tooth edge. Twisting this way and that as his hands
clawed at my back, he scraped that tit harder into my mouth. I bore
down and gave him the chewing out every bad young marine deserves.

I was so busy with business that I hadn't been listening to him
talking shit and groaning away like a TJ whore. When I crunched down
on that tit and started to gnaw, though, the very desert itself heard him
scream out in perfect, pent-up pleasure.

I tore into his other tit when the first had been rubbed just the right
way -- and then left it in ruins to lick my way up into his armpit, the
unquestioned font of eau de grunt. His massive arm locked around my
head again, trapping me in the wellspring of his sweat and scent and

savage sexuality. I sucked dry the chestnut hairs that tickled my fancy and kneaded his ass through his sweat-soaked cammies while I did it. After what may have been minutes but seemed at once a lifetime and but a second, I knew if he was going to respect me in the morning, I'd have to do a little training of my own.

When I got a grip on his nuts, he released his hold on my head. A quick tug at his tits pulled his face down hard against my wiry, rust-coloured chest fur. Sodden with my sweat, it was ready to scrape against his face until he sucked and tongued and lapped my fur dry and titillated me besides. Standing there at parade rest with the Saudi sands stretching away into infinity and Miller sucking at my body like a leech with a free lunch, I did what any desert defender would do: I unbuckled my belt and dropped trou.

Troy may be a sergeant, but he wasn't completely retarded. His face slid down my pelt to tongue my belly-button for a moment and then worked his lips around the tip of my lizard to slurp up the stream of pre-cum oozing out of my foreskin. For a long moment, I let him dig deep into my cocksock and ease it back so he could get at the love-honey and sweat and built-up musk I'd been saving there for that special someone.

I suddenly jerked it away from him with the warning I was going to dick a different hole; his job was to lick the sweat from my balls and, if he was lucky, lick my nasty asshole until it sparkled.

I'll never know how I held off as long as I did. That tongue on my tool had been lethal to my virtue. By the time I shook him off, I was far enough gone that when I felt his tongue lap at my nutsack and his lips suck my balls down into his mouth, my guts exploded. I was too busy having fun to take critical notes, but I know that, righteous though it was, that nut was unlike anything I'd ever known. My dick was free to frolic, but as my guts clenched tight I was able to stay sufficiently con-scious to see one glob after another of gleaming Jackson jism spurt up into the air like some alien UFO space test. A few landed on my chest, but most arced high and wide over Troy's bare back to splatter against the desert.

Once I'd started shooting, I held his head tight, nearly castrating myself as he gulped for air and got gonads instead. The last several globs of my jarhead jism splashed onto his back and joined the rivers of sweat flowing down across his gleaming, muscle-cobbled back.

Once I'd started breathing again myself, I reached down for a handful of my sweet, slimy spooge and smeared it where it would do the most good: along the crack up my ass.

My waking wet-dream had been wild, but I was anything but drained. My sergeant was still between my legs, licking my thighs and balls and crotch; but when I barked at him to lick my ass, he hove on the double. Miller's perfect nose parted my cheeks and gave his tongue room to work. At first, he concentrated on scooping up the fresh marine manmilk I'd left for his lunch, but when that was gone, he dug deeper. The slut's sandpaper tongue slipped between my hard cheeks like a Panzer column. I clenched tight despite myself, but that slutty tongue coasted along the sweaty depths of my most secret country. Miller traveled that secluded landscape like a native going home for Thanksgiving, relishing each precious feature and nuance both for its own sake and for the banquet which lay at the end of his journey.

I was bent over by now, bracing my arms against what passed for our guard shack, my ass arched outward, presenting my proud, pulsing pucker for whatever punishment lay in store. Troy's face just kept pressing harder and deeper up my ass until, like a thunderbolt, his tongue tore into my shithole and shut my dirty little mind down hard. I've always had a thing about tongue up my ass. I read once that if you massage an alligator's belly, he won't attack. I guarantee the same holds true for a marine's asshole.

I felt every bump on his tongue as he drilled its tip into my pucker and lapped at my hole like a spaniel with a new dick for Christmas. One distant corner of my mind heard myself talking shit and groaning in delight. My ass ground backwards into my sergeant's cute all-American marine face, but I was powerless to do anything but enjoy. My body had mutinied and was acting on its own. After weeks and then months of hell, my ass had found a small stretch of marine heaven -- and it intended to enjoy it.

He kept that tongue tearing up my ass forever. At one point I came out of a daze to feel Troy's ass-licking lips locked tight around my shithole, sucking hard as he drilled deep. My hands were on his head, trying to stuff that face up my ass where in belonged. His hands fluttered up along my sweat-soaked flanks as he worked, licking and sucking and drilling and caressing me, at once his sleek desert stallion and the luscious man- flavored ice-cream bar he yearned to chow down.

As the milk-colored air simmered around us, drawing streams of sweat from every pore, the heat was so enervating I wasn't sure whether I was passing out from heat prostration or tongue penetration. That tongue was so demanding, so terrible and insistent, my balls clenched tight again; I was only moments away from another desert accident, but this time it was going to be on purpose. I'd had enough of trying to see him work on my ass. The ass-licking faggot had had his chance to do me hard up the butt. If he wasn't going to use his marine manhood on me as was his right as senior man, I'd drill his ass hard enough to strike Arabian crude.

He looked stunned when I pushed him back onto his butt and fell atop him. For a moment, my lips met his and I tasted my ass for the first time in my life while our chest pelts ground our pecs together and our hips poked pricks into the other's furry belly. The airborne oil and the gushing sweat made our hard bodies slip together on the sand until our arms and legs and slick marine bodies were writhing like bait in a can of Crisco. I felt his tits digging across my stiff fur and mine boring into his soft, chestnut down; his hands slid down to my ass, forcing my dick harder against his belly. Then we both knew it was time.

We both had our trou around our ankles, but stopping to unlace our boots was impossible. I lifted his legs towards the sky and slipped my shoulders between his calves. His belt buckle pressed against the back of my neck, but just then I'd have challenged a guillotine to bury my shank up his ass. Rolling about on the ground, he'd picked up a dusting of sand so I slapped his ass clean before I settled my dick against his hole. His eyes flashed with every slap until one bred another and I was half tempted to take time and teach him some manners before I fucked him. Just then, though, I was out of time. We both were.

His hard cheeks clenched tight to pull back my foreskin as I dug deep. After waiting patiently for so long, the tender tissues that lurked deep inside his pucker lurched outward at the first scent of dick, clutching at my cum-slit and urging me to drop in for a visit. A hundred images combined in one as I hung there, savoring a last grand moment of anticipation before I did him: the feel of the hot desert sand on my knees, the clank of his buckle and sodden clammy feel of his cammies on my shoulders, the tight luscious depths of his steamy asscrack, the feel of his strong hands on my back as he pulled me downward to our destiny, the way his lips hung slightly parted, glistening sweat and gasping in rhapsodic expectation. Most of all, though, I remember his eyes: the hungry eyes of a wild cat out for a mid-day stroll who finds a sweet, juicy young gazelle struggling with a broken leg. Unable to believe his good fortune, the cat sits for a time, relishing the delights to come, postponing his inevitable pleasure until sublime satisfaction ceases being a surprise and becomes a present fact of nature.

The eyes were Troy's, but I pounced to end his rapacious rever- ie with a quick, brutal marine thrust. I answered his butt's craving with a single savage stroke that tore through his tight, tender tunnel and kept reaming on until I was buried dick-deep in his ass, my stiff pubes were grinding the living fuck out of the ruins of his shithole, and my cum-slit was scratching a need he'd kept so hidden from the world that he'd even forgotten it himself.

At the instant we became one, I saw his hungry eyes slam shut, but they opened almost at once. My hips had no sooner slammed his body hard against the desert sands than those blue-green eyes found mine. Now no longer hungry, they were triumphant. His lips moved slightly in a pant or nervous twitch as his system got used to have nine thick inches shoved up his guts. In a moment, though, I discovered it wasn't a twitch. He mouthed the word again: PLEASE. The slut want- ed more.

Between the trou trapped behind my back and his boots digging the living fuck out of my ass, Troy didn't have much chance of making a quick getaway so I settled in to tend to business. The first stroke up was almost as fine as the stroke down, but his ass was soon awash with liquid love, slicking my pre-cummed way through his guts. As my hips remembered what to do, I made them our master. They drove my thick, butt-breaking dick deeper and harder down into Troy's trapped marine asshole with every stroke, tearing grunts from him and making me whimper as though I were the faggot-assed bitch getting the ream- ing of a lifetime. As I looked down, recording forever in memory every flinch of his boy-next-door face and splash of my sweat onto his chest, I realized distractedly where we were. I'd probably done a company's worth of marine butts before, but for was the first time in my life, I was fucking another marine up the ass and we could make all the noise we wanted. When you're used to dark corners on base or a quick poke in the back of a `track, you don't even think of letting yourself go.

As I shot my load up Troy's ass, I tore loose with all the howls and screams and SHITs I'd repressed over the years. The bitch would have jumped atop the guard shack if I hadn't had his ass nailed down tight. For the next minute or so, I was busy blowing my load up his ass, grinding my bush against his hole, and yelling at the gods to get a gander at what GOOD feels like.

The slick feel of my own jism up Troy's tight marine ass was such a turn-on, there was no way I was about to leave home. I'd never been harder. Sweat was pouring off me in buckets, but at least it was good, honest sweat that I'd done something to earn. Besides, I wasn't getting stuck with it; Troy was the poor bastard awash. When he saw I was going for another inning, he stopped being shocked and returned my boot camp noise decibel for deafening decibel. I'd give his ass an especially vicious prostate pounding and yell as loud as I could into the face three inches away from me: "Take that you faggot, shit-bag excuse for a marine!"

He'd clench the whole length of his shitchute around my massive marine meat and slam back with "Give me something to work with, Needledick." We kept it up, fucking harder and screaming louder like butch marine drill instructors gone wrong as I pounded his body against the bedrock, pushing him slowly across the desert as my dork drilled his ass and his boots rode my butt as though we were at Santa Anita. I'd fucked him dry by the time my next load was ready to launch, but it was the best of the day -- maybe the best of my life. The slick feel of another marine body trapped below me in the desert wilderness was almost as much a rush as the tight dry fuck-friction heat toasting my tool on the inside as we steamed on the outside and the glorious raucous marine noise we made as we rutted were the best fucking time I can imagine having. Just before I lost it again, I pulled myself -- and Miller -- to my knees so I could hold him in my arms while I shot my load up his ass. My teeth tore into his dusty, sweat-soaked shoulder and my hands tore at his hard back as my hips drove my dick home where it belonged: into the deepest, most secret reaches of my sergeant's guts.

It was there I left my load as we thrashed and howled in the middle of the Saudi sands like psychotic savages on speed. It was there that I found my true home, my true marine core. When I was finished with his ass, I collapsed back atop him and lay for a moment trying to catch my breath. He was patient for all of a dozen seconds before he said, "All right, lance corporal. Let's get these weapons cleaned." Needless to say, he intended me to start on his. The bitch expected me to suck his dick!

Fortunately for us both, I wanted nothing more. He was trimmed meat, but the horn-dog bitch had been oozing pre-cum for hours. By the time I sucked his balls flat and chugged down his first load of the day, I couldn't resist sticking around for another serving. I insisted that this time around, while I was proving what cocksuckers lance corporals could be when they had a sergeant like him, he should get that talented marine tongue of his back into action up my butt. The feel of that bumpy tunnel tickler is better than any possible narcotic -- and impossibly more addictive. My mind slipped into neutral as we used good old marine teamwork to make sure these desert maneuvers came off just right.

By the time dark and our reliefs were due, we were rubbed so raw by the sand and each other, it was time to stow our gear and stand down. Now that I'd discovered what an ass-lick my sergeant was, I was looking forward to the next several months. We couldn't always howl at the heavens while we drilled for desert cream, but we'd be together. Life had turned a corner and was looking pretty fucking good. When the night team showed up, they must have wondered what we were so happy about. After all we'd been through in the previous months, being happy didn't seem natural. After that day, though, together and alone, happiness was the most natural thing of all.

THE DRILL INSTRUCTOR

Men become marines for many reasons. When I was 18, the studly uniforms and call to adventure were at the top of my list. By the end of my third week in boot camp, though, I discovered the glorious savagery which waits hidden, patient and ever-faithful, within us all. When you're lucky enough to live around men like yourself, every day is both a hunt on the wild side and the timeless struggle for survival. Once you know how it works, the Corps is the best fucking career in the world.

Nearly three weeks of sleep deprivation and 25-mile humps and the brutal physical abuse the Corps likes to call "thrashing in the pit" had built up muscles I'd never heard of and then made them all ache at once. Through the agony of cramps and general exhaustion, I was proud that my body had shaped up like a Spartan recruiting poster. Despite my body, I was still only 18 and knew nothing about sex or life. Then, during that third week of boot camp, my drill instructor worked overtime to train me hard.

I was dragging my ass from the shower towards my rack just after taps when I heard my DI's dogfaced bark. "RECRUIT JACKSON!" stopped me dead as I tried to straighten to attention in my towel. He was in my face about hauling my worthless recruit ass into his office before I found myself back in the pit for the night, but I had no clue what had set the crazy bastard off this time. Once he had me alone, there was a lot of screaming about how I was a worthless waste of my daddy's cum. Marines had to have guts and stamina. I was a pussy-assed faggot and would never be a marine so why didn't I get out of his life before I pissed him off. I figured the psycho was just fucking with my head so I said all the right things complete with "Sir, no, Sir": I could hack anything. I was a marine-tough gungy killing machine and good to go.

When he snatched the towel off my waist and told me to grab my ankles, I felt more foolish than afraid -- but I had already learned when to obey an order. I wasn't sure what lame high school game was coming next, but sure as shit knew when it arrived. The paddle didn't look lethal later, when I saw it abandoned on the floor, a 2-foot piece of rough-cut, unfinished redwood with holes bored at irregular intervals. That first blow, though, was the single most exquisite experience of my life. Looking back, I see now that the various parts of my body endure it on different levels. All I saw was the floor coming up at me as the impact sent me toppling. I don't think I ever heard the brutal SMACK of the rough wood tearing into my flesh. By that time, every fiber of my being was so busy being stretched and grated and incinerated that the rest of my senses just shut down. Oddly, my ass itself didn't hurt more than anything else; it just happened to be the tortured ground-zero of the detonation which blinded me with one indescribable seizure of pain after another. My soul was stripped as naked as my butt, and I teetered helplessly towards the dark, welcoming edge of consciousness.

The DI's sneers jerked me back. I was struggling to my feet again when I noticed his dick trying to burrow its way out of his Charleys. His tits pointed hard up beneath the olive t-shirt stretched tight across his pecs. I'd read about sadists getting off on inflicting pain. Two things came to mind right off: being a DI was the perfect job for the fuckers and I was in a world of shit. As I scrambled, the bastard just stood there, gently swinging the paddle against his leg, impatiently waiting for me to reassume the position or slink out of the room in defeat. However sick my DI was, I meant what I'd said: As a matter of pride, I could take anything he could sling my way. What I couldn't do was separate the pain in my ass from the mind-numbing fireball that was my all-consuming torment. Then, bent double again and bracing myself, waiting for the second blow to land, I had another surprise.

My dick had swollen so thick and long that it was pulsing just inches from my face. What the fuck was happening to me? I'd done plenty of jerking off and even used the thing on a couple girls in high school, but I'd never felt anything like this hard-on. Why were my nine inches standing tall now? The paddle landed again, replacing thought with another bolt of redwood lightning that ricocheted up my spine and outward to fry every nerve I had. I managed somehow to stay on my feet, gasping for breath and fighting off the darkness that threatened to snuff out the white-hot fireball searing my flesh. At first, I fought off unconsciousness just because I'd be damned if I'd give the fucker the satisfaction of passing out on him. Then another blow landed and yet another until I found myself focusing on the pain, using it for my own twisted satisfaction. When the darkness caught the glow and burned as bright, I knew I had conquered unconsciousness and learned to love the brutal honeyed sweetness of my agony. One butt-ripping blow blended seamlessly with the next, flaming my ass and soul from fire to fission to fusion as my mind misread the signals of torment and discovered the secret beauty that dwelt within.

After a time, my eyes eased open to hurry the paddle and found another target. My dick danced in my face, a huge B- movie cyclops, throbbing purple and gushing a torrent of crystalline rheum from his single eye. Like a Zen martyr, I set one remote corner of my soul watching the beads of love- lube splash away from my dick and fall to the floor in slow- motion threads of perfection. Slipping by easy stages from pain to pleasure to an ecstasy of unimaginable rapture, I was sure nothing could be better.

Later, I watched my DI initiate others into the Corps and studied the way he waits until the ass hungers for another taste of the paddle before he stops. I know now that every muscle in my hard young body was knotted tight, that I was gasping for air, and that I was slipping rapidly towards shock -- but all I felt then was fine. I was even too deep in ecstasy to notice when he moved from the paddle on my ass to a more ancient and wonderful torment.

Without warning, the delicious feast changed courses. The appetizer was gone and it was time for me to get the meat. Now, instead of the intermittent SLAM THWACK of the rough paddle, my butt felt the constant fire of being ripped apart from the inside. I didn't feel his zipper slashing at my raw cheeks as his swollen dick dug deep up my exit-only shithole, but that auto-da-fe sent my spirits soaring to heaven. I didn't feel his hands ripping at my hips or tits, holding me fast against him as he raped me faster up the ass. All I felt was the unbelievable fullness in my guts. I was a virgin. How was I to know his huge marine weapon was using my recruit hole for his pleasure?

I know now how he brutally ripped my virgin ass open. I know how he stretched my shitchute like rhino fucking a gnat's nostril. I know he slammed and reamed and mangled my ass -- but I also knew even then that whatever he was doing, I'd never felt more alive. Everything about the scent of his sweat and his slick touch and the rasping savagery of his breath seemed so perfect I wasn't interested in tedious questions about what was going on.

After seconds or a lifetime having of his bull-sized buttfucker up my ass, grating across my prostate and smashing into my liver, he let up for long enough to slam my head against a full-length mirror on the wall so he could see the meat he was fucking. As my eyes opened again and I came face to face with my violation, I jerked myself away from the delicious agony that had flooded my soul. I had to do something. The bastard was raping me -- fucking me up the butt. No man could just stand there humped over with a guy's dick up his ass and take it. However glorious that grunt shank felt smashing my guts to tapioca, this had to be sick and wrong and perverted. Instinct drove me forward towards escape; but inches before I could wriggle my ass off the his rail, a hand slammed down to snag my balls in what felt like a bear trap. Once he had them, he squeezed and twisted until I my guts started to surge out my ears. Through the blood pounding and my stifled screams, I heard his whisper: "Try that again, Boot, and you're dead meat." All the while, of course, he raped on, pounding that gut-busting dick harder and deeper up my ass with every brutal stroke. As I watched my rape reflected in the mirror, scruples and shame gave way to the realization that he meant what he said. Besides, his marine meat felt so fucking good up my ass, I wasn't sure I could bear losing it. Far from escaping or just letting him take what he wanted, I became his accomplice. I joined him in my rape and, in that instant, joined the spirit of the Corps for all time.

My body was in shock, but my spirit had never felt so alive. This was more than brutal rape. It was a transcendental fucking experience. I suddenly saw that life shouldn't be about car payments or mortgages -- not with pleasure on this scale available for the taking. Civilization tries to strip away man's beastial nature until he's tamed, deodorized, and safe. But the civilization is fucked in the head; we're all still really just animals at rut. We need to mount and conquer to show our power and, sometimes, even to be taken when we deserve it. That's the marine lesson my DI was drilling into my tight recruit hole. Just then I was taking it up the ass, but I knew I'd be on top soon enough. When I was, the world had better fucking look out.

Meanwhile, I yearned to memorize every sight and sound and smell so I would have them forever: the way my lust-struck dick was

pumped so tight it threatened to split down the middle, the savage grimace on my DI's sweat-streaked face, the way his whole body convulsed against mine in rabid fuck- frenzied thrusts, the hungry look in
his eyes as he used me harder and deeper, and the way my own
marine-recruit body glowed studly lean and hard and tasty-ready as I
slammed off the end of my drill instructor's gut-busting bone.

An especially vicious thrust stopped my bout of self- admiration
as surely as it stopped my hole. I jolted back with the program to the
rules changed again. The DI's reaming had ripped away the golden
glow of pleasure he'd beaten into my butt. Now I could feel every
relentless ram of his rod as though my ass read Braille. Beyond his
massive fulfillment and the shrieks of pain from my hole, I caught the
feel of his trigger-ridge slamming up against the inside of my shithole.
His huge blue vein pulsed the length of his shaft as my slick guts rippled across and begged for more. The hard, swollen head that had broken so many recruits over the years now ground away at the dark end
of my shitchute as his downy blond pubes scraped away the ruins of
my ass.

My hands flew back to his butt, stripping down his trou and
pulling his naked hips hard against me in reassurance that being raped
hard up the ass was this recruit's idea of a dream come true. He was-
n't in the least worried about my feelings, of course; but it's always easier to bust a nut when the hole wrapped tight around your crank has
decided it likes being there.

As I watched in the mirror, he slammed his dick into overdrive,
rolling his hips upward to pound home his point. My fingers held tight,
following his rhythm as they separated his powerful cheeks and worked
their insubordinate way into the sweaty crack of his ass. I was looking
for adventure and found it. His mouth was already gaping open, panting and slavering like a cheetah at a greyhound track. When my fuckfingers slipped across the tight, tender pucker of his jarhead ass, his
face twisted into yet another reflection of beastial brutality and the
chronic savagery of man.

The craving to feel his hot, hard chest scraping across my back
pulled me upward to grind against his iron-tipped tits. His tongue
slipped up my neck and into my ear where it flicked madly about like a
short-circuited electric eel. His olive t-shirt was sodden with sweat that
dripped down my back to splash a first hint of lube onto his monster

marine dick. That hint was buckets too little and half an hour too late. I was too far gone to worry about having my ass torn up, and the way his DI cadence was going to shit told even a cherry- boy like me that the bastard rapist was ready to nut.

His tongue slipped from my ear as breathless pants grew to feral growls that echoed my jungle grunts of dick-bred satisfaction. His teeth sank deep into my shoulder, pinning me tip to tail against his man-hungry grunt body. I'd been too busy making the best of being raped to mess with myself, so I thought I was safe. But my bootcamp butt didn't know how to handle dick yet.

I was instinctively bearing down on his bone to milk it dry. My hands slipped from his asshole to cup his marine-built muscle and glide up along his flanks as his hips rolled harder and faster with every frantic fuck-thrust. The smell and feel and noise of our rut filled my consciousness the way his dick crammed up my ass. I could even have withstood the pounding pressure up my butt and the grating across my prostate if I hadn't looked into the mirror again. What I saw reflected back was too much for me: his hands sliding across my helpless body as he reveled in his absolute power over me, our bodies locked together like cur dogs in the street, and, most of all, the look of absolute power and total triumph on his face as he used my virgin fuckhole and the hard young marine-recruit body that held it. My balls cinched up and sent the load of my life blasting upwards.

Always before, I had gradually pumped myself friendly, climaxed for several seconds, and then coasted back to earth. That night, something about having a buttful of dick changed the program for the better. One moment I was focused on the fire up my ass and wondering if I'd have toothmarks on my shoulder; the next I was blown straight through space-time. I'd thought the paddle had beat me to a frazzle. Then I was convinced my DI's thick dick had bred perfection. The blend of pain and pleasure, of being done and doing, of rape and eagerness picked my ass up and threw it over the abyss I'd been skirting all night. I don't suppose I completely lost consciousness, but I sure as shit wasn't in any shape to take notes. My guts turned inside out and fired off white-hot shards of peter-plasma that flew like shrapnel -- into the mirror, up onto my naked belly and chest, across onto the wall, and in great pearly gobs onto the DI's deck. I was so busy having my best time ever, I didn't care what my seizure was doing to the meat up my hole. As I clenched and cinched and spazed like a firehose, my guts bore down onto that DI dick like a battalion of Iraqi EPWs onto a lunch wagon. As I'd locked and loaded, I was being dry-holed to a frazzle. By the time my last spurts of recruit cream were dribbling out to join the rest of the mess on the deck, my ass was awash with enough lube to make every man in the barracks a slick customer.

All that was left for me to do as I watched the rest of the show in the mirror was bear down even harder on that overgrown bone, partly to keep it happy, partly to keep that mammoth marine load of jism up my ass where it belonged. When the DI finally finished grinding and twitching up my butt and pulled his monster meat out of my hole, I was ready to play again. He wiped his dick on my ass, zipped up, and said, "Dismissed, recruit."

He wasn't interested in love. The gorgeous bastard just liked raping young recruits. The problem was, of course, that I'd been given a glimpse of a world I'd never dreamed existed. I wasn't about to lose it without a fight. Two nights later, the worm turned.

I got up about 0200 to pee and heard noises in the office. When I eased the door open, he had Jenkins pinned down over a table and was humping the living shit out of him. Jenkins was a hopeless wuss, whining about how he hurt and how guys fucking guys wasn't right. Now and again, he'd try to squirm away and the DI would inflate another inch as he slammed the kid back onto the table. I stood watching the show for about two minutes, but my dick was swollen hard enough to hurt -- and I had just the hole in mind.

I had him in a nelson and was up his ass before he realized I was in the room. We probably almost fucked Jenkins to death the way we thrashed around, but my hold was so firm and his hole was so hungry that the fight didn't last long. I was only up his ass about thirty seconds before he splashed Jenkins and finally let him slink off to the head to shit out his creamy memories. After we lost Jenkins, the bashful bastard tried to roll me off, but I managed to hold on until his DI butt was full and overflowing with Jackson jism. I thought he might try to beat the snot out of me, but I'd no sooner pulled out of his ass than he pinned me onto the deck and took his revenge the way I craved: he raped me again -- twice.

We tangled five more times before I moved up from recruit to marine, but I won't bother you with the scores. By the time I left boot camp, I was ready for life among men in the Corps. In the years since, I've sailed with the fleet, been stationed from Okinawa to Europe, and have drilled more holes than OPEC. Whenever I must wrestle a marine to the deck to get what he has, I think back on my drill instructor in boot camp and have to admit that, when it came to drilling, he taught me well.

THE GLORY THAT WAS GREECE

Every graduate student in the field was fighting for a chance to work on the dig at Nauplion, the Miami Beach of ancient Myceanë, but the Greek Department of Antiquities had only two slots for Americans on their team. That summer was especially important because finds made the summer before had threatened to revolutionize thinking about the origins of the all the Heroic Age ruling houses. When the invitation telegram arrived from Athens, I knew my career was made. Even if I spent the summer just sweeping up, having the dig on my resume would get me a lock on any tenure-track job I wanted. Besides, when you're a young archaeologist looking forward to your first real season in the field, you're sure you will be the one to uncover the next Troy or Tut. Excited and optimistic as I was, I had no clue just what I was to discover about Greek culture.

The grad student from Berkeley was a woman, so they assigned me one of the Greek grads for a roommate -- a kid we'll call Skippy because that's what everyone else called him once they saw him tear into the American team's peanut butter the first week in camp. I could tell you his name, but it's very long and, these days, very famous in grave-robber circles. Skippy will do.

Our first week, everyone was more or less sweeping up most of the time, doing the thousand things that needed done before we could get down to our real work. By our second week, camp had taken shape at last. Skip and I were finally assigned to do something interesting: make a test trench into a hillside below the megaron. The bigwigs were eager to finish up on shaft graves left over from the previous season, so we had almost no supervision. Skippy was almost as excited as I was; and we tore away at the slope, cutting through the detritus until the dust flew, but always careful enough that every sherd was preserved.

The humid summer sun of Argos quickly worked up a royal sweat. We stripped our shirts off and dug our high-class ditch in shorts and sneakers, working away like road gang convicts through the afternoon.   What chatter there was was romantic crap about how Agamemnon or Orestes might have been on the very spot during some distant summer holiday. Skip's American improved, but we waffled back and forth between it and Classical Greek, depending on the topic of conversation.

Several times I looked up and saw Skipper looking at me with his head askew and a goofy expression on his face, but at the time I thought he was just excited. Now, of course, I understand that he was excited, all right -- by what he thought I had to offer. I was 23 that summer, with rust- coloured hair and a body born for ditch-digging. My massive pecs were already covered with a thick growth of red fur, my stomach was flat as a dean's jokes, and my butt was never better. Skip seemed preoccupied with my shorts. To be fair, they were skimpy and didn't do much to hide my nine thick inches of archaeological excitement.

After we'd knocked off, Skip and I went back for a quick shower before dinner. When I came out of the john, drying my hair with my towel and chattering about some pottery sherds we had found, Skip went all weird again. He walked over to me, put out a hand to stop my towel action, looking deep into my innocent young green eyes, and said life was more important than jars. He seemed so eager and earnest, I had no clue what to say -- until, his bottomless brown eyes still locked on mine, I felt his dusty hand on my clean American nine-inched crank.

Before I could get my mind out of the 13th Century BC, Skipper was on his knees at my feet and was licking my lizard! Eighty-seven thoughts zipped through my brain at once: Skipper is a faggot -- but that does feel good. I'm going to have to live with the guy all summer. How am I going to get out of this? Jesus, that's good! Does the Director know? Are all Greeks queer? I thought that was just ancient Greeks. He's such a nice kid, too. Christ! His lips are so fucking fine I --

That was about as far as I got with rational thought. I felt my hands latch into the fleecy black texture of his dusty hair and just tried to hold on. He was as old as I was; if he wanted to suck my dick, I'd be an idiot to say no. I think the last remotely sensible thing to flicker through my Bedlam of a brain was that Greece really was a very friendly country.

He'd started lapping at my dickhead, bouncing it off my thighs. His hands had slipped around behind me and were cupping my butt, pulling it forward to grind his mouth against my knob. As my dick started to fight back, his mouth slid open and hot, wet lips worked in rapid strokes across my dick. Within seconds, I was harder than a calculus exam and twice as fucked up.

As I wriggled his face down my swollen dick, I knew only that my joint had never felt anything like Skip. I somehow stopped worrying that he was a guy or that life would be more complicated. I just knew I needed to shove my thick nine inches deeper into his mouth -- and then deeper still. Skip was in no hurry. His lips were spit-slicked skids of satisfaction slipping across the hard bumpy country of my cockhead. As he sucked on and shock gave way to appreciation, I made out distinct sensations: the flutter of his tongue under my head, the nibbling around my snout, the slight twisting of his tight lips just behind my trigger ridge. Each moment brought new, incredible surges of bone- shattering pleasure that made me forget my provincial American priggishness and groan aloud in surprise at each new, miraculous sensation.

At the time, I missed most of the subtleties of his technique; I knew nothing about having my dick sucked except that it felt better than anything I'd every dreamt possible. As my hands worked his face harder down my pole, Skip gave up polishing my knob with his lips and let me slip his curly head harder along my swollen shank. Once I was inside his tight, tender throat, he hunkered down for some serious Hellenic honing.

I must have opened my eyes because I remember looking down at his head as I pumped it along my shaft, fucking my hips up into his classic young face. Just beyond those curls lay the body of a man in his prime -- soft, olive skin stretched tight across shoulder muscles and lats that led down to a butt jutting out far below me. I may have admired his muscle briefly while he was munching mine, but my first view of a man's ass while he was gnawing on my bone reminded me of something. After a moment, I remembered an unhappy experience I'd had years before fucking a girl's tits. She'd freaked out when my dick had gone off and laced her with a month's worth of my slimy jism. What would Skip do if I shot off inside his mouth? The image was at once revolting and, yet, a kinky turn-on. An hour before, I'd have thought that only a really sick bastard would try shoving his dick into another guy's face. Not only was I that sick, Skippy was pretending to have one hell of a slurpy good time. His head was twisting this way and that to work my crank farther into his throat and the cute little pervert was so happy he was wagging his tail.

Somehow those olive-skinned glutes looked a world more interesting than tits -- harder and more ësthetically formed. A hand coasting down the cleft in my own ass brought me back to my senses. I wasn't sure how far this Greek kink of Skip's would go, but I knew he wasn't about to let me slide my dick along his asscrack until I shot my load up onto his back. The idea of stroking my dick along some shitty asshole was gross enough, but the image of my jism dripping down across Skip's hard naked flesh was so wicked that, now I'd gone bad, it had the delicious thrill of perversion.

What was I thinking? Guys interested in men's butts hung out in prison showers -- I knew so because I'd seen it hinted at in movies. Those hands up my ass jolted me back to the present quickly enough. He'd added a second by then and they were slipping along my wet asscrack, prying my cheeks apart and massaging them at the same time -- or maybe I was doing the massaging. His hands up my ass made me aware how I had been clenching up, pushing my hips forward against Skip's eager, young cocksucking face. I felt his lips digging against the harsh texture of my red pubes and tried to pull back politely, but those fingers halted my retreat with a new surprise.

His touch of my butthole was like a bolt of Olympian lightening that sent shivers ricocheting up and down my spine. He didn't push inside my hole, but skitted around it like a gang of butch butterflies on a rumble. Between the tight, hot torment of his throat and the guerilla warfare against my butt, I lost track of myself for a moment. When I came partly to again, his finger was lying hard in my crack, sliding along my butthole just as I'd fantasized doing to him with the same stiff dick now shoved hard down his gullet. His other hand had slipped below my legs and was playing catch-me with my nuts.

Guided by destiny or Skippy's cocksucking young face, we'd somehow maneuvered closer to his bed. He pushed me backwards with his mouth and pulled downwards with his hands until the worldwise little slut swept me right off my feet and down where he thought I belonged. He kept his curls bobbing along my shaft for another several seconds and, just when my balls started to clench up and even I knew he was about to be gagged good, he escaped my load by easing his slutty face off my dick. I came close to hosing us both, but his fingers slipped over my dickhead and pinched me into submission. I knew why he wouldn't want to get caught in my splash and had, in any case, long since given up trying to run my life. Skippy did a much better job.

I lay there panting, trying to figure whether it was good manners to thank somebody for sucking your dick. Skip sidled up along my body, lapping here and there to keep me interested, until his lips were nuzzling my neck like a colt looking for sugar, His mouth on my dick had given me an intense glow, but those lips, half-tickling, half demanding, send shivers back down my spine to cinch my butthole up tight.

His lean young body was atop me now, one leg curled up across my stiff dick. As he sucked on my neck and ear, his hands learned the language of my landscape, running through my thick mat of wiry chest hair, grinding his palms into my hard tits until I really felt them for the first time in my life, slipping along my trembling flanks, and sliding up through my hair. All the while, my dick was arching upward, seeking new fields to plow.

His fingers on my asshole and lips on my neck had been a thrill, but the rush I got when his tongue torqued deep into my ear would have shocked me rigid if I weren't long since already as hard as any young archaeologist can get. The unforgettable scent of man cascaded down off his dusty, sweat-soaked, body like some Olympian gift. Strangely, the stench of armpits and Greek grime didn't reek of body odor, but wafted an erotic elixir whose sweet cloud conspired with the touch of his rabid young body to make me forget the priggish, provincial preconceptions about love that had, so far, kept me from finding anything approaching happiness in my own century.

While my body sucked in great lungfuls of his glorious musk the way a corpse rescued from Death's Welcome Wagon would clutch at air, Skip's wicked dervish of a tongue fluttered and flapped inside my ear, raping me even more insensible. His hot, savage breath roared through my consciousness like the voice of a god and sent me over the abyss into a stupor of complete, perfect, mindless satisfaction. When he finally took mercy on me and pulled the fucker out, I stopped twitching and writhing about long enough for him to ask: "See, you can like?"

Fucked up as I was, I was still able to come up with a couplet of

Rick Jackson USM

Homer's Ionian which translates to something like:

The mighty Akhaians' camp, strong-greaved warriors all
Took pleasure in their company, celebrating life together.

Skippy grinned like a fiend incarnate and asked me, essentially, whether I wanted to try. He was obviously what today I'd call a bottom, but I suspect he wanted me to feel my own way so I could get a handle on every aspect of male love. I was willing and then some, but completely ignorant of the possibilities a man's body possessed. Skip lay beside me on the bed, gazing up like Ganymede with his deep brown eyes and a smile of such absolute trust that I felt I could do no wrong. His doe-length lashes slid shut in pleasure as my fingertips mimicked his, tracing the lines of his classic male muscles on the soft, olive-colored skin stretched over them. Shivering slightly, his body told me I was on the right track. As my palms slid down his firm flanks, I remembered the touch of his hands on my pecs and slipped my lips down to suck gently at the tits stood tall and firm above his chest.

A groan from his lips and a firm hand behind my head were all the encouragement I needed. My lips and tongue and, eventually, even my teeth slipped along his tender manstalks until my Greek boy-bitch was humping the air like a cur dog with a fresh leg. Much as the form and texture of his nipples fascinated me, once his scent had been sucked off, I was eager to move on. Skip's chest was as hairless and soft- skinned above as it was firm below, but some perverse instinct drove me towards his pits -- the living font of his studly smell. He raised his arm to let me snuggle close against it, licking my way to the rough black hairs that lived there.

I could have stayed locked between biceps and lats forever, snuffling out the salty taste of his sweat, its musky brew spinning one sensory delight after another. I lapped and licked and sucked at bold folds of muscle and long, stringy clumps of hairs that held what I needed. I would likely be there still if he hadn't run low on pit-power and been high on other attractions. Once both pits were polished, I moved for a time to suck on his lips and discover the wry character that lived in his face: his innocent dimples, the ironic arch of his right brow, the boyish allure of his pug nose, and the open, friendly gleam of his smile.

I couldn't get the taste of his flesh out of my mind. For a moment, some inner reserve held me back. I knew only one store of musk was left untapped, but -- was I a cocksucker? I must have always been and just not noticed. When I slipped down to his crotch and slipped my tongue across his balls, I knew my world had changed forever. This was no quirky walk on the wild side, no one-time experiment to regret later. Anything that felt and smelt and tasted this good must be right. My lips captured his nuts and sucked them hard like sweet jawbreakers designed with adult tastes in mind. Again, I slipped my tongue across his tender, arching flesh until no trace of manmusk lingered.

I'd been putting off his dick. It was eight inches long and thick, crowned with a huge head almost completely hidden by a mass of wrinkled foreskin. I may have seen `skins in passing -- in gym locker rooms or frat house showers -- but I'd never looked at them before. I hadn't known how fine dicks could feel. His pulsed like a metronome against his hard belly, begging for the feel of my lips, daring me to suck cock -- to admit to myself I was a faggot.

I gobbled his joint with an enthusiasm and ignorance of technique that still make me smile today. My tongue found its way between his tender cocksock and the hard purple meat the hid underneath, but rather than taking it slow, scooping out his glory in easy stages, I tore into his bone like a starving hound. His `skin slid back along that thick Greek column and my mouth exploded in a riot of savory sensation that made his pits seem bland as a parson's handshake. As my lips slid down his column, my tongue explored the nooks and crannies of his capital, digging out the last particle of Greek glory while my hands continued their ceaseless search across his thighs and belly and flanks.

Suddenly he pulled back and flipped over onto his knees, shoving his butt in my face. I hadn't thought about licking the musk from his ass, but moved in to check out possibilities like the slut I had become. Looking back over his shoulders, Skippy turned on his wide-eyed charm and begged for my help. His true nature cried out for relief: "Please fuck me. Put your dick up my ass. Use me hard."

How could I say no? From that angle, the similarity to tits wasn't as great, but his butt still looked just fine. I slid my dick along the crack of his ass, much as he'd slid his fingers along mine. The thought flashed through my mind that he'd want to fuck me after I'd done him -- but that just turned me on all the more. The image of his lean Greek boy- bitch body locked across my back, pounding those thick eight inches up into my ass, sent blood rushing to my heads and made me feel woozy.

Skip threw me a bottle of sun-tan goop and suggested I slather it down my shank to make it slide better. Now, of course, I know he didn't want me to do irreparable damage, but I can't blame the little shit. In the years since that summer day of discovery, my dick has been too much to handle for more men than I can count. Skippy was only able to take up his ass at all because lust can teach the flesh magic past understanding.

I didn't slam right in. I played with his asshole, sliding my slick dick across it, prying his cheeks apart just as I'd fantasized. The feel of my bone sliding between those firm mounds of man-flesh while Skipper clenched his butt and wagged his fanny at me like a Vegas stripper was only the latest in an endless supply of surprises. When he reached back to grab my joint and almost shoved it up his tight little Greek ass, I thought we would both pass out. Skipper's whole body went rigid; every muscle seemed to stand out beneath his soft skin like an anatomical model of the perfect human body. My meat was almost as bad off. This wasn't some slack snatch; Skip's shithole locked around my lizard like a hot iron cuff.

For one panic-filled moment, I remembered how comical dogs looked locked together and wondered whether I could reclaim my rod if I wanted to. The moment passed when I knew I never wanted to leave his body. The tight heat of his ass on my head, the slick feel of his guts greeting my shank as I slid slowly home, the clench of his cheeks, the feel of his hands on my ass as they pulled me harder against him, the soft feel of his skin against my wiry chest thatch, the quail-like moans of pleasure that slipped steadily from his lips -- all these and a thousand sensations besides melded together in one perfect cataclysm of bliss.

Long before I was ready, Skip's butt started sliding up my slick joint, fucking himself up against my stiff red pubes, grinding into my crotch like the original whore of creation. His cooing was so eerie in its absolute fulfillment that I forgot my own greedy sensation of the moment and went to work. I enjoyed the feel of my shank slipping through Skipper's guts and slamming into the hard end of his shitchute; but I knew so little about a man's body or how to use it, that I could have done much better. I only discovered his prostate by accident; but, after Skip leapt half way to Hisarlik as I slammed into the sucker, I kept discovering it. The feel of my arms wrapped around Skip's sleek male body as it heaved up and down my dick was epic; the smell and taste of his sweat was a rush worthy of Olympos. The way he grunted each time my dick slammed home and the way his body shook from the fierce impact of my pelvis was something I'll never forget. In almost every sense, this was the perfect first time. Only one thing was missing. Draped across his back, I didn't feel I was fucking Skip, but some ancient sacrificial beast. Doing him hard up the ass was hot as a hekatomb, but I'd started to like the kid as more than what today romantics would call "a piece of tail."

My lips nipped affectionately at his ear lobe as I slammed my dick harder and faster up his perfect young butt, feeding the fuckfrenzy that we had bred but which now ruled us both. Skipper must have sensed my longing for a personal connection -- or maybe he felt the same way. Whatever his motive, he let out a fierce grunt and then pulled away from me, twisting like a wrestler of Olympia. Almost before I sensed his movement, he had twirled about on the end of my dick, scraping the insides of his butt the way a drill scrapes through hard oak. He was on his back, though, his feet locked in the small of my back and his eyes boring up into my soul. His hands on my back pulled me down against him, locking our bodies together as our hips crashed together and apart like indecisive Titans at a neighborhood brawl.

Now the moment was complete: this was sex the way sex should be: my lips on his, the smell of fucking and man clogging the thick summer air, the THWACK and SMACK of two hard, heaving male bodies, my groans and his blending together in unconscious harmony, the glow of our fuck-friction spreading from my match to his tender kindling. Our bodies were smashing together with too much speed and violence for our lips to stay together. Not knowing what else to do, I dug my elbows into the bed beside his chest and parked my face a foot above his, watching every flicker of pleasure fly across his face, while our hips smashed hard together. My eyes strayed once, down between our bodies. I saw the sweat dripping from my hairy chest onto his smooth skin; I saw his balls bouncing on either side of a cock so swollen it seemed momentarily to split its skin down the middle. Just beyond, magic beyond belief, I saw about seven of my nine inches rise for a moment from Skipper's tight fuckhole to gleam slick with lube in the hot evening air and then slash back down into his guts, pounding its way home, finding destiny's direction to a knowledge of life and love that was already old when Myceanë was young.

The sight of Skipper skewered on my pole, of that thick dick slamming up and down, fascinated me in ways beyond reason. Somehow, the dick wasn't even mine any longer; it was ours -- a yoke that bound us together. I had no more control over my hips or the unit they were ramming deeper up Skipper's ass than I had over his hole. Nature or fate or the gods themselves were in charge now, and I was only a spectator in the audience, hypnotized by the slash of my pole down my roomie's hole, the SWOOSH of bone through flesh, the heat and smell and glorious feel of man-sex.

I was still lost in the beauty of dick sliding into ass when I felt Skip's arms clench even tighter around my shoulders. He had been grunting and howling stuff in Greek for minutes, as his hands polished my ass, but now he shattered the room with a cry that sounded the very torment of Hades. Something caught the corner of my eye and I slipped my gaze up to see his dickhead explode and pearly frenzy of jism that spurted up onto my chest to drain in glorious white threads of summer tinsel down onto his hard body. His nuts were clenched tight on either side of his thick dick to pump up other globs of Greek man-seed that splashed past me onto the bed and, finally, just dribbled up onto Skip's classic sweat-streaked torso.

The spasms of animal pleasure that racked Skip's body were too much for me. I could have kept fucking along if he'd just clenched his ass tight. I could have ignored the shrieks of frenzied, lust-struck ecstasy run amok or even the clutch of his arms. I might even have ignored the scent of jism in the air or the feel of his load dripping with coy little tickles of my chest hair down to land back on his studly young body. All at once, though, coupled with the glorious sight and slick sensation of my dick reaming out his cute little Greek fuckhole, they were too much. I felt my own guts contract in unutterable fierceness and then immediately heave as the world collapsed into the void that exploded out of my dick.

When my soul slipped from a birth of Dictian blackness and slid into conscious pleasure as profound as those of Olympos itself, I could but hold on to the form locked tight by mutual need beneath me. My balls finally ran dry; my hips eventually stopped their rampage. My eyes returned to his, wider now than ever, but glowing with the triumph of conquest and the heat of a secret shared. I collapsed, a sweaty but very contented mass of young American manhood, into Skippy's arms.

I lay there, contented if out of breath, until he rolled us over to sit astride my rod, tickling nine inches up his ass with my dick and grinning like a fool with a secret. The slut took a finger and scraped a white glob of jism off his belly and put it between my lips. I liked the taste of his natural dick better -- but I managed to choke his spunk down that afternoon -- and evening, and for the rest of that glorious, eternal Greek summer.

Skip and I became quite a team on the site, too. Between us, we did more valuable work than all the other grad students put together. Something about the land became part of us and we understood, in ways others seemed not to do, the meaning of what had been left behind. In the years since, Skippy and I have gone our separate ways but keep in touch. Once or twice a year, we'll meet at some convention or congress and that Greek summer of our youth will warm our lives again for a few nights before the cooler days of middle age reclaim their own. I've had many men since our dig at Nauplion, but even when we are continents apart, Skip and I can never lose that part of ourselves we shared together and will share forever, that part the land taught us -- the real glory that was Greece.

POGEY BAIT

A lot of the grunts I run into think that just because I'm an admin office puke what jarheads call a pogue that I'm likely to be some simple shit-bag drone, processing paperwork and letting my proud Marine-built body sag soft. I suppose there are some pogues who don't keep themselves lean, hard-charging fighting machines, but most of us have too much time invested in pumping our bodies to tight, Corps-bred perfection to let them grow slack and nasty. Besides, we have to keep ourselves hard for our fellow Marines.

Most Marines deal only with men in their own units from fire teams up to the platoon level. I have to handle not only my own unit, but Marines company-wide, and often up throughout the battalion. Back in the rear, when Marines come to me with their bodies safely hidden away in thick cammies, I can generally tend to business without losing my bearing. When we're in the field and especially deployed underway on ships in the Gulf things aren't so easy.

Ships are hot and unpleasant so we're allowed to wear our "alternative tropical uniform": a T-shirt that clings to every tight, hard muscle a Marine has and UDTs khaki-colored swim trunks so short they're also called "Daisy Dukes." The things barely cover a man's butt and are always crushing a good pair of nuts as we sit down. Wearing underwear might help solve that problem, but if a man can't put up with having his balls crushed now and again for the sake of looking good, he's not Marine material to begin with.

When PFC Buckner came into Troop Admin yesterday, he was the perfect proof of how dick flashing in the field can distract a good Marine from doing his duty. He asked me to verify an allotment for his truck loan, but as I sat at the computer screen and he stood close beside me, his pay numbers were the last thing I wanted to crunch. I should explain that Buckner is a young dark green Marine what a civilian would call Black with a face like the boy next door and a body sweeter than living sin.

As he towered just inches from my tongue, the rippled muscles of his abs and lats seemed to writhe with elemental power beneath his thin tan T-shirt. His ass jutted out behind like some ancient monument to male perfection, and his dick was so long and thick that the head hung down below his shorts. Since there is a limit to how much a few inches of cotton can hold, Marines generally have their cranks or nuts hanging out of their UDTs part of the time, but there was nothing average about Buckner's bone. It was huge and uncut and trimmed with enough soft, purple, wrinkled skin to haunt a stoic's dreams.

I've always been a sucker for an ebony-and-ivory wrangle. The way hard white and black legs and dicks and fingers look as they prod in or around or through each other is just the maximum possible rush. After about ten minutes of fumbling around with my keyboard as my corporeal unit stood tall and taller in my lap, I realized PFC Buckner had been intentionally fucking with me.

His tits were towers of tan-clad flesh, and his best head was swelling so much even his floppy foreskin couldn't guarantee to keep his piss-slit under cover much longer. I accidentally brushed against his bone with my hand and was seriously tempted to gobble his grunt dick right there. I didn't want the LT coming in and getting jealous, though, so I asked Bucky when we could get together later so I could give him what he wanted. He flashed me a grin that tore into my guts like a fragmentation grenade and admitted he had the midwatch in Upper Vehicle Storage. Midnight to 0400 amidst the amtracks and trucks sounded like a good place to be. I told him I'd research the details on his allotment and bring him what he needed after midrats.

The ship echoed its emptiness as I slipped down into the humid welldeck about 0100. The air-conditioned spaces of the ship had been stifling for months, but with only exhaust fans to vent the heat into the Somali night, the welldeck had a temperature above 110ß and humidity serious enough to stun a piranha. I threaded my way through the vehicles to find Bucky leaning against the ass-end of a truck, naked but for his boots and socks, with streams of sweat rippling in rivulets down across his firm flesh as he pumped away on his huge, swollen shank. The faint red glow of the welldeck lights gleamed off his shiny black jarhead dick, but, as my lust-struck eyes adjusted to the darkness, I saw more than a glistening shadow. For a long, timeless moment, the silken slide of his purple cocksock up and over and around his pulsing knob entranced me like a sorcerer's curse. Bucky's swollen dickhead was the savory image of a huge, ripe plum, distended with pent-up juicy goodness ready to splash free and sweet. Somehow, though, the tender ripeness of that fruit managed to survive being gobbled again and again by the relentless ravenings of the serpent slashing up and around his shank.

I moved over to him and tossed my T-shirt and UDTs onto the deck beside his. My lizard was long since threatening to explode, but Bucky had so much firm muscle and hard meat I didn't know where to start. After a moment of awestruck indecision, my fingers took charge, slipping up across his flanks to ride a hot layer of jarhead sweat to his tits. Once they were on station anyway, I let those swollen purple tit-stalks feel the fierceness of my need. Buckner's thick dick slamming against my belly as he jacked away brought my knees crashing down against the unforgiving metal of the deck. I'd intended to do him hard and rough up his magnificent Marine ass and then leave him with my load buried deep to savor the memory, but the heat of his body, the wet feel of his sloppy shank against my belly, and the smells of blended mansweat and precum and crotch musk redefined my mission in one serious fucking way.

I slipped one hand around the broad base of his bone and used the other to cup his low-slung balls like the holy relics of Marine manhood they were. His hips shivered as my fuck-finger slipped past his nuts and up into his tight, sweat-slicked asscrack. While he humped my hand like a stray cur, I was kept plenty busy dealing with a faceful of dick. His `skin slipped back up and over his throbbing purple head until it was a perfect paragon of soft skin and chronically slurpy precum run acutely amok. Dick-honey gushed out of his shiny purple cum-slit and slathered its way over the fleshy thrum of his cocksock before drizzling down his dick in a slick, sweet symphony of Marine glory that made Guadalcanal and Iwo Jima look about as impressive as the dog's lunch.

When I slipped my tongue between the softest tissues of his tool and slurped up his dick lube, the clear, crystal threads that chased after my tongue became magical spun sugar. As fast as I slurped and sucked at his dick, his throbbing, twisting, ramming Marine trunk always managed to come up with more sap. My tongue tore deeper, prying his soft cocksock away from the hard, slick purple knob that lay beneath. Every flick of my bumpy tongue across the super-sensitive landscape of his lust brought new tremblers of pleasure reverberating up his rod until his whole body shivered in delight.

My lips locked tight around his soft cocksock and, as my tongue whirled about his head, his swollen knob was lured farther up into my mouth. I know you'll agree that nothing on earth tastes quite so fine as uncut dick. I took my time sucking up every atom of his essence: the perfect taste of mansweat aged deep inside a natural dick, the hint of musk, and the gloriously wicked taste of Marine man-sex unleashed at last.

Buckner's hands were all over my head, pulling my face farther up his crank even as he ground and wriggled against my body with his knees. My hands returned the compliment, sliding up along his oak-trunk thighs, polishing the huge, hard Marine bubble butt that boot camp had built him, and ultimately dipping my fingers down into the sweaty gorge that separated those two massive mounds of man-muscle. From early on, Bucky had been moaning and talking dirty, but the farther he fucked his way to my throat and the more my fingers felt up his tight ass, the louder the dumb grunt got. Before I'd even touched his asshole, he was making so much noise that even the whir of the ship's ventilators could no longer drown him out. His animal yelps and frenzied moans rumbled down across the welldeck until I was sure someone was bound to hear us rutting away like recruits in a shower. Buckner's dick tasted so good shoved down against my throat and his butt felt so fine wriggling in my hands, that just then I wouldn't have turned him loose for a Commandant's inspection.

Sweat splattered down onto me as his hips humped my face, driving his swollen knob hard against the back porch of my throat. A guy doesn't get to be a corporal in the United States Marine Corps without being a world-class cocksucker, but Buckner was worlds too big to ream his way as deep as he wanted to be. I let my wet lips and meat-beating tongue make it up to him while my fingers pried his gluteus to the maximus. Hard as his narrow hips were humping his dick through my face, when my fuckfingers found Bucky's tender butthole, his body went wild.

He screamed. He moaned. He slammed more inches of impossibly thick dick through my facehole. When I felt his balls clench up against my chin, though, I knew he was getting out of hand. I didn't mind choking down his hot, frothy load. In fact, the idea seriously appealed to me almost as much as taking everything he had up the ass. As my fingers pried his shithole wide, his lean belly tried to buck me senseless and I knew for sure that I needed that huge first-class private slammed up my tight ass more than I'd ever needed anything in my life.

I somehow managed to pry my face off Buckner's heaving bone and left him speechless in shock and loss and, perhaps, incipient outrage. I was off my knees and draped over the tailgate of the truck before he could begin to find voice. He had no trouble at all finding my hole to fuck, though or deciding what to do with it once he did.

I suppose that maybe some creature somewhere in our long evolutionary climb from the ooze may have felt the kind of pain Buckner's impossible bone bred in me as it slammed against and through and up my tender asshole. Maybe a saber-tooth's cruel claw flaying a field mouse could have caused such agony or the hot, sticky tar trapping an ancient brontosaurus as it trickled down into his lungs and seared his suffocating doom.

Nothing in our epoch, though, could have torn through animal flesh with the vicious frenzy of Buckner's ass-wrenching Marine weapon. Nothing could have reamed wide a shithole as quickly or surely as his lust-driven dick. If it had, the screams of agony would be reverberating still. Oddly enough, I didn't scream out in agony not at first. I couldn't scream or breathe or even think. Every particle of my body and scintilla of my soul were wrapped tight in a whirlwind of such horrible grandeur, that pain or thought or life were all distant irrelevancies to be considered another time.

When, finally, the grating of Bucky mammoth grunt cock up my shattered ass began to jolt and slam and crash its brutal way into focus, I was fucked far beyond simple torment. To keep even the most tenuous grip on sanity, my soul's slut-center converted every searing, nerve-shattering cataclysm into ecstasy even more profound. The harder that huge dark green dick broke wide my shithole or slammed off my prostate, the tighter my body convulsed around it, at once nursing my own doom and breeding bliss beyond mortal comprehension.

Bucky had been about ready to nut down my throat so he couldn't have fucked me up the ass for very long yet it felt at once an eterni-

Rick Jackson USM

ty and an instant. Before the end, I came back to myself enough to feel his huge hands locked hard onto my hips, holding me tight and help-less against the brutal hunger of his eager onslaught. I felt his sweat splash down onto my flesh and his breath snarl in my ear. The taste of the metal tailgate and the stench of mansex lurked just on the outskirts of awareness. Oddly enough, though, my ass was worlds above the fray, awash in an oblivion that was as absolute as it was unsuspected. No single sensation was strong enough to rip its way through the chaos that huge cock was causing deep within my shuddering guts. Instead, I knew only that my whole torso was consumed by a relentless inferno that spread ever wider with every rampaging crash of Bucky's body against mine.

My hands reached back to hang around Buckner's huge neck as he fucked me harder against the unforgiving metal of the truck with every brutal, bestial stroke. Then my fingers slid down low to claw at his butt, the fierce, relentless engine reaming my ass wide with an ecstasy bred deep in our warrior brotherhood. I heard, finally, my cries of animal ecstasy echoing off Buckner's rhythmic grunts of Marine sat-isfaction and the harsh clanging of the truck's tailgate as my body slammed helplessly into it.

I had no sooner struggled back to semi-awareness than Buckner's body exploded up into mine. I cannot truthfully say I felt the gush and spurt of his jism off my tortured guts as he blew the nut of his young life, but I did feel the cooling balm of his slick seed flowing in soothing layers between his grating grunt dick and the tormented tis-sues of my ass he had rubbed so raw. I had more certain signs that Bucky was nutting than a slight slaking of the fire up my ass, though.

His dick had been doing me deep all along, but now it change direction, slamming up and forward, arcing high inside my ass until my feet were lifted off the deckplates and I was temporarily riding impaled aloft on Bucky's spurting bone. His hands had left my hips and seemed everywhere at once, slamming my pecs and belly and shoulders down against the fiercesome good time he had humping.

He kept slamming away until his body had so flushed itself up into mine that he just had nothing else left to give me. Even then, his hips couldn't resist grinding against the shattered ruins of my ass as his lips tore at my neck and ear lobe and his hands used my tits for illicit R&R. When he eventually dropped my feet back to the deck and

– 134 –

popped his triumphant tool out of what was left of my ass, we both knew I'd been fucked.

He leaned against me, sweat pouring off his beautiful body as he gasped for air, but he obviously didn't suspect how good I was to go. I hadn't ridden as a bottom in ages; but now that I knew afresh how good being possessed, totally and absolutely by another human being could be, nothing could stop me from sharing my discovery with PFC Buckner.

Buckner sputtered something about how I was a "tight little pogue," but he didn't get very far. He may have been startled when I eased behind him and slammed my stiff nine inches of eager Marine up his ass. As his body crashed hard against the sweat- stained tailgate and I bent his chest down to elevate his tight hole, I heard him start to gurgle something else. He didn't have time for more than a start, though, before the first waves of outraged ecstasy burst up through his brain and launched him off into a world of his own, bred by Marine brotherhood and the adventure of the moment and rammed home by my stiff pogue dick.

By the time my nuts were empty and aching, Buckner wasn't good for much more fun that night. I pulled my dick out of his tight, spooge-soaked ass and wiped it across his butt. I was buttoning my UDTs before the glaze left his eyes and he remembered to ask about his allotment. I just reached low to give his perfect ass a proprietary pat and said I would have a fire watch tonight. He promised to be there to keep me company while I stood it, but something tells me that many come up, but his allotment isn't likely to be one of them.

SHIP MATES

Everybody in the Navy knows that divers are an odd bunch. Pilots are zany, marines are a hoot, and SEALs can be plain spooky but when it comes to unabashed, old-fashioned, off-the-wall rowdiness, nobody on the planet can outdo a navy diver. Most of the time, our reputation is deserved; we get away with outlandish crap because we can. With the possible exception of a marine infantry platoon, no unit going relies so much on support from the men in it than a dive det. Most of our dives are long, cold, dirty, mundane chores; but a thousand unpleasant faces of death lurk behind every coral head and screw shaft. Relying on a buddy every minute we're wet builds a bond that lasts even when we dry out.

The Cape Cod had been deployed for four months by the time we hit Hong Kong. Most of our det was ready to party and didn't give a shit how the sedate British would react to our cutting loose. Oddly enough, they fucking ate us up. By our second night in port, we'd more or less moved into a popular pub in Kowloon and turned it into our Animal House zoo away from home. We drew so many Brits in to scope out the crazy Yanks, the management not only delayed tossing our rowdy asses out into the gutter, they kept us awash in drinks to make sure the show kept going. That first night, I even had to turn down three very attractive British waitresses with the fiction I was married. The real story, of course, was that I had a meatier need: HMSN Rob Weston.

I'd craved Weston from the day he came aboard, but my initial hunger grew more ravenous as I saw his hard, lean body hanging out of his UDTs day after monkey-spanking day. He still had an eager, chicken-delight freshness despite the way the Nav had pumped up his body, every muscle bulging into the next until any normal man's teeth ached at the sight of it. His blue eyes and boyish shock of blond hair and goofy grin all kept my crank inflated.

In the shower and changing for dives, I couldn't help noticing a world more than his broad shoulders and narrow hips. His seven thick inches of circumcised meat may not have measured up to mine, but that pale marmoreal blue-veined shank always looked good to go. Besides, I was more interested in the classic Michelangelo-quality ass that guarded his tight fuckhole and gave me dreams night after lonely night. Our daily PT had molded those twin mounds of manly muscle into cantaloupe-sized spheres that whispered of savage pleasure and secretly begged me to pry them apart with my nine inches of thick diver man-hose.

Our second night at the pub turned out to be one of those rare times when men shed all pretense of civilization and do what they fuck they want. A pack of us had taken over a table and were making more noise than the Normandy invasion when Weston disappeared into the head. A few minutes later, I was in the process of having my Foster's refilled when the waitress looked over my shoulder and let slip a "Oh, my God!" as her chin dropped to her waist. I looked up and saw Weston and Davey Balboa strolling towards the door stark naked and with their clothes neatly folded under their arms. As he passed the table, Rob gave me a wide-eyed come-hither look and reached down to shake his shank at me. The navy probably has more gay corpsmen than any other rate, but I still wasn't sure of the signals. Whether he was really interested in being fucked hard up the ass or was just jerking my chain, though, you can bet your pension that by the time he reached the door, his awesome ass still grinding away like a sackful of cats on their way to the river, I was rising to meat the call.

Hong Kong isn't Thailand or Subic Bay. Well-built American men generally don't hang out on the street corner. I still don't know what happened to Balboa. He has always been a stolid, pussy-whipped drone so I suppose he found some dark corner to slither back into his clothes and rejoin the party inside. Rob didn't have the opportunity. I grabbed a fistful of firm dick and dragged it around into the alley behind the bar. We were shielded from view by an over-sized dumpster, but just then I'd have done him in the middle of Nathan Road.

By the time I flung Robby up against the wall, his unit was swollen to a new personal best and throbbing away in cadence with my racing heart. I reached down to grab a handful of his fuzzy, low-slung nuts and clenched up tight. His lips parted as though to beg for relief, but the glorious bastard had the sense to keep quiet. My free hand traced its way down from his strong neck, across his broad shoulders, and over the tattoo of a cat's paw-print centered over his left breast to find the stiffest tit a man could ever want to chew. I examined his strong, hairless pecs and was content just to run my hands across his naked body.

Much as I wanted to dig in, I knew I should make Weston take care of me first. After all, I outranked his ass. My fingers locked around his tender tit-stalks and pulled him down onto his knees to kneel naked at my crotch. My ball-hand locked behind his head and ground his goofy bootcamp face into my basket until his teeth pulled open my 501s. Just to show I could help a buddy out, I jerked my pants down to my knees and slammed his pretty face against my swollen nuts. His tongue fluttered out to flick around my hairy balls, slurping and slashing their way to contentment. Powerful hands tore at my ass, forcing my crotch even harder against his face as his tongue and lips ripped along my thighs and took turns busting my balls and licking my crotch clean of the man- musk bred of a very long and even more humid Hong Kong August afternoon. Every slash of his spaniel-like tongue past my `nads sent shivers shuddering up my spine to echo through the very bedrock of my being.

Robby's fingers, so practiced at medical examinations, pried my glutes wide, digging deep into the hot, sweaty crack of my ass. Then he prodded across the trip-wire that slammed me shut tight around his fingers. He felt so good tickling my fancy, I suddenly changed the battle plan. My dick would feel fine down his throat later. Just then, though, I needed to have his fine navy tongue tearing away at my shithole,

Rob was still busy eagerly chewing away on my nutsack so I had no trouble tipping him off-balance and tossing his naked ass onto the filthy pavement of the alley. By the time he'd opened his mouth to whine, his nose was buried deep up my sweaty buttcrack and I'd shoved my shithole halfway down his throat. I squatted low over his head, grinding my ass up and down across his eager mouth, playing bang-the-balls with his stubbled chin, and tweaking his tender, hairless tits until I was sure he was a good enough suck-ass to succeed in the United States Navy.

Young Rob didn't let me down. His wet lips locked around my puckered fuckhole so he could slurp and suck and tongue his way even farther up into my affections. Already slipping into a daze, I rocked slightly back and forth as his tongue darted up and out to conduct his most in-depth proctological examination ever. He hissed and smacked and sputtered like a snake with a stuttered lisp, but I was past noticing much of anything. Nothing shuts my brain down faster that the eager feel of a man's bumpy tongue up my butt; and Rob was sucking my ass fine enough to qualify for a Navy Achievement Medal.

Instinct convinced me to unhand his tits and slip forward onto my knees so I could inhale his dick while he gave me the rimming of my young life. Fortunately, for a born slut like me, blowing a buddy isn't something that requires a lot of conscious thought. I easily slurped my way across his throbbing head, siphoning up his sweet, gooey strands of crystal pre-cum as I went. I felt his unit throb and buck in response, but he kept his face held steady on station, buried tight up my ass, and that was all that counted.

Although the hypnotic flicks of his tongue prodding deeper and faster into my butt and the sloppy slurps of his lips tight around my tender hole quickly lulled me into semi-consciousness, some remote corner of my brain never completely shut down. At the time, I was aware only of the hard strength of his dick throbbing away down my throat and the velvet torment of his anal abuse, but some flickers of memory sparkle through in exquisite ecstasy to give me a sense of what went on as we rocked back and forth together in the alley and time between us slid slowly to a stop.

I remember the taste of his sweet pre-cum coasting down out of my throat and across my tongue as his joint jolted deeper down my gullet with every upward thrust of his hips. I remember the savory scent of man-musk and sweat rubbing against my nose from his balls and crotch as we bounced together. The constant slurp of his spit-slicked lips at my ass and my grunts of dick-fed satisfaction echoed across the darkened alley as though in counterpoint to the animal noises drifting back from the bar. Robby's hands drifting up under my T-shirt and across the hard, furry country of my belly and chest seemed the perfect compliment to the slick, sweaty feel of his hard, naked body trapped below me. Most of all, though, I remember the feeling of absolute contentment as though I could have coasted forever back and forth in perpetual motion, impaling myself onto his thick, throbbing dick on the down-stroke and onto his twisting tongue on the rebound. Somehow, even sprawled across that filthy alley in exotic Hong Kong, I had never felt so perfectly at home before. In the sterile, bureaucratic naval world, Robby and I were a perfect match. We had the same needs and yearnings and fears for the future. Was I in fucking love?

I snapped back to consciousness to find Robby's hands clawing at my thighs as he struggled to keep his face up my ass while his hips slammed dick down my throat in a rhythm so syncopated only a drunken three-legged goat tap dancing down an escalator could begin to mimic it. Instead of his velvet tongue and eager lips around my asshole, I felt his teeth latched hard onto my right glutes like some lovestruck, if incredibly inept, tomcat. His slurps had changed to butt-muffled grunts of "Oh, FUCK!" and "JESUSSSSSS, SSHHHITTT!" Robby's tasty dick had swollen big enough to stick in my craw, and his balls were clenched tight, hard under my nose. A guy didn't have to be Ben Casey to figure out that I was about to get a hot seaman injection.

Ever the caring lover, I grabbed Robby's nutsack with one hand and shoved my other up his ass-crack. My fuckfinger had no sooner prodded against his shithole, that Robby's dick exploded in a barrage of bone-blasting jism that should have registered on the Stanford seismograph. I pulled his ass upwards off the pavement and slammed my own down harder onto Weston's face because the fucking slut was howling like a bull becoming a steer. Besides, as he gasped for air and tried to make noise, his face felt really fine against my flaring asshole. By the time Robby's crank had started to run dry, I had his ass nearly three feet off the ground and was eager to taste some of the cream he'd been force-feeding me. The last few wads of his load bounced off the back of my mouth and drizzled down across my tongue like a dream come true. I slipped my suction into overdrive and prodded a last spermy thread or two out of his cum-slit, but Rob's rod finally just shut down and was of no further immediate use to anybody.

Since I already had his ass off the pavement, though, I was able to think of one more way the gorgeous horndog could be of service. I eased my ass off his face and twisted around between his legs. My T-shirt was already gone somehow, so I just had to kick off my jeans to give me enough room to work. Looking down at Robby's panting, bewildered face, I knew for sure I must be in love.

I lifted his ankles towards the stars and gave my tongue a final wash of his tasty wad before I drooled it out to drip down his ass-crack.

My thick nine inches of naval lust jimmied Robby's firm, pale buttocks wide and smeared his jism all along the bottom of his ass-crack. I looked down into his big blue eyes and knew I had to hold him in my arms while I did him hard up the ass. He'd already locked his heels on station at my butt, so I had no trouble lifting him into my arms. The taste of my own ass on his lips was a major rush, but nothing like the crinkled look of terror in his eyes as I dropped his torso down onto my shank. His bootcamp ass was too tight the first time around, but when I fucked his back up against the wall and slashed my hips forward with the speed of a man in charge, his sea-pussy popped open and swallowed everything I had.

My eyes were on his as they slammed shut with the first waves of pain. Every muscle of his body seemed to knot tight at once and then hang suspended in time as my thick dickhead slipped up through his guts with no lube other than his own sweet spunk. If his shithole wasn't virgin-tight, it was the next best thing. Every inch of his slick guts rippled along my rampaging rod like a homecoming parade, yet his sphincters just couldn't get a grip on reality. By the time his shithole was impaled on the thick base of my bone and his nuts were piled onto my pubes, I knew neither of us had ever had it so good. I just stood with my buddy's body in my arms, my dick up his ass, and my lips on his neck until he finally started to breathe again.

Rob's eyes opened with in a mixture of terror and regret terror that I'd pull my knob out of his ass and regret that he'd taken so long to get it shoved up there in the first place. When I felt the ruins of his fuck-hole flutter to life, I slipped about six inches back from him and took that much of my meat with me. Then I rolled my hips forward again, crashing back up through his guts, ricocheting off his prostate, and slamming the swollen shank of the evening into the secret depths of his being.

This time around, his eyes stayed open, and he gasped for air to handle the terrible pleasure I was fucking up his ass. My lips and tongue found his and ground out yet another good time. I had my hands full of his ass, but his fingers fluttered about my body like a glutton locked in the chow hall. He twisted my tits and the thick red fur that grows across my chest and belly. His hands careened along my flanks and joined his heels prodding and prying at my ass. I was soon shafting my way faster and deeper with every rampaging inch. His moans on the out-stroke and grunts when I slammed home grew louder and more desperate with every gut-reaming fuck-thrust.

His jism had long since rubbed off my rod so every jolt of my joint up his ass sent the temperature up another few degrees. My twirling log felt as though it had a boy scout on one end and a campfire on the other so I knew damned well young Robby was feeling the heat. Somehow though, what with the taste of my ass on his lips and the scent of his sweat mixing with mine as out bodies heaved together through the night, with the fire up his ass and the feel of his balls as our bellies slammed together, with his moans and grunts and the way his hands were clawing at my body somehow with all that going on, I didn't much give a shit whether we both went up in fucking flames or not.

My mistake was pulling my mouth away from the ear I was tongue-fucking and looking into those wide baby blues to watch him enjoy me doing him hard up the ass. His eyes met mine and our souls clicked together in an instant of understanding. I felt as though I knew every thought and fear and hope and dream he had. As our spirits merged together, I felt wave upon wave of desire and admiration and love.

Without warning, my guts flared white-hot and exploded up through my heaving dick to jet into Robby's tight navy ass. My body slipped from spasm to spasm as I pounded my gusher so far up my buddy's ass he should have had a nosebleed. His shoulders and head slammed against the stone wall behind the bar, but I was as helpless as he was. Somehow the only thing that mattered just then was to breed his corpsman asshole so full of my jism that he'd always carry part of me with him. I heard a savage voice growling from afar and discovered only as I flailed to a finish that it was my own.

Pulling my joint out of Robby's ass was the single hardest thing I'd ever done and I don't mean just because we were both cramped up. The hour we spent in that filthy alley in Kowloon moved us from gut-wrenching lust to a love I've never believed possible. We wiped ourselves off and pulled on our clothes, but just to walk the few blocks to the park. The night was so hot and humid, we knew we could lie together, naked and alone in the heart of that great city, until the Star Ferry began again at dawn. Dawn came years too soon, but we knew there would be other nights together long, slow, easy nights hidden away in secret spaces aboard. After all, the navy doesn't call us shipmates for nothing.

SQUID PRO QUO

I noticed his hard, bare belly first and then his hair, but when I spotted his cute little sailor butt, I knew I was in love. I'd only been aboard about two weeks before we pulled into Fujairah and had our ship's party, so I had never seen QMSN Scott Forsee in mufti before. The few times I'd seen Foreskin around the ship, he'd impressed me as a chicken farmboy type that I might like to do sometime if the opportunity came up. Since I didn't sleep in his berthing back then, all I could do was wonder about his nickname: Did he or didn't he? After I saw him at the ship's party, I stopped worrying about whether or not he was trimmed meat. I had something more solid on my mind. My passing thought of doing him hard up the butt ripened into the goal of my young life.

He was on the Tropicana's dance floor, shaking his butt to the tunes of a Filipino group mislabeled "Hot Duo." They weren't, but that ass was. That night, though, the belly struck me first because he'd cut his t-shirt off just below his tits. As he bounced around, that flat, tanned belly of his flashed at the room like a searchlight in the desert twilight. His tits were pointed, dime-sized numbers that made my teeth ache. My eyes followed his rippling muscles down into his cotton shorts and my mouth started to water.

way his hair was cut pumped my `nads next. His sides and back were cut marine-short, but his shock of blond hair was almost as long as my dick. Later I learned he was able to keep his hair long by always wearing his ship's ballcap aboard, but that night I was amazed anyone who looked as fresh as Foreskin could sleep in a berthing compartment full of squids without having his furrow plowed and seeded every night. Later on, when I came to know him more intimately, I learned the truth about what went on in berthing, too.

That first delicious night, though, my nasty little mind kept coming back to his choice butt. Forsee is only about 5'7", but every inch is prime stuff. His hairless chest and belly rippled with muscle, green eyes flashed sex with every lewd, sailor glance, even his pug nose and firm jaw etched out the glory of young manhood and made my dick twitch like a carillon's clappers at noon. I couldn't take my eyes off the way he slunk around the room, alternating flashes of tanned navel appeal and butt-clenched grinding fuckthrusts wasted on the air. The few women in the room noticed Scotty plenty, but he seemed more interested in enjoying his little leprechaun dance than in putting the moves on babes.

Over the next hour, I kept my eye on his hard, gyrating young butt the way a glutton watches a desert cart. As soon as I got the chance, I bought him a drink -- and then another. I was charming, he was thirsty, and before my cash ran out we were fast friends. The little bastard didn't get drunk as he tossed back drink after drink, he just got cuter and more lovable. His smile widened between a classic set of dimples and, when most men would be sprawled unconscious in a corner, Foreskin lit a tomcat twinkle in his eyes and asked me when I'd last gotten any. We shouted our exchange of sailor confidences as carefully as we could over the racket Hot Duo were making -- and moved from talk of unsatisfactory hand jobs to how hungry we both were for a good solid fuck. When Forsee said he'd give anything for just a blow job just then, I told him what he was full of. He might give ten or fifty or a even hundred bucks, but he wouldn't give anything. He wouldn't give some babe a year's pay, for example. He wouldn't re-up in the Navy just to get sucked off. For a moment, his smile faded and the hungry twinkle in his eye was replaced by a far-off gaze of almost etherial longing. He shook his head as though to clear it and said again with the desperation I knew so well, "No, right now, tonight, I'd give anything to blow my load into somebody's face."

We sat silent for several minutes as the world partied about us while I tried to decide whether I needed his ass enough to risk my naval career. I knew there was no question and finally broke the silence: "If you're serious, I think I know someone who can help. Follow me."I headed out onto the bar's patio and up across to the caban*p 8*~a on the Gulf beach behind the hotel. The November breeze was almost chilly as it whipped whitecaps against the sand. I led Foreskin down the sand until the laughter from the bar began to blend with the night. Except for the occasional Pakistani groundsman skulking about the bushes, we were alone. I sat down on a retaining wall and pulled

Scotty against my face. The soft cotton of his shorts didn't hide his need. I sensed his surprise, but however fresh Scotty looked, he was no blate and blushing bootcamp. His hard dick had forced itself belly-up; the top several inches against his hard belly. That hard meat ground its soft underside against my mouth while my hands clamped tight onto his firm butt. His slim hips started rocking desperately forward, fucking my nose with his fine young meat.

Now that I had him alone, I intended to take my time. My lips jacked up the underside of his stalk and found a bonus at the top. The squids in berthing had known their stuff when they starting calling him Foreskin. You don't see many `skins in the Navy, but his was big and floppy and, even hard and throbbing as he was, crowned his cock like an Easter Island topknot. My lips sucked his `skin up like saucy pasta al dente and set about stripping it clean. I moved one hand around to jack loose skin up his joint and, before I had really gotten going, my mouth was filled with the tender tip of his tool. Like any born cock-sucker's, my mouth waters at the first whiff of manhood; now it was gushing torrents. As my tongue tip muscled deep between the soft layers of his cocksock, feeling blindly for the savory man-meat I knew lay below, my spit drained deep to carry away his sauce. As I burrowed deeper, his manmusk filled my mouth with the best philter made: aged manmusk cooked with a hard day's sweat. Foreskin's body was grinding away like a Tijuana whore on a pay-day weekend, and he was starting to make pretty much the same racket. His hands locked around my ears and forced my face down over his dick -- just where I wanted to be.

By the time I'd cleaned his cock, that soft, tender `skin lay folded back along his pulsing crankshaft and his swollen dickhead filled my mouth with meat that throbbed its craving for a good basting. I kept giving his pecker the spit- polish of a lifetime, tearing my bumpy tastebuds across the tender flesh as Scotty's slutty hands clutched at my hair. When my lips locked hard around the back of his trigger- ridge so my tongue could really lash his lizard, Foreskin used language I wouldn't let my own mother hear -- just before he rammed his dick all the way down my throat. I felt my eyes bug out and considered gagging, but his thick dick down my gullet didn't leave me enough room. Instead, I slipped his shorts all the way off his ass and started prying it apart. For the next several minutes, I was one busy cocksucker. I managed to latch the tight, tender tissues of my throat around his ramrod and switch my suction into overdrive. The feel of my nose slamming into his soft, blond pubes as he used my face, the scent of his full, sweaty balls banging hard into my chin, and the animal noises tearing out of his throat were all enough to give me one very good time. They didn't stop me from letting my fingers walk down butt alley, though. His cleft was as hairless as his chest -- and felt even better. Every thrust of his dick down my throat began with an instinctive clench of his ass that drove my fingers down deeper towards his manhole.

Just about the time I was sure I was going to smurf, I heard his breath turn to a growl and felt his cadence go straight to shit. The way he jerked and twisted and torqued that thick dick of his into my face guaranteed I was about to get a hot seaman injection. His hands trapped my head where it belonged, but I knew what I had to do. The second his cum- tube started pulsing, I slid my fuckfingers through his twitching little pucker and twisted like a taffy-puller at the state fair. He was too far down my throat for me to taste dick, but his lupine howls at the moon told the world he wasn't bored. I let him spurt while I con- centrated equally hard on sucking up his load and opening his ass for my squid pro quo. I made sure he got his and enjoyed it, but, as soon as he ran dry, I was going to break his hot stallion ass to the saddle and ride him to a fucking lather.

I kept sucking and twisting my throat along his crank until his fin- gers unclenched my hair and I knew the pump had almost run dry. The craving for air and the longing to taste his seaman semen grew until I was able to unscrew my face up his driver. The instant his jism-jet jolt- ed free of my gullet and I felt his thick cream splash against the back of my mouth, I knew I'd be back for more of his cream cocktail before the deployment -- or the night -- was over. His hips tried to pull his super- tender tonsil-tickler away from my tongue, but I held onto his lizard like a leech. Until the last sweet drop of sailor spooge had worked its way across my tongue and down to join the rest of his load, my lips were sealed -- and the fingers up his ass kept digging new sensations out of his rapidly stretching fuckhole.

When his dick finally wasn't any more good to me, I let him pull it out, but I kept my fingers up his butt. As I looked up to see his goofy grin sparkle moonlight, I told him I was ready for him to do anything for his blow-job. He clenched his asshole around my fingers to show he understood and admitted a first-class cocksucker like me deserved anything he wanted. I unhanded his ass and stood beside him in the moonlight. I'd long since unbuttoned my trou to give my lizard some air, but now I slipped them off and threw them to the sand. My hands turned him around and bent him over to rest his hands against the retaining wall that partly hid us from the blind eyes of the hotel. His naked butt looked even better than it felt -- smooth and perfect and soft on the outside, coiled bands of carbon steel on the inside. I dumped some beer across my thick eight inches to suds my way into his affection, but we both knew I'd be hard to take. I kicked his ankles apart, grabbed his shoulders, told him to hang on, and slammed my swollen butt-cleaver hard into his twitching butt pucker. I saw his body surge forward, but had to pull his ass back. The shithole was shy. I thought about loosening his ass up, but I was past foreplay. Instead, I checked the angle to make sure I wouldn't break my bone and then pulled his ass back onto my joint until the tight-assed bastard started to slide down my dork. The solid ring of man-muscle just inside his shithole stretched wide enough for me to get my snout in the door. After that it was all over; I pried and stretched and shoved my way home where I belonged.

It wasn't easy going; I could feel the muscles of his back knot up solid as I slid my thick dick up shaft alley. His slick silken guts gripped at my pole, rippling along my joint, almost teasing me to drill deeper. But I didn't need any coaxing. His teeth were clenched and he was panting like a woman in labor, but as I screwed his torso up my dick, there wasn't the slightest doubt he needed to be there. I reached down with first one hand and then the other to grab his bare thighs and pull him the rest of the way up my rod. By the time my stiff red pubes were grinding into the ruins of his asshole, Foreskin was JESUSing and SHITting into the night, but his tight ass was wrapped around my dick as solid as a post in concrete.

I gave him a few minutes to accept the inevitable while I played with him like the little fucktoy he was. The back of my nails slipped up his spine until gooseflesh swept across his flesh. My butt-stained hands slid up his flanks to molest the iron-hard tits I'd seen on the dance floor peeking out from under his t-shirt. My tongue slipped up his neck and found an ear lobe. As soon as my tongue slid into his ear, I felt his body quake and finally knew for sure that I had a live one. He let me have my way for a minute or three, but when he couldn't take any more aural sex, I heard a soft, earnest whisper bubble from his very depths: "Do me."

He didn't need to ask twice. I was a young sailor on liberty and in the mood for love. My hands slid back to his shoulders and, once he was anchored tight, I jerked my joint nearly out of his ass. This guts were packed so solid around me, they started to come, too. As my trigger-ridge scrapped backwards along his shitchute, I felt his slick innards trail across my dickhead and fold vacuum tight as soon as I was gone. Once I had snagged my pride on his sphincter, my hips flew hard ahead and fucked his butt solid enough for the ages. I only half heard his scream as I tore back into his hole; I was already on my way up again before it registered. Almost before I recognized the signs, I had slipped into the instinctive fuck-frenzy that comes to young men once or twice in their prime. My heart was pounding; my mouth was dry. I couldn't breathe. My whole world was wrapped up in my dick, tearing along the inside of my shipmate's shit-chute. The distant music, the nearby ripple of the ocean or night screams of my mate sounded distant as the next galaxy. All I knew was the hard feel of my hands on his shoulders and the soft, tight, incredibly perfect feel of his body around my crank. My hips took control of my destiny, fucking harder and deeper with every stroke. I felt them ram into the hard mounds of man-muscle I'd admired so much. Now I was using them for my pleasure as though I were a cur dog and he were my mongrel bitch. What had felt tight began to flame as my fuck-friction fed the fire in our loins. Some distant corner of my soul must have registered Foreskin's grunts and moans and prayers of gratitude, but I only knew about the way my firestick was flaming his tail. My butt clenched tighter with every brutal stroke until even before I felt my balls cinch up, my guts exploded white-hot squid-juice up through my butt buster and out into Scotty's ass. The first few blasts of foam greased the skids of love and set my piston plunging harder than ever.

I came fully back to consciousness, I found my teeth gripping Foreskin's neck like a tomcat in love -- and my butt was drilling dick deep down Scotty's spooge-soaked shithole. I hadn't had any in weeks, though, and wasn't about to stop with one load. I eased up for a moment to catch my breath and concentrated on stirring my little honey pot. I pulled Scott back against my body and lifted him slightly with my dick, seating the base of my bone tight in his butt. I sat down onto the retaining wall and twisted my little buddy around like a top on a spindle until he was facing me, his feet by my hips and my tongue down his throat. For a few minutes, I was content to hold him in my arms and explore his flesh with my hands while I whipped my cream up his ass. Tight as he was, I started to feel my load leak out of his ass and drain down onto my balls. Even as I cuddled his butt in my lap, we'd been rocking back and forth like lamas in a trance. Now, I knew it was time to show him what a buttfuck could feel like when administered by a real dick.

I started by arching my ass upward, driving my dick back its full eight inches up his butt. Almost at once, though, I reached down to grab his ass from below and lifted us both into the air. I fucked my way across the beach, driving his body backwards before me, until we reached the near wall of the caban*p 8*~a. My arms circled under Foreskin's knees to force his hole even tighter against my dork while I used the wall as a backstop, slamming his back off the wall with every stroke. Bouncing between my crotch and the unyielding cement behind, Scotty's hard young body felt the full fury of my need as I used him harder and faster than I had from behind. Now I was in less of a hurry for my nut; I took my time watching his face twist in delicious agony as I used his ass for my pleasure. I savored the way he clenched his eyes tight whenever my spooge-slicked sex pole scraped across his prostate. His hands around my neck made me feel almost as good as his ass around my joint -- almost. As my dick dug deep, I sucked at his pouty lower lip and licked the sweat from his neck. Scotty pulled me even closer and hung onto me almost as much for his salvation as for his satisfaction. My first load had lubed his butt enough for a lifetime so this trip there wasn't any road burn, but only the feel of a well-greased fuck machine purring away through the night. Even machines have their limits, though.

The sight of his cute, virile bootcamp body in my arms, the sound of his grunts as I did him hard, the feel of his back bouncing off the wall and sliding down my slick dick, the smell of his sweat filling my face as my meat filled his guts -- these and dozens more sensations conspired to lure me away from the individual particulars of our love. Once more, the thrill of the rut took control and I became a mindless jungle savage again, fucking what was mine by right of conquest, taking what I wanted and leaving my seed behind. I felt my arms cinch tight around his flanks and shoulders. His heels were wrapped hard around my waist, but they couldn't hold my hips still. As I held his body tight against the hard cement, my hips tore upward, stabbing hard bone up his hole, twisting it tight, and pulling out to tear north again. For a moment, I seemed to be looking down on us from a distance to see my ass hammering Scotty's body against the wall like a steam engine run amok. His head was twisting this way and that as he mouthed soundless, gaping oaths of submission and sublime satisfaction. Once more my teeth clamped onto his neck, this time where it met the shoulder, digging in to hold back the inevitable. This time around, though, I felt my balls rise. I felt my body clench tight to squeeze my sailor spooge up through my dick like nitroglycerin through a toothpaste tube. When the first load was primed and ready, my dick exploded up his butt, slamming him hard enough against the wall to knock him breathless. Every gusher of sailor spunk jolted upward with more fury than the one before until I was jackhammering jism up his spooge-packed sea-pussy. When his guts ran out of room, my second load started backflushing onto my belly and balls, but I was too far gone to notice.

Sometime later I found myself dry-humping his hole. I'd long since tapped out, but his slick shithole felt so good I just couldn't bring myself to stop. Foreskin's chin was resting on my shoulder as mine was upon his while we heaved together through the night. Fine as his butt was, my arms were tired of holding his ass up so I slowed to a grind, gave him a last buttful to remember me by, and lifted him off my dick. His legs hit the deck but didn't hold him up; he was too wobbly to stand so I held him tight in my arms until he got his breath and feeling flowed back into his legs. I spent those moments basking in the warmth of his body, savoring his smell and the texture of his skin, and memorizing every muscular curve. When he was able to stand on his own, I suddenly felt silly standing there in my t- shirt and Top-Siders but I wasn't about to let him go. I pulled his dick down the beach where we lost what clothes we had left and took a long playful swim in the Gulf. Quite soon we were grab-assing naked in the surf and splashing each other with salty globules of glimmering moonlight. I had a hammerlock on my little fuckbuddy when he let loose the world's biggest, sloppiest underwater fuckfart and gave billions of my whip-tailed semen recruits their freedom. I pushed his careless ass backwards into the cloud and told him we'd just have to start over again.

We did, too. I could tell you about savory salty dick is or about what the foxy Pakistani gardener found us doing later that night -- or about what the three of us did back in his shack -- but I wouldn't want you to think I couldn't keep a military secret. Let's just say that Foreskin and I started out to have a good time and have been swapping one up on another ever since. I don't know which turns me on more, the cute little farmboy face I see as I do him hard up the butt; that soft, savory `skin with its primitive taste of man; or his tight, jism-hungry sailor butt. I'm going to keep working on him until I find out, though -- no matter how long it takes.

TEAMWORK

I couldn't take my eyes off his ass. You don't serve in the Corps for five years without seeing asses of all shapes and sizes and colors. I'd never paid them much notice before, but Dave's ass was keeping me awake.

As I lay watching him sleep, the moonlight shimmered off his tanned body and the pale butt that seemed its masculine center. The girl's arm was draped across the back of his head so, for me, his hard, grunt body began at his massive shoulders and the back that grew down from them like the sheer face of an unconquerable alp, left stark and raw by the snow-colored sheet along the crest of his side. With the easy rise and fall of his breath, muscle folded and rippled upon muscle down across that monumental back until they narrowed at hips as tight as a parson's pocket. Then his butt exploded out in twin mounds of marmoreal muscle that slowly flexed open and shut as he breathed in dreams. One nut, peaking out from under a bent leg, hinted at what other wonders must lay hidden from sight.

His butt was the main thing preying on my mind, but I'd spent plenty of time watching him work, too. We'd found the whores in a Patong bar and brought them back to our hotel room to do. What's the point of being a young marine on liberty in Thailand if you don't get shit-faced and laid? Until that night, I thought fucking whores was what young marines did. They were OK, but Jesus Dave's butt was fine. Even as I was humping away, my eyes kept straying across to Dave's bed, watching the way he slammed his dick home and twisted his firm little fanny in the air. The way that ass clenched as he ground his marine meat home got me harder than I'd ever been in my life. By the time we'd collapsed for a nap, Dave had tossed two full rubbers onto the deck beside the bed. I'd done three and was nowhere near satis-faction.

That ass was the biggest turn on I'd ever seen until I looked down at those rubbers by his bed: sloppy twisted plastic bags overflowing with my best buddy's thick creamy cum. Was I turning queer? I'd never shared a fuck-room with a guy before, but the process opened up a whole universe of feelings and questions. The thought of that dick buried deep in snatch, shooting off one studly blast after another, got me hard all over again. I was about to reach for another rubber when I felt the bed shake and my employee head for the john.

As I heard the shower start up and knew I had some free time, I remembered a fuckflick we'd seen in berthing just days before. The plot centered on what two overgrown cowpokes did in a hay loft to the village schoolmarm. Suddenly I knew what had to be done. I slammed my babe's pillow against Dave's ass to wake him up and demand he lend me his bitch.

Dave's a PFC; I'm his corporal. He didn't even hesitate, but that didn't mean I'd take advantage. As soon as the whore was bobbing up and down, working my newest load up into rubber number four, I took care of my marine. He was leaning on one arm and watching with a worshipful grin on his face. All I had to say was, "OK, Marine. Front and center. It's Cowpoke's Delight time," and he was between my legs in search of a hole to plug.

I wasn't sure what he'd do, but when I felt his dick slide up inside the snatch with mine, I nearly came   Only my super semper-fi dedication and the sublime tightness of that grunt-packed pussy kept me from it. Well, OK, maybe a general case of whiskey dick and the month's worth of jism I'd already blasted loose didn't hurt. Dave had lubed his log like a wildcatter with a fresh gusher so our rubbers didn't drag against each other. Instead, as we bobbed our bitch up and down on our bones, we raced for the finish. We had too much dick for the hole so both our swollen heads couldn't fit all the way in at once; the second man up had to settle for a snug shaft press. I felt his balls slam against mine and the torturous tenderness of our dick's undersides grating, one raw marine dick meating its match. If the tight heat of that slick, gushing hole and grinding motion of my buddy's bone along my underside weren't enough to pleasure a grunt good, the goofy look on Dave's face would have melted any DI's heart.

His mouth gaped open in almost sublime ecstasy, gibbering clever things like "Oh, SHIT" again and again and again like some mystic marine mantra. As I looked into his wide, brown, boy-next-door eyes, I wondered if I could ever feel as close to another human being. I slipped my hands up to grasp Dave's powerful flanks, pressing my palms around to fill them with his iron-tipped tits, grinding them down as fiercely as our dicks were grinding along each other up inside that tight rental twat. His eyes locked on mine, wanting direction or reassurance or congratulation. I just shoved in more dick, harder and faster with every frenzied upward thrust of my hips. Each stroke was more frenetic than the last, climbing towards a peak that remained forever hidden in the clouds of our young lust.

I slipped my hands into the small of his back and jerked my torso upwards, rubbing my tits against my buddy's hands as I licked at his strong, broad marine shoulder. With Dave in my bed, the whore had become irrelevant except as a safety valve to keep contained the true feelings I was afraid to face.

My buddy's angle of entry put him at a disadvantage. His legs must have cramped up big time, for he pulled his bitch backwards onto his suddenly supine form and left me to roll forward atop them. Now I had more room to work, my nuts couldn't help splashing out. If anything, our new position was even more of a rush. My ass could roll up to gather speed and then slam my dick deep down along his sloppy shank. We were both having fun now, grinding our dicks together when we met deep down. I kept my face above Dave's, looking down at the open young face of my powerful PFC. I had never really seen them up close and personal at that point, but I could tell his privates were first class. Now that I had room to maneuver, I slid along his shaft like a snake with a warm branch, using XY lube to help teach the lad a lesson above love.

I wasn't sure how experienced young Dave was, but he definitely needed help like with where to put his hands. He wanted to be cool, but was awkward as hog at a horse race. First he slipped his hands around my neck to pull me down against them. That seemed to spook him, so he dropped me for a moment. Then he crossed our sexual Rubicon.

His hands found my ass, cupping and stretching it wide as he pulled me tighter against the two of them. Those strong government-owned hands on my up- tight marine ass were so illicit, so unexpected, and so fucking fine that they felt more like high-voltage cables. Their every touch sent shockwaves rippling through my being and confused the shit out of me. His legs were spread wide as he tried arching upwards into our mutual passion pit. Some distant corner of my brain realized the sound of the shower had been replaced by festive splashing in the bathtub, but the last thing our game needed just then was another player. Keeping track of the rules and players was hard enough as it was. We were all making enough noise to stampede trees, but Thai hotels are fortunately known for their discretion so I made the most of my opportunity to learn about life.

I heard myself grunt with every slam of my bone and flesh. Dave's voice rang out like the baritone barks of a beached seal. Flat on his back, he'd stopped his SHITs and was yelping like the horndog he was. Every downward thrust of my hips grated my dick along Dave's, splashed deep into our mutual fuckhole and dug out enough satisfaction for a marine battalion. Somehow our rhythm had changed, too. We weren't slamming deep at the same time, but taking turns in her depths, bouncing her up and down like a deranged tandem yo-yo. The more I tried to file away what was going on for retelling later, the more I was distracted by Dave's hands on my ass.

They grew bolder and more knowing with every shared thrust of our marine units. His fingers soon weren't happy with pulling my ass down; they had to pry my cheeks apart and work their way into my crack. I shifted this way and that, rolled forward and down, but try as little as I might I couldn't escape his grasp. Was he just trying to hold on or was I imagining a hidden agenda? Was the kid playing with my ass? God knows his fascinated me. I was still driven by the strange sexual power of his body but driven where? What exactly did I want to do? I wasn't hung up on priggish dogma or social dictates. I just didn't know myself what I wanted. I wanted his strong arms to hold me tight and let me rip my lips along his. I wanted to lose myself in his brown eyes and feel his scent in my soul and suck his tits until he cried for me to stop and begged me not to. I wanted to fuck him deep and hard until we came together and his body was mine forever.

When I felt his fingers at my asshole, I knew I had to do something. Given our gymnastic gyrations, the goofy grunt was obviously straining to reach my ass. I humped on, waiting for a clue and reading only excitement in his eyes. If he needed more, if I was going to help us both out, I'd have to hurry. Drained whiskey dick or not, I was only mortal. Even a marine can only fuck so long before his dick goes off. The time had come for me to be a leader.

I slipped out and away, both from the whore and from the hands that begged me to give more. Dave's hands moved down to mangle my asshole. He didn't have much time to get fancy before I'd changed rubbers and was lubed slicker than a defense contractor at audit time. I'd heard what guys did in prison and the Navy. I knew what I wanted. I lifted Dave's legs and took it.

Once Dave's ass was up in position, the girl managed to finally get a clue and ambled into the crapper to let us have some real military service. I was amazed how right using his tight jarhead ass felt. Easing my dick into his ass- crack as I held his ankles wide was so obviously the thing to do that it was second nature from the start. Dave's butt clenched around my shaft, holding it tight and guiding it towards his hole. For a moment, I pounded his perineum, but his hips leapt upwards, driving his shithole around my swollen shank. His lurch petered out before I got my hole in one, but I followed him down, pronging him insensible with every brutal thrust.

His body seized up tight, locking his hot ass muscles around my joint while jerking away in a paradoxical paroxysm bred of pure boyish reflex. He'd asked for what I had, but he'd gotten more than even he could handle without flinching. Once I was buried hilt-deep up his ass, he took my nine thick inches like the game little trooper he was. I kept his legs spread wide and worked wonders. Dave's cute face was a chronicle of every cock-thrust up his tight marine ass as I bred him to the bone.

He squirmed in tight, noisy pleasure on the end of my joint, jolting my motion forward, echoing my fuck-thrusts into his own dick's movement hard up against his own belly. I felt his ass milk my bone, fiercely clutching my cock as I tried to pull up and away. Every down-stroke brought my crankshaft a tighter cylinder with compression exploding up into Dave's guts like the very spark of Doom. His hands reached up to claw at my neck and shoulders, forcing my upper torso down hard towards him while leaving my hips free to drive home every inch of pleasure we could stand. Fortunately, marines are trained to withstand a lot.

My pace picked up speed as my cock found its ancient cadence. The faster and harder and deeper I slammed my non-com cock up my buddy's butt, the more he bellowed and squirmed and tried to hold the fuck on as I bucked and pounded and buried my bone home. Amidst the moans and grunts, consciousness fogged and I lost track of the details of that bareback ride. At one point I had hold of his ears and was pulling his head up towards me, smearing his face into mine because those ears were the only thing I could reach. I also remember latching onto his hard tits and the selfish dog-face moving his fingers to tweak my nipples. I think it was the feel of this stiff titillation and the slick, sweat-soaked pecs below them even more than the open eagerness of his All-American face that sent me over the edge and flushed my white-hot liquid guts up into his tight, jism-hungry.ass.

I snapped back to awareness to find myself bent double, my hands wrapped under Dave's shoulders, my dog tags flopping in his face, and my balls ready to file a complaint with Amnesty International. Dave was in pretty poor shape, too. He'd long since lost his rubber and had splattered a massive blast of balljuice up across his hard grunt belly, covered his broad pecs, and splashed up onto his chin. Drifting off for a nap in Dave's arms was the perfect cap to the most interesting night of my life.

Morning came early when Dave's tongue deep in my ear jolted me awake. Our bodies were sticky with love, but eager as ever and good to go. We rubbered up for another, slower wrangle and made the most of everything we'd learned the night before about what a man can do with another man's hard young body. That time around, I started with Dave's lips and moved south at a more careful, leisurely pace. I'd never thought much about how a marine's body would feel to my tongue, but before the morning was over, I had discovered plenty. We spent the next three days together and even left the room a couple of times to lie on the beach and swill some beer with our buddies. The bars quickly grew boring, though; and we always left our buddies, explaining that it was time to "pleasure our bitches." We didn't bother to tell everyone that we were our own best bitches. Among the countless things I discovered that liberty in Thailand, one stood out like an honest politician: Dave was not only tighter and better looking and more fun than any girl on the planet, he was free. What more could any young marine ask?

SIESTA TIME

The small, one-bedroom apartment in Chula Vista I shared with my steady bitch seemed coldly cavernous and lonely as a lunar landscape when he sailed off on a six-month deployment. I found myself spending more time aboard my own ship, hoping work would keep me sane until he got back -- but not really believing it. I knew I'd miss drilling Darren's tight butt; what surprised me was how much I missed having the rest of the gorgeous goof around. I started to worry I might be growing up. Even when I was home, I escaped the mournfully silent apartment and spent as much time as I could manage at the pool, trying to broil away the desperate loneliness that now hung over my life like a premature pall. Darren's deployment still had 162 days left the afternoon I noticed Jeff.

He was obviously another squid; but in Chula Vista, you couldn't swing a dick without hitting squid. A year or so younger than my 23 and considerably smaller of build, the kid was cute as a bug's ear. I kept my eye on him from across the pool, the way one does any fine piece of studflesh on display, but I made no move to approach him. I considered it for awhile -- until I got a look at his hands. Jeff was cute, I was horny enough to tackle a knot-hole, and, worst of all, those 162 days stretched like forever into my future. Maybe I'd just been with Darren so long I'd forgotten how to pick up fine looking young men. No, I didn't believe that myself. I knew deep down I wasn't going to last until Darren got back. He was probably already doing some young seaman every night and fooling himself into hoping he could live without my thick nine inches up his ass.

I saw Jeff a few more times over the next week and liked more of what I saw. He was about 5'7" but more compact than slight. When he moved, you were reminded of a panther: muscle tightly coiled and ready to explode. Like a lot of squids, he had a moustache to make himself look older and more worldly. It didn't do dick -- but I think his overt innocence is what first drew me to him: his naive, open, wide-eyed farm-boy quality. Just the way he sat by the pool made you like him. He had a toothy grin for everybody and a bright sparkle in his blue eyes that promised an easy disposition. If I had to pin down my two favorite physical turn-ons, they would be his cute little chipmunk nose and the hard, well-built ass that made my dick twitch with every twist. My major turn off was the wedding band. That was what kept me from ambling over to suggest a trip up to our place for an afternoon siesta. At least "siesta" was what Darren always called them; I called them rabid, low-down, no- holes-barred fuck-and-grunt sessions.

The ring didn't keep me from being amiable when Jeff came down to the pool on D-day minus 153 and took the chaise next to mine. He started chatting in the easy-going way two squids do when they don't know each other. Something about our shared experience allows us to skip the typically defensive mode one would use with a stranger and open up to another squid more as a cousin one hadn't seen in years. We chatted about our ships and the weather, about the Padres and a dozen other things. He mentioned in passing that his wife would-n't be joining him until Thanksgiving; this was August. The rest of the building knew about Darren anyway, so I mentioned what ship my bitch was on and that the deployment already seemed like forever.

Jeff was silent for a minute and then asked, "Fags, huh?" He was neither censorious or, especially, congratulatory -- speaking the term in the way we squids use with it, much as most would say "Protestant" or "Black" or "Nebraskan." I gave a grunt of affirmation, knowing both that he meant no offense and that I didn't feel especially "gay" just then anyway. We chatted on for a time, but now I had the ill-defined feeling the climate had changed. He was as friendly and open as ever, but now something seemed to be preying on his mind. As the afternoon slowly aged, we slipped easily and alternately between con-versation and the reptilian stupor which possesses creatures as they bask in the sun.

Jeff hopped up at one point and did a few laps. I watched, with mild regret, from my chaise as his compact muscles stretched outward and pulled him through the water with an easy, masculine grace that kept his ass grinding away like pistons. When he padded back for his towel, he dried his hair and then, the water still dripping from his fine, hairless chest, he sat back down and grew suddenly solemn. He liked

me. He was horny. I was alone. He was alone. He liked girls, understand, but that didn't mean he minded "messing around." So, he said,
hopping to his feet again and ready to bolt, I felt like giving him a call,
we might . . . .

I was up and grabbing my towel before he could finish. We were
in my apartment and I had stripped him naked before his dick could dry.
I hoped the little woman appreciated what she had gotten. For a man
his size, eight inches was impressive -- almost as impressive as the
overall sight of him standing before me, naked and defenseless and
perfect as a mustang colt. For a moment, I didn't know where to begin.
His dick was belly-up and bouncing like a bass drum pedal against his
belly. His balls hung low and heavy in the tenderest looking pouch I'd
seen in ages. His tits were hard -- and not because his swim had
chilled him to the bone. His massive chest heaved in nervous confusion and pent-up sexual excitement, waiting for me to make the first
move.

I reached my hand to the back of his neck and pulled him against
me, letting the damp coolness of his skin feel my sunburnt passion. My
hands eased down across his hard back, following the rocky valley of
his spine to that gorgeous butt. They cupped it and pulled upward, driving his dick into my belly, smearing his wet crotch against me. His
body trembled against mine in eagerness and, perhaps, a touch of relish at the wicked thrill that comes from sex you think is slightly kinky.
His body held nothing back. His hands were all over me, sliding along
my flanks and ass and shoulders, pulling my body against his as if only
together could we find salvation.

I wasn't sure how fast to go; my lips started slowly, tenderly on
his neck as our hips rocked together. I eased upward, seeking his ear
lobe and the tender zone just behind it, lapping and nibbling and sucking up his chlorine-flavored mansweat. I reached down to hold his
bone and discovered pool water wasn't the only thing smearing my legs
and crotch. The slutty horn-dog was dribbling out enough sweet, crys-
tal- clear pre-cum to lube the Tsarist army at Borodino. His lips were
on my tits, sucking like a starving calf; but when my hand wrapped
around his crank, he lapsed into another frenzied shivering fit -- as
though he were ticklish and every tickle turned him on even more. I
held on, feeling the power of his young manhood too long denied surge
out and envelope me.

I used his dick to man-handle him to my bed and fling his ass down. Rubbers quickly covered both our rods; my head was between his pilose thighs almost before either of us could breathe. My lips eased down across his thick, throbbing knob; he quivered like an aspen in a cyclone. I'd already straddled his face and stopped only long enough to make sure he was gnawing on my bone before I coasted down into a cocksucking frenzy of my own. His hips rolled up to greet my face as I slid down his crank, my lips wrapped hard around his crankshaft and my tongue twirling like a dervish the whole way. By the time my nose was sunk in his ballbag and my chin grinding against his damp, chestnut curlies, the head of his lance was locked in mortal but hopeless combat with the tight bands of muscle that live down my throat. His hips had instinctively rolled farther forward, arching his ass upward as it drove his dick even deeper down my gullet. I reached around and held on, at once cradling his powerful mounds of manmuscle for the treasures they were and using them to lock his squid dick where it belonged. As my lips and throat and fingers used his studly young body, I felt him making progress between my legs. Darren always claimed I was a thoughtless shit who would nail a guy's head to the mattress with my nine inch spike, so I'd purposely kept my crotch above Jeff's face and made him reach up and beg for meat. He had not only given my cock a preliminary cleaning, he was sucking on my nuts like a persistent squirrel. When he saw at length that they couldn't be cracked directly, he pulled my naval weapon back down into firing position and stuck the muzzle back into his mouth. I knew it wasn't ready to go off, so I let him have his fun while I turned my suction function up to MAX and did some serious bobbing up and down his crank.

My hands and his had the same idea at about the same time. We eased our fingers down the tight defile that led to the others' shitholes. I think I was first by a few strokes, spreading his cheeks wide and slipping my fuckfingers down into the clammy, chlorinated trench where I knew I'd find one fucking good time. He was anything but blate, though; I felt his fingers holding my cheeks wide, scraping the sweat from my fuckfurrow, and feeling my ass up until he was able to put his finger on exactly what he wanted. My ass nearly ate his hand. I was stroking along on his crank, minding my own business, when my butt lurched upward like a dolphin leaping towards the clouds. A finger slid into my hole and stayed, prodding gently, twisting slightly, making a home there

-- for itself or for some thicker, meatier digit.

I kept about my cocksucking business, puzzling over the ins and outs of pick-up etiquette. Darren and I knew each other so well, a single look or touch would convey volumes. He loved having me up his butt; I could take him up mine on special occasions. But usually he splashed his frothy seaman semen into my throat, and we emptied his rubber to lube mine before I shoved it up his ass. He got off on having jism up his ass and, even though we'd been together a year, I wasn't in any hurry to take chances.

Young Jeff was another matter. Did he think he was going to fuck the queer and bolt before I got mine? He was cute enough I probably wouldn't mind as long as I got off -- not then, anyway. Since I liked the guy I needed him to understand I was up for anything, as long as both ganders got a good goosing. By the time I was sure how I felt, he had two fingers up my ass and was prying and stretching away while his face worked my crank like a 110 milking machine operating on 220.

I did his asshole slowly -- first gliding across just above his pink pucker, then stopping to bait it with a healthy hit- and-run poke, and finally staying to dig deep and party. My fingers eased into his fuckhole and felt super-tight muscles but no resistance of the will. His ass pressed against my fingers, wriggling slightly to worm my way up into his hot, hunky guts. Every twitch and wriggle of his ass brought another, involuntary, shudder of needy pleasure from the body trapped beneath me. We reached a stand off -- sucking fine dick, but knowing we both wanted to blow our loads into something tighter, darker, and more demanding.

Since it was my bed -- and I was the worldly fag, Jeff may have been waiting for me to make the first move. I pried my face off his crank, took a few well-earned and much-needed breaths, and asked whether he wanted to go first. He gurgled for a moment, so I raised my hips and stopped humping his head to the mattress. He said I should go first. He had done a couple of guys, but he'd never been fucked and didn't know how well he could take a pole as big as mine. Just in case I had too much, it was only fair I go first.

I'd found a stray stud squid with scruples -- and the gift of blarney! After that speech, I'd have let him ream me out without even a handshake in return. He was a good enough cocksucker, though, I knew I wouldn't last all that long. If he reamed me out first, my load would settle and I'd ride his ass into oblivion. If that sounds like ratio-nalization, it is. My other head was shouting out loud and clear: stop dicking around -- buttfuck the cute little bugger before he changes his mind. I tend to think too much, so this time I gave up and listen to my conscience.

Once I eased off Jeff and saw anew how hunky and eager he was, I thought about sucking his tits or sliding my tongue down his throat. His cute chipmunk nose was wriggling in anticipation; he was so young and fresh and gorgeous, I knew I couldn't wait. His ass was already arching into the air so I lifted his legs to my waist and reached for the lube. I spilt it all over him and me, but sliding my crank up and down between those two fine cheeks was such a rush I almost didn't need to fuck my way inside to get off. Almost.

As I parked against his hole, I realized Jeff was the first guy I had ever done who had admitted to being cherry. This was a moment he was going to remember forever; I was guaranteed a kind of immortali-ty. Knowing how hard even Darren sometimes found me to take, I leaned down for a last nibble of Jeff's ear and whispered, "If you change your mind, let me know." I saw his wary tongue flick out ser-pent-like across his lips, but the eyes knew what they wanted. Then I realized, much as he needed to shoot a load down some tight hole, he was also living out some long-suppressed fantasy. He said he'd done guys. Now, at long last he'd know what it felt like to be fucked -- what a man's thick, hard dick shoved up into his guts was like. Maybe he'd even noticed my basket at the pool and picked me because of my size. If that was the case, I was sure as shit going to make his lesson as memorable as it was satisfying.

My head pried gently at his fuckhole, burrowing inevitably, remorselessly, but gently up into his guts. I kept my eyes locked on his face and can still plainly see every flicker and flinch the next few moments bred between us. His butt arched and pressed against my dick, begging for what I had to offer, demanding the whole, chicken-lickin' bone. Jeff's hands slipped down from my shoulders to pulled against the small of my back, urging me on. Just the pressure of my dick against his hole had him moaning like a Tijuana whore. I pressed still harder and was soon bouncing into his butt, ready to ram through at the first sign of weakness.

When it came, I crashed inside in one swift, relentless soul- shattering stroke that sent his body into a seizure of pain or pleasure -- or each inextripably fused with the other. His eyes clenched shut in agonecstasy just as his butt first pulsed open in disbelief and then latched down around my log like a leech with lockjaw. I lay still inside him until his legs relaxed their grip on my hips, his eyes eased open to shine with new a knowledge of life and love, and his butt realized there was yet more to come. Then I started sliding slowly in and out, working my way even deeper up his ass with every stroke, being careful not to strain his body past the breaking point. My red pubes ground into his shithole and received a little wriggle in return. My log lurched against his prostate and tore shivers up from his very center. When I reached my nine-inch limit, my knob was so swollen with lust and pride in the way Jeff was giving up his cherry, that I almost shot off. I took another time out to play with Jeff's bare chest, sliding the back of my nails down along his quivering flesh, gently tweaking his tits a lesson, and reaching down to squeeze his swollen ballbag and dick.

My eager little love-monkey had come too far to be put off. He wanted a reaming; he had one coming. I slipped slowly into gear, this time building up speed that surprised even me. I knew I was horny, but I'd never felt so furious, so beastial a savagery before. My ass clenched tight, driving my dick down harder with every stroke, deeper and faster. I twisted this way and that, meating new territory with every frenzied fuckstroke. The SLAM and SLAP of flesh and muscle and my moans of pleasure and Jeff's animal grunts blended together until I thought I might pass out any time. Perhaps I did for a moment; one deep butt-wrenching stroke blended with the next as I reamed and rammed and pounded Jeff's tight virgin hole with all the pent-up frustration and loneliness and maybe even an illogical sense of betrayal. Darren's desertion had left me more alone than even I realized until that moment. With Jeff's hard young body wrapped around my harder dick, his tight guts slamming past every exposed nerve-end in my dick, blending sensation and truth with the frenzy of discovery, I knew suddenly I could come to terms with Darren's deployment. I would make it.

Suddenly I didn't even need Jeff's butt the same way I had before. I wasn't reaming his hole as a substitute for Darren; I was drilling my dick through his hot guts like a demon on fire because I wanted to. I liked Jeff himself -- as a person, not just as a mass of muscle around a tight hole.

I was thinking too much again. Maybe I had fucked myself into a stupor, because suddenly I jolted back to the present. Every impulse in my body told me I was about to take care of business in a big way. Jeff was screaming profane shit at me between the grunts; my moans and snarls echoed off the walls. Then, suddenly, I had to latch hard onto Jeff's shoulders to keep from fucking myself into the next county. My hips drilled out of control, rolling up and back like a stapling machine run amok, sliding every inch I had into the tight, eager meat wrapped around my bone.

I zoned out for sure. When I came to, Jeff's butt was clenched around my dick, trying against reason to milk more sailor spooge out of my joint, but he was wasting his time. My balls had pumped a week's worth and then shut down on strike. Somehow I managed to stop dry-humping Jeff's hole and collapsed into his arms for a well-deserved rest. He held me tight for a time, brushing the hair from my forehead and talking in soft, lovers' tones about how good I'd made him feel and how sorry he was he hadn't give it up sooner. As soon as I'd started to get my breath back, though, I knew I should roll over and get back to business. I knew if I could take Darren up my ass, I could handle Jeff. I hadn't counted on what a live-wire the little bastard was. He started off pleasant enough, but once he was galloping along in the saddle, he nearly rode my ass ragged. Looking up at that compact body of his humping up and down, watching his dick crashing in and out of my hole, and, especially, seeing the demented, dick-drilling smile that spread across his cute, young-stud face -- I knew I could keep him busy until his wife showed up.

Later on, after we had showered and were lying in each other's arms, waiting for another load of jism to percolate up close enough to tap and do the nasty again, he talked about his wife -- and how much she liked three-somes. I was fun by myself, of course, but would I mind coming over to hump him up the ass while he did his wife? Maybe after this Darren fellow got back, he could join us? With all those dicks and holes, he said with a grin as he held my dick in his hand, the possibilities would be practically endless.

R & R

By the time we pulled into Bahrain for R&R, I'd been in the Navy for five years and long since learned about what marines were like. That first day in port, though, stunned even me and gave a whole new meaning to R&R.

If you've never been to Bahrain in August, you'll have to take my word that it's warm. Sailors and marines who have been floating around the Gulf for four months don't much enjoy waiting in a pier-side parking lot for the superannuated school bus that was hired to haul them to the beer. They get especially pissed off when the 1400 bus is still there waiting at 1415, filled with sweating, very thirsty bodies -- but without the Pakistani driver who has wandered off somewhere by himself.

I gave patience a try, but was quickly as disgusted with the sheep-like mentality of most military men as I was with South Asian varlets who can't be bothered to do their jobs. I'd watched the driver stroll down towards some warehouses just before 1400 and decided somebody ought to go drag his ass back to the bus. With the prospect of chilled Foster's on tap, I decided I was just the somebody to take charge.

As it happened, he wasn't hard to find. I'd stomped about a block when I passed a plywood-and-tin shed the size of the average packing crate. Even through the plywood, the little grunts and moans told me the little bastard was up to no good -- and on my fucking time. The minute I opened the door and stepped inside the dark hot-box, though, I saw I owed the guy an apology. He was tending seriously to business after all. This was no Pakistani jerkoff caught red-handed, but a serious inter-cultural sodomite of the first order.

The light streaming in behind me gave my presence away, but obviously neither of the guys gave a shit; they were too busy having a good time. The Pakistani had his slacks down around his ankles and his long white shirt-tail bobbing up and down across his gaunt, brown ass as it slammed back and forth. He looked OK for a guy about 4'8", and another time I might have been interested enough to see what he had hanging. Just then, though, I had more important things on my mind -- like the gorgeous blond United States Marine he was fucking up the ass.

The marine's blouse and T-shirt were lying on the floor; his camie pants were down around his boots. The light filtering through the single dingy window way up in wall wasn't enough for me to tell much more than that I wouldn't mind fucking him myself. Letting the door slam behind me cut down on the glare and gave me a better view.

Even from across the little room, I could tell that my countryman wasn't challenged. Before the driver eventually left us, I got a good look at his shit-covered dick and was impressed. He was much bigger than I'd expected someone his height to be. The marine, though, had felt big bruisers up his ass and knew better would come along -- like me, for instance. At first he just looked over my way while the Pakistani pounded away and I stood watching the show and loving every stroke.

Gomer was about 19, with a great body even by grunt standards and a face that would make a Hollywood agent's whole year. His head was close-cropped on the sides with a tuft of golden hair that he wore like a surfer-god's crown. His eyes sparkled blue above a pug nose and boyish grin, but the strong brow and jaw were all marine. At first I couldn't see nearly enough of his body to satisfy my prurient urges. I saw plenty of shoulder and a flank tapering down to no waist at all, but between the angle and the Pakistani and the streams of sweat glittering in the indifferent light, my view could have been better.

It quickly got that way; the grunt bastard decided to show off what he had. He left the scrimmage-line posture and stood erect so I could see every ripple and hair and glistening river of man-sweat. The poor Pakistani clutched tight around Gomer's waist and shimmied up his legs as he felt himself being lifted aloft, but he wasn't about to let himself be bucked from this fucking stallion's saddle.

As Gomer reared high on his hind legs, his pizzle proved sweat wasn't the only fluid he was leaking. He was swollen thick and long, but still had enough wrinkled foreskin across the top of its head to make my mouth ache. Crystal strands of slick love-lube spun between his bare belly and throbbing bone as each beat of his racing pulse slammed the two together to weave a glistening invitation. The kid's balls, hanging low with enough jarhead jism to last a Nebraska winter, swung between bare, powerful thighs as the bus driver shifted his stick, desperate to find a higher gear.

The hungry look in his eyes told me Gomer was a typical marine -- pumped into a perfect man-machine but with all a grunt's needs. The typical marine craves many things, but having a big, stiff dick slammed hard up his ass heads the list. Men will give a lot of reasons for joining the Corps; but, once he stops fooling himself with the patriotic bullshit, all those reasons boil down to two: to live day and night with hundreds of other sweaty men in prime condition -- and to be abused 36 hours a day. From the first day of boot camp, a marine's world cycles from insult to maltreatment to humiliation and back again. For a powerful male animal, the ultimate shame is also the most ancient and the delightful. For a grunt to be really happy, he must yield up all control over his body. Another man has to possess him completely -- to shove his stiff dick hard up between those powerful marine-built cheeks, to hold him down and slam through his tight asshole until his very body is violated with one frothing gusher after another of his conqueror's seed. The Pakistani was doing a fine job of satisfying himself, but he wasn't reaming nearly hard enough to give Gomer the kind of gratuitous grief he needed. I knew I had both the equipment and the attitude to do the job. First, though, I was going to take care of that leaky dick.

I lost my shorts and T-shirt on the short trip across the floor; but once I stood two feet from the kid, I had to stop again to watch. Some day I'd be old and wrinkled and, as I took myself in hand, I'd be able to summon up his image and remember the classic grunt I'd done in my youth. If anything, he was even more outrageous close up. Gomer smelled like stale crotch-sweat blended with the savory scent of man-sex. His puerile, farmboy face looked especially foxy set above his massive killer-machine body. A thick wrestler's neck led down to broad shoulders which eased their way into a set of arms Paul Bunyan would be proud of. Powerful biceps just made his pecs look all the more pumped. Every pore was open, gushing sweat that stippled his body in shimmering beads that soon answered gravity's call to streak his body with sweaty rivulets. His massive chest was as hairless as it was magnificent. Twin russet disks erupted in nipples that pointed downward, dripping great golden drops of sweat begging to have my teeth rip those tender tit-stalks loose in punishment for the sin of being his.

Below that perfect chest, muscle rippled into knotted muscle as his torso cascaded behind a pair of clanking dog tags down to narrow hips and strong legs. I'd done enough marines to know what his powerful bubble-butt would look like even without prying buttfucker number one off. Two brown hands still clutched tightly around Gomer's tighter belly just above his dick -- still gushing love-lube and praying for my attention. The thing had seemed like a freak of nature from across the room; up close, it was even better -- but I knew enough about marine psychology to know that for Gomer to really get off, I'd have to put my own cocksucking on hold until I'd taught Gomer his place. OK, so you don't believe all that. I admit the obvious: deep down, I was less concerned with whether the grunt got off than with the wicked, sadistic thrill of giving someone built like him a world of shit.

Step one was putting his ass at risk. Even though the Corps knows what goes on when the lights go out, they pretend to be as dumb as they look. Just to prove its hypocrisy, the Pentagon picks several hundred grunts a year to kick out because they love to love sweaty men up the ass. When he let me reach up and grab his tags, Gomer put his future absolutely in my hands. I had to squint because of the lousy light, but he stood, silent and grinning, as I read his tags. Even the Pakistani prick up his ass seemed to take advantage of the moment to find new purpose in life. Now he was Gomer no longer; I had a name to go with the dick. He was PFC HAMMOND, JASON S, an O+ Roman Catholic who was good enough to eat -- later.

First we had to convince young Jason that he was at the bottom of the food chain: "OK, Boot, I know what a faggot like you wants. Go ahead, choke on it." I hadn't gotten past his name before my hands had wrapped around his Corps- cropped head and shoved his face down to my crotch. The Pakistani finally popped fully into view, but I had eyes only for the top of Jason's blond head as it opened wide to gobble my joint. He went all the way, choking my swollen knob far enough down his throat to tickle tonsil before he stopped to let his lips graze among my stiff red pubes. His mouth and throat were hot and tight and eager--full of high-suction enthusiasm that threatened to do too good a job. The tight, tender muscles of his throat stroked and pulsed and pulled across my swollen knob, ripping loose one soul-shivering sensation after another. The feel of his lips locked tight around the thick base of my bone and of his tongue slipping along the underside of my shaft was good enough to market to the good people at Disney as the ultimate E-ticket ride. I had wanted my first load of the day to blast up his ass, but unless the bastard learned self-control on the double my rocks would pop high.

His throat convinced me that breeding his cute farmboy face was just as good as doing his asshole, anyway. Down his gullet, I wouldn't have to settle for sloppy seconds -- though blowing my load into another guy's jism is always a special kind of rush. I'd more or less ignored our Pakistani cohort all along; but as he saw his marine boy-toy gobbling down my first class privates, his South-Asian dick erupted in the ass-clenching, nut-busting jism-jet of his young life. He was still holding tight to young Jason's belly, but his hips drilled that dusky dick into Jason's tight desert- defender butthole like a run-away sewing machine. The faster he fucked, the louder he howled and gibbered away in Urdu until any sensible person would have worried about having our tryst disturbed by eager groupies or censorious shore patrolmen. None of us was the least bit sensible by this point; but isolation worked in our favor and we were left to rut away, undisturbed but by our own dick-driving demons.

When he felt his ass flush full of frothy Pakistani ballsap, Hammond firmed up even more on his hole. I saw his butt clench tight, determined to milk out every drop and keep it deep inside him. The bus driver heaved and slammed and twitched and writhed up Jason's ass for while seemed an hour as my cocksucking marine kept my knob polished better than ever. When the Pakistani finally opened his eyes and slipped backwards out of Jason's ass, I got my first good look at the dick that had done him. It looked fine -- bigger than most Asian bones, colored a deep brown and streaked with pearly white seeds of life he'd illicitly smuggled out of Hammond's ass. The foreskin was almost black, still stripped back behind his café au lait knob and wrinkled down along his shaft. The smell of Jason's manhole and of his own unwashed crotch blended together until I almost lost interest in the man-beast with my dick down his throat. Almost.

I've never enjoyed being fucked; most squids don't. With that fine hard dick in full view, though, I couldn't help wondering for a minute how good it would feel up my ass. The idea of Jason's butt-juices blending with mine as the bus- jockey who had jizzed him full gave me a twin helping felt oddly wicked and, consequently, exciting enough to be a turn-on. He could do me while I fucked Hammond's face and then, after I'd blow one load, I'd turn the grunt around and bust my second nut up that tight marine ass, blending my cream with his while he did pumped me full.

As often happens in life, though, I was too busy dreaming around and not busy enough reaching out to grab a handful of dick. Before I could bend over and motion him up my ass, the Pakistani's other head took over. His eyes widened to about the size of the Arecibo telescope as remembered the busful of sweaty Americans who were doubtless ready to rip his nuts off. Having bred his American for the day, he was out the door, his shirttail flapping behind as he tried to stuff his stiff, gooey dick back out of sight. Even though I am a life-long top, my ass-hole felt a tickle of remorse as the door slammed behind him.

You can believe, though, that Hammond was enough man to keep me busy. In a way, having his hard, sweaty grunt body to myself was a bonus. My tongue had been twitching over his dribbling dick since I'd first seen the thing; now that he didn't have anyone up his ass and had shown that he was the low-life, shitbird cocksucker by choking down my bone, I was free to feed my own face.

I latched onto his cute little ears and took the con. He'd been doing an outstanding job of working my load north, but it never hurts to remind a grunt who's in charge. As I picked up my cadence and rammed my rod rougher through his perfect lips with every brutal stroke, I added just the sort of verbal abuse that makes a desert defender bloom: "Suck harder, you fucking faggot -- or you can kiss my dick good- bye. Fucking shitbird cunt! I don't have a fucking clue why I should waste my time on a no-load piece of shit boot like you. I'll bet your bitch of a mama could handle me better; whores usually can." There was much more of the same, but with a body like his munching off the end of my bone, I wasn't really listening. I do know that the more I tore into him like a drug-crazed DI, the happier and horiner and hard-er he got.

When I thought he'd bite by balls off, I pushed him backwards onto the filthy floor so his cute little head would be trapped against the deck and I could fuck it the way I wanted. He still managed everything I shoved into him, but I could tell the angle of my elevation was giving him trouble. Switching around to the time-tested 69 mode not only matched the bend in my bone to the drop in his gullet, but exposed his sweaty, love-lube soaked crotch to my mercy for the first time. Even after we shifted about so my head was in his crotch, I kept my hips pounding my point home down his throat where it belonged, deeper and faster with every instinctively cruel, conquering, dicktatorial stroke. By this point, I was operating purely on auto-pilot. Some small, remote corner of my brain kept the tape running, recording the tight warmth of his throat and the snicker-snack of my joint down his jarhead gullet; but below the waist, my small head was definitely in charge.

I was much too busy sorting through sensory overload that lay a tongue-length away. Hammond's narrow hips rocked forward, fucking the air in time to my tool. Now and again, when I took a moment to grind my coarse, rust-colored pubes into his chin, his ass would jerked up a tad so his dick could mimic mine's motion. Hovering just a heart-beat above his hard, messy belly, his joint would shiver and wiggle and shudder like a strangling python in its death throes. Then, as my stick shifted out of neutral again, he'd spin loose another crystal thread down to join the pool of dick-honey on his belly.

That marvellous mire of man-sugar begged to be my first target, but even I wasn't greedy enough to slurp it all down. I knew my limita-tions and realized that once I started, I wouldn't stop until he was dry as the desert around us. To prove what a nice guy I was -- and to get his ass ready to wrangle, I dipped my right fuckfinger into his puddle of petrine ooze and came up with enough slick sap to grease a hundred grunts his size. On the way past, I palmed his balls and was tempted to stop, but the hot syrup starting to thicken on my finger needed to get kept warm. By the time my hand was prying his hard marine-built cheeks apart so my finger could slither up the hot, hairless valley of his ass- crack, the grunt slut was rolling those hips up to meat me good. My finger slipped across his tender pink pucker on a cushion of his own sauce, but I didn't have a chance to stuff the gander. His hole reached out and grabbed my hand, gobbling it down without so much as a burp. I knew his shitchute had to be slick with Pakistani cream, but all that was far down in the dark, secret well of his ass. Up high, where I could reach and where he wanted me to stay, his hole was hot and dry and starving for more. The slut let slip a long, dick-stifled moan of pleasure at having another man up his ass. Even then he wasn't satisfied until one finger followed another and I had three up his hole, stretching this way and twisting that. All the while, his throat scraped along my shaft and that beautiful jarhead joint kept oozing a steady stream of honey.

I had him pegged head and tail, but his belly and dick finally got what they deserved, too. I started out slowly, savoring every tongue-tingling drop of his crystal pre-cum, but was soon slurping him down at lightspeed, careless of anything but my own piggish pleasure. When his belly was lapped tidy enough to take home to mama, I started on the real source of his nectar -- his thick, throbbing uncut marine dick.

I used my tool down his throat and hand up his ass to hold him steady for a moment and then out-flanked his swollen head with my lips. My tongue hooked inside his cock-cowl, lifting it slightly away from his belly so I could get a good hold, and then my lips closed tight, locking the first couple inches of his meat inside my mouth. At first I couldn't concentrate on anything but the mind-numbing meld of pre-cum and man-sweat and crotch-musk that exploded across my tastebuds. As my tongue slipped lower into the silken caress of his cocksock, working its way between that soft `skin and the hard, smooth knob that throbbed beneath, the ephebic tenderness of his flesh was at odds with the raging animal marine strength of his bone.

Hammond loved having his dick in my mouth. Not only did his already thick flow of pre-cum gush into overdrive, but the slut somehow managed to gurgle up groans of pleasure from around my face-fucking shank. I didn't give a shit whether Hammond was having fun or not; I was. My lips tore at his crankshaft, working more and more of his baby-tender skin up his pole, across his knob and the tongue wrapped tight around it, and into my face. My mouth was watering like a Niagara and his `skin seemed to melt away to nothing in the hot bubbly spit swamping my mouth. I should have swallowed, of course; but his studly scents and salacious tastes were too fine to waste in a moment's pleasure when I could save savor them again and again while I dug deeper down into the secret country of his cowl-clad cock. The deeper I drilled, the more musk his marine meat had waiting for me to scrape loose. Soon my tongue was so far up his tender cocksock that there wasn't room for his organ and mine, too.

His `skin ripped back down across his head and nestled behind his trigger ridge like a convertible top caught by a summer squall. Suddenly the full glory of his grunt dick was open and exposed and ready to action. I scraped and slashed and sucked his joint until one wave of satisfaction after another made me forget myself. The smell of his crotch, the soft blond pubes stroking my chin, his hard feel and soft touch -- not to mention the suction of his mouth on my shank or his butt's brutality towards my fingers -- these and a thousand other sensations swept away my will-power and caught me unawares in their silken web of hunky man-sex.

One moment I was chowing happily down on Jason's joint, the next I was busy blowing my load. I didn't just pump sperm, it exploded up out of my balls, stretched the walls of my cum-tube until I thought my dick would split down the middle, and blasted out through my cum-slit and straight down Hammond's gulping gullet. Any decent person would have gagged and sputtered and coughed up my crank. Hammond was no decent person. The grunt whore let me pump enough protein down his throat to feed an African family of six for a year -- then he doubled the suction and shanghaied every squid sperm I had hiding out in reserve. He kept sucking until I was sure that I'd ruptured a nut -- and until my dick had stopped pounding down past his Adam's apple and my hips had finished grinding away into his Dick Tracy jaw.

When I felt myself regain control, I reluctantly spit out his dick for awhile to give him shit -- for ruining my fun, for taking my load without permission, and for any number of other bullshit offenses the few working cells in my brain were able to invent. He had to be punished -- and I had just the EMI to keep an asslick like Hammond busy while my balls churned out another load to shoot up his ass.

I sat on that cute farmboy face and warned him that if I didn't feel his tongue up my nasty, dirty squid asshole on the double, he'd be the sorriest cocksucker alive. The slut was still licking gobbets of my jism off his chops and didn't look especially sorry, but the idea of licking my sailor ass was just the thing to make his world a fucking utopia.

Some guys approach assholes with disgust; some work their way up slowly as though a tapeworm is likely to leap out at any moment. Hammond did give my hairy ass-crack a quick sweep with this tongue, but mainly to make sure he wasn't missing anything. He dived into my pucker like Santa Monica Boulevard pro and didn't stop until his lips were locked tight around my hole and his tongue was buried deep inside me. The rough texture of his bumpy tongue up my tender ass was almost painful, but so soporific and entrancing that what could have been pain bred the purest pleasure beyond description. I felt every bump and grind of his face up my ass, but I felt them through a vein of otherworldly enchantment that held me spell-bound above the dark, grimy deck where my ass rubbed along his United States Marine face like a dog's tail across a carpet. I relished every rapacious, butt-raping stroke of his tongue, every slurp of his wet lips, every manly touch of his hands as they pried a firmer hold up my crack. His tongue taught me great sagas of contentment and absolute peace. I might be there still, grinding my ass against that cute grunt face, if his ass hadn't gotten in the way.

Hammond was holding his own up my ass, but wanted me to hold it everywhere else. I slipped to the crest of consciousness to find him rubbing his right tit against my hairy leg and humping my hand with his asshole. I was doing everything but jacking the jarhead off -- and, great as he was with his tongue up my ass, I knew from experience how much better he'd feel with his ass wrapped around my rod.

My ass popped loose from his lamprey-like suction with a sloppy SMACK as I stood up to show him what happened to grunts to amused themselves without permission. He lay still on the floor, his camies still down around his ankles. They had to go, so I ripped his boots and trou off and threw them across the small room. His sweat-soaked wool socks stayed in place as I grabbed his ankles, lifted his feet towards the ceiling, and put my joint on station. I'd thought about doing him from behind, the way the Pakistani had, but I never waste a cute marine. If the grunt is built good enough to do but has a face like a goat's shithole, I'll sometimes hump him from behind. Hammond was choice, USDA farmboy goods. I wanted to see his blue eyes crinkle shut in pain as I slammed my throbbing, reproductively dick-advantaged nine inches up his shithole. I wanted to him struggle and twist on the end of my joint; I wanted to hold his feet wide, to be in total control of his body while I used him and it for my pleasure. I was going to enjoy owning his ass. What's more, he'd enjoy it, too. Crudely put, he had to watch me fuck him up the ass and know what he was -- an easy piece of ass, a butt-fuck, a convenient hole to take my load. He had to feel he was the lowest piece of crap on the planet or he wouldn't be happy. Only a totally degraded grunt can have a good time -- and that's what was written on my dance card: one fucking good time.

If anything, his face was even better than I'd hoped. The Pakistani had opened him up some; my three fingers twisting and prying up his ass had helped -- but few men can take the head of my swollen nine inches without shrieking like a skyful of bats on their way to the blood bank. My knob didn't go in at once so I reared back and slammed forward harder at the same time I spread his ankles up and out, stretching him like a wishbone and fooling his faggot ass into thinking it had a chance. By the time his brain knew he was fucked, my dick had sliced through the gates guarding his doubtful virtue and slammed down the well-worn path that led to his guts. My knob ricocheted off his swollen prostate and sent shivers echoing across the firm landscape of his rock- solid body. By that time, though, I was buried hilt-deep, the thick base of my bone stretching his asshole to the breaking point, my cum-slit was teaching the blind end of his fucktunnel to get out of the way, and my shank was dripping with hot, frothy, Pakistani jism.

His cute lips parted in a moan and then opened wide to suck in great lungfuls of air that made his powerful chest convulse as though my dick weren't enough and he needed my teeth to tear at his tender tits. I ground my pubes into his tender asshole and then jerked my dick upwards until the bottom of my head slammed into his tight sphincters and bounced back down into his prostate. His guts clutched at my bone, stroking slick jism across every inch as I slid up and down with a cadence that was born charging and learned speed with age. The slut's hands were everywhere at once -- stroking the back of my head, latched onto my shoulders, pulling at my ass, sliding along my flanks.

As his ass rose to meet every downward plunge of my piston, I dropped his heels and felt them take up station on my ass, spurring me ever faster, ever deeper. My balls strained to flush up a load, but they had been so drastically drained that this fucking evolution was going to take some time. Fortunately, I was in no hurry at all and since every upward stroke of my pole brought more jism up to lube his hole, I knew a buttfuck grunt like Hammond could take what I had all afternoon if necessary -- and love every second of it.

One I was galloping along in the saddle, I let my dick do the driving again and hung motionless above Jason's face, watching the flinches blend into a pattern of ecstasy. A low, deep grunt echoed every SLAP of my hips against his ass, every muffled BUUUP of my dickhead up into his guts. When I couldn't resist the lips another moment, I slipped low and sucked his pouty lower lip between mine. I tasted the musk of my own asshole and dug deep between his lips with my tongue, searching in vain for some lingering taste of my load. He had long since swallowed my first blast of jism, but wouldn't have to bother with the second.

My lips and tongue tangled with his until I had to let him breathe. I moved across his neck and shoulders and then up to tongue-fuck his ear until he was crying for relief and I'd drilled pleasure into such exquisite torment that Torquemada looked as charitable as Mother Theresa. I lifted one arm so my lips and tongue could find his hairy pit and lick the day's scent from the long stiff hairs that hung there hidden from sight, as though ashamed to defile his glabrous grunt body with a man's hair. My teeth sunk low and scraped across his blood-gorged tits until both were numb with pleasure and our bodies were slipping and sliding together in a sea of sweat, writhing and thumping and heaving together with the ancient rhythm of the rut.

The heat and the smells of sex and the slippery texture of being done hard up the ass were too much for young Jason. His dick had sent out for more pre-cum and brought in a gusher. The honeyed crystal dripped and splashed down onto his sweat-streaked belly until something had to be done. I leaned sideways, balancing myself on one elbow, and scooped up one finger-load after another to drizzle between his lips. As his sucked his lube from my fingers, I kept at his ass, harder and faster than ever until the fierce power of my thrusts was fucking his naked body across the dirty floor, leaving a dark, wet stain behind as though some gigantic slug had been out for a stroll.

The taste of his own dick-wash, the torment of my tongue and teeth, the prostate pounding pleasure up his ass, and the rising temperature of our fuck-friction all finally got the better of my boot PFC. His eyes clenched shut again as his body slipped into convulsions. I saw him reaching for his dick in time to slap his hand away, but he didn't need to whack off. His body knew when he'd had a good time and launched one thick blast of pearly jarhead spooge after another up between us. Most of his load caught in the thick red fur that lives on my chest and belly, but some splashed past to land on the floor or on his shoulder or in his face. I bent low to lick a glistening white strand from his cheek and moved my tongue into his mouth so he could enjoy the taste of his marine seed as well. I kept the globs of grunt goo on his shoulder for myself, but made him suck his jism from my fur.

Unfortunately, the taste of his load, the sight of his body wracked by uncontrolled ecstasy, and especially the way his shithole clamped down tight around my bone as he slipped into the first throes of his cum-convulsion all conspired to drop me into the abyss as well. I barked something nasty at him and grabbed his head and shoulder to steady myself before I turned my dick loose to batter and bludgeon and slam his ass as much as it deserved. I was still at it, a minute or an hour or a lifetime later, when my balls brought me back to earth, burning with as much exertion as my bone was with the glow of a job well done -- and a marine well fucked.

I had just pulled my raw meat out of his ass and was wiping my dick against his balls when the door flew open and our Pakistani driver dashed back inside, his run completed. Now that he had some more free time, he was all rabid excitement and rapid, incomprehensible English. Pretty clearly, he was ready for more marine tail. I knew I would regret not sticking around myself, but sometimes the flesh is too weak to give the bone what it wants. I needed to slink off for a day or so and recuperate -- and that cold beer was still waiting. On the other hand, now that I'd found Hammond, I didn't intend to let sleeping dogfaces lie. I lifted his legs so that our friend could sink his shaft back up Jason's jism-choked ass and top off the sperm cocktail he kept there. I even slid forward enough that Hammond could take a few stray licks up my ass-crack and suck on my tender balls in case he'd missed anything the first time around. My nuts were about to implode, though; I had to leave. Before I did, I reached down for a tit to get the slut's attention and leaned low into his ear to say, "OK, Buttface. I'm finished with your slack ass for today. You and your little friend here can play your faggot games all you want. I want you back here at 1500 tomorrow, though. This time, bring two of your grunt buddies so I can show them what a faggot-assed piece of shit your are."

The next day, he was there at 1500 -- and his two buddies were with him. I see now that I'd made a mistake including them. Having them watch Hammond being fucked up the ass by a squid was a righteous turn-on, but if young Jason had worn my bone to a frazzle the three of them kept me going until nearly midnight. You can imagine more or less what came up, so I won't go into details. Let's just say I've never been so fucking happy to get underway as I was the next morning. Sometimes pulling into port for R&R just takes too fucking much out of a guy.

THE OLD GREY FOX

As I lay in my rack with Burton's tongue darting between my sweaty toes, I had a hard time keeping my mind on training him to be a good marine. He was cuter than fuck with his eager green eyes and that pouty lower lip that liked to stroke along the bottom of my crank as I nailed his face. His ass was the tightest in the company -- and knew the most tricks. In the weeks since he'd reported to the rock, I'd managed to help whip his lean body into serious shape until he became the kind of gungy, hard-charging young marine I get off training. Even with Burton hunkered down between my legs, though, my mind was drifting.

For one thing, this was the hottest summer Okinawa had seen in years, and my quarters weren't air conditioned. I'd dragged my company's asses back from a 25-mile hump across the island just an hour before, and Burton and I had been much too busy to shower off our smelly bodies. The trickle of sweat dripping in steady rivulets across my naked body tickled almost as much as the tongue flicking between my toes.

For another thing, Burton had already gagged down so big a load I'd almost ruptured a nut -- but I kept reaming away inside that foxy young face-hole until my marine weapon felt raw as any recruit. We both knew who was going to get the next one up his tight PFC ass, but not until he earned it.

Mainly, though, the combined sweat of summer and savory scent of man-sex had lured me away from Burton's green eyes and tight holes to another, sweeter summer when life was simpler and I was the boot being broken in. Something about the heat or the smell of sweat or the soft, tender texture of Burton's nearly hairless skin made me real-ize the trick the years had played. I'd unconsciously ignored the dam-age life did to my shaving mirror's reflection, but suddenly I was outside myself looking at the boot licking the colonel's stinking feet and time turned inside out. I had become the old grey fox -- I had become Gunny

Grant and the recruit inside me was forever gone, but hardly forgotten.

Gunny Grant had retired from the Corps and moved in next door to my parents sometime while I was away for my freshman year in college. Our houses were separated by hedges and huge fences so I might never have noticed him even after I came home for summer vacation if he hadn't been out front one afternoon trimming his hedge. I noticed him plenty -- almost as much as he noticed me. As our eyes locked, and we each took stock, I knew my life would never be the same again. I'd jacked off and done some guys at school, but Gunny Grant was a man. The look in his eyes told me the difference.

He was standing on a ladder, naked except for the khaki shorts the Corps calls UDTs. They're tight as fuck across the ass and just long enough in the legs so your nuts don't hang out -- if it's a cold day. In the face-off that followed, I eased closer to the ladder and got a look up his left leg to see huge ball and even huger dickhead peeking out at me. The rest of his body didn't bother peeking. Muscles rippled from one tanned triumph to the next, down from a thick neck, across a broad chest covered in thick grey curls, down to a flat, hard belly that disappeared into size 32 UDTs.

Gunny's face was even more powerful than his compact body. It wasn't hard or mean, you just knew straight off that people did what he said. His grey hair was still cropped Corps-close as though to be ready for every morning's formation. Clear blue eyes and a strong brow and jaw made him look like a jarhead DI poster-boy.

Only his right tit upset the image. It was pierced through by a gold-plated arrow. Now it's hard to find a platoon that doesn't have at least a couple pierced tits, but this was 1964 -- when Beatles-length hair was outre. Weeks later, he told me the story of how the doctor had saved the Pathet Lao bullet so he could have it made into his good-luck piece. That first day, though, I was more concerned with the way the sun glinted off that golden arrow and his silver chest thatch to make my dick stand at attention.

I was shirtless myself so I wasn't really surprised when I felt his eyes on my naked torso. As they slid down to the bone-bulge in my jeans, I realize he was rating my potential as though I were some especially stupid mule he'd been stuck with. He must have found me worth a trial ride, because he let out a long sigh and barked, "You must be the cum-stain from next door. I'm going to finish this hedge. Grab a beer from the fridge on your way through to the pool, but leave your clothes in the house."

The beer and the pool may have been an off-hand invitation, but the last bit about my getting naked was pure military order. Who did the geezer think he was? The guy was old enough to be my father. Did he seriously think I wanted to fuck his wrinkled old hole? Sure, his body was obviously in good great shape and he had a raw, animal power that fascinated me almost as much as it turned me on; but if he thought I was going to do everything he said, he could go fuck himself. As he went back to trimming the hedge, I stomped off -- to his pool, leaving my clothes in his house, but I showed him. I didn't touch his fucking beer.

I lay naked in the sun and swam and wondered what I was doing. The guy was obviously the kind of pervert my mother had always told me not to take rides or candy from, and here I was, buck-ass naked waiting for him to finish his yard work so I could ream him out. With my luck, he'd probably just blow me and keel over with a coronary. The cool beads of pool water turned to sweat in the strong summer sun and I drifted in out and of sleep, accompanied of buzzing bees and the blended smells of chlorine and freshly mown grass.

I came back to consciousness to find a stronger, more ancient smell had engulfed me. My first sensation was of something tickling my chin, then acrid clouds of stale man-sweat billowed through my uncertain consciousness like a half- remembered dream. The scent clogged my lungs and grew still stronger, adding an exotic muskiness that forced my heart to pound. I opened my eyes to brush away the fly tickling my chin and found a very different outrage. The old geezer's hairy ballbag was bouncing off my chin as he straddled my face, but all I could see was his ass planted two inches from my face.

I couldn't raise up without shoving my nose up his asshole, so I started flailing about in outrage, asking him what the fuck he thought he was doing. I wouldn't even have managed that if his eyes had been on me, but his smelly butt-pucker didn't seem too commanding. An instant after he saw I was awake, though, he got busy on the double. First his paw wrapped around my nuts the way a congressman goes after a cash bribe. If that hadn't been enough to shut me up, the way his shit-hole planted itself against my mouth had to.

His firm, hairy ass slipped down on both sides of my chin as his hole smeared itself across my lips, grinding and twitching away like some soulless science fiction creature from beyond. I tried to escape, but his ass was locked too tight around my face -- and the smell and texture of his gunnery sergeant shithole held me in an even firmer embrace. I'd sucked enough dick to know what a man's crotch smelled like, but assholes were virgin territory for me that summer. I marvelled at the way his pucker pursed against my lips, sometimes flaring wide to let me inside, sometimes clenching tight to demand some tongue. The musky scent of his ass was the pure taste of man, refined and distilled throughout the generations.

Suddenly, before I knew it myself, my hands had stopped flailing about and were locked around his hips, pulling his butt down even harder onto my face. My tongue gave that asshole what he wanted, slipping out of provincial priggishness into a new world of delicious delights. As I slipped the bumpy blade of my tongue up into his pink folds to taste everything he had, Gunny's hands dropped my nuts. I felt his body echo my pleasure of discovery, wriggling and shuddering with every flicking swipe of I gave his shithole. With him sitting on my head, I couldn't hear very well, but amidst the moans and throaty grunts of satisfaction, I heard him mutter something like "Fucking asslick boot." I didn't understand the "boot" reference at the time, but my transforma-tion into a young asslick, determined to give my elders the respect they deserved, was complete.

I didn't just give him respect, I ripped it out of his asshole. My tongue tore up into him, hooking inside his sphincter and grating along that marine-muscle rim until I was sure we'd both OD on pure pleasure. The way my mouth was watering, I had no trouble keeping my lips wet to coast across the tender suburbs of his ass while my tongue went seriously to town. My hands tore his tight cheeks apart so I could get everything I needed; my chin ground hard into his perineum, anchoring his hole just where I wanted it so my face wouldn't slide along his ass-crack until I wanted it to. Once I tasted what a man had to offer, I could-n't get enough, slurping and sucking and scraping away. I lost myself in a greedy struggle to gobble up everything Gunny's grizzled ass had stored away over the years, but he didn't much notice. Within moments of my attack, he was slowly rocking back and forth on my face in the ataractic trance I would come to know so well when, years later, I set about training my own boots to lick grunt asshole.

I'd still be under Gunny even now if my untrained jaw hadn't finally locked up on me. I pulled out and let his ass massage my face while I reached up and felt for the first time what he had standing tall against his belly. The thing wasn't a dick, exactly. The shape was the same as a swollen, throbbing, uncut dick; but the size was all wrong. Dicks are six or eight inches long and narrow enough to get your fist around. This sloppy serpent was more like a python in rigor mortis that seemed to go on for fucking ever. When I finally found its mouth, I also found the source of the slime that had drizzled down his throbbing stock. While I'd been up his ass, the dick had been oozing salacious torrents slick, sweet, crystal pre-cum. I couldn't help thinking how nice his love-lube would feel as I jacked him off while I did him hard up his tasty shit-hole. After the fun I'd given the geezer, there was no way I was going to let him off with just sucking my dick. A moment later, I discovered he didn't have sucking my dick in mind, either.

When the nickle finally dropped into the depths of his subconscious and he realized my tongue had gone UA out of his ass, Gunny let out a bellow about "fucking shit-for-brains boot pussies," leaped up off my face, and had me flipped over with my legs in the air even before I could check out the freak of nature growing out of his groin. He spread my ankles wide until I was about to pop like a wishbone and then told me again at length what I waste of the milkman's cum I was. He used even more pressure on my hip-joints to help me learn out to say, with feeling, "Gunnery Sergeant Grant, Sir. Fuck me, please, Sir." I kept saying it until he was satisfied. Looking back, I suspect the grief he caused my hip sockets was the only thing that kept me from going into shock when he reamed me out.

My hole wasn't exactly virgin, but I'd never let anything approaching my eight inches up it. Gunny's marine weapon made my howitzer look like a snub-nosed .38 -- and, since he didn't bother fingering me wide to accommodate him, when that monster slammed up against my ass, I wasn't surprised he didn't get inside. I suspect he probably had a long history of problems with tight, young assholes. At any rate, he didn't bitch me out other than with an off-hand "Faggot." He did worse -- and better. His muscular hips slammed back and then crashed up against my ass, driving and twisting his impossible dick down through the ruins of my asshole and far enough up into my guts to dislodge my liver. After Gunny Grant worked his way up my hole, I knew why it's called "screwing."

The pain was indescribable so I won't bother trying. Even all these years later, the first jolt just isn't something I like to think about. Gunny didn't appear to give a shit how felt, though. He was no sooner buried shaft-deep, grating his short, silver curlies where my asshole had been, than he was on his way out again, leaving a worse vacuum behind. Within thirty seconds or so, he had found his cadence and was stroking away as though he'd always been up my ass. Fortunately, not long after, the red waves of agony that washed through my soul diffused into a golden glow of cosmic acceptance. The tidal forces inside my guts answered the rise and fall of his marine mass and soon relearned the ancient rhythm of the rut.

I tried to bear down along his rampaging shaft -- partly because I wanted to salvage some remnant of an asshole, but mainly for the feel of my searing ass slipping along his love-lubed shank. I almost never ooze pre-cum myself; call it a failing. When I find a man who does, though, he always reminds me of Gunny Grant. I swear the guy could fill buckets. I guess maybe he was always just horny; I know every time I saw his dick over the next three years, it was awash in joint-juice. I like to think that was because I was around then, but I like to fool myself, too.

The more I bore around his reaming pole, the harder and faster he slammed into my ass. My guts were numb, but even through the shock I could feel his shaft grating across my prostate until I knew I had to piss or shoot or something. His swollen dickhead somehow found a home in the very farthest reaches of my shit-chute and burrowed bone there about twice a second. How he kept up that light-speed pace given his length and the tightness my ass, I have no clue. My job was just to be there -- to hold on and take everything he slammed my way. I took plenty.

As he slowly increased the fuck-friction up my ass to blast- furnace levels, I watched him work -- and admired. My feet had locked into the small of his back; my hands were on station on his butt, polishing his powerful gluts as they clenched and flexed while he fucked me hard up the ass. My fingers slipped deeper into his crack with every thrust until every back-stroke shoved his shithole up against my fuck-fingers. My spit was still slick along his hairy crack so I slipped and slid over his hole until he needed me up his ass the way he needed to be up mine. Locked tail-to-tail, we bounced about on his pool deck more like one of those mechanical dogs bobbing up and down in the back window of a car than anything human.

The shock of his entry had been so fierce that I couldn't even scream. Once he was stroking pole, though, I felt a low, almost subsonic moan rise from my soul and seep out across the world. My long, animal yowls were punctuated by an involuntary grunt every time I was force-fed more marine meat. The dick in charge only grunting a little, not with my forced, soul-felt fervor; but with little nasal grunts of satisfaction, as though complimenting himself on a job well done. Between us, though, we were making a considerable racket even aside from the sweaty SLAP of his hips slamming into my ass. While one remote corner of my consciousness was glad my parents were working, another wondered what the people on the other side of Gunny Grant's must think if he entertained often around his pool. Something told me he didn't give a shit what anybody thought. From the look in his eyes, I was sure that if any herald of virtue showed up to complain about what today would be called "family values," he'd just fuck him hard up the ass, too.

Gunny's eyes squinted slightly at me as he worked, boring into my eyes as hard as into my ass -- almost as though to gauge my limits and keep my butt always on the boundary of a breakdown. Those bright blue eyes burned with a determination at once terrifying and reassuring. Gunny Grant got what he wanted, but somehow that was all right -- it was the way the world should work. The faint Mona-Lisa on his mouth was the only indication he was enjoying himself.

What I remember most, though, was the uncanny sense of being enveloped by the perfect male animal. His hard muscles were unyielding, doing with my body what they knew needed to be done. His wrestler's neck and broad shoulders were almost motionless above me as he, resting on his elbows, kept his piston pumping like Parnassus with one powerful pëan to manhood after another shoved up my ass. His muscles were everywhere -- in the broad sweep of his shoulders and pecs, the bulge of his biceps, and even the strong grip he had on the nape of my neck so he wouldn't fuck me forward out of his monster reach. His chest especially fascinated me, covered as it was in a thick thatch of grey hair so dense that one nipple was lost temporarily from sight. Only the tit with the arrow through the middle stood tall above the fray. It was some distance below, but I managed to twist my body enough to reach him with my lips. I slipped my tongue across to wet them and tasted his asshole again.

When I sliced my tongue across the tip of his tit, his asshole clenched up tighter around my fingers, telling me I was on the right track. I slipped around his nipple, trying to sort flesh from fur, and finally knew the best way to get his attention would be to eat his arrow. It was almost an inch long, so I had no trouble wrapping my lips around it and tugging upward, tenderly, worshipfully at first but then with a fierce fury bred deep up my ass. I strained his tender tit to the breaking point, pulling and tugging his tender tissues until one shudder after another rippled through the firm bedrock of his marine body.

The grip on my neck grew suddenly more desperate as the cock-cadence up my butt pounded from canter to gallop to run. The golden glow his dick had taught my ass now flamed out of control until I felt like a Boy Scout's kindling. The harder I tugged at his tit, the harder he used me for his whore. He fucked me loose from his golden arrow, but it was too late by then. I knew I was going to shoot any second and feared he would.

My face slipped up tight into his armpit, snuggling deep to enjoy the font of his sweaty man-smell as I blew my first load in days. I'd kept my hands on and up his ass, but the torment he was giving my prostate was too much for man or boy to bear. The moment I wrapped my lips around the acrid, grey pit-fur that smelled like an antique jockstrap collection, I felt my balls contract and blow my load. It splashed up between our rutting bodies, coating Gunny's grey chest with thick splotches of pearly white. I held on and let the waves of agonecstasy buffet me about, forever insensible. I know my teeth locked tight around his hair, because I pulled some out by the roots before I was done. I know my fingers stretched his hole wide and tight, because that was what finally sent his dick into terminal overload, gushing his load of jarhead jism up my ass until I was even swamped with enough of his creamy Corps spooge to spume out the fire in the guts. Mostly, though, I know we convulsed about on the deck like a lab experiment involving kittens and electricity run horribly amok. We torqued this way and twisted that -- and then found a third way to twitch and wriggle as our bodies satisfied themselves, each with the other.

I saw a one quick flutter of satisfaction cross Gunny's face before his eyes hardened again. No, I said to myself, I wasn't going to be cuddled and praised for having the tightest ass he'd ever done. We both knew he had busted a bigger, better nut up my ass than he'd had in weeks -- maybe since he fucking retired and left all those firm, young marine assholes to do without -- but he wasn't about to tell me how good I was. To him, I was just a "cum-stain faggot shitbird" piece of ass to be reamed and demeaned before he kicked my ravage butt out in the street as damaged goods. I didn't understand it at the time, but, somehow, his approach suited me just fine. For the rest of the afternoon, he went through his well-tested catalog of dirty tricks -- starting with making me suck my load, now turning all runny in the summer heat, from his silver chest pelt before he put me over his knee and paddled my ass for shooting off without permission. To this day, I don't think my dick had ever been as hard as it was pressed into his thighs as he spanked me good.

When I limped home that evening, leaving him sipping beers by the pool in what must have been a much better mood than he let on, I knew I'd be back for more the next day and the next. He put me through my paces all that summer. By August, I knew I had to sign up for ROTC. If a has-been, gunnery sergeant could be such a fucking psycho, I couldn't feature the fun a grunt officer could have.

I've had it, too. Sometimes over the years my NCOs got pissed off because I did so much of the disciplining the men myself, but the boots were young and able to take it from both ends. Besides, in the early days when I was a Second Lieutenant and the Gunnys or First Shirts were very good, I'd let them help keep me in training. Over the years, that happened less and less as the wrinkles set in and my own hair sprouted in unexpected places and turned silver. The senior NCOs steer clear of me now, but they keep referring gorgeous young grunts with attitude problems to my attention. I suppose they want to keep me busy with the young meat so I won't work them over. A good NCO knows his commanding officer.

ffffffffffffffffffffffffffffffffffff

Burton snapped me off memory lane with his tongue tickling the sole of my left foot. He'd probably been licking my sweaty feet for half an hour; but when marines get an order, they follow the fucker whether the colonel's paying attention or not. The beautiful boot obviously needed a reward so I decided to bring his immediate supervisor into the picture. I kicked Burton's ass off the bed with a, "Bitch, get on the horn and get Sergeant Stewart over here on the double -- and tell him to bring some chocolate syrup if he knows what's good for him."

As Burton rushed to my desk to `phone his sergeant and I admired the tight young bubble-but I was about to ream while I waited for Stewart to join us, I ran through the other possibilities for the evening in my mind -- and thought for the thousandth time that day how training and disciplining fresh-faced, tight-assed, cum-clogged farm-boys for the United States Marine Corps was the best fucking life a man could have.

NOT-SO-INNOCENTS ABROAD

Most people in the West know Sri Lanka from newspaper stories about the current trouble with Tamil bombers. Science fiction readers usually think of the stories of Arthur C. Clarke, who has lived there for years and uses the place as the setting for some of his best novels. When I look back on my two weeks in Sri Lanka, though, I just think of Butch.

That's not his name, of course, but I have a western prejudice against memorizing South Asian names longer than my dick. To be fair, since he never wrote his name out for me, I can't say I've measured Butch's name against my nine and a half thick American inches, but I took his measure in plenty of other, more important ways. After he came up to my room, I did ask his name and after he'd finally finished pronouncing the sucker, I decided that Butch would have to do.

I'd checked into the Mount Lavinia Hotel just outside Colombo because it seemed a happy compromise between the big city and the beach. Sri Lanka has some dynamite beaches in the South and East, but these days I saw no reason to risk the dynamite just to work on my tan. The Mount Lavinia was only about thirty minutes away from The Fort (downtown Colombo) but had a fine beach of its own where one could sit watching the Indian Ocean waves roll up as lads fetched you cool drinks from the bar. Butch was probably one of the beach squad too, but I first noticed him at dinner.

If you've never travelled in Asia, you have no idea what "service" can mean. The hotel and its restaurant are left over from the Raj -- all white columns and plush red carpeting. Most nights, the restaurant had half a dozen customers at a time -- and at least 30 waiters. Unlike their colleagues in the West, these guys wait -- next to your table. If you want something, there isn't any "catching the waiter's eye"; all you have to do is look up and they are ready to fight over the honor of bringing you whatever you crave.

I looked up plenty the first couple days I was at Mount Lavinia.

Rick Jackson USM

Asians don't generally inflate my crank, but something about Butch did -- probably because he's so different from the studly type I usually do. Sri Lankans are generally small; Butch only stood about 4'10" high in his white shirt and stretch black pants. He was small-boned to boot, but what there was of him was perfectly formed in a foxy sort of chocolate brown that made me wonder how sweet his cream would be. Since I knew little of the mores of the country, though, wonder was all I did -- at first.

My fourth night in the hotel, I called down to room service for some ice. Butch knocked on my door about two minutes later with ice in a bucket and a fire in his basket. I was almost ready for bed (which turned out to be good planning on my part) so I was wearing nothing but an old pair of beach shorts I bum around in. I didn't know much about the ins and outs of gay life in Sri Lanka, but one didn't have to be Nostradamus or Margaret Meade to read the looks I got as Butch put the huge silver ice bucket down onto my table. His eyes were all over my chest and flat belly and the way my dick and ass filled out my shorts. I could have felt cheapened and degraded, a mere piece of meat being ogled; instead, I fumbled through a pile of the nearly worthless local currency, gave him a fistful of rupees worth about a dollar, and waited.

I wasn't surprised when he didn't take the tip and run. As I lounged back in my chair and crossed my bare leg to give him a view up my shorts, I knew where we were headed and made up my mind to enjoy the trip. He said if I wanted anything else, to call. I said I would. He gave the bed a bodeful glance and asked if I was alone. I said I was. Wasn't I married? No. I won't bother you with the rest of the fencing match that followed. Eventually, we got round to my agreeing that he could "keep me company" as long as he had "something I wanted." His dark brown eyes locked onto the crotch of my shorts and gleamed as he tentatively pulled off his shoes and slowly started unbuttoning the starched white shirt he was trapped in all day. He was at once shy and starving for dick. His side-long glances at my pole making a circus tent out of my shorts and the nervous tongue that darted across his lower lip couldn't hide the bulge in his own black stretch polyesters. He needed it bad. I hadn't been laid in nearly a week. We were made for each other.

By the time he was to his shorts, I was hard enough to ream out an oak. His briefs glared so white against his deliciously Dravidian skin that they almost hurt my eyes. He stood nervously before me, both of us getting harder by the second, until I told him to shed the shorts if he wanted to suck my dick. I leaned back in my chair, stretching out my legs to make room for him between them. Skittish as he was, he was naked and between my knees almost before I could see his six uncut inches flying towards me like a bullet.

I didn't help him with my shorts. He didn't need help. Once my meat was clear, he took a few moments to worship my bone as though it were a holy relic. His hand snaked under my balls and hefted them lightly, afraid they might go off at any moment. Young Butch had a point; they were swollen tender and heavy with a week's load, packed and ready to travel. When he eased his face down to relish the musky scent of my crotch, a hand behind his head was enough to smash his face into my nuts to warn him what he would have coming.

The slut started licking my nuts, sliding his tongue deep between my ballbag and thighs to gather up the day's scent. I felt his lips nip at my sack and knew my hand could be put to better use. I sent it off reconnoitering: across the nape of his neck and shoulders, down the cobbled road of his spine to the twin hard mounds of muscle that lay at the other end. The second my fingers touched his coccyx, a crotch-stifled groan bubbled up from his depths to proclaim himself a born bottom. He needn't have bothered. The way his perfect ass twisted beneath my touch, meating my fingers wherever they went, shivering like a country-bred colt, told me that whatever his birth certificate said, his name ought to be Butch Buttfuck.

As I slid my fuckfinger between his dusky muscles and felt the moist heat bred by a polyester day in the tropics, I knew that much as I wanted to, there was no way I was going to do him up the butt. Half the full-sized American assholes who try my dick can't manage to swallow my oversized head; those that do remember the experience for a very long time. Maybe Butch thought he wanted the same thing I did, but in his case Rick Jackson was be the dictionary illustration of too much of a good thing.

I played with his crack anyway, sliding deeper along while he smeared his face along my crotch, snuffling like a spaniel. He felt soooo good I finally had to unfinger his ass and simply collapse backward in my chair to let him work. I'd no sooner shut my eyes to enjoy his tongue-lashing when the slut got tired of licking the sweat from my balls and wanted meatier goods.

His tongue wasn't shy; it slipped up the underside of my shank, bouncing it against the coarse rust-coloured hair on my belly. I felt tickle on one side, slurp on the other, and damned fine all over. When he reached the V where the two lobes of my head parted tender company, his tongue did some ancient dance of welcome, darting deep into that canyon of cockmeat, flashing here and slashing there like a swarm of migrating gnats caught in a tornado. All the while, his lips had locked about my meat, nailing me tight against my belly so he could rape my rod at his leisure -- except leisure seemed the one lesson he hadn't learnt. His wet lips slid wider as his tongue tore along the super-sensitive underside of my log, dragging me willy-nilly from ferocious pleasure through delicious torment to blissful and abject surrender.

When I knew I had to escape his tongue or go mad, I reached down for a handful of hair, jerked him up away from my milk bone, pried my thick dick away from my belly, and shoved his cocksucking face down onto my knob. The bitch locked his lips around my cum-slit and used the stream of slick pre-cum oozing out to lube his way to satisfaction.

Like a hyena, once he had a good grip on my bone, his touch turned even more feral; but what he did to me was no laughing matter. Soft lips and his bumpy tongue slid along on a mixture of spit and pre-cum, working their way down across the hot swollen flesh of my throb. I found my hand back on his head, smearing the musk of his ass into his curly black hair as I tried to screw his face down my pole. Whether because of its size or Butch's insistence on eating my wiener with relish, he was determined to take it slow.

I must have slipped unawares into that blessed, mindless fog that comes over men when they're having their dicks sucked. I know I was gone only because I was jolted back to consciousness when his tongue-tip started prying its way into my dick-hole to work out every last drop of lube. Even then, though, his lips had somehow worked themselves behind my trigger-ridge and were twisting away like a washing machine agitator on the "heavy duty' cycle. More to the point, he was pulling upwards with them to force his tongue deeper into my dick than I thought I could handle. I'd had guys take a swipe to open up my piss-slit to give me a thrill, Butch was drilling tender red fucking bedrock. I hadn't thought I had any virgin territory left, but the catheter-like feel of his mouthorgan down my dick made me squirm like a fleet whore on payday Friday.

I wasn't sure whether my dick hurt or felt so fucking good it amounted to more or less the same thing. I grabbed his ears, trying to ease him off my dork so I could take stock of the situation; but he had my stock just where he wanted it and wasn't about to turn loose. Since I couldn't pry him off -- and wasn't really even sure I wanted to -- I did the next best thing: I shoved his cocksucking face hard down my throbbing, cum-clogged cock. His tongue unreeled out of my dick all right, but in the process I slammed my swollen meathead so far down his gullet I knew I'd have to Heimlich the fucker out. Fortunately, I was in no hurry.

Stretched out in that chair in Sri Lanka, Robert Frost's New England woods popped briefly into my head because Butch's throat was so lovely, dark, and deep. I felt his breath stirring my short curlies and stopped what little worrying I'd been doing about him and went to serious work. In reality, there wasn't much left for me to do, though. I was stuck in his craw, but Butch was somehow able still to slide his face up and down my shank while the tight, tender tissues of his throat pulsed and prodded my pride and joy.

Consciousness slipped easily away, lost in a chorus of muffled grunts from Butch and deep slow groans of contentment from me. How long I lay there with him bobbing up and down my shaft, I'll never know. One glorious sensation blended seamlessly into the next until all I knew was a soft, diffused glow of perfect contentment. Looking back, I think I felt his hands gliding up across my chest to play with the thick thatch on my chest. He may have played with my tits. Mostly, though, I just drifted through the soft, wet fog, suspended above the earth like a god.

Mortals have their limits, though. I reached mine years too soon and found myself cresting up toward consciousness at lightspeed, just seconds behind the biggest, richest, juiciest protein injection any young Sri Lankan ever had pumped down his gullet. Butch had done his groundwork well. My nuts felt like balls of molten lava spewing forth new worlds; my cum-tube was rubbed raw and ready; every nerve my dick had flared to life to explode down Butch's throat.

I woke to find both my hands locked onto his head, grinding and twisting his nose into my rough red curlies while my hips arced upward, fucking my cream up through his face until he'd been force-fed enough to outlast a Tibetan winter. I kept humping his face-hole even after I'd run dry, just because the hot, creamy feel of my own spunky backwash inside his throat felt so slick and soothing. His hands were latched in the small of my back now, anchoring him fast around my waist as though he longed never to leave. Finally, though, he discovered the load he'd choked was keeping him from breathing and, after a time, almost mournfully, he loosed his hold and eased his grinning face up and off my hard joint.

His dick was small but perfect, like a Baroque miniature. He was still panting when I pulled his crotch against my face and inhaled his dick, stripping the `skin back as I slid him in. I'm sure he'd started out clean that morning, but the day's sweat had blended with his natural musk and, perhaps, just a hint of some mid-afternoon piss to conjure a concoction worthy of any Olympian table. It was salty and sweet and tangy all at once: the taste of a natural man in love. I wanted to tease him along, but choking on my load had turned the little bastard on something fierce. My nose was no sooner buried inside his stiff pubes, his slit scraping the back of my mouth, than I felt his balls tighten against my chin and knew I was in for a Ceylonese cream sauce.

Butch was wriggling around off the end of his crank, screeching shit in some heathen language or other. He broke momentarily into English to yell "Wait," but telling me to wait was a lost cause. His nuts wouldn't listen. I did what any considerate cocksucker would have done under the circumstances: I picked up my suction, ground my face against his crotch so his unsheathed dickhead grated hither and yon across the soft back of my mouth, and reached around to shove my thumb up his ass.

From the way the little bastard carried on, you'd have thought it was the main lead from Hoover Dam. He let out a breathless yelp, started twitching like a fiend, and splashed one jet of juicy jism after another off the back of my mouth. I've done enough uncut dicks to know how untouchable they get when they fire. Nothing sends the natural man up the wall farther than having anything touch his stripped meat after he's started to splash. My dry finger had some trouble with his asshole, but sweat and the excitement of the moment overcame any tight-assed hesitation. About the time his load was rolling down across my tastebuds, I'd was doing the Jack Horner number to his ass. Butch's twin clumps of butt slammed shut on my hand like a vice. He was so light I was almost able to lift him off the floor to dangle suspended butthole and dick. The only thing that kept me from it was the way he was thrashing about. As it was, I had my hand and mouth full just keeping him from flying off fully cocked. I sucked and chugged and slurped until he had run dry and the base of my thumb was stretching him wide. Was it wide enough? No way. Still. . . .

I knew I had to give it a try. I had sucked out a generous mouthful of sweet Sri Lankan cream. As soon as Butch stopped carrying on, I eased my thumb out of his butt and my mouth off his bone so I could spit out most of his load into my palm. I'd already rubbed it around my egg-sized knob when he saw what I was thinking. The bastard ran for his pants -- not to make for the exit, but to fetch a tube of some red-coloured muck that smelt like my third-grade teacher. It was slicker than an insurance salesman, though, so Butch squeezed out another generous load to keep his company on the end of my dick.

I pulled him towards me, sat him onto my thighs, eased his feet up into the chair, and dragged his lips to mine. He wasn't sure about that at first, so I just sucked at his lower lip and neck and ear lobe. When I slid my tongue into his ear, he went ape-shit, crying out like a bat in a blender. The farther I did him up the ear, the louder he went and the more his ass squirmed about in my lap. I locked on tight, lifted him up, and eased myself against his fuckhole. I knew I wasn't about to slide right in, but even I had underestimated how hard it would be. I rammed and shoved and bucked and prodded. Finally, when all I'd managed to do was smear his jism and lube all over us both, I gave his shoulders a savage push downward at the same time I dug for his brain with my tongue.

The distraction may have helped, but every muscle in his lean body knotted up at once in pain become ferocious pleasure past endurance. His lungs struggle for air enough to scream, but nothing came. I moved my lips around to his. When the tremors eased and his face unclenched, I lost myself up close and personal in his bottomless brown eyes and eased farther in. We kept at it, slowly wobbling his butthole down my thick American dick until the straining lips of his butt were grinding along my stiff red curlies.

I'd never felt an ass so tight and probably never will again. It wasn't just the butthole that was tight, the whole length of his shit-chute nine inches in was stretched around my ramrod as hearty as a car dealer's handshake. Every beat of my blue vein's pulse seemed to echo back at me from his slick guts; every ripple of my rod reverberated throughout his being. Movement was impossible, but somehow it happened anyway.

His butt slowly shuddered its way back up my pole. After a few inches, he slammed back down against my crotch, boning his body hard. Then he started up again, his arms around my neck for balance so he could push upward with his feet. I felt his stiff little dick against my belly, prodding me hard -- but nothing like the way I was prodding him. He held himself tight against my body, hugging me close to keep the world at bay. As his butt learnt the rule of my rod, he moved more easily. Hard against me, I heard his moans of inexpressible pleasure grow until he was shouting again to the heavens, as though daring the gods to have such bliss up their butts.

Cranking up and down my shank six or seven inches at a time now, he would rise until my swollen dickhead snagged the inside of his butt and then he'd collapse his legs, letting gravity pull him back to earth, spearing my monster meat up into his liver. The feel of his ass on my legs was too much temptation. I grabbed him by the butt and stood erect, too. He was unbelievably light sliding up and down my crank. I spread my legs and held him out a bit so I could watch his face as I lifted his ass up my dick and then dropped it back down. Every time I boned him home, his eyes would crinkle shut for a moment and then open, radiant with satisfaction. For the first time now, my hips were able to use what they knew about fucking, rolling forward and back, slamming my dick up into his hole like some primitive machine.

That's really all we had become: a primitive fucking machine, two moving parts locked together, swinging back and ramming forth, a nature-powered engine of perpetual pleasure. His chest heaved as he struggled for breath; sweat streamed off both our bodies despite the air conditioning. The purr of the fans were lost to the slick SWOOSH of my bone sliding through his tight hole and blended with the echoed THUMPs of his butt crashing against my hips. Now and again, as though to prove our humanity, I'd skip a beat and grind my pubes into his asshole; sometimes I'd double-stroke him to see his mouth gape wider in surprise.

Soon, we were both little better than savages, rutting in the jungle of instinct our ancestors thought they had left behind forever. The dark mists closed in yet again and I let them swallow me, eager for the cool shadows of mental oblivion. I know we continued our drumless parody of Shiva's dance of creation; we were powerless to do otherwise. As muscle glided along muscle and bone speared flesh, time slowed to a stop, the drumless beat ended as we each pounded on to lose ourselves in the union with the other.

The cool, timeless shadows of mind-numbing night exploded without warning. I came back to find we'd somehow moved against a wall. Butch was still in my arms, my hands full of his perfect butt, his legs wrapped hard around the small of my back, his feet digging into my butt like a Derby jockey in the home stretch. My balls were clenched tight, spewing out my second load of the week -- and of the hour. I was out of control, slamming his back into the wall with every frantic stroke of my hips against his ass. Our mingled howls and animal grunts echoed off the walls to taunt our pretenses of humanity. I consciously tried to ease up, but my pile- driving hips were governed by a higher power than the mere mortal mind. After a supreme struggle, I was finally able to pull him closer against me the way a mother would clutch her child in times of crisis -- and so we fucked on until, moments or eons later, I collapsed backwards onto the bed, Butch still boned up the butt and loving life.

The slut stayed there until I carried him into the shower and made him ease off my joint so we could rinse off for another round. We had countless rounds after that, but no matter how many times we went down, it never seemed to be for the ten- count. By the time my vacation ended, I was sorry to leave, but knew I had to. My dick was rubbed raw and I needed a rest. I hadn't seen the national museum. My tan was already on the wane. I hadn't seen a single shrine or jungle ruin. During the last nine days of my stay, though, I had more room service than the rest of the hotel's guests put together. I'm sure the management figured out what was going on, but they didn't seem to give a fuck. We took care of that.

MILITARY ASSISTANCE

I was horny enough to look and admire, but I wasn't cruising. My mate of two year's standing was on maneuvers on the Big Island for a week, so I was just bored. I came down to Waikiki to get some sun, scope out the Japanese honeymooners, and generally hang out. We're both marines stationed at Kaneohe on the other side of the island, which means that we don't spend a lot of time in tourist heaven. You might think that since Uncle Sam keeps his marines in good shape, a jarhead couple would have super, bone- crunching, back-breaking, knock-down, call-home-the-cows sex. You'd be right. Most of our time off base is spent in bed doing things that I'll probably write about some day. The problem is that once I start, the thing will run to so many volumes that I won't have time to do any more research. For now, let's just say that since Trent had only been gone for two days, my lusts had not driven me amok in search of tail, but since Waikiki has plenty of great bodies stroking around more or less naked, I didn't especially mind watching what came my way, either.

About 1600, I stopped to pee in the head at the Royal Hawaiian Shopping Center. The john there is in a weird place: at the end of a long, twisting hallway used mainly to connect the retail stores with stock areas. You follow the "rest room" signs into the corridor, take a couple of 45˜ bends in the hallway and walk another hundred feet before you finally get to the crapper door. Except for the stockrooms even farther along, there isn't dick down the hallway. You feel you're at the end of the earth. I mention all this, because I had needed to tap a kidney for an hour, and I almost splashed a puddle in that endless corridor from hell.

Once I was drained, shaken, and restowed, I had to deal with the trek back to civilization. When I finally came back out into the world, I sat down onto a bench in the sunshine to watch the fountain, gawk at the passing tourists, and generally let life slide past in its easy, careless

Hawaiian way. I'd already done the beach thing that day so I was just trying to decide whether to take in a movie or head back over the Pali to our empty condo of sin.

As my mind drifted to this and that, I checked out a well- built guy wearing only a set of black boxer swim trunks. He was slowly working on the ice-cream cone he had bought at the Burger Hut at the end of the mall. Seeing people in Waikiki shops in swim gear isn't unusual, but this specimen was fine enough to make me notice plenty. He was about my size and age -- twenty-four. His sun-bleached blond hair, fried complexion, and, most of all, his red, peeling nose proved he was one of those unlucky blonds who burns rather than tans. Surfers are scarce in Waikiki because the waves are better other places, so this dude stood out all the more. His fine upper-body development, two-day's growth of beard, and general shifty look started to turn me on. I guess the best way to describe his compact, slightly disreputable sex-uality is to say the thought crossed my mind that if Clint Eastwood ever made a spaghetti surf flick, the Ice-Cream Kid would be perfect casting.

The way his long tongue flicked out to lap at the side of his cone didn't do anything to deflate my crank. I slipped into a waking fantasy about what Trent and I could do with a sex- monkey like Sam Surfer. He was in no hurry to move on so I had time to drift easily in and out of my daydream as I sat in the afternoon sun and watched him lap the smooth, creamy surface of the cone almost as though he were practic-ing up for something closer to home. Now and again he would look at the door of the Burger Hut behind me and then let his eyes wander again. At first I thought he might be trying to attract my attention and wondered whether he could possibly be as rangy and wild as he looked -- but the idea passed.

Trent and I were enough. I would turn him down even if he put the moves on me, but it would be a sacrifice I'd make Trent sick of hear-ing about. The guy's studly sleaze would have to be the stuff of great adventure. Then, smiling at my inflated ego, I decided that maybe he wasn't after me at all. Since I was a pumped jock marine, I automati-cally figured every dick I saw must want to swing my way. Perhaps he was only waiting for somebody.

In between serial fantasies involving Sam Surfer, I checked out other folks as they shambled past. Japanese honeymooners heading back to their hotel rooms laden down with macadamia nuts and sou-

venir T-shirts were the biggest draw on offer that time of day. I saw
plenty of old couples from the Middle West in ugly but matching
Hawaiian print costumes, and, now and again, a pair or trio of local
teenagers would wander past in search of a life. One family of five
passed me, arguing in some Slavic language. As I smiled at the way
the hen-pecked husband was trying to convince his wife about something, I noticed Sam Surfer's dark green eyes were focused on them,
too. Something about the eyes made my flesh crawl. The phrase "a
lean and hungry look" popped into my mind from Junior English.

Sam was a hunter. He could have been pushing drugs, but
somehow I didn't think that was it. Dopers are zoned out of reality;
Sam's beam was tight on focus. Maybe a purse-snatcher? I looked
after the woman, but both she and the man had those ubiquitous and
odious strap-on biker fanny-pack contraptions. Whatever his game
was, I knew from his eyes that I wouldn't like it. He ceased to be an
object of fantasy and became the enemy.

I moved around on my bench to look in the opposite direction
and, after a few minutes, had managed to temporarily forget him. The
Japanese held possession of the Burger Hut for a time, but their reign
came to a sudden and noisy end.

A mob of mainland tourist kids swarmed up off the beach and
filled the place with their youthful chaos, crowding the formal, once tran-
quil Japanese back into the corners. When they'd ordered, one boy
broke off from the group and headed out of the joint and down the corridor for a head call. As he passed me, I was suddenly saddened. Just
then I realized at a gut level that I'd probably never have children. I've
always liked kids and am good with them. I don't know why I'd never
really thought about dying childless; but I guess when you're 24, you
assume you have time for everything.

The kid was somewhere between 15 and adulthood. He looked
a lot like my son might have been -- the type of kid whose hair you are
driven by instinct to muss -- the typical American paperboy, the Dennis
the Menace who lives down your block and rides past on his bike on
the way to school. He had reddish-blond hair, a thousand freckles, a
cute little nose, and still a full measure the bounce and vitality that die
a slow death late in one's teens. My new fantasy made him the mirror
image of the son I would never have. I'd never teach him how to play
catch or drive. I'd never help him with his homework or take him camp-

ing to write our names in the snow. We would never conspire to slaughter Bambi's daddy, go to ball games, or char steaks outside on Sunday afternoons --and I would never live to see his children running wild on Christmas mornings. Or would I? Why not? I'll grant I'm not likely to knock Trent up, but if he and I are still together in several years, why couldn't we adopt? For that matter, we could hire somebody and take turns planting her. Then at least one of us would be the biological father. We're enough alike that if the woman had an intermediate hair color, we need never know which of us had done the deed. We could parent a whole lot better than many of the traditional breeding pairs I've seen. My thoughts wandered randomly down that path as I noticed he had turned the first bend and was gone down the hallway and out of sight -- out of my life. I don't think I had ever felt as alone as I did at that moment.

I looked over at his friends tearing the Burger Hut apart and decided to talk to Trent to see whether he'd thought about having a kid if and when we eventually left the Corps. I suppose the laws of most states are down on gay couples adopting, but priggish convention had never bothered us before. Out of the corner of my eye, I saw the black trunks disappear down the hallway and wondered why for the hundredth time they didn't have the john more centrally located. More people would use it then; but I suppose that would cost them more in paper towels and ass-wipe. How much does an up-scale shopping center probably spend on butt-wipe in a year? At a quarter a roll, it must mount up. Yeah, I thought to myself, as the gang of kids got the chow, Trent might just go for adopting. I might as well ask. Nothing ventured, nothing . . . .

Then I remembered those eyes. How long had the kid been gone by now? A minute? Three or four? I'd been daydreaming in the late afternoon sun and had lost complete track of time. His friends already had their food, but there wasn't any reason to worry. The guy had just needed to take a dump. After all, kids shit, too. It took a minute or so just to get to the head. I glanced around where Sam had been sitting. In an ashtray by his bench, part of his ice cream was forming a pool of chocolate under the uneaten cone. I stifled the urge to puke. I had to be wrong. It was 1630 of a sunny day in paradise, for chrissake. Then I remembered the Slavic family. Their eldest had been about 14 or 15.

I knew I was one sick, suspicious son of a bitch, but there was no way I could just sit there. I'd hike back down to the fucking john, check to make sure the kid was OK, and then head home. Mourning my unknown, unborn, unconceived son had put me in no mood to sit through a movie.

The bare cement walls and tiled floor seemed to stretch out forever like some nightmare by Dali. I felt like a total ass, but broke into a trot anyway. I knew I was being stupid, but sometimes you just can't help yourself. When I got to the john door, though, I heard a squeak. As I opened the door, the image of what I saw seared its way into my brain. This was nearly a year ago now, but Trent tells me I still scream in my sleep when I dream about it.

They were both in front of the middle urinal. Sam had his right hand on the kid's swim trunks, trying to get them down off the kid's legs as he tried even harder to escape from the horror's clutches. Sam's black trunks lay tossed into the corner. I couldn't see much of the boy, but I could hear him begging Sam to leave him alone. The man was bare-assed and hard, and I was close to puking again.

The boy's pleading had drowned out the sound of the door, so Sam was surprised when he felt my arm around his neck. For good measure, I'd reached down past his ass and grabbed hard onto his ball-bag. Sam dropped the kid, who landed with a hard splat on the cold blue tile. As I pulled Sam away and shoved him into the tiled wall, the kid collapsed into a heap of shuddering scrawny limbs and sobs. That moment was the closest I've ever come off the battlefield to killing another -- no, I started to say "killing another human being," but the term hardly applied. He started to say something, but I tightened my grip, paying special attention to his nuts, and banged his head into the wall as hard as I could, given my uncertain leverage.

I waited for a minute or two, hoping the boy's panic would fade. The sobs died away, but he didn't move. I told him it was over, barking louder than I'd intended. The bare, harsh cement walls of the room echoed like a tomb. I asked if he was all right, and he minutely nodded his head and sniffled. I asked if his mother or father was around, and he shook his head. Finally, I asked if he was strong enough to leave on his own. I had to hold onto Sam. Could he go back to the Burger Hut and send one of his buddies for a cop? They could `phone for one, or just go out into the street and flag one down. He needed to move, though, because my arm was already starting to twitch.

The kid started sobbing again and begged me not to tell the police. He was consumed by terror. His parents would be angry. What would his friends say? Just the idea of anyone knowing his shame was unthinkable. I tried to tell him that his parents wouldn't be angry with HIM; that he hadn't done a thing -- but I knew I was wasting my breath. He was obviously too upset to listen to logic and I was probably just making his trauma worse. Shit, I would be beyond reason. I had two choices: I could carry Sam out into the mall until I could get a copy to take the kid's story, in which case the boy would have to relive the episode again and again, but could be checked over at a hospital and would probably get counselling later on to make things easier -- OR I could send the kid on his way and hope that he could put the horror behind him on his own. To this day, I don't know whether I made the right choice in the few seconds I had to decide. I did what I hope some-body would do for my kid. I asked if Sam had "gotten inside" him; the kid shook his head. I'm no lawyer, but I suspected that because I'd arrived in time, Sam could probably hire himself a shyster slick enough to keep him out of jail. I asked the kid if he was SURE he didn't want the cops, and he almost nodded his head loose. By this time, he did seem all right, but I knew he wouldn't be later. I told him to splash some water onto his face and wring out his trunks, which had finally landed in the corner. In a few minutes he looked more or less normal except for the red in his eyes and a big bruise forming where he'd landed on his tail-bone.

Sam croaked again. I made the mistake of letting up on his throat and heard him say, "Look, stud, I saw you. There's enough for both of . . . ." I shut him up by clenching the fist with his nuts inside. I looked over to his trunks with the idea of using them as a gag and noticed they had one of those little pockets inside. I told the kid to look inside. He didn't want to get near the trunks, but after a few moments, bucked up and pulled a little wallet from the pocket. The boy had guts; maybe he would be OK after all. Inside the wallet, we found Sam's dri-ver's license, a VISA card, and some cash. His name wasn't really Sam, but since that's how I've always thought of him and since lawyers are the last refuge of the scoundrel, we'll stick with that to protect the guilty.

When the boy assured me again he was all right, I offered him a deal. I wouldn't insist on the police now if he would promise to tell his father what had happened. He said he was with his mother; his father wouldn't be flying in from Maui until that night. That was fine. Would he promise to get his father alone tonight and tell him what had happened? He thought for a minute or two, shaking his head, afraid of what would happen and, finally, looked at Sam dangling in my arm and then at me. I saw a little of the youth flow back into his eyes, but there was strength there now, too. He had begun the transition from fear and shame to anger. The tough little bastard said he would tell his father the whole story. I told him to take the driver's license and give it to his father. Sam didn't like this development at all. He bucked and tried to kick his way free, but when I tightened my grip, he didn't know whether to gurgle or scream. He compromised and shut up.

By this time the boy had rinsed out his trunks and was climbing back into them. For some reason, I flashed back to the thrill and satisfaction I had felt after I had lost my cherry. I remember pulling up my jeans after my first fuck on a beach not that far from there and how I felt grown up at last. Today was this kid's introduction to sex -- the day the kid who wasn't my son would remember for the rest of his life. He wouldn't remember a circle jerk in his teen clubhouse or a fumble with panties in the bushes. He would remember only terror and disgust and guilt. Rage tightened my ball-handling claw until the slime started to scream. I had the lad tell me once more he was OK, and that he would give his father the license. Then I told him Sam would be sorry before I turned him loose -- I promised him that much. It was time for the kid to split; I didn't want him to be there when I made good my promise. On his way to the door, I told him he was a brave kid and had handled himself like a trooper. When he finished growing up, he should join the Marines because we needed tough young men like him.

He gaped, "You're a marine?" When I said yes, nodding down with my chin at the green T-shirt with USMC partly visible above my UDTs before Sam blocked the view of my chest, the little guy's eyes widened for a second in the look of admiration and hero-worship I'd never get from Rick Junior. Then he smiled, moved towards the door, opened it, and turned around for a second to say, "Thanks, mister. My name is Joey." Then he was gone.

I was alone with Sam. The first thing I did was to loosen his balls so I could flick the lock on the door. We weren't likely to be disturbed back here, but I was taking no chances. Besides, the lock would make it harder for Sam to bolt. With my right arm -- now starting to hurt as I was then unaccustomed to strangling strangers -- I pulled Sam even closer tome and leaned forward to whisper into his right ear: "You like chicken? Did you ever make it with a man, or do you only get off inside hairless little butts like Joey's?"

He relaxed a little, thinking that I hadn't cared about the kid at all, that I just wanted to nail him myself. "Sure, I like men, too. I really wasn't going to hurt the . . . ." That was as far as he got. I needed him off guard so I could turn loose of his neck before my arm fell off. I started in with three rabbit punches to his left kidney and, at the same time, butted his head into the wall. He collapsed into a limp heap on the floor, a careless parody of little Joey's pile of shuddering flesh. The comparison was obscene enough to piss me off anew. To keep him quiet while I reconnoitered, I rolled him out of his pseudo-fetal position and forced him to lie dick-down on the cold tile floor. He was only half conscious, but I told him in the serious voice a marine uses when he means business, that if he moved an eyelash, I would kill him. To guarantee I was serious, I planted my sneaker-shod foot hard into his crotch. He puked and heaved in pain, but lay quiet, shivering in the puddle he had made.

I suspect now that if he had given me any trouble, I probably would have killed him. I had heard of the beast which lurks just below our civilized veneer, but had never appreciated what that meant until I felt my blood pumping hard through my veins and roaring in my temples. Why not off the bastard? There was no way they could identify me, and after Joey's dad got hold of the police, they probably wouldn't bother to look very hard anyway. I could easily twist the fucker's head, leave him face-down in the trash, and walk away having done the world a service. If I hadn't been sure Joey would deliver the license to old dad, and that dad would turn it over to the police, I think I might have finished Sam there to make sure other Joeys were safe. At least if the police knew about Joey, they could keep an eye on Sam. Waikiki has cops the way Africa has flies. Once the word was out, at the very least Sam would have to find somewhere else to lurk.

No, I was too civilized to scrag his ass, however much he deserved it. I was animal enough to make him sorry, though. I wanted to hurt him -- bad. I considered cutting his balls or dick off. To be technical, I thought about biting his cock off; I didn't have a knife handy.

Losing his dick would not only hurt him plenty and would continue to do so forever, but it would ensure he would never use it to fuck any other little boy. Had there been others before Joey? How many times had the marines not been on the beach? Aside from making me feel good, though, there wasn't much point. The sexual demons which drive men are armored against reason. If they weren't VD wouldn't stand a chance. If he couldn't use his dick, he would use his fingers or dildos or God knows what. My task should be to make him sorry, all right, but to do the job in a way that would show him that raping children wasn't a turn-on. I couldn't make him want to nurture children, but I could sure as shit make him understand rape. I looked around the head for something to use. There wasn't much.

The first order of business was to make sure he wouldn't feel frisky. I up-ended the trash can and used the plastic bag inside to tie his wrists together behind his back. I had to pull on his expensive-looking Seiko to keep the knot from slipping, but he wouldn't need to know the time. Once he was trussed, I let him rest while I finished exploring. Aside from the bag, I only found three other remotely useful items: a plastic bottle filled with detergent, a toilet brush, and a plunger. Before I could get creative, though, I knew I had to get to the meat of my presentation. I was going to fuck the shit out of the asshole, just to show him what it felt like. My main problem was that I wasn't feeling romantic. I never have problems getting stiff around naked men, but now I was angry and disgusted -- and about as far from turned on as I could get. He obviously fed off the terror of his victims; I've always gotten off by giving pleasure. The idea of finding satisfaction in brutalizing someone had never occurred to me before that day. If I was going to rape him, I needed to change that. I needed to be as savage and hurtful and selfish as he could be.

He was starting to come out of his daze. I emptied the detergent into a sink and filled the bottle with cold water which I squirted into his face. Although I just wanted to wake him, the traces of soap left in the bottle found their way into his eyes. He woke up hurting. I flipped him over onto his back, careless that he would find his bound wrists an uncomfortable cushion, and dragged him out of the puddled muck on the deck. Another jet of water washed away most of the puke staining his face and left him handsome again. Maybe this would be easier than I thought. After all that had happened, could I still find him physically appealing?

He squirmed around trying to get comfortable and started to bitch, asking what I was going to do to him. I told him more or less the truth: I was playing that by ear. The one though he could take to the bank was that if he pissed me off, he'd be sorry. I tossed of my T-shirt and stepped out of my UDTs, freeing my tools for the work to come. I started making my point, asking him if he was turned on. His limp dick shouted that he wasn't. He hurt; he was cold; he was uncomfortable; he was afraid. "A stud like you," I said in a low, kind tone, "must be into S&M. Otherwise you wouldn't get off hurting kids. I'm not into chicken, but I like giving a hunky dude a thrill." I lied, reverting to the classics for the second time that afternoon to prove myself a true warrior-scholar by paraphrasing Dromio's pun: "You're bound to like me more than any boy. You DO liked being reamed hard and long up the ass, I hope?"

"No way, I'm a top."

"You were, stud. You were. You were a lot of things. Now you're a bottom. No, you're not even that. You're a hole I'm going to fuck until my dick blisters, then I may just fist you to dead too raise a smirk." He started to whine, so I gave him a quick taste of my foot to the kidneys as I straddled him. I shoved my butt into his face and reached out to grab his nuts again. He got the idea and started rimming me like a protein-hungry pro. I rocked my crack along his mouth, using his nose as a stylus to guide my groove as he played sweet music. Besides making plain that he was just an object I was going to use for my pleasure, the rim-job had the added advantage of getting me hard. Much as I hated to admit it, the dude knew his stuff. That a hunk with his technique went after chicken in public crappers blew me away; but I suppose that was the point. Sexual cravings are like religions -- the other guys' always seem silly at best and harmful at worst. I just wanted to get his attention enough so he would realize raping hairless holes was not nice. As he tongued on, I almost forgot why I was there. He was good. He even managed to suck on the stiff red tussock at my asshole. He would slow now and again, and I'd pull up on his nuts to motivate him again. Soon I was putting my weight onto his face, grinding my ass into his nose, mouth, and chin. When I twisted his balls and told him to, he dug through my hole and used the flicking tip of his tongue to make me even harder. The blond beard stubble excited me almost as much as his tongue. Then at one point his tip found a surprise as fate took another hand. I discovered the need to fart and saved up to make it a good one. When his tongue reached new territory on one grind of my ass, I let fly, filling the room with a green cloud which bubbled past his tongue in the grossest possible imitation of a kiss. It was ripe enough to make me shake my head in admiration. I could only wonder what he must feel.

When I was stiff enough to ream molybdenum, I stood up and warned him the party was on. I rolled Sam over with my foot, lifted him to his feet by his bound wrists, and aimed his body at the same pisser Joey had tried to use. The pissers in this john are the kind with the usual upright part along the wall and then a water-filled trough which juts out about eighteen inches into the room. I bent him double and aimed his head at the upright. As his head hit porcelain, I put the eye of what Trent calls The Monster against his hole. My body kept him from backing up and the walls of the pisser dissuaded him from much sideways movement. I grabbed his bound arms, leaned forward to whisper into his ear, "This is what you were going to give the kid. Of course, his hole is a lot smaller than yours, so you won't have as much trouble as he would have. How does it feel?"

I pushed my thick, throbbing, unlubricated nine inches up into his guts in one swift, relentless, terrible stroke of retribution. He felt his body seemingly break in half and shrieked and moaned and begged me to let it rest a minute, but I reamed on with as much brutality as I could find. I kept one hand on the bag binding his wrists, using it as a fuck-rein. I kept the other near my dick to put it back into his hole. Almost every stroke, I'd intentionally pull my rod all the way out so his hole would have to accommodate my over-sized passion-plum twice on every stroke. Having my head pop out every time almost meant that the blood and butt- juices which would normally help lube my log had a chance to dry a little with every stroke. Once my weapon was buried to the hilt, I ground my rough, red pubic forest into the shreads of the asshole's asshole. The rhythm of thrust, grind, pull, pop, re-fuck, and thrust slowly grew as I took care to change my slant from time to time so no one part of his guts could grown numb to my abuse. When I found his prostate, I sent my bone crashing into it at full force and taught him the true meaning of marine fury..

Sam was one hurt puppy from the beginning. I don't like being fucked myself, so I knew the pain he was in. As the first shock of rip-ping muscle became a slowly spreading friction burn deep inside his guts, he bitched and begged even louder, promising he'd do anything I wanted if only I'd let his ass alone. I leaned forward and whispered, "I'd kind of like to try fucking hairless hole myself. Does chicken feel dif-ferent? Let's see." I moved my dick-pointing hand around to his bush and started thinning, pulling loose several hairs at a time. His blond pubes were too firmly anchored to come away in handfuls, but when I wrapped ten or twenty hairs around a finger and ripped, they popped up like little scallions, their white root bulbs shining. I couldn't snatch him bald because I was too busy fucking and holding, but by the time I'd reached all I could, the fur floating in the pisser was considerable. I wondered in passing whether they would grow back. I hopped not.

Inspiration was kind to me later again when, to balance myself as my hips picked up their reaming rhythm, I put my hand up to the pipes above the pisser. I found my hand resting on the flush lever and, since those messy hairs were floating around below, I flushed the fuckers. Besides, his head was crashing against the pisser on each stroke, and I thought a shampoo would be nice. When I saw how he accepted the repeated dousing without much added hysteria, I reached in and grabbed his hair, pulling his head back so his face smashed against the smooth white wall. Soon, though, the thuds of his face against white turned to red. The fierce fuckstrokes of my hips had smashed his face into the pisser so hard his nose began gushing blood down into the water. I released his hair and let the bastard slip back into his original position just about the time the virginal tightness of his hole took its toll and my balls rose to deliver their payload. The tensions of the last hour exploded through my dick and deep up into his guts as I shot out the biggest blast of cock-snot I'd felt since the first time I'd done Trent. I fucked and rammed and twisted and reamed and ground and pounded until I thought I would pass out.

Amazingly, when I came back to full consciousness, I was still hard. My head is normally super-sensitive after I've shot off, but the warmth of Sam's hole and the lubrication my juice had pumped kept me gungy and good to go. I started again from scratch. Somehow I think it was only then, when he felt me begin again after I'd already cum, that the real danger he was in dawned on him. I'd hurt him before, but in some weird way, the pain and humiliation were a turn-on. He could look back on them as fuel for jerk-off fantasies for years to come. Being drilled for load after load and hour after relentless hour, though, was another matter. He wasn't having fun anymore and tried harder than ever to escape. I moved back to his balls, but even that didn't stop him entirely. The bastard ended up doing little except smacking his head against the side of the pisser, I kept at his ass and returned to his bush with minor variations on the theme for another ten minutes or so. Then I decided we needed a change.

Lined up beside the pissers were four sinks, sunk flush into a counter placed at about thigh height to accommodate the wheelchair-bound. I pulled back on his reins and kept my dick firmly planted up his ass while I prodded him over to the counter. As he lay his torso onto the counter top, he could see himself in the mirror -- and me in total control up his ass. I pulled back on his hair again to make him look at his bloodstained face and to watch every shockwave that rippled through his body as I pounded my dry, stiff log up into his hole. Seeing him reflected in helplessness below me made me even harder. I began to wonder whether I wasn't as vicious and savage as he. My only con-solation was my rationalization that I was raping him to teach his ass a less, not just to get myself off. Looking back, I have to admit I was probably fooling myself. By this point, I was pounding on and on because I enjoyed the feeling of absolute power his domination gave me. His reflected image of abject powerlessness under the ravages of my rod's rule interrupted my musings and set me off again. If possible, I enjoyed myself even more this time because, as I got ready to shoot, I could watch the whole process reflected in the mirror and savor Sam's terror as much as my own pleasure.

When I'd pumped the bilges dry again, I opened my eyes to find him praying I was finally finished. In the real world, prayers aren't always answered, though; I wasn't nearly done with him. My hips switched back to ramming speed and slammed the hope from his eyes. No longer the hunted, now the prey, old Sam was not having a good time. He saw his humiliation and pain stretching endlessly through the night. Tears ran down his face as he begged me for mercy. The more he cringed and whined, the more the bastard just pissed me off. I kept pounding and said only -- "Like you gave little Joey?"

After he collapsed into sobs, I decided I was wasting my time. He was fucked so loose that not even The Monster's eye was keen enough to find much traction. With one hand on his wrists to keep him flat against the counter, I pulled my dick back into the light. As hope revived, Sam's head sprang up to see what I was doing.

Once again, he was disappointed. I started in with my hand. First I just slapped his ass as hard as I could until red paw-prints shone on his blond, freckled cheeks. I needed relief from the stinging in my hand so I stuck it up his ass. I went in with three fingers but, before you can say "hand- job," had my wrist stuck in his hole. I could feel the blend of blood and prime USMC-spooge lying dormant in the floor of his fuck-tunnel. Always one to clean up my messes, I scraped my fingers along inside his ass, gathering my seed. I folded the fingers tightly to pull them out again, careful not to let them drop their load. My cock nestled tight in his crack as I reached the hand around to his mouth. He was-n't interested in a high-protein snack, so I helped his mouth open by holding his nose. Seconds later, Sam was licking everything I could deliver. I made several trips up his hole, fisting bigger each time until you could have housed a family of Munchkins up his ass with room left over for a few local Rotarians.

My hand-prints had faded by the time Sam had finished his chow, so I looked around for something better to spank him with. The toilet brush was a natural. Its thick, stiff bristles tore into his tender blond cheeks as though I'd found a porcupine. Within seconds, the bristles awoke every nerve in his ass and he was howling to the heavens for pity. Agony unlike anything he'd felt since I first crashed through the gates of his virgin ass now flooded through his brain. Then the deter-gent bottle caught my eye and fancy. Since he was next to the sink anyway, I made him fill the bottle and hand it back to me. After I stuck its mouth into him, I would squeeze what water I could up his ass and then make him refill it for another round. We kept at it for a lot longer than I'd expected. Anyone with the wits of a turnip would have shit out the water as fast as I was pumping it in. I think he probably just didn't want to have the shitty water run down his legs, but he must have know that it would eventually -- and that the more water he had up his guts, the more dramatic the flood would be. When the surge happened at last, I was impressed. Tiny globs of shit, water, flecks of blood, and floating islands of feather-like cum blasted out of his butt and halfway across the room. The back of his legs looked as though he'd taken a stroll through the Okefenokee and lost his way in the process.

I should have gone on longer and been a lot more creative, but I was sick of torturing the asshole; I was sick of looking at him. There was no point in stretching the farce out any longer. If I'd made my point, fine; if I hadn't, another nine feet of dick wouldn't have done it any better. It was time for me to book, but before I left, I needed to come up with something special for a finale. I also needed to slow him down a tad since I didn't want him running wildly out into the shopping center and attracting attention until I had gone. What would be an apt finale for raping a rapist?

I pulled him off the counter and dropped him onto the floor, belly down in the pool of puke and shit. From there, I could reach the stuff strewn around the floor. The VISA card and cash Joey had dropped out of his wallet were closest at hand. I saw four twenties, a couple of tens, and several fives. Wadded into a little ball, they went up his hole with no problem at all. I almost put the VISA down, too, but figured it would be a breech delivery on the return trip and he'd have to go to the hospital to have it removed. The last thing I wanted was for him to seem the victim. I had another inspiration of something even better to take its place: his gold Seiko was next down the hole. It would be easy enough for him to pull out on his own, but the thing would take some massive cleaning before he wore it again. More importantly, every time he checked the time from that day on, he would remember his pain and humiliation. I'm not normally the creative type, but if I say so myself, that day I was on a roll. I needed wadding to hold everything in place. The swim trunks did that just fine. It took me forever to get them down his hole because they were cotton and soaked up everything in sight. There was just no way they were going to slip in easily, but that also meant he would have to do some serious shitting to get them out again. The beauty of using the trunks was that until he got them out again and cleaned them up, he was stuck in the crapper. In the end, I had to prod them down his hole with the end of the plunger. I didn't get the whole two feet of handle down his hole, but I'll bet he thought I had. I'd never played baseball with anyone's prostate before, so the experience was educational as I batted homer after homer and he writhed and squirmed about the in the muck. By the time I was finished with his stuck-up ass, I was certain he would remember the afternoon for a long, long time. More important, even though he had begun by treating the rape as a lark, I was sure he had learned how being the victim felt. I used his hair as a towel to rub the shit off my dick, stepped back into my UDTs, pulled on my T-shirt, and was history. As I stooped to free his wrists, I put my shoe atop his nuts and said, "If I ever so much as think you're cruising chicken again, I'm going to cut your dick off and shove it up you ass. If you wonder whether I'm serious, give it a try."

It was 1853 when I walked back down the passageway. I was shocked to see young Joey sitting alone outside the Burger Hut, waiting for me. I grabbed him by the arm and more or less carried him down the stairs and out onto the sidewalk: "Are you crazy? The guy's still in there. You need to get back to your hotel room."

"I just wanted to make sure you were OK. You were in there a long time. I was worried."

That did it. Now I had to do what I'd craved all afternoon. I mussed his hair and gave him a paternal pat on the head: "No problem, kid. He was a piece of cake. I don't think he'll bother anybody again soon." At least not until he gets his wardrobe out of his ass, I thought to myself. "Don't forget your promise to tell your father what happened. If the police don't know about him, he may go after other kids when I'm not around. You wouldn't want that, would you?"

He renewed his promise, this time with eager civic duty positively shining on his face. I walked him the three blocks to his hotel just to make sure he didn't have any other adventures along the way. When he got there, I could see he wanted to say something else, but couldn't find the words. I took off the green, sweat-stained T-shirt with USMC blazoned proudly across the chest and slipped it over his head. He beamed as he straightened it out until it reached about to his knees. Sure, it was years too big for him now, but I knew a kid with his pluck would grow into it. He would have to be the only kid on the block to have one -- and that gave me an idea. I asked him for address, but wouldn't tell him why. Before we parted, I asked him to tell his father at the end of their talk that I thought he was one lucky man. I mussed his hair one last time, gave him a manly slug in the shoulder, and sent him inside -- out of my life forever.

On the way back to the car, I passed a military shop and went in to see what they had. I found a flak jacket and red T- shirt with the Corps' seal in gold, both in Joey's size. They would be waiting for him when the family got back to Nebraska. Now that I had a kid to shop for, he would get presents now and again from odd parts of the world. He wasn't mine, but that wouldn't keep me from pretending a little. I had no idea how his parents would feel about his having all the junior jock grunt shit thrust upon him, but I didn't really give a fuck. I was sure he wouldn't let a few parental objections keep him from being cool. I also made up my mind to sit Trent down for a talk when he got back.

As I tossed his gear into my trunk, it occurred to me that the kid didn't even know my name. To Joey, I would always be that big, friendly marine who had helped him out. I rather liked it that way. Now I would live on, changeless, frozen forever in the amber of his memory as a friend when he needed one most. That's not as good as being a father, but it isn't a bad beginning, either.

SUMMER LOVE

Fuckflicks have the wrong idea about pool boys. We don't even call ourselves "pool boys" anymore. The job isn't anywhere as laid back as it looks in movies, and the pay stinks. The main thing porno movies fuck up, though, is the idea that we stroke from one poolside hose session to another -- all with tanned guys who have huge, uncut dicks and look like a cross between Tarzan and Hercules. For starters, in Florida, most pools are owned by chubby oldsters who about as attractive as a wisdom tooth extraction. Even when you finally find a dude you'd like to do, he almost always ends up claiming to be one of those straight guys you read about. I've had dozens of old ladies and grizzled geezers put the moves on me, but it took me three years in the business to run across Tad.

He was worth the wait. When I showed up, he was lying on a chaise with his arms draped down onto the cement and his ass in the air. Sweat glistened on his lean young body and I knew I was in some serious love. I was so stunned to finally stumble across a fuckflick-quality stud that I stood just inside the gate, holding my gear like a goof. After what was probably two or three minutes of brainlock, I finally managed to squawk "pool service." He opened an eye, gave me a look, and said, "Service away."

If I could show you a picture of that butt, you'd understand how servicing was just what I had in mind. For the next fifteen minutes or so, I tried to get on with my work -- while keeping both eyes on his body. He told me later that he was on a 30-day leave from the marines. I should have suspected. His body was like tanned marble, every bold muscle leading naturally to the next. A wrestler's neck broadened into strong shoulders. They stretched into a knotted back and firm flanks that tapered to a waist the size of politician's heart. That perfect butt of his lifted upward into the air, twin mounds of flawless manmuscle. Proclaiming the glory of man as they gleamed in the sunlight, they seemed to lack only one thing to make them perfect and complete: my stiff eight inches shoved up between them.

If possible, his face was as much a pecker pumper as his butt. Tad's blond hair was trimmed skin-close on the sides but grew out into a lavish sun-bleached, blond topknot. His brows were darker, almost chestnut, and grew together across the top of his pug nose for form a single, powerful, gut- clutching focus to offset the lower part of his face: a jaw was so chiseled it belonged in a Saturday-morning cartoon. Later, I saw his cat-green eyes and gleaming smile, but I'd long since seen enough to know I would try to do him. I thought of one line after another until I chose the middle course between the insecurity I was feeling and the cockiness someone like him would expect: "Do you mind if I get comfortable?"

He opened one eye again and looked at my t-shirt and shorts, already distended by my thick dick on the rise. Giving his head a shake to keep sweat from dripping into his eye, he said, "Do what you want," and dropped back into his sun- struck daze.

If he only knew. He was obviously too young to own a house like this; but since he was bare-assed, I figured his parents were working or dead or something. I was naked in a flash and spent the next several minutes trying to do my job with my dick throbbing against my belly and my eyes raping his ass. The bastard didn't give me a second thought. I might as well have been a tree. Finally, I had had enough. I was going to make a move and if he didn't like it, he could clean his own goddamned pool. I eased over to his chaise for a close-up look, hoping he might come to. His butt wasn't the kind of thing you could just look at.

My hands brushed lightly along the crack in his ass -- just above the skin so I could gather the beads of sweat that lived there. My fingers lifted to my mouth so I could lick them clean of the salty sweat off his ass. He tasted like pure man. On the next pass, I eased a fraction of an inch lower, caressing his skin like a fly skidding across the shadow of an impure thought. I slowly added more pressure until I was firmly sliding along the sweat-slicked groove of his butt. My palm caressed his ass; my fuckfinger found his hole and felt it quiver in welcome. His pink pucker nibbled at my finger like a colt on a winter's morning. I held his hard ass for a moment and knew that wasn't enough.

The angle was tricky, but I was just able to straddle the chaise and get my face up his butt. I suppose I must have looked like an idiot, but I was too far gone to care. Bracing my hands on the chaise, I prodded at his butt with my nose and slipped deeper until I had pried apart his muscles and was face to face with his eager fuckhole. My tongue slurped up the sweat out of the long trench leading up from his nuts to his shithole. I felt it quiver again as my hungry mouthorgan began darting and dancing around it, only now and again slithering near enough to make it jump. As my raids down his butthole grew more frequent, I locked my lips around his manhole and began to lightly suck. My head kneaded his muscle the way my tastebuds needed the flavor of his sweat and the savor of his manmusk. The harder I sucked and slurped and drilled his butt, the more ravenous I was. His ass was like some fatal narcotic, easy to use but impossible to give up. Soon I was smearing his ass into my face, moaning like the original whore of creation and loving every slutty second of it. He finally started to react, arching upward to give me better leverage and let my tongue slither deeper up his shithole. His hard muscles flexed tight against my face, trapping me where I wanted to be -- forever up his ass.

After forever, his moans were louder than mine and I heard his deep voice through the cascade of my slurps and smacks say, "You'd better be good. Go ahead and do it."

I knew what It was and I was ready -- but I wanted to do him on my terms: face to face with me locking into his eyes as I slammed everything I had up into his guts. Some passing god gave me the strength to pull my face out of his butt and stand up. I told him to turn over so I could see what, if anything, he had. When he flipped over, I knew the guy had enough raw sexuality to boil beryllium. Aside from those delicious green eyes and his goofy marine smile, he had a thick dark-blond mat of hair that covered his pecs and led down across a flat, hard belly to find his crotch. His dick was almost as long as mine -- but even thicker! The fucker lay pulsing and pounding against his belly fur, waiting, hard and inevitable as a tax collector. Passion-pointed tits poked through the fur, begging for my fingers to twist and torment them into a good time. I slid my palms down to cup his pecs and felt how much he needed what I had to give. My fingers traced along his flanks and felt his body quiver like a stallion's. Every particle of my slutty being needed to suck his dick and tits and go back to lick his butthole until it bled. Then I would do him up the ass. His perfect male body shone like some holy relic; by worshipping him, I would be worshipping life and manhood and even my own nature. Long before I knew he was a marine, something unspoken told me he was no seeker of adoration. He wanted to be used and abused. He had lain naked before me, hoping I would hump him hard to satisfy my vilest animal pleasures.

I moved up until my balls dangled in his face and didn't have to tell him what to do. His mouth inhaled my cum-clogged nuts and pulled at them so hard my lizard slammed down against his forehead. His tongue and lips and jaw all seemed to surround me, sucking my cum-pods ever deeper into his face so he could give me marine-quality licking. The sharp edge of his teeth closing around my nuts sent a delicious shiver of danger shooting up along my spine; when his mouth opened enough to slide his tongue up the back of my nuts toward my asshole, I didn't wait for more of a clue. My balls popped out of his face and flopped down into his hair as I raised up to reposition my shithole over his lips. I slid down to find his tongue already out and darting up to lick my butt. I reached back to pull my firm cheeks out of the way for him and skidded my asshole between his chin and nose like a dog on a carpet. His tongue followed along, digging up my ass, twisting and turning as he went. I put my hands back on his chest and just sat on his face while he did the work. An a universe where a lifetime was restricted to one sensation, I think I would choose the delicious soul-numbing torment of his mouth up my butt, finding every itch within me and scratching it away into oblivion. As I rocked back and forth on his face in the sunlight, I think I knew complete bliss for the first time in my life.

As the afternoon aged and I felt sweat pouring off my chest and belly and down into Tad's face, I knew it was time to give the ass-lick what he deserved. I was off him and had his feet spread wide before he could lick me from his chops. As I put my eight inches of need against his shithole, I leaned over his face and lost myself in his eyes. Then with no lube but the day's sweat to slick my dick, I was inside him -- where I belonged. His face contorted as I did him -- first into a mask of pain, then of unhurried, careless contentment. By the time I had ricocheted off his prostate to slide my crankshaft along the slick, cock-hungry tissues of his guts and slam my swollen dickhead deep up into his marine innards; his eyes had opened with a clear, green sparkle that loved life. When I felt my balls slam hard against his ass, I took a moment to scrape my cum-slit along the blind end of his heaving, twitching shit-chute and grind my stiff red pubes into the ruins of his asshole.

His butt awoke from its long, yearning sleep. His sphincters gripped the base of my bone the way a drowning man clutches at a life-saver. The grasping heaves of entry soon gave way to a knowing, sin-uous series of wave upon wave as his craving, talented fucktunnel slipped and slid along my joint, coaxing my cock to swell even larger, begging me to bore even deeper into his most private, most delightful secrets. Tad's hands clutched at my back and shoulders; his heels dug into my butt, as though he were trying to cram me completely up his ass. His moans and the feel of his slick flesh around mine and the sun on our naked, rutting bodies made me wish the moment would never end; but I had hole to ream. When I jerked back hard for the first time, pulling my hips toward the sun until my swollen trigger-ridge caught on the inside of his straining shithole, I sensed his guts follow my dick as they slammed shut in the vacuum. My own ass crashed back down like a pile driver, slamming my raptorial ramrod through the gates of his soul and jarring our bodies together like elks at rut. The webbing of his chaise stretched tight, sending Tad's butt towards the ground, only to snap up at me again, a frenzied slingshot-driven fucking machine. His butt bounced up, pushing my dickhead with it, until he ran out of power. My lizard kept leaping, though, until its head was once again trapped by Tad's hungry marine butt. Then my ass knifed deep again and start-ed the whole fucking process over. Every brutal thrust and glorious grind of my dick up his butt ripped a soul-felt grunt of impact and moan of pleasure from Tad's parted vulpine lips. I heard myself talking dirty as I did him, but my mind wasn't really on chit-chat. In fact, my mind wasn't much of anywhere. I had shut down my top head was using my lower one for more important things than thinking. Tad's hard butt had stripped away the civilized veneer; now I was a jungle savage, acting on instinct alone as the primordial mists of conquest and lust blinded me to all the world except his slick, hard guts. I half remember holding tight onto the chaise frame as I used it like a trampoline, nailing Tad's ass down with Olympic-quality precision and feeling his hard, sweat-stained body fly back up to meat my dick. Some corner of my soul recorded the sound of our moans and the wet SMACK of wet flesh against flesh as I nailed his ass. Mostly, though, my world was filled with the dark fire in my dick as I drilled ever deeper down Tad's shithole and time slid slowly to a stop.

An eternity later, the blackness shattered into white-hot shards of blinding light that cut the mists from my mind and made my heads explode. I came to consciousness to feel the searing plasma gushing up from my nuts to cool a frenzied fire of fuck-friction up Tad's ass. Every thrust of my thick tool up his butt brought more creamy relief until his ass was overflowing with the milk of manly kindness and my balls and thighs were frothy with the blend of my own jism and our mingled sweat. Long after I was pumped dry, I kept slamming home where I belonged, unwilling to let the moment end. His eyes were open now, as full of satisfaction as his ass was full of spunk. Tad's hands lay strong and tight in the small of my back, pulling me hard against him while he grinned that foxy marine grin of his as I used his body for our pleasure. At last, I pulled my hard hose out of his ass, knowing that I'd be back soon. While he licked my crotch clean, I lapped at his balls and soon sank my face back up his butt. When all I could suck out of his shithole was my own spit, I swallowed his dick and sucked like a slut until I felt his hardy body convulse. I pried my face up off his flailing crankshaft and caught a mouthful of the sweetest, thickest jism a young man could dream of. His hips kept slamming upwards into my face as he screamed and swore and tore at my hair with his fingers. When I felt his flow slacken, I shoved three fingers up his butt and spread them wide and he erupted again. I chugged like a sailor trapped in a brewery, but even I couldn't keep up with him. I let his dick slam back down against his furry belly and tried to lick him clean as his firehose run amok made my job impossible. I got dark blond belly fur stuck between my teeth and probably gained a pound from all the high-calorie man-cream I lapped up, but I wasn't much worried. I knew that before the afternoon was over, I'd work it off. By the time Tad's leave was over, I felt as though I'd been through boot camp myself. That's why I'm not worried about the future. I've given up the pool trade and leave for basic training next week. After learning from Tad how the Marine Corps builds men, I be a fool to spend my life just hosing pools.

THE PLACE TO DIE
by Mick Jackson, Private Investigator

In the eighteen months since I'd moved my office down to West Hollywood, I made do without a vacation. When you're the only private dick in the office, you can't afford to be out of town. You may go months without getting anything but routine divorce tails or missing husband jobs, but just try spending the day at the beach and you'll come back to your answering machine to find you've missed case -- and fee -- of a lifetime. I'm not kicking too much, understand. Since I moved to West Hollywood, I've had my share of entertaining cases and have met some very colorful characters. Still, I was plenty glad to hear about Jean-Pierre's pesky murder problem and the working vacation that went with it.

Private dicks need to know a little about everything, but even I had only heard vague rumors about La Place. That was the way Jean-Pierre liked it. He and his partners craved anonymity the way a marine sergeant craves a sailor gang- bang. I sat back in my chair that July Tuesday afternoon and let him fill me in. La Place was part Club Med, part health spa, part whorehouse, and part nudist camp stuck out in the Nevada desert about 45 minutes from Las Vegas. Jean-Pierre had a 5% share in the resort, but the big money came from a Franco-German syndicate. Jean-Pierre's major role as manager was to keep his rich guests happy -- and to keep what went on at the resort away from the outside world -- especially from the press. Most of the guests were either rich Europeans tired of the paparazzi at Nice and Cannes or rich American dowagers interested in spending their husbands' legacies on a good time. The last thing La Place needed was the supermarket tabloids getting wind of murder among the rich and idle.

Franco Montini was the name of awkward corpse Jean-Pierre had on his hands. He had been a "waiter" at La Place. The morning cleaning crew found Franco, extremely dead, on a bench in the weightroom with a metal necktie across his throat and a very unpleasant expression on his face. Everyone assumed he had been lifting without a spotter, missed the rack, and accidentally dropped the barbell with its 180 pounds of weights onto his neck. The bench he was lying on was padded metal so it held up pretty well; Franco's throat wasn't so lucky. After trying for several hours to figure out some other ploy, the resort reluctantly called the coroner out to write a death certificate. He took one look at the tidy way the bar was balanced across what had been Franco's throat and called the county sheriff. It was possible that the bar could have dropped so perfectly across his neck to stay balanced in the ruins, but nobody with any sense really believed that story. When the cops dusted the bar for prints, they were sure it was murder. The bar was clean: not even Franco's prints were on it.

Jean-Pierre had sucked enough figurative dick that the sheriff was already walking softly on this one. Vegas and La Place had several things in common, but one of them stood out: they lived off money. Neither wanted the kind of publicity a messy murder in a wicked jet-set playground would guarantee. The sheriff sniffed around, interviewed those close to Franco, and drove back to Vegas to start running background checks with the FBI and INTERPOL. Jean-Pierre knew that unless the murderer turned up soon, the sheriff would have to start rooting around into La Place's nasty secrets -- then the word was sure to leak out. Once the tabloids got wind of the story, Jean-Pierre would be lucky to find a job as a substitute clerk in an Arkansas trailer park. A very satisfied former client of mine from my days up in the Bay Area happened to be at the resort over the weekend and suggested Jean-Pierre fly down to LA to hire me and solve all his problems.

The staff were mostly French, Spanish, Italian, and Greek. The owners found dealing with fellow Europeans to be less expensive. Besides, rich American dowagers feel they're getting more for their money if they are waited on hand and foot by dark-eyed, young Mediterranean types with continental names and exotic accents. From the way he was pussy-footing around, I knew La Place was special. Jean-Pierre blushed and outlined how very understanding their staff was. If a guest took a special liking to a waitress or golf pro, to a bell-boy or a gardener, he could easily arrange for the employee to be released from his usual duties for as long as the guest wished. Of course, the resort added a discrete -- but very large -- fee onto the bill.

The employee involved received only about a third of this fee in addition to his regular salary, but no one ever complained. Guests who received special attention almost always lavished gifts upon their companions. The relationships sometimes even led to marriage -- and occasionally even to romance. Many a lonely Connecticut widow had checked into La Place one week and had checked out the next with a new husband who was willing to give up his profession as a poolboy to devote himself full time to spending his bride's money. Straight European men generally left their companions behind when they flew home, but it wasn't unusual to find lasting male relationships formed in the bedrooms of La Place.

Jean-Pierre said the county sheriff had seemed most interested in Franco's friends. I interrupted the story long enough to note that 90% of murders are committed by family and friends. He fervently hoped so. If one of the staff had killed Franco, the management could throw his ass to the wolves without attracting much publicity. If some German industrialist or French count had put the iron into Franco's spine, inquiring minds would want to know all about it.

Franco had shared a large apartment on the grounds with another waiter, a lifeguard, and a bellhop. The waiter was named Juan, a 20-year-old young man from Barcelona everyone seemed to like. The lifeguard was 24, named Dieter, and from Kiel. The bellhop was a 19-year-old Greek everyone called Mikos because pronouncing his real name was too much work. Dieter wasn't as close to Franco as the other two. Then again, when I met him I was surprised he was ever close to anyone. The boys were so popular it was unusual to have more than two of them sleeping in the apartment at a time. When Franco wasn't being of service to a guest, he was also "seeing" a Greek maid named Elena. In fact, he had seen her so much that she was rumored to be having his baby. The sheriff had talked to each of them, but apparently hadn't gotten much.

About all Jean-Pierre knew about the "accident," as he kept calling it, was that it must have happened about 2 A.M. the previous Sunday night. Juan and a "guest" had heard loud words and laughter as they were heading into the steam room at about 2. Juan thought the voice was Franco's and that he sounded at first angry and then amused. The kid also said, though, that he was too busy to pay much attention. By the time Juan and the 52-year-old New Jersey trucking tycoon were finished with the steam and came out to hose off, all was quiet out in the adjoining gym. They scampered back to their bed in the tycoon's room and kept on trucking until past dawn. The sheriff had verified Juan's alibi, so he seemed a good place for me to begin.

Jean-Pierre suggested I register at the resort undercover and nose around. He didn't even ask what my fees were, so I jacked them up for his benefit: $500 a day plus expenses. The bastard didn't even blink. I should have asked double that. I wasn't sure about the under-cover angle, though, so we agreed to play the situation by ear. I booked myself onto a Vegas shuttle that left the next morning and flew off to exotic Vegas for my working vacation. When I got into the resort's limo at the airport, I was even sorrier I'd been so modest in naming my fee. The resort limo was the size of my apartment and furnished like a cross between the Arabian Nights and the Sharper Image catalog. My only fellow passenger was an aged overweight woman who dressed like a whore and smelled like a Chanel experiment gone wrong. As we picked up speed and headed out into the desert, I lay back to work on a chilled Foster's lager and my battle plan.

A realization began gnawing at me as I checked in at the desk, but by the time I had looked around my room, I was sure the gods had made a mistake somewhere: I should have been born rich. Here was the life I was meant for. When I went to the window and looked down at the pool and the lawns and tennis courts beyond, I got an eye full of more than landscaping. Jean-Pierre had told me the outdoor athletic facilities were clothing optional, but he hadn't prepared me for La Place. The staff were trolling for guests with their long dicks and bronzed tits swinging in the sun. I'm no expert on what makes women sexy, but I assume the babes inflated straight crank the way the guys inflated mine. The guests, on the other hand, were unwise to have taken the clothing optional route. Bellies and butts sagged everywhere you looked, exposing more nasty, wrinkled flesh than you'd find on a Kenyan elephant reserve. Something told me the boys would be happy to see a guest who wasn't quite 27, had kept his Navy SEAL muscles where they belonged, and had eight thick inches to play with. Since even my whoring expenses were on the house, I was determined to get to the bottom of everything in sight.

I spent an hour getting the lay of the land and decided it was time to give the hired help a thrill. I got naked and lay out by the pool for half an hour or so, swam some slow laps to show off my form -- and my stroke -- and, belatedly, made up my mind to buy some sunscreen. About the time I realized I was frying my ass, it occurred to me I should see what the sheriff had to say before his office closed. Jean- Pierre had lent me a car for the duration, so I dressed and was coasting into town before you could say "desert adventure."

Life in Vegas had made Doug Slater easy-going. The average cop puts a private dick somewhere between a jackal and a hyena on the evolutionary ladder. Slater may not have wanted me to marry his sister, but he didn't get that "I've just stepped in dog-shit" look when I told him who I was. He gave me a smile and firm handshake, kicked out a chair from me to sit in, and welcomed me to town. His position was pretty clear: La Place was trouble. Eventually he had to do some real digging, but if the resort could hire some private goon to solve his problem for him, so much the better. He had no clue yet who the perp was, but he'd rather have me turn some jet-set bad-guy than him. When I asked if I could see the coroner's report, he did everything but suck my dick. He gave me copies the report, the crime scene report and photos, investigation notes, and everything else short of his personal blackjack system. My major find was that young Franco had been providing special service to a Mrs. Maude Malinowski, a Chicago widow apparently intent on spending her late husband's sausage fortune. Mrs. Maude checked in about two weeks before Franco's death and had been scheduled to leave later this week. After the shock of losing her "very dear boy" she went back to Chicago to mend her psychic wounds. She confessed that she didn't sleep well sharing a bed so young Franco had delivered the sausage sauce and left to work out around 1:30. She drifted off to a satisfied sleep not knowing her main meat was about to be permanently tenderized. No one witnessed her dreams, so she could have followed the dear boy down to the gym to roll 180 pounds onto his neck, but no one saw her walking about late that night, either. Maude Malinowski prowling the weightroom at 2 AM would have stood out. Besides, she had no motive. If she'd tired of Franco, all she had to do was replace him. Slater didn't much like the theory of Grandma Malinowski as a deranged weightroom murderess; somehow neither did I.

Since I didn't want to fly all the way to Chicago unless I had to, I paid special attention to the notes of Maude's interview. She had definitely decided young Franco was good news. He made her feel young (among other things) and needed. She couldn't imagine he was gone. Whatever would she do now? The one question Slater didn't ask was whether she would have ultimately asked young Franco to help her spend the sausage millions; but I got the idea if Franco had lasted out the week, he'd have been in hot-dog heaven. That guess gave me a motive Slater hadn't mentioned, but the case was young. I needed to check out the boys Franco roomed with before I jumped to any conclusions. They were all Europeans so I had to take my time and give them the kind of penetrating, in-depth survey the sheriff's department was too busy to handle. Since the night I happened across a young marine on Okinawa back in my SEAL days, I have had a serious thing about foreskins. At $500 a day, I was in no hurry to stop working over Jean-Pierre's young Eurostuds -- and that was before I saw them.

I was back at the resort in time for dinner so I asked the maitre d' to put me at one of Juan's tables. He grinned so little I got the idea others had used the same ploy before, though doubtless for less noble reasons than fighting crime. When Juan came to take my order, I almost gave it to him on the spot. His nametag said "Juan," but his face cried "Use me." He was only about 5'8", but had a Latin charm as lethal as plutonium plasma. He looked something like the Beaver's brother Wally except for his perfect nose, slightly stronger jaw, and enough curly black hair to outfit the Turkish army. I made no bones about the way I slid my eyes down his body. Well, OK, so I made one. His muscles were compact and perfectly in proportion to his frame, but Juan was obviously more into aerobics than lifting weights. About the time my eyes locked onto the crotch of his black slacks, he asked again how he could help me.

I took my time moving my eyes back up to his smile before I said, "Right now you can get me a menu. After you get off, I'd like to, too." When he brought the menu, Juan said he'd made arrangements to leave after his break.

If anyone ever kicks off and leaves you enough money to buy Nebraska, you might consider dinner at La Place. I don't usually get off on bits of French cooking arranged on a plate for $200, but then waiters don't usually look like Juan. From what little I remember, the food was good, too.

I waited for him out by the pool. Except for some loud Germans oozing their asses over stools along the outside bar, the pool area was mine. I slipped out of my clothes and stretched out in the cool desert moonlight to watch my peter pump against my belly as the dry desert wind fanned my pubes. Just the thought of what lay hidden beneath his white shirt and black slacks had me ready; when he stroked out and suggested we move to the opposite side of the pool so we would be hidden in darkness, my lizard did everything but lurch into the lambada. We found some towels piled by a caban*p 8*a and spread them out on the well manicured grass just beyond the pool.

Our grassy knoll was so dark, I couldn't see much of Juan's body at first. He knew what a young man wanted, though, and jumped right to work. My waiter started serving me in his savory continental way by lapping my ballbag, tonguing my heavy loadstones like a rock-hound in polishing class. He kept at it, snuffling and snorting, until I felt my hips instinctively rise to let him to slide lower. His face dug deeper, tonguing the dark crack in my ass while he felt me up with his hands until the Iberian ass-lick realized I wasn't going to roll over to give him a good time.

His snout snuffled back across my skinsack and up the underside of my throbbing joint. When his fingers slid beneath my pride to pry it away from my furry belly, I realized for the first time how really hard I was. I'll never know how my little Latin lover kept from breaking me off at the bone. As his wet lips slid slowly across my egg- sized dickhead, I felt the bumps on my hard knob slide along the grooves of his lips as though they were cast from the same pattern. His body snuggled against my legs and one hand played along the rust-colored mat of fur that covers my chest and belly -- but my every brain cell was busy with the tender touch of his lips sliding across my crank.

He was in no hurry. His lips circled the very tip of my dick until, his mouth filled with spit, he eased gently forward on a thick cushion of his slick fluid. Then he sucked back, drawing his spit and then his lips hard against my pulsing purple prick. His tongue drilled into my cum-slit as though to sink a foundation he could use to mark his advance and retreat across my tender tool. That tongue burrowed slightly as his lips slid farther south, widening just enough as they went to wedge me inside. My hands found his curly hair and grabbed his ears to urge him harder down my pole. It wasn't until his jaw had stretched wide enough to lock his lips behind my trigger-ridge that he turned on the suction.

His tongue had long since abandoned my jism-jet and was torquing around my tool like a Kansas twister, ripping terrible waves of delight from the exposed nerves of my bone. When the suction hit, wet slurping sounds slid out across the still blackness of night. Impossible though it was, my dickhead seemed to double in size as the blood rushed to my heads and my hips began to heave upward. My arms pushed his face down along my best asset until I'd bucked him all the way down my dork. When I felt his nose tickle my short curlies, some secret switch hidden deep inside me slipped on and my ass started bouncing up off the towel like a rivet gun, pounding my tortured dick down Juan's tight throat.

The horn-dog didn't even begin to gag as I reamed his gullet open. The tender insides of his cocksucking throat locked around my dickhead like the collapsing walls of Doom, twisting this way and that as I thrashed up and down beneath him. Some part of his body locked around my shaft to keep my throbbing trigger-ridge from sliding out. Pound and heave as I would, I knew my meat was his for the duration.

The tight pull of his cocksuction eased my load up from my aching nuts. His fingers kept busy twisting a tit and rubbing my butt-hole as though a genie was due to momentarily pop out. My hips lost their rhythm and began slamming up and down almost at random; my ballbag shrank up against my body. Juan's nose pounded into my pubes. His throat tightened. Slick, tight muscles gripped my bone and squeezed. My legs slashed out straight. The night exploded -- and I held on to that curly black head as my only constant comfort in a universe ripped apart from the inside. My guts seemed to gush up through my dick, stretching me from within as I was sucked thicker and stronger from without. For the next minute, I knew nothing but the glorious feel of tender, torturous flesh gliding across my tender dickhead and the uncanny sensation of having my guts unspool to be sucked out through the end of my dick.

When I more or less came to again, I felt Juan's chin still slapping madly at my balls while he tried to keep my bone stuck in his throat. His suction pump was still cranked up into overdrive, but I was drained dry. I lifted up on his head, partly to stop the loud slurping noise from attracting attention, partly to get a better look at the naked body hunched between my legs. I finally managed to work him up off my pole, but he gave me a wounded, hungry look that shouted betrayal. I was here to find out about him, though, not for cheap, simple sex. If I was going to get anywhere with the case, I had to start investigating.

I started on his lips. The lower one stuck out in a permanent pout, making him look a little like a young Ricky Nelson. Others have complimented me along the same lines, so we were a matched set and able to make the most of our lip action. He still smelt of food, blended now with sweat and the musky scent of my crotch and a distant hint of cut grass. My dick was still hard and, as I lay atop him to suck his lip and tongue and the tender lobe of his left ear, his cock ground into my belly. I felt him humping his ass upward, stroking his rod along my crank as his whole body shuddered in excitement. I suppose good whores always seem excited, but if Juan was faking how he felt, he deserves a fucking Oscar. My hands slipped along his flanks and locked behind his back, pulling his dick up harder than ever into my fur-clad belly while my mouth used his ear for my pleasure. My legs wrapped around his, trapping us together. I'd been around enough uncut belly-fuckers to know what he was up to. The slut was pressing his meat against my belly until his head popped out. Then he was forc-ing his bone up and out so his tight Spanish `skin would ripple along his soft dickhead. In short, the dick was using my belly to jerk himself off. What I didn't know, because I was so wrapped up in tongue- fucking his ear, was how far along he was. Just about the time I stopped sucking and blowing and drilled my darting tongue into his ear canal, my tongue work was too much for him. His body started thrashing around below me as though someone had slipped the main line from Hoover Dam up his ass. At first I thought his spastic jerking and loud yelps were a sim-ple reaction to my aural sex; but when he calmed down a little, I felt the unmistakable slickness of jism sliding between us. Fine as he was, I wasn't going to let him get away with spooging all over my belly and chest.

I grabbed a handful of black curls and shoved his face down to clean up his mess. When his right paw started to reach for the root of his trouble, I put a stop to his nasty handiwork. I had plans for that gooey dick and they didn't include his manhandling his business. The little bastard took several minutes to work his cream up out of the stiff thatch that covers my chest and belly, but he needed to be taught a les-son about picking up after himself. I was willing to wait.

That cock was worth it. When Juan had finally finished lapping up his suds, I eased him onto his back and lifted his dick for inspection. Still hard, the slut's meat was completely covered by olive-colored skin tender enough to eat. The wrinkled thrum of `skin that crowned his head was a frothy, white mess that overcame his cock and drizzled down his shaft until he looked for all the world like a rabid weasel. The jism running down his joint was still fairly stiff in the dry night air, laced through with creamy white threads of man-seed. I took my time slurping them up as I lapped my way along his lizard heading for home. When the outside of his cocksock was clean enough for company, I started on the inside.

My fist locked around his crankshaft, just behind his head and slowly eased down, pulling his beautiful `skin back along his long, rippling shaft. More and more of his secret store of jism came into view, glistening in the reflected lights from the distant bar. When his hood was stretched all the way back, nestled behind his trigger-ridge, I gave his super-tender dickhead a vicious grating stroke of my tongue. He let out a spasm that shook a few last drops of bone-cream up out of his hole to join the rest of the family. His cocksock had kept this part of his load nice and warm, thinning it to a milky consistency. Gravity seduced his frothy cream down his shaft. It was time to take steps. My lips engulfed his silken-smooth dickhead and latched tight around his member about three inches from the end. Then I started upward, stripping the last of his load upward across the throbbing veins stretched inside out along his shaft, up over his tender, musk-laden trigger-ridge, and across the smooth meat of his dickhead. Once my lips closed tight in an inside-out kiss behind his cock to swallow his jism, only the stray strands of spooge soaked away in the secret folds beneath his head needed to be ferreted out.

Dinner had been tasty, but if The Place could charge $200 a plate for mere food, the combination of Juan's jism and sweat and musk all cooked over the course of a summer's afternoon in the heat of his crotch were worth enough to bankrupt a Midas. When I had started on his dick, the slut had moaned and grunted and talked dirty to me, but I ignored him. Now that I was out of jism, the rest of his body was more interesting. I rammed his dick back into my mouth and eased his `skin back over his head so my tongue could give one last twirl around its insides, stripping away one final, glorious dessert to finish off my meal.

My tongue eased up from his pubes, sliding up to his belly button to dart and play in its solid dimple. His belly was bare and hard and shivered under my touch like a colt on a winter's morning. Once again, his body made me forget myself. I tore into him, careless and greedy and driven wild with the thrill of the rut. My tongue danced around his bare, iron-tipped nipples until they needed the firmer lessons only my teeth could teach. I slid my face upward again and buried it in Juan's right armpit so I could lick the musky stench of dried mansweat from his black curls. Our bodies were writhing together again, arms and legs intertwined like an Escher drawing.

The smell of his body drove me on, past his pits to lap at the muscles of his back. His bumpy spine led me south to the best butt I'd seen in months. Juan obviously worked out, but his ass was more than good muscles. It was a blessing of the gods. Those two mounds were clad in soft, olive skin but had hard, unyielding man-muscle at their core as they tensed and relaxed: the butt of a born bottom. I licked down his spine, and his whole body shivered like an aspen in an earthquake. His butt loomed higher and higher. I reached up to pry his ass apart with my fingers. When that asshole came into view, I slipped the last bonds of consciousness and became an animal, pure and savage in my lust. My tongue darted down the dark, dusky trench between those glorious soft-skinned cheeks, lapping at the musk that lurked there hidden away from the world. His butt was clean and tight and pulsed its hunger. Working my face up his ass wasn't easy, but I was past stopping. When I finally felt my nose clip his asshole and his whole body heave in response, I tore down with my tongue until I made hard contact. Now it was my turn to feel an electric charge shoot through me as I clawed at his hole. I had to pull his ass up into doggie position to get enough leverage to do him justice -- or to do him at all. His muscles relaxed a little and my lips were finally able to clamp around his shithole. My cocksucking tongue dove and twisted and hooked inside his manhole, eager for every glorious, wicked thrill two young men can have naked outside in the dark.

My tongue drilled deeper and harder into his ass, stretching him wider with every sinuous twist. Great dollops of my spit followed my mouthorgan down to drip into his ass as I slurped and sucked at his hard ring of party muscle. By now we both knew what was about to happen, the only question was how much longer I could delay the inevitable. His shithole was so perfect and I was so far gone that I might be there still with my head up his butt if he hadn't started whining for me to give it to him -- to use him up the ass. I didn't have any complaints about Juan's service so far, so it was time for him to have a tip.

I put that tip right against his shithole and let his tender pink lips nibble at it, sizing it up, inviting it inside to play. My hands slid upward again, across Juan's back and down again along his lean flanks. Finally, I grasped him hard under his chest, holding his shoulders tightly enough so even I couldn't fuck him off. My dick began pressing, gently at first but with more savagery with every forward, clenching thrust of my ass. My dick drove harder and faster until his outer defences gave way and I was inside his foxy little Spanish butt.

Short guys have small, tight buttholes. Juan was short, tight, and apparently determined to strangle my chicken before my cock could crow. I've had tight-assed guys clamp down hard with their sphincters; somehow Juan muscled me into a corner the whole length of his shit-chute. The sphincters were tight enough to give me a swelled head, but his slick guts flexed and pressed around all eight inches of my shaft like a hoard of IRS agents swarming about a TV preacher. I felt his prostate skid along my bone and his ass churn, pulling me ever farther down into his dick-defying depths. His butt was so fine I almost found religion myself. In the cool night air, the heat of his body trapped below me and the feel of his flesh as I snuggled closer fed the flames of my fuck-frenzy until my lips and tongue returned to his ear. His hole took all my attention, though, so I just gripped the back of his neck and held on as my private dick dug deeper into the case.

The slut was moaning every time I eased up thick dick up and grunting like a hog with adenoids on every sharp downward stroke. Once I really got to work, he sounded more like a clogged storm drain but was obviously loving every inch I had. His hands alternated between my head and ass; my butt won out as he tried to pull me completely up into his gash. Slick guts rippled and tore at my pole; his body arched at all the right moments. I was having more fun than would be legal for any dozen guys, but one thing was missing: I couldn't see my love-monkey's cute little face while I did him.

I stopped reaming his butt just long enough to grab a leg and flip him over onto his back. I felt shitchute torque around my tool like a wrung-out towel. Once he saw what was up, a slutty smile slid across his face and I wondered for a moment how I could make one murder investigation last a lifetime. His feet wrapped around my butt and spurred me to action. I pounded my dick up into his butthole like a panzer column through a gnat's nostril. I'd already opened him up, but the surge of meat mangled his manhole enough that every muscle in his hot young body seized up at once. I reached down to suck at his lower lip again until his eyes opened -- and then gave it to him again. I kept on giving it to him, harder and faster and deeper until I lost all track of space and time. My world consisted only of his eyes with their mirrored need and the glorious sensations of my dick wrapped inside his tight, slick asshole. Our bodies arched together, trapped by lust like stray dogs, hoping to make the moment last forever. Hands slithered along my back until our bodies began crashing together so hard he had to grab tight just to hang on. The SMACK THWACK of solid flesh pounding hard muscle drowned out the animal snarls and whimpers escaping both our lips, ignorant of any need but satisfaction, mindless of any law but our own pleasure. My shaft reamed his butt and his hands clawed at my back as we bucked together through the mind and into eternity.

Even eternity has a down side, though. Ours came to an explosive finale of nearly thermonuclear proportions. One minute my heads were screwed on tight; the next, I'd blown the next thing to my very soul up into his tight Spanish ass. When I came back to consciousness and felt his butt milking me like a machine and saw his cocky young grin, I knew I was going to fuck him senseless if it took the rest of the night.

It did, too. Just to show him who was in charge, as soon as I had finished pumping that load up his butt, I pulled out and picked him up off our towels of sin. I threw his cocky ass over my shoulder and started back to my room. He said something about our clothes and the management not liking nudity in the lobby, but I was determined the whole resort to know what a little whore he was. Rather, I was determined for everyone to know whose little whore he was. I suppose scoring off a whore isn't hard, but Juan was such a perfect fuck I knew it was more than work. He got even better as we took a long, messy shower and as we ate strawberries and drank champagne -- without using our hands. We finally both passed out about dawn and slept, wrapped in a very messy jumble of arms and dicks and legs until about nine.

When he licked me awake, I got serious enough to ask him some actual questions as I was humping and pumping. We soon made it a little game, me asking the question just as I slammed my bolt home. Rather than bore you with a blow by blow account of the next six hours, I'll just summarize. Juan had liked Franco, though they seldom shared secrets. Juan did get the idea his current "guest" was going to take him up to the big time, but he couldn't say why he thought that. Franco was just unusually cocky and made some remark about slipping his "bitch one hot sausage." Juan told me about the trucker -- who apparently didn't begin to measure up to me -- and that he didn't really know anything more that would help me, with the case at least. When I finally got tired of pumping information out of Juan about three, I patted his little behind and threw him and a towel out into the world. We 27- year-old private dicks need our sleep.

Unless my memory is going, too, when I was 18, I could fuck for weeks at a time. As I rolled out about dinner time, I knew I was over the hill. Juan had been fun and gorgeous and mind-numbingly glorious -- but the last thing I wanted just then was sex. My dick was dragging so low I should have looked into mineral rights. I was one hurting, over-the-hill unit.

Dieter, the lifeguard roommate, was next on my list, but I knew I needed solid food first. I'd had enough calories of liquid protein to feed Pakistan, but a steak and baked potato were next on my list. I didn't feel so bad when I got to the dining room. The maitre d' gave me a severe look and said that young Juan was having to take the evening off. By the time I'd downed the French version of meat and potatoes, I was feeling chipper enough to sneer at how frail this younger generation was. Why in my day . . . .

When I checked in the office to get a lead on where I might find Dieter now that the sun was down, I wondered what was up. The girl behind the desk made a little face and shivered, asking "Whatever would you want with him?" She gave her head a shake to clear it and suggested in a funny tone that I should try the weightroom. I saw almost at once what she meant. Dieter looked like a Nazi recruiting poster: about 6'3", blond and blue, high cheekbones, perfect nose, Superman jaw, and muscles out the ass. His body was the sort of steroid malformation folks used to think of when they heard "body-builder." He was terse, arrogant, cold, and a pain in the ass. I started in friendly enough, explaining I was looking into his roommate's murder for the resort. He kept lifting and grunting away as though I were on Mars. Finally, when he'd finished his set, he rolled his head in my direction and said he didn't care who had offed Franco. He used "pansy" and an offensive ethnic term to do the job, but I got what he meant. I also saw I wasn't going to get anywhere with him using my usual Dale Carnegie approach.

I looked at him for a second and got the overpowering urge, for the first time in my life, to use sex as a weapon. Every ounce of my being loathed everything about Dieter; the idea of pounding him to fucking tapioca was too agreeable to deny myself. Besides, I was on vacation.

I kept smiling at him for another two minutes or so and then said I'd buy his time. He got a shocked look on his face and babbled, "You mean. . . ." When I nodded, he looked down at the bulging basket in his Lyrca shorts and smiled. I gather some guys like getting it up the ass from these clowns, but I had something else in mind. It took him ten minutes to make the arrangements, but he was back with a grin. We were more or less alone in the weightroom, so I told him to drop trou.

I watched his face as he tried to have a thought. It was fierce work, but finally something registered and he said, "You want it here?" I motioned for him to strip. When he had, I circled around as though admiring my new stud and put a hand between his grotesquely muscled shoulders to push him forward against a universal weight machine. The mirror across the room reflected one emotion after another: shock, outrage, anger, shame, and, finally, that Teutonic teeth- clenching "I can stand any amount of torture" resolution war movies are so famous for. I kicked his feet apart to get his butthole down into striking position. Even before I unbuttoned my jeans, I was surprised at how hard I was. Under normal circumstances, I wouldn't have given a jerk like Dieter a second look. Some inner rage, which I then little understood and which puzzles me even more in retrospect, surged into my dick and I was ready to take all my petty frustrations out on Dieter's fuckhole.

Except for my hips and dick, I don't think I even touched his body. My hands gripped the machine he was leaning against, I put my thick, dry dick into position and went to work. In a way, Dieter wasn't even there. I was using his hole, but most of my brain was wrapped up in the porno flick reflected in the mirror across the room. The clamped jaw of outrage and determined squint in his eyes evolved to an expression unlike anything I'd ever seen. He could have stopped at any time. He wouldn't get paid for the fuck, probably, but I wasn't even sure of that. In any case, I'm sure he didn't need the money. What hurt was that I was fucking with his mind as much as his butthole. He'd rented himself out thinking I loved his body as much as he did. Now he knew I only wanted a hole to spunk off in. For a beast his size, Dieter's butt was tiny. My dick must have felt like a sequoia slamming up his shit-chute -- but he was determined to take it however loathsome it was.

Just to fuck with him some more, I played my little game again, pounding him with a question with every thrust. He found my eyes in the mirror and almost spat his answers at me. He had slept alone the night of the murder. He didn't like Franco. He didn't talk to Franco. Franco was nothing -- the implication being he was as unimportant as I was just then. By the time I'd gotten tired of being nasty, I was astounded to find my balls had been working overtime. Juan had taught them to be prepared. I hadn't spumed sperm in almost five hours and found I had a man-sized load lurking low between my legs. The first couple blasts up Dieter's butt were a surprise; but once I'd given him something to remember me by, I pulled my eight inches out, grabbing around the middle, and jetted jism all over Dieter's pumped up back and ass. I've always gotten a childish satisfaction from watching my load arc through the air, so I almost forgot what a jerk Dieter was. When I was done, though, I wiped my spunky monkey on a dry patch of Dieter's ass, buttoned up my pants, and told Dieter to let me know if he thought of anything that might help. Without another word, I walked off, leaving him leaning against the weight machine dripping my creamy white jism.

I needed to talk to Franco's sweetie Elena, but more than anything I needed rest. Since I was being paid by the day, I figured Elena could wait until morning. I had a drink or two at the bar and went upstairs to wash any hint of Dieter off my dick. After an endless night with Juan, I stretched out naked between my cool white sheets, happy to be alone in my king-sized bed. I started to watch something mindless on the room's huge television set, but was asleep before a commercial. Later, dreams and memory merged and I awoke to find the TV off and Juan's curly head resting against my chest. I turned slightly and threw a left over his body and gave his head a pat. By unspoken agreement, we drifted off to sleep again without so much as a kiss. Grateful as I'd been to have the bed to myself, I was even happier to have him share it. His simple presence was all I needed; we'd both had rockets enough for awhile. When I awoke after eleven hours of deep, satisfying sleep, I was alone again but Juan's sensuous scent lingered in my bed and made me smile.

When I was up and around, housekeeping told me where to find Elena. She didn't look especially pregnant, but then I'm no expert. Tears began to gush the moment I brought up Franco's name. When I suggested that the her baby might be the result of some extracurricular service to a guest, she stopped crying and started sharpening her talons. For the rest of our interview, she wavered back and forth between grief and indignation. One minute she was telling me how she'd kissed her beloved goodnight as he left her bed to go work out, the next she was irate the resort had hired a "cheap shyster" to harass her. The shyster gaffe told me a lot besides that Elena had seen some gangster movies and didn't understand all the English slang she'd heard. She droned on at tedious length about how I shouldn't believe gossip about Franco and ended by bemoaning her fate. If only he had stayed in her bed and slept with her that night, poor Franco would be alive today. At least her "poor orphan" would know his father loved her. I thought about telling her the difference between an orphan and a bastard, but took a close look at her claws and thought better of it. Being a private dick is a dangerous enough job that we don't go asking for trouble.

By now I was sure who had orphaned the little bastard, but when you're paid $500 a day, you don't rush to blab everything you know all at once. Besides, professionalism demanded I make sure the last roommate, young bellhop Mikos was innocent -- of murder. He sure as shit wasn't innocent of much else. I'd seen the gorgeous bastard lounging around the lobby like a tomcat in heat even before I knew who he was. Leaning against the desk or wall with his hands in his pockets, he gave one the impression that he was merely humoring the resort management until his meal ticket checked in to be bedded and wedded. When he had to tote luggage like a common bellhop, he rolled his eyes and grinned, as if to say he was willing to play along with the charade -- but only because he was a good sport. Mikos was only a year younger than Juan, but while my tight-assed Barcelona bedmate was suave and confident and knowing, Mikos was cocky. Except for his classical good looks and engaging smile, Mikos would have been a punk. As it was, he was so charming and wicked even the resort management were usually more amused at Mikos than pissed off.

Since I wasn't paying the bills, I asked Juan to arrange for Mikos to join us for a little group interrogation that night. According to my Spanish spunker, their clients had kept the lads so busy -- and so drained -- they'd never gotten around to doing the dirty together.

My dick was already belly-up when the pair arrived looking for all the world like bookends. I greeted them wearing nothing but one of the resort's fluffy terry robes with the belt tied tight across my joint to keep it from getting too greedy. After one look at the two of them, sluts with the faces of angels and bodies of gods, I suddenly knew where I was going to start. I pulled up a chair and leered while they got naked. Mikos' muscles were as fine as Juan's, but his chest was covered by soft black curls that contrasted with Juan's hard, hairless pecs. Both their thick uncut dicks were already hard and oozing pre-cum. The came towards me, probably expecting me to suck their bones dry, but I just slid my hands along their smooth thighs and cupped their heavy nuts in my hands. I squeezed slightly and felt their bodies tremble in anticipation of the fun ahead. Juan reached down and pulled the cord on my robe, releasing my lizard with a leap. I'd long since memorized every soft wrinkle of Juan's foreskin and traced every throbbing vein on his shaft, but Mikos' member was strange, wonderful, undiscovered country. I wanted the boys to put on a show for me, but Mikos was drooling dick-lube so fast I couldn't resist giving his sperm-spigot a tickle with my tongue. That tickle bred a slurp which gave birth to a frantic cocksucking session. Juan's leaky dick slapped against my face, begging for equal time and smearing his young love across my cheek.

I left my hands between their thighs, cupping both young butts in back while my mouth toyed with Mikos' meat. The lads had their hands all over me, fluffing the fur on my chest, pulling at my log, grabbing great handfuls of hair. My mind was on the floppy `skin that covered Mikos' monster. What was a kid not 5'7" doing with anything that long and thick and fine? My lips kissed his dick's before my tongue slipped between them, lunging deep into his head looking for a tongue. His tool was mute, but every inch made its feelings known clear as a clarion. Mikos' smooth, hot dickflesh bounced inside me to the beat of his racing pulse and almost escaped my mouth. His pre-cum was such good news to my tastebuds, though, that I'd have done anything to keep his hose where it belonged. My tongue slithered faster back, stripping clean his supply of dicklube and manmusk as I slipped back his `skin to leave him naked and defenceless inside my mouth. I didn't take the time to savor the little slut the way I had with Juan, but he was all set to shove his thick dick down my mouth anyway.

I wasn't ready to taste his load -- not yet. There was time enough for that later. Now that I'd had my appetizer, I was content to let the lads lead the way and show me what two professional studs could get up to. I had them turn around so I could slide my hands up the cracks of their asses and massage their buttholes. Both butts were perfect bundles of manflesh, just waiting to be used and abused. Perhaps the greatest rush, though, was the feeling of power I got. Both these perfect studs was ready to satisfy my every whim. Standing before me, naked and defenseless as meat in a Roman slave market, the two powerful young men sent delicious, depraved shivers of lust deep into my soul. My cock had long been oozing love-lube and so swollen with need it felt ready to split open. My hands left their grinding butts and tight puckers to slide up their spines to strong shoulders and down again along their flanks. Those hard bodies could have stood before me forever and I wouldn't have had enough, but the impatience of youth beat beneath their muscles. I decided they were right. We had some long, rough rides coming up. The sooner we saddled up and hit the trail, the better.

I turned Mikos around to face me so I could lick at the underside of his dick and gooey, low-swinging nuts like a spaniel. My palms pressed against his full pecs, delighting in the feel of his passion-pointed tits drilling into my palms as his curls slipped through my fingers. Juan must have been playing the perfect asslick, because Mikos started moaning and grinding like a Tijuana whore with a crotch full of crabs. His sweet dick was tempting, but somehow I knew I would enjoy watching my own private little fuck-show more. When Juan had tongued open Mikos' Greek glory, he stood behind him and reached his hands around to grab Mikos' hips. I leaned back in my chair and concentrated on the bright, black eyes that blazed his excitement. I was watching those eyes when Juan jammed everything he had up Mikos' tight fuckhole. At the time, of course, I didn't realize how really tight it was. That didn't come until later. There wasn't much mistake, though, from the way those eyes bugged out of his head and then clamped shut that Juan had made a pretty fucking dramatic impression. Every muscle Mikos had seemed to stand out, knotted and defined, until he looked like the kind of statue I'd gone to museums to admire as a kid -- but no statue had a dick like his. Juan's joint was no sooner up Mikos' butt than the dicklube flow oozing out of his cum-slit doubled, dripping down his throbbing, heaving shaft to mire his nuts with glistening good news. I watched Mikos wriggle on the end of Juan's hook, scratching the secret itch he had buried deep inside him. Juan returned the favor, pricking even deeper up the tight Greek ass wrapped around his rod until he threatened to lift Mikos' feet off the floor. His thrusts and grinds were so fine and furious that I almost felt his hips curl up to drive his meat this way and that inside Mikos's butt. Parted Greek lips and rolled-back eyes told the story of how good his guts felt shished with Spanish kebab.

I rose from my chair and wrapped my robe around the three of us, greedy to share the heat of their olive-skinned bodies. Mikos' chest curls and hard tits slid across my belly like a Christmas wish come true. My own leaky dick fucked itself up against Mikos' flat belly, but I felt his meat throbbing and trickling away at ball level as Juan's reaming rod kept him bouncing. That demanding dick dug harder up Mikos' ass with every thrust until grinding turned to bucking to serious all- out, world-class butt-humping. Within moments, Juan was pounding into our friend so hard I lost my balance and sprawled back in my chair to watch the show.

Mikos bent over to raise his fuckhole and give Juan more room to work, but he needn't have bothered. I could tell from the expression on Juan's face that he intended to take anything he needed. By this time, his hands gripped Mikos' shoulders, his hips slammed furiously into Mikos' butt, and his thick dick was giving that Greek studhole a marine-quality reaming. Every brutal thrust sent shockwaves charging up through layer upon layer of muscle. The racket of flesh meating flesh was soon drowned out by Mikos moaning and crooning against the background of Juan's harsh snarls and animal growls. Entertaining as they seemed locked together just inches from me, I had to get a clearer view of the action.

I swiveled around on my chair and let my head down to the floor between their legs. My dick was still in the chair, pointing right at Mikos so he didn't waste any time. Any other time, having my dick sucked by a Mediterranean hunk would have been the high point of my week. Now, I barely noticed his lips sliding across my bone or his tongue whirring its way around my swollen knob. If you'd seen the view I saw up close and personal, you'd understand. I couldn't have had a better view of the action. Juan's thick meat slammed smack through Mikos' shithole and then magically reappeared in a moment to begin the cycle over again. His slack-skinned dick was shiny with butt juices and pre-cum; Mikos' buttcheeks glistened in the shadows where they'd stripped off the pellicle off Juan's perfect pounding prick. Just watching those two powerful pairs of thighs crashing together like elk in rutting season was enough to give me jerk-off memories for my old age. The sight of Juan's `nads swinging hard up into Mikos' was something I'll never forget. My hands slid upward along their legs. One found the dark secrets of Juan's butt-furrow. I slid my fuck-finger inside the trench and splayed the rest of my hand out across his epic ass, glorying in the powerful, surging thrusts and tight clenches of will that propelled his shaft up into his buddy's guts. The other hand took turns pulling down hard on nut-sacks. Three times I felt the cadence turn serious and knew sperm was about to fly, so I yanked down on Juan's `nads, dragging his load back away from the firing chamber. More and more, though, the tongue- and throat-work Mikos was using on my joint tore through my concentration. He was just too good.

I gave up being a spectator and threw myself into the battle. Getting my dick back so I could slide up to lick Juan's tight asshole was-n't easy, but I managed. My face shoved itself up Juan's ass so I could tongue-fuck him on the backstroke and lick his ass-crack when he clenched shut to drive his point home up Mikos' meat locker. Six or eight thrusts were all I needed to know Juan was about to blow again so I stopped fucking around and started fucking around. The slut was so far gone, I don't think he even noticed my thick eight inches of fury slam up his ass. Juan's body was paying more attention than his brain. I know Mikos felt Juan's instinctive reaction, though. The extra torque tore out an extra yelp louder than anything in Nevada since open air testing. Juan slid back and forth between Mikos' shithole and the butt-busting base of my cock for another ten seconds and then went ape-shit.

Mick Jackson, Private Investigator

His rhythm was the first to go. Then the screaming started -- terrible grunts and squawks and howls in Spanish by way of hell. If Mikos' hadn't braced himself against the chair I'd crawled out of, he'd have been fucked flat. As it was, we staggered forward, Juan clenching his butthole hard enough to make gravel, his slick, hot guts gripping my crankshaft along its whole swollen length and dragging it forward with him as he tore up Mikos' gorgeous Greek hole. Juan's butt would bounce back for a millisecond to grab some of my stiff red pubes in his cheeks and then slam forward again, fucking us down hard against the back of the chair until Mikos was bent backward like a circus freak -- and loving every terrible, tortuous twist of the dick up his ass.

I was so busy trying to keep myself in the saddle and having fun that I lost track of Juan's pleasure pumping. After what seems like forever but was probably only fifteen or twenty thrusts, Juan's body seemed to deflate like an escaping balloon. He collapsed with a wet sigh onto Mikos' body and started to give him a kiss on the back of the neck -- as though I had time for any of his sensitive continental romantic crap. I tore Juan off Mikos and me at the same time, reached down to drag Mikos to his feet, and shoved my eight inches up where they belonged. I am so much taller than Mikos that I practically fucked him airborne with every stroke, but my hands locked through his crotch and kept him from straying too far from what he needed. His butt was tighter than Juan's -- even after all it had been through. It was sure as fuck slicker, too. Juan had pumped enough Spanish sauce up into Mikos' cockbox to lube it for the entire Greek Army. The thought of that dickload of sweet Spanish cream sliding along my crank made my tongue twitch, but I knew Juan had more in reserve for desert.

I half noticed him in front of Mikos, his face dangling off Mikos' joint, while I pounded him up the butt. Juan flopped around like a rag doll, but his suction was strong enough to keep him where he needed to be. Meanwhile the slick cushion of spooge up the ass made Mikos a buttfucker's dream come true. He was tight and loud and active enough to be a good time, but cool and slippery enough to last forever. I slammed and pounded and reamed and tore up that tight Greek butt, twisting this way and that for what must have been twenty minutes before my dick whipped his cream enough for the party to start. One moment I was warming myself from the satisfying glow in my dick, the next second my heads were coming off.

I heard myself screaming as though at a distance and felt molten glass shoot through my dick and up into Mikos' sperm bank. As I held on, letting my hips do the fucking while I tried to remember every sensation, I felt Juan's greedy little mouth still clamped around hard cock. When, minutes or years later, I drifted back into the world, I eased my teeth off the nape Mikos' neck and gave him a last few good jets of jism, grinding my dick deep up his ass and stirring our loads together for the ages.

Only when I was finished did I realize Mikos had been having fun, too. Sometime during the blackout, Juan had gotten a hot protein injection of his own and was just sitting back on his haunches, licking his lips, and grinning profanely at the sanctity of my love.

Before we headed for the showers to rinse off the ruins of our first round, I had to have more time with Mikos' Greek dick myself. I unpricked his cum-soaked butt, picked it up, and threw it onto my bed. Then I moved between his legs and started taking my time coaxing up the next cream delivery. Since my ass was in the air, Juan shoved his tongue up it and went to work. Except for a few detours up to use my mouth on the best tits ever to leave Athens, that's more or less the way we stayed until Mikos spewed another load -- this one down my throat.

I could tell you what we did in the shower, or what happened the next morning at the riding stables when the three of us went bareback riding, but you're not interested in my personal life. You're interested in the case. I'll admit it rather slipped my mind for awhile.

When I finally remembered to ask Mikos whether he knew anything about Franco's murder, he gave me that earnest, open look of his and said, "Gee, no." What more proof could a guy ask for? He didn't have an alibi, but with a body like his, he didn't need one.

You've probably long since figured out who did the dirty deed -- murdered Franco, that is. As with 97% of murder cases, the key lay in the motive. I was fairly sure before I talked to anyone at the resort, but when Elena told me of her tender farewell as her beloved went to work out, I knew she was going to make Jean-Pierre a very happy man. He wouldn't have to bother the guests with indictments and could probably avoid scandal if whatever lawyer the resort hired for Elena could convince her to plea bargain.

Elena and the sausage widow both said Franco left their beds go to work out. One of them was obviously not remembering right. Since

Franco had seemed certain to wiener his way into a fortune within a few days, it didn't seem likely he was still doing Elena. She'd probably been whining at him about Franco Jr. -- just exactly the last thing he'd want to hear under the circumstances. While I couldn't see the Widow Malinowski traipsing around the weightroom at 2 AM, Elena was staff. She could go wherever she wanted without being noticed. Whether she followed him from the sausage queen's room or just happened upon him working out didn't really matter. The argument Juan had heard was almost certainly Franco telling Elena what she could do with her brat. He may even have suggested the same thing I had -- that the baby could be a momento from some fat industrialist who had checked in for a few nights of fun. Juan thought he heard laughter. That would have made Elena snap. A woman wronged taking revenge, she could have easily shoved at the barbell and knocked it down onto Franco's surprised throat. She might only have intended to scare him. The lawyer would probably recommend that approach, anyway. Once the job was done, she would have panicked. In seconds she could lift the barbell back onto Franco's throat with the mistaken idea it would look more like an accident that way. She knew all about fingerprints from television, but wouldn't have been thinking clearly enough to realize what a completely clean bar would mean.

The next afternoon, when I pulled myself away from the boys long enough to confront her in Jean-Pierre's office, she denied every-thing -- until I told her about the single print the sheriff's office found on the barbell. The murderer had missed it because it lay against the ruins of Franco's throat. When I whipped out my ink pad with a flourish and demanded her prints, she crumpled into a very unpleasant heap of tears. I have to admit she was right about one thing. Franco was a skunk. I can't really say I'm sorry he checked out of La Place before the Widow Malinowski.

On the other hand, without Franco I'd never have known Juan and Mikos. They've both learned to stay at my place for cultural and protein exchanges whenever they're in LA. Jean-Pierre was so thrilled with the way Elena shuffled quietly off to serve five to ten that he offered me a retainer to handle any future troubles in his desert paradise. Rather than money, we agreed on a free weekend twice year at La Place.

When the sheriff came out to pick up Elena, he was confused by all her ranting about the fingerprint he'd found on the barbell. I pulled him aside and confessed I'd made it up. What I didn't tell him was the reason. Given the choice between taking the whole afternoon to break down a girl already lapsing in and out of hysterics -- and one you felt sorry for in the first place -- or winding things up so you could get back to bed, which way would you have handled the interrogation? Before you answer, keep in mind that Mikos and Juan were in bed alone at the time -- waiting.

REEL TEMPTATION
by Mick Jackson, Private Investigator

When I left the Navy SEALs at 25 and started a detective agency in San Francisco, I was sure I'd seen every kind of critter alive. Then a few months ago I moved my agency down to West Hollywood and discovered how diverse people can be. Even industrial espionage cases down here take a queer turn when you least expect one.

We'll call my client Ralph. You would probably recognize his real name if I used it, but I don't violate client confidences even if they are assholes. I picked "Ralph" because I knew a Ralph years ago who was such a total waste of his daddy's cum that ever since I've measured other jerks against him. Let's just say that if assholes were earthquakes and Ralph came to town, the Pacific would now extend east as least as far as Nebraska.

Our first meeting should show you what I mean. Naturally I'd heard of Ralph even before he called for an appointment. He's one of the top five gay fuckfilm makers in the business. His movies tend to rip off a lot of William Higgin's style, but he uses the same sort of cute young guys as his "models," so I've always managed to overlook his lack of plot, dialogue, direction, editing, or focus. Although I've made enough interesting surveillance videotapes of my own to know what to do with a camera when there's naked flesh around, Ralph was the first "movie mogul" I had met in Movietown USA. I was starting at the bottom of the barrel when it came to class. His first words as he dropped his fat ass into the chair across my desk that Thursday morning in July were "I heard you did OK for a fag. They didn't tell me you were pretty, too. Why don't you stop by for a test. I go through you guys like a fat bitch through buttwipe; I can always use somebody fresh."

I suppose he hit a sore spot. I'm not pretty, but I have to admit

I'm good looking. Even at 6'1", I don't look like a private dick who's almost 27. A friend of mine once claimed except for my bright red hair, I was a cross between a young Kevin Costner and Tom Cruise, with a little Ricky Nelson thrown in around the mouth. Growing up gay and six years in the SEALs had given me plenty of time to prove I could handle any problems that came along. Besides, since he'd gotten rich off gay movies, I didn't like the way he used the word "fag." I was to discover he used it a lot. If he had used it a little less, he could have saved himself my fee -- but that's jumping ahead of the story.

Once we decided I wasn't interested in making him richer, he got down to business. Hoping to improve his choice of words, I told him I made videotape records of all my interviews and pointed toward camera purring away. He didn't give a fuck what I did. He was sure someone was bootlegging his tapes and he wanted me to find out if he was right so he could take care of making sure it didn't happen again. The problem was he was short on specifics -- but long on story. Most Fridays he takes home a box of half-inch tapes to screen. Sometimes the tapes are tests for new talent, sometimes rushes or rough edits, sometimes completed cuts of unreleased films. He uses the weekends to view the tapes and approve them or, more usually, decide whose butt to haul over the coals the next week. His secretary always packs the tapes into a grey metal case roughly a foot square. The thing has a flimsy lock, but he never bothered to do more than latch it because "any retard faggot with a nail file" could open the lock.

The weekend before, he had the final cut of an especially important cinema epic called Football Huddle starring his new head boy, who had the unlikely sounding name of Lance Stallion. The tape master had to be expressed to Mexico City for duplication on Monday if he was going to meet the advertised release date, so checking the cut that weekend was a must. Other tapes included screen tests for new "models" he was considering using. Out of curiosity I asked why he was using a Mexican duplicator, but since his explanation that they were cheaper involved details that were offensive not only to gays, but Mexicans and Jews as well, we'll skip over the details. Ralph was not a nice man.

His problem had come to light on Tuesday afternoon when the secretary got around to unpacking the case so she could decipher his notes on the screen tests. The cassette box that had held Football

Huddle was empty. He assumed at first that he'd left the tape in the machine or somewhere in his den. The master had been sent off; the release date was five weeks away. If someone in the office had stolen the tape, bootleg copies could flood the market before he could get his slow but cheaper Mexican duplicator to deliver. Ralph had already heard other filmmakers were sniffing around Lance, but he hadn't wanted to offer "the little faggot" a decent contract until he saw what Huddle's sales were. In short, he had his financial dick in a wringer if anyone had stolen the tape.

He tore home early that afternoon and ripped the den apart looking for the tape. He grilled the maid about whether she'd let any of her "third-world" friends into the house. By the time his wife came home, he was frantic. The only other person in the house had been his 19-year-old son Greg, home from Stanford for the summer, but he had been out most of the weekend. Except for the maid, the house had been empty nearly all day Sunday while Ralph and the wife were at a big society wedding. Ralph stormed back to his production facility and went bug-fuck. The secretary, whose name is Marge and at 64 is about as much like your image of a fuckfilm maker as Mother Theresa, went over the story again for him. He'd brought the case in Monday morning. It had set in his office until just after lunch on Tuesday. She brought the case out to her office and, after being distracted by visitors and `phone calls for about an hour, discovered the tape was missing. Sure, she said, anyone could have gotten to the case either while it was in his office or on her desk -- not to mention overnight.

Ralph was upset. He terrorized the staff sniffing around for a lead on who was shitting on him. After he gave up on them, he went home and tore into the maid again. She was Mexican so obviously, he reasoned, guilty of something even if not of stealing the tape and trying to ruin him. When she didn't confess, he called me for an appointment Wednesday morning. Thursday, on the way to lunch, he heard a rattle and found the tape under the passenger seat of his BMW. He hadn't taken it out of the case except inside the house. Obviously some snake in the office or one of the maid's many relatives had swiped the tape, dubbed a two-inch quad copy, and thrown the original into his car hoping he would think it had been there all the time. My job was to prove who had the copy now so he could use legal -- or other -- means to keep them from releasing his hard-hunked jewel on the underground market.

We spent the next two hours going back over the story, but since we didn't accomplish anything except pissing me off even more, we'll skip over the details. I asked questions like who had access to the office after hours, did his house have an alarm system, did he have a gardener, was the Huddle originally shot on film or videotape, and so on. I didn't have to be Hercule Poirot to see that whatever happened was an inside job, but his theory about tape piracy didn't add up. If the perp worked in the office, he could have dubbed a high-quality master. Why settle for borrowing a shitty half- inch copy? Someone using the house for access might have settled for that, but he wouldn't broken in again just to return the tape.

My usual rate is $350 a day plus expenses, but I didn't like my client. Since he was in a hurry, I offered to put all my other (nonexistent) clients on hold for $500 a day plus expenses -- and a $1000 bonus if I could tell him whether a pirate copy of the tape was in unauthorized hands and another $1000 if I delivered the thief. The bastard didn't blink; I should have asked for twice that.

The next three or four days, I did the mundane background work that is 97% of detective work. I checked his office staff and maid out with credit bureaus and a friend with access to LAPD's computer. I did a basic security check of the house and grounds. The place was up in the hills and about the size of Windsor Castle, but furnished mainly in red and gold with mirrors and tasseled throw-pillows spread around. Over the sofa in Ralph's den hung what has to be the world's largest black-velvet painting, featuring three big- breasted babes and a jungle waterfall. I could go on, but you probably get the idea. The alarm system was an expensive infra-red number good enough for Fort Knox. Ralph's black velvet was safe.

The maid was an over-worked frazzled out woman who looked 50. Her naturalization papers said her name was Alicia Romero -- and that she was only 36. Ralph didn't give her time to get laid and since she was a citizen, I figured blackmail was out. The wife was named Blanche, a hennaed caricature of the society matron she longed to be. After meeting her, I couldn't decide whether she or Ralph had decorated the palace. She knew nothing about any tape and knew even less about her husband's filthy business. Her only concern was using the money he raked in. The son finally wandered in from the beach as I was about to leave. Old Ralph had done at least one thing right in his life: making Greg. He looked a lot like Charlie Sheen except for the blue eyes. The kid was cute as a bug's ear, but those eyes especially interested me. Young Greg tried to hide it, but he kept glancing back at me -- sneaking glances at the way my crotch hung, looking at the line my pecs made in my shirt, and so on. As I admired the way his swim trunks were filled out, I asked him about the tape; he asked me about being a private dick. I wondered what he had done Sunday; he wondered what being a Navy SEAL was like. After about ten minutes, I saw I wasn't getting anywhere -- with the case -- and decided to pack it in. I gave Greg my card and asked him to call if he though of anything that might help out his old man. His attitude told me two more things as I headed out the door: helping out his old man was about last on his list of things to do -- and I might well be hearing from him again.

The next morning, I headed out to the "studio." Paramount or MGM it wasn't. The place was essentially a warehouse, with four small office spaces in front and a combination sound stage, editing facility in back. A few storage rooms and a couple of closet-sized dressing rooms completed the tour. I let Marge repeat the story, checked the security system, nosed around, and finally kicked back to watch them tape part of Ralph's next epic. The set was supposed to be the berthing area of a Navy ship, but looked about as much like one as I look like Millard Fillmore. Taping wasn't going well. The bottom was a cute, curly-headed kid just old enough not to be jail-bait. He had a surfer-quality tan and muscles and radiant sun-bleached hair. Flashing his baby blues at his master and wriggling his butt in the air like the original whore of creation wasn't getting him any, though. Something about the kid reminded me of something else, but I couldn't place what it was.

The top had a problem placing something, too. He was a lanky hairy number with a chain dangling from a tit-ring. The supposedly "gay sailor" top was watching TV monitor out of frame that showed a lesbian 69 orgy. When the girls got their tongues going, his dick stiffened up; the director would start taping, the top would start to stick it to Kid Precious, and his dick would deflate like the Hindenburg.

You wouldn't think fuckflicks would be boring to watch, but after about twenty minutes, I decided anything would be more interesting than the chain gang trying to stiffen up. The editing crew came in from lunch so I asked about how the Huddle was shot and edited, discovered they thought Mexican tape duplicators were sub-standard, and finally asked if I could look at a copy of Football Huddle. They racked up a timing print for me. I had to admit that Lance Stallion was good enough to eat, but the plot wasn't especially savory. We saw Quarterback Lance in the shower and locker room with the team rookie. Then we cut to Lance at the pep rally -- in the john with the towel boy. When they got to the scene with Lance giving the coach what he needed before the big game, I said I'd seen enough for one day. I believed it, too -- until I headed out to the parking lot to reclaim my wreck.

I was walking past the kind of brown van that litters the landscape of southern California when my detective ears picked up the sound of young love. You would probably have kept walking, but we professional detectives must be ever alert for clues. The windows were covered by a curtain and I wasn't about to climb up to peer in the sunroof. I did what any self-respecting dick would do: I opened the door and asked if they needed any help. They didn't, but I went on in anyway. The young bottom from the sailor epic must have gotten tired of waiting for something stiff, because he was doggie down on the floor with Lance Stallion up his tight little butt. Lance started to object, but he stopped as soon as he saw I OK myself. Besides, young Curly did everything but swoon. As he slid those bright blue eyes up and down the lizard trying to escape from my crotch, he practically drooled precum. Those worshipful blue eyes finally clicked the missing element of the case into position. I put my knowledge of dicks and assholes together and suddenly saw how things had to be. At $500 a day, though, I figured I'd take the rest of the week to wrap up the loose ends, especially since I was going to be out one of my thousand dollar bonuses. In the meantime, I had some tight ends to worry about.

I later discovered Curly's stage name was Brice Savage. As I slipped off my clothes and shoved my thick eight inches into his mouth, I didn't much care what his name was. He was one fine pug-nosed little cocksucker and that's all that counted. Those cute, wet lips of his slid across the swollen head of my throbbing dick like a private dick's wet-dream come true. Before they reached my trigger-ride, his tongue had followed along, whipping around my tender tool like a fleshy weed whacker. The horny bastard didn't stop at just giving me head. He gave me crank, too. By the time my hips were shoving all I had into his pretty-boy face, he'd slicked me up enough his throat could come in for the kill. I felt a SWOOOP as he slipped his suction into overdrive and inhaled my best asset. His tongue kept plenty busy stroking up and down the underside of my shaft, but the tight, tender tissues of his throat took charge. I felt his gullet ripple and pulse, using the vicious thrusts Lance was delivering up his ass to massage my meat. The throat wrapped tight and sliding along my rod felt like some starving prehistoric worm that, having swallowed me whole, was determined to suck my nuts dry. He only had one hand free, but it started sliding from my balls, along my thigh, and back to cup my ass while I fucked his young fuckfilm face. I was no cinema expert, but it looked to me as though Ralph was missing the boat on these two.

I later discovered that Ralph didn't hold with "non-scripted fuck-ing" on the theory the boys should save their loads for the camera. After the morning young Brice had been through, though, his ass was thirsty enough to satisfy the Pacific Fleet. Lance was trying to meet his needs in a big way. I gave Brice plenty of attention as he swallowed my pride, but Lance was a hard young man to ignore. I liked the way his hips were bucking up into young Brice's butt, but Lance had more than brute lust. As his piston pulled up and snagged on the tight insides of Brice's sphincter, he gave his own butt a stylish little wriggle to repo-sition it for the next stroke. Every bone-crunching thrust of Lance's pile-driving butt followed a different path, scraping against new nerves as his massive member drove deeper and harder up his buddy's butt. Brice tried to grunt and moan his pleasure, but my thick eight-inch gag was giving him a lot of trouble.

You have probably noticed I've put off trying to describe Lance, but as I fucked one end of Brice and he reamed out the other, you can believe I watched him plenty. A typical police-style description would-n't help much: white male, about 20, six feet, 180, light blond hair, very muscular build, brown eyes. If I talked about the way his tuft of blond curls dropped down over his strong brow, or how his puppy-dog eyes seemed seductively out of place in his blond body, you might get some idea that he was good looking. Talking about his perfect teeth or the cleft in his chin, his dimples or the way his perfect skin glowed as he drilled deep might help. His muscles were even more developed than mine and rippled across his flesh like a real stallion's beneath hairless skin. Let's just say Lance had looks -- the kind of body and face and self-confident bearing that made your guts clench up when you saw him for the first time. Some of his charisma filters through onto tape, but if you run out to rent Football Huddle to see what the fuss is about, you just have to take my word he looks about 90% foxier in person than he does on the phosphor screen. I know, because even though Brice was as good as a human male can get and sucked dick like sword swallower with the hiccups, Lance was better. He was like some god come to earth to fuck with the mortals for fun. I could have gotten off just watching his muscles ripple. When he clenched his jaw or grinned after an especially good thrust up Brice's ass, his spaniel eyes sparkled pure, glorious lust unlike anything I'd ever known.

I kept one hand locked in Brice's curls and stroked the other down his heaving spine. My fuckfinger worked its way between the hard mounds of muscle that guarded his fuckhole. I prodded deeper and felt his ass shudder with the impact of Lance's hips. Half an inch more and I had my fingertip on Lance's dick as he reamed in and out of Brice's hole. Soon I had a finger on either size of his thick tool, stretching the way open and getting off on the frictionless lust-log he was using to fuck his needy buddy's body up onto my dick. Lance was so good I released Brice and used my other hand to trace lines of worship across his perfect pecs, to touch his hard tits with the same wonder a child feels at his first snowfall, and finally to lay my hand on the knotted muscles of his shoulder.

Lance and Brice had been riding the monster before I crashed their party so it's no reflection on Brice's cocksucking that Lance lost his load before I did -- just. When I saw those gorgeous brown eyes roll back into his head, heard his breath turn to savage snarls, and felt Brice's throat learn a violent new rhythm, I didn't need a road map to know where we were. Seeing Lance's butt bang forward to shoot jet after creamy jet of jism up Brice's lovehole, hearing his screams of JESUS and OH, FUCK, YESSSSS, and feeling Brice's the already tight throat around my tool clamp up like a vise was too much of a great thing. One minute I was admiring Lance's body and fucking style the way you would admire a Michelangelo statue or Montana pass, the next my guts had turned to molten glass and I was blowing crystal chandeliers down Brice's grasping gullet. We rode him backwards and forwards, pumping our creamy seed into his body until we were drained flat, streaming sweat in the stifling summer heat of the van, and loving life. I reached back to glide my lips across Lance's mouth and felt his tongue burrowing in. My hand still lay on his shoulder; his wrapped around my neck and pulled me to him.

Even without noticing Brice had worked his face off my joint, I must have straddled his body, instinctively drawn to slide my slick, sweaty flesh against his. I wound my arms about his waist and slipped down to feel the butt I'd seen driving his dick home in the Huddle. Brice wriggled his forgotten, sperm-soaked ass off Lance's lizard while I got comfortable and proved what a hard, nasty private dick felt like. My lips sucked on Lance's tongue until he was ready to go again. My lips gnawed at his neck and ear lobe and, finally, his sweaty bare tits. I had my head under his right arm, lapping up the glorious taste of his musk, when I felt Brice's tongue up my ass.

The slutty little bastard didn't waste time licking the sweat from my balls. He shoved his tongue up my fuck-furrow and dug hard against my hole. His whole face was up my ass: his lips wrapped around my pucker, his tongue digging through into my musk-locker, his nose digging for thrills like a hog in a truffle warehouse. With studs fore and aft, I had the good sense not to move. When Lance saw I was distracted, he turned the tables and tongue-fucked my ear until I knew what heaven and hell must feel like. Brice was an even better asslick than a cocksucker. My brain shut down about four seconds after his tongue slid up my butt and stayed that way until the world was older and Lance's aural sex fucked through the haze and seemed the brain out of my head.

I started yelling and thrashing about, trying to get control of the situation and secretly hoping they'd keep up their sweet torture forever.

Brice knew when to move on. I looked down to see him leaning against the wall of the van, ass twitching and feet spread. One of my dozen or so weaknesses is the idea of sloppy seconds. I'd almost rather slide my joint where another stud has reamed cream than do the source up the ass. I probably need professional help -- but, then, I had a couple professionals right there. I twisted away from Lance, patting his hard butt to show I was grateful, and slid my rigid ramrod through Brice's butt in one, swift, vicious stroke. I bounced past his prostate, felt Lance's lizard milk engulf my goods, and kept on drilling until I hit the hard wall muscle eight dark inches up his butt. My cum-slit dug around, stirring the hot pot holding Lance's cream while my stiff red pubes ground into the tight rim of Brice's butthole. His slick shit-chute trilled and heaved along my crankshaft, urging my bone home. I felt my ballbag nuzzle is butt and reached forward to hook my hands under his thighs and lift him harder up my horn.

I hadn't paid much attention to his gear, but when my hand bumped against his piece, I was impressed. A lot of the bottoms I'd known weren't what you would call huge. Brice was nearly as long as me, was hard as a tax-collector's heart, and had something I didn't: a juicy foreskin oozing pre-cum. Now it was Brice's turn to get his ear lobe sucked; while I was within whispering distance, I told him what I was going to do to his `skin as soon as I finished reaming his ass raw. The slut just clenched up tighter and started sliding up and down my rod, raping his ass with everything I had. Lance's sweet lube made my dick do everything but sing as I torqued and twisted and slid in and out of Brice's hole. The whore made a sound that told me my baton was conducting the right score. I sunk my teeth lightly into his shoulder, slid one hand tight around his belly, and started to hump his hard, fuckflick ass like a mongrel dog doing a cur bitch in the street.

I had humped about two dozens strokes up his ass, when I was Lanced from behind. Except for whatever juice he'd dragged out of Brice's butt and the stray drops of our sweat that dripped down, he was bone dry. He was also longer and thicker than he looked on TV. Either that or the guys he humped with such ease in the Huddle were alien freaks from outer space. When that thick Hollywood dick broke through into my shitchute, every nerve in my body called a foul. A wave of shock and pleasure so intense it was painful ripped through my soul even before his thick, Hollywood member had finished ripping through my guts. My shitchute knew what to do with a dick like him, though: I clamped down tight, wriggled my ass into his soft, blond curlies, and hunkered down for a ream come true.

Swinging back and forth between Lance and Brice was one of the top two or three experiences in my life. Brice was tight and juicy and begging to be used, with enthusiasm out the ass and inventive sense of timing that wouldn't quit. Lance was hard-driving, domineering, and cared only for his own pleasure. Together, they made a team that couldn't lose. I just hung on while they slid along on nature's best and bumpiest ride. I felt pierced through by a massive log that left Lance's body and slid through mine to end up Brice's ass. I was battered back and forth while Lance built up enough fuck-friction up my ass to ignite a sequoia. His hands were all over me, sliding along my flanks, tearing at my tits, grabbing great fistfuls of my hair to use as reins as he bucked my bronco long past the eight-second bell. As they fucked me back and forth, mindless pleasure took over and my mind just shut down. My body was too busy with bliss to keep track of reality.

In the end, though, the heat was too much for Lance. Within six or eight minutes some remote part of my brain felt his body shudder and heave. The fire up my ass flushed itself out in the surge of sperm that made Johnstown seem like a clogged storm drain. By the time Lance had jolted me all the way back to consciousness, he was screaming and pounding my ass in the last blast of his affections. Since I'm a nice guy, I kept swinging back and forth, concentrating my talent up Brice's sodden sluthole. By the time I felt Lance finally give up my ass, I was ten seconds away from lift-off and counting down. I unplugged Brice, whirled around, laid him up in a full nelson, and fucked him hard up his ass. I was more prepared than he had been. Aside from Brice's butt- juice, I had about six quarts of my own pre-cum and about six acres of Lance's own seed farm still on my dick. I slid through his tight ass like snot through an electric fan. Lance obviously liked to think of himself as a top, but his skill as a bottom was hard to beat. He wriggled his ass back up against me, clenching and twisting and torquing his fuckhole until I thought my bone would break off at the joint. I dug up his ass in hard, sure, vicious strokes of butt-fucking conquest, counting how each one aloud so I'd have the pleasure of knowing exactly how many times I'd nailed a film legend up the butt. At stroke number thirteen he let out a bellow and I reacted by launching my first load. I kept seriously juicing his hole until stroke twenty-seven. From there on in, it was all dribbles and goo so I unplugged Lance and let Brice have my sloppy seconds.

By the time I'd finished up Brice's butt and sucked his gloriously musky uncut dick dry while Lance lapped up everything we had, it was starting to get dark. Ralph's studio wasn't in a neighborhood I'd want my wreck setting out in at night, so we exchanged `phone numbers and I made a hurried farewell. As I was almost out the door of Lance's van, though, I had a thought. I asked them what they thought about Ralph. They both looked at each other and smiled. Finally Lance said he was an arrogant, money-grubbing, shit- for-brains bigoted, homophobic asshole with the class of a drug-pusher's pimp. Although Ralph didn't know it yet, Lance was moving up to a good director and was starting shooting a dude ranch fuckflick the next week. I suggested Lance stick close to a `phone on Saturday and left them as Brice was telling Lance what he'd do for him if he could get him a job on the dude ranch set.

The next day, Wednesday, I called Ralph and told him I was one step away from wrapping up the case. I'd be back in touch on Monday. Then I took the next couple days off, at Ralph's expense. On Saturday, I was knew Ralph and the Mrs. would be leaving for a society bash around 5, so I took a drive up the coast for a few hours, clearing my head and putting the finishing touches on my strategy as the ocean zoomed past. I was parked outside chez Ralph when they pulled out in his BMW. I waited about five minutes and rang the bell. Alicia remembered me so there was no problem giving her a bogus story about how I was back to check on the second-story security system. The family was out, but she didn't give a big rat's ass; she had problems of her own. I told her my good-looking assistant might show up later and that she should send him up.

I like snooping through other people's houses. I suppose I'm sick, but I can live with that. Since Ralph was a client, I'll just spill that he and the Mrs. had separate bedrooms and not talk about her vibrators or what I found under his bed. Finding junior's room wasn't hard; the All-American boy even had a Stanford pennant on the wall. Finding his stash wasn't hard, either. The VHS VCR was on his dresser next to the TV; his 8mm camcorder was in the top dresser drawer along with nearly twenty tapes. Some of them were marked with red dots on the cases so I slid one of those into the camera and hooked up the TV. It wasn't Football Huddle, but what I saw was damned good stuff. I needed two more tries to get Huddle up and running. For shits and giggles, I kept looking for the magazines I knew would be around. They were -- under loose carpet and a lift-out board in the back of the closet. It was 5:30. I just had to wait for Greg to straggle in from his day at the beach so I stripped off my clothes, took a couple magazines to Greg's bed, and watched some more of Lance in action. Speaking as a lover of fine cinema instead of someone he's fucked up the butt, the guy is good.

The look on Greg's face when he came through the door was classic. I'd decided I needed the shock treatment to make my point effectively, but I guess I was too brutal. He looked at me, first turned on like a big dog with a fresh pant leg to hump, then terrified when he saw His Secret was out. His first glance went to the closet, then to the TV, and he seemed to crumple. I stroked over to him and threw his ass on the bed. Then I laid out the plan. I wasn't here to drag him out of the closet. I knew pretty much what the story was. He knew his old man was an asshole and thought the old buzzard would throw his preppy collegiate butt out into the gutter if he let on he craved dick. Probably up at Stanford he got plenty -- or maybe he cruised up into town to get it. At home, the long hot summer stretched on forever so he started borrowing tapes and copying them for company along his single-handed cruises down the palm drive expressway. When he'd heard about the wrangle over the Huddle, he'd gotten spooked and tossed the tape into the BMW, hoping the old guy would think the tape had just fallen out of the case. Was I right or was I right?

The kid was astounded. Who told me? How did I know? When I told him I was a detective and paid to know things, that didn't go far. His plan was to keep his heads down until he finished his masters and then let the old guy know a few things about these faggots he was always on about. Greg couldn't believe I wasn't going to stake him out to dry. What did I want to keep quiet?

I just wanted him to rent tapes from now on and leave the old man's alone. Anything beyond that was up to him. I wasn't going to make him put out to keep his ass out of trouble, but on the other hand, I was a virile 26-year-old three-day virgin who wouldn't turn down a young college boy if he threw himself at me. In fact, if he wanted to get really down and dirty, I had a friend who'd like to fuck him hard up his Stanford butt. Was he interested or should I slip into my clothes and out of his life? He was on his knees and at my dick so fast, I practically had to drag him to the `phone. Lance was at home. I asked if he'd like to nail a cute young college kid who just happened to be Ralph's only son? You can figure the answer. He'd be over in a flash. Meanwhile, I had enough to do that I wasn't bored.

I let Greg suck my dick. Since he was already clamped on, I couldn't do much else. Greg's body was typical jock college material: soft skin stretched over a frame of solid muscle. For a 19-year-old, he had an amazingly thick pelt of chest and belly fur -- soft, thick black curls that stretched from his hard pecs, down across a flat belly rippling with good news, and down into a crotch so well-stocked it was criminal to hide it away. His balls swung low and heavy below a swollen dick that pounded upward against the black fur on his belly. Except for his blue eyes, he looked even more like Charlie Sheen with every movement of his head and wry crinkle of his eyes. He looked up at me with something near hero- worship as he stoked my pole, a black shock of hair drooped rebelliously down over his right brow. If he was going to suck dick, I was going to join in.

His day at the beach had stewed his crotch in sweat, bringing out the second-best taste in the world: man musk. I licked his ballbag and felt his hips wriggle in appreciation as he smeared his `nads into my face. I took my time sucking them clean and moved on south, slipping into the deep, hard crevice of his ass. He'd showered before going to the beach so the only thing up his crack was the best musky set of butt fur you could want to shake a tongue at. The boys in the van had shaved their holes for professional reasons, but I could live with Greg's fur just fine. When I latched my lips around his fuckhole and started prodding my thick tongue up his ass, twisting and turning to screw my way into his affection, his ass danced in my face like a highlander who'd just inherited a distillery.

My hands tore his ass apart so I could get my face farther up his butt, but soon it wasn't enough. Greg had already moved from my pole to my hole and was doing some awesome ass- licking for a closet case. I had to envy what those Stanford boys must get during the school year. Fine as his tongue- lashing was up my ass, I was ready for action. I reversed on him again, flipped him onto his back, lifted his legs, and told Ralph's spawn to hold tight. His shithole had enough of my spit inside it, he didn't need lube; but since he hadn't been getting much lately, I knew I'd be one tight fucker. He took it like a man, though. I saw his blue eyes flicker when I eased through into his ass, but he kept focused on me the whole time, either to show he could take everything I had -- or that he was having one fucking good time. When I was finally buried up to my hilt and his guts were latched around my lizard for the duration, I reached down to suck his foxy lower lip into my mouth. My hands slipped beside his ribs and, as I went to work, Greg gave me an open-mouthed kiss that spoke volumes. Soon, though, we were both grunting and moaning too much to be caring, nurturing partners. This wasn't "Love Me Tender." Once Greg's guts found out what I had, he seduced me into something more akin to jungle rape. My butt arched upward as it crashed down, ramming his hole body off the bed as my arms held him down. Every time I powered my ass backward, dragging my trigger-ridge along the slick inner surface of his manhole, his guts collapsed around my joint, begging me not to leave. Now and again, I pulled completely out of his ass, just to feel the thrill of stretching him wide when I left and slammed back inside. His hands tore at my back and butt and hair as he thrashed beneath me, made insensible by lust finally allowed to run wild in the real world.

Every stroke was better than the last and I felt I could drill his hole forever. His cute frat-house face and firm body and perfect fuckhole all blended together with the circumstance of the moment -- and the knowledge that I was fucking Ralph's son in his own house -- to make our tangled, frantic rut as fun for me as it was special for Greg. We humped and heaved for what seemed like eons until his heels dug deep up my butt and made contact with my fuckhole. That did it. My ballbag clenched tight and three day's worth of private dick cream shot up into my client's tight jock ass. It kept shooting while I ground and huffed and puffed and did everything but blow his fucking mansion down. When I had finally splurged all my sperm, I pulled out of his ass and gave his chest a furry pat. While I was in the neighborhood, I latched onto one of his tits towering above the fur and began fucking with it -- while I made myself useful between his legs by sucking his collegiate cock.

I didn't hear Lance come in, but when Greg saw his fuckfilm jerk-off model standing naked beside his bed, he gave my head a grateful grab and pulled Lance down across his face. I could tell from the gleam in his eyes that Lance was happy with his blind date and didn't want to waste a lot of time. I unpronged Greg's pole enough to tell Lance that I'd already done him; he was too late. Lance gave me a grin and said he didn't mind -- now he'd do him right. Once I got out of the way, Lance lifted Greg's right leg toward the ceiling, picked his ass up, and sank a shaft that was sure to bring in a gusher.

When I saw Lance and Greg going at it, I kicked myself for being so stupid. I always tape all my cases; here was the photo opportunity of a lifetime and I was letting it slip by. I padded over to Greg's camera, found a blank, and clicked it inside. Once the camera was set and purring along, I went back to the bed and shoved my face up Lance's bounding butt. His shaved ass tasted tamer than Greg's sweaty shithole, but was just as much a turn-on. By the time Lance had set his rhythm, he'd pulled Greg to his feet and the two of them were doing great things. I bent down in front of Greg to chew his tits and suck his dick, but suddenly the rhythm of their love got to me, too. I turned my back on the two of them and gave Greg his chance to use his daddy's employee for something more constructive than chasing down phantom tape pirates. His dick had the driving need of youth -- and the ram-jet tail engine of Lance up his butt to push him even harder. This time it was Greg's turn to spooge my locker, but Lance wasn't far behind. When they let go at almost the same moment I was tempted to jack a quick joint myself just to be neighborly. I kept my hands off -- but only because I knew I'd need every drop I had before the night was over. I was right.

After the horn-dogs finished doing the dirty and I was able to pry my ass off Greg's preppy peter, I reminded him that the old folks would be home within a couple of hours and suggested he and Lance come over to my place to spend the night. I had beer, we could order in pizza, and life needn't need any more than beer, pizza and the two of them to be perfect.

As we were dressing, I told Greg about the tape we'd just made and suggested he stash it away until he was ready to jolt the old man senseless. It would probably be years before he was ready, but Lance and I both felt good knowing that eventually old Ralph would get a double shock. He was bound to find out Greg's secret anyway -- and the sooner the better for all concerned. Exactly when Greg chose to tell him was none of our business. You just had to love the idea, though, that Ralph would see his private dick and leading man doing his kid up the ass.

Lance and Greg finally left my place about 3 the next afternoon. It was a Sunday, so we'd "slept in," though it would be more accurate to say we only passed out from time to time. After a few winks, one of us always woke up to try something new. I'm happy to say they've been over a lot since. Greg went back to Stanford in August full of the craving for knowledge and quarts of jism. Football Huddle was such a big hit that Lance was able to get a percentage of the profits from his dude ranch epic before the thing was even released. And, yes, I know you're curious about young Blair. Lance got him a bit part in the jerk-off scene but when the director saw what he was jerking off, Blair was promoted to the foreman's assistant. You can guess what he assisted with.

The next Monday, I filed my report with Ralph. Under the terms of our deal, he owed me $500 per day plus expenses -- and the thousand dollar bonus because I'd discovered none of his competition had a bootleg copy of his tape. He could safely wait and release the film on schedule. I also told him I'd solved the puzzle of how the tape ended up in his car but, in a phrase I picked up in my Navy days, he had "no need to know." He fumed and bitched, but I told him I'd done what he hired me to do. He had gotten all he was going to get -- and if he didn't like it, he could suck my dick.

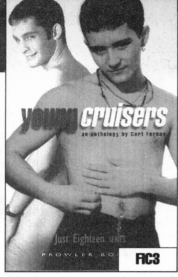

Slaves (FIC2) Slaves is the tale of Jack's sexual encounters which begin as he joins the mile high club. Cumming off the plane he falls headlong into one horny sexploit after another.

Diary Of A Hustler (FIC1) Follow the escapades of 18 year old Joey as he goes through his hot'n'horny training for his first hustling jobs. As Thane shows Joey the ropes they soon realise that Joey's a natural.

Corporal In Charge (FIC4) Twenty short stories of hot and sleazy sex. Fritscher details each story down to the last drop of cum. From teenage wank sessions to college locker room fun to hard sex in the army.

Young Cruisers (FIC3) The third novel to cum out of the Just Eighteen series is a tantalising selection of short stories on sleazy first time adventures.

£5.99 / $9.95 each

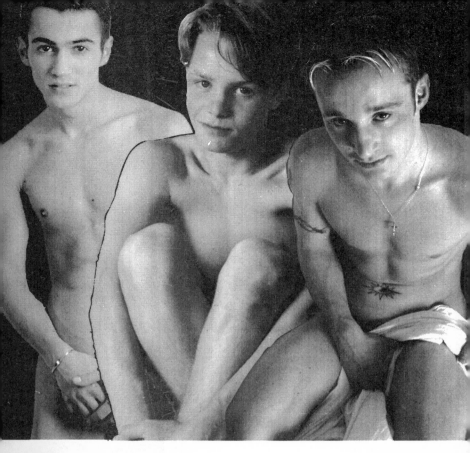